LOVE REMODELED

SEEKING PROVIDENCE

BOOK THREE

JILL BURRELL

First edition: July 2025
Library of Congress Control Number: Forthcoming

ISBN: 978-1-955507-19-6 (eBook)
ISBN: 978-1-955507-20-2 (pbk)

CHAPTER 1

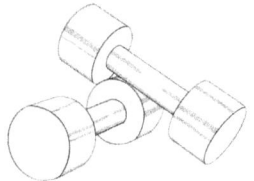

Happily ever after, here I come.

Paige put her car in park then used the rear-view mirror to check her hair and makeup. She fluffed her limp hair. She'd gone to extra lengths this morning to look nice for tonight's date, but keeping up with thirty second graders had taken its toll.

Her cell phone rang as she reached for the lip gloss in her purse. She pulled her phone out instead and grinned at the sight of her cousin's name on the screen.

"Hi, Riley. Happy Valentine's Day!"

"Guess what Daniel gave me for Valentine's Day?" Riley's voice was positively giddy.

"Chocolate? Roses? A slinky nighty?" Paige couldn't resist throwing in that last one.

"Well yes, but that's not what I'm so excited about." Riley's voice rose in pitch. "He gave me a new saddle!"

"Don't you already have a saddle?"

"Yes, but it's twelve years old. My new one is so pretty. He even had my initials engraved into the leather."

"You're giddy because your new saddle has a pretty little H for

1

Hamilton instead of a W for Winters?" Paige laughed as she rolled her eyes.

"Yes. Isn't it the sweetest gift?"

"It's perfect. For you." Paige wondered if she'd get to change her last initial from Y to E soon.

Paige Ellis.

She liked the sound of that.

Paige wanted the kind of lovesick happiness Riley and Daniel had. She was already lovesick over the perfect man. She was just waiting on the promise of forever that she hoped was coming very soon.

"Please tell me Phillip made special plans for tonight," Riley's voice pulled Paige from her daydreaming.

"As a matter of fact, I'm meeting him at Tulio's." Paige looked at the upscale Italian restaurant on the corner. It was one of the most popular restaurants in Seattle. "We're having an early dinner because he has a work meeting later tonight."

"On Valentine's Day? Seriously? His bosses should be fired."

"Such is the life of an international business consultant. He often has to cater to clients in other countries." Paige applied a coat of tinted gloss to her lips. "But he did say he has something important to discuss with me tonight."

Riley let out a little squeal. "Do you think he's going to propose?"

"I hope so." Paige bit back a squeal of her own as a rush of giddiness swept through her.

She melted every time she recalled the smoldering look in his hazel eyes and the husky timbre of his voice when he told her last month he couldn't imagine his future without her in it.

"I can't wait to hear all the juicy details," Riley said. "Call me when you get home."

"Deal."

Paige checked the time on her phone before dropping it into her purse and getting out of the car. She was a few minutes early, but Phillip had told her to ask to be seated in case he ran late, which he often did. His schedule was unpredictable.

A nippy breeze blew her hair across her face as she walked the twenty yards to the stop light at the corner. She wrapped her arms around herself to ward off the chill.

The friendly maître d seated Paige in the already crowded restaurant without question. She sent Phillip a text saying she'd arrived and couldn't wait to see him. His prompt response said he was ten minutes out.

She slipped her phone back into her purse, intent on enjoying the soft music and tantalizing aromas that added to the ambiance of the classy restaurant.

"Are you...Paige Young?" A beautiful redhead with a death grip on the strap of her oversized handbag, sat across the table from her. Her red-rimmed eyes looked like she'd been crying.

"Do I know you?" Paige's head jerked back in surprise. She tried to place the woman as a parent of one of her students, but she didn't look familiar.

"No, but I know you." The redhead shook her head. "Well, I know *of* you." She grabbed the water glass in front of her with a shaky hand and took two large gulps.

Paige gasped. Her shoulders bunched as she scrambled for the words to tell the rude stranger to take a hike without making a huge scene.

Water dribbled down the woman's chin and onto her blue silk blouse. She replaced the water glass, grabbed the napkin off the plate, and dabbed at her shirt. "How embarrassing. Look at me. I'm such a mess. I've been a wreck all day." A sheen of tears filled the woman's eyes before she quickly blinked them away. "I never thought I'd find myself in this position."

A twinge of sympathy pricked Paige's chest. The woman was obviously upset, but she couldn't fathom what it had to do with her.

"What position?" Paige asked slowly. Cautiously.

"I never thought I'd find myself sitting across the table from my fiancé's...girlfriend."

"Your *what*?" A chill swept over Paige as a lead weight settled in her stomach. Her mouth turned dry, but she resisted the urge to grab her

3

own water glass. She'd probably be just as clumsy as the woman across from her if she attempted to take a drink.

Phillip's engaged?

"There must be a m-mistake." The words rushed out of Paige's mouth before she could even think about stopping them.

"Oh, there's been a mistake alright." The other woman's voice turned hard. "Lots of them. All made by Phillip."

Surely, she's not talking about my *Phillip.*

The clank of silverware on ceramic plates and muted voices faded away as Paige's mind raced. She recalled the times Phillip had canceled their plans because something came up at work. How he always stepped out of the room to take work calls. He even had to travel out of town over the weekend occasionally.

But that was just the nature of his job. Wasn't it?

She'd wondered at times if he had commitment issues, because he had yet to take her home to meet his family in Colorado. But maybe he was already committed to someone else.

A squeezing sensation hit her chest, stealing her breath. She gripped the edges of her chair as she focused on drawing air into her lungs.

"I'm sorry. I'm probably doing this very poorly." The redhead twisted the napkin in her hands. A large princess-cut diamond ring flashed on her left hand. "I promised myself I wouldn't make a scene, but I had to say something. And I must admit I'm crazy jealous. You're very pretty. I can see why he likes you." She smoothed her hair back with a still trembling hand. "Listen to me. I'm so nervous, I'm rambling." She drew in a deep breath. "I need to know how serious your relationship with Phillip is."

"Wait a minute. What makes you think I'm your fiancé's girlfr—" Paige shook her head, unable to put those two words together in reference to herself. "That I even know your fiancé?"

"Phillip kept getting messages on his phone last night after falling asleep on my couch." The woman laid the napkin on the table and attempted to smooth the creases she'd created. "I checked to see if it was something worth waking him up for, since he often gets work calls and texts all hours of the day and night." Her hands stilled. "I used to think they were work calls, anyway, until I looked at his phone last night and realized he's been communicating with you for months." Tears filled her eyes again.

"How do you—" Paige shook her head in confusion. "Why would —" Her mind jumped tracks. "What do you mean?" A flood of questions swirled around inside Paige's head, but she couldn't seem to articulate them.

"I don't know what Phillip has told you about his job, but he's led me to believe that ever since he was made a supervisor at Emerson, he's had a lot more responsibilities that require his attention around the clock."

"Wait?" Paige held up a hand. "I think you may have me, or rather my Phillip confused with someone else. My boyfriend is an international business consultant with McKinsey."

"Is that what he told you?" The redhead's eyebrows shot up, then she shook her head vigorously. "Phillip Ellis is not an international business consultant. He works in sales and distribution for Emerson Office Supply."

Ellis. That's my Phillip.

Paige's stomach twisted as tight as the napkin the other woman had been mangling moments ago. If she had any food in her stomach, she would have lost it at the realization of what was happening.

"And it turns out, he wasn't made a supervisor at Whitlock eight months ago. I verified that with his boss today."

Eight months?

That's how long Paige had been dating Phillip after repeatedly running into him at the gym. He'd spent as much time flirting with her as he did exercise most days, yet he had a great physique.

"I think he lied about being made a supervisor, so I wouldn't be suspicious when he suddenly had late meetings and took calls from you at all hours of the day and night."

Still reeling and not wanting to believe this was happening, Paige scrambled for a way to prove the woman wrong. She recalled Phillip mentioning a crazy ex-girlfriend who had been stalking him for years and sabotaging his relationships. That's why he avoided social media.

Or did he avoid it for other reasons?

"Are you Noelle?" Tamping down her doubt, Paige leaned forward and pinned the other woman with a stare. He'd said Noelle would try to drive Paige away if she found out they were dating.

"Goodness no. I've met Noelle." The other woman shuddered. "That woman is psycho." She reached into her handbag and pulled out her driver's license and laid it on the table. "I'm Avery Buchanan. Phillip and I have been engaged for almost a year. We were getting ready to set a wedding date several months ago, but then he decided we should save for a down payment on a house first."

Paige thought of all the dates Phillip had taken her on. How on earth could he save for a down payment on a house with the kind of money he'd been spending on her? Or had he just told Avery that to string her along, like he'd apparently been doing to Paige for months?

Paige didn't know it was possible to simultaneously feel anger toward one person, sympathy for another, and an overwhelming sense of loss for herself. The emotions roiling around inside swirled like a tornado in her stomach. The knot growing there expanded to epic proportions. Had Phillip really cheated on her?

No, he used me *to cheat on his fiancée. The man was engaged to another woman this whole time!*

How had she not seen through his lies? Was she really that naive?

Heat flooded Paige's face as she realized the couples at two nearby tables stared at her, their expressions a mixture of condemnation and empathy. Her body grew hot all over as humiliation swept over her.

"I'm sorry." Sympathy covered Avery's face. "I'm sure this is quite a shock to you. It certainly was to me last night when I read Phillip's texts." Her chin lifted. "I hated you immediately for trying to steal my fiancé, but I read far enough back in his texts to know Phillip is far from innocent." Her gaze dropped to her lap where she fiddled with her purse strap. Then her head popped up. "I...I need to know if you've slept with him."

"What?" Paige's head jerked back again. "No, of course not."

Although Phillip *had* been pressuring her lately for an intimate relationship. Thankfully, he backed off each time she said no.

"I don't want to forgive him or hurt you, but I have more than just myself to think about." Tears filled Avery's eyes again.

"What do you mean?" Icy dread filled Paige. The boulder that had taken up residence in her abdomen made her want to vomit. How could the woman even consider forgiving Phillip?

Avery pulled a series of ultrasound pictures from her purse and slid them across the table.

She's pregnant?

Paige quickly spotted Avery's name and the date near the corner of the top image. They were dated three days ago. A staggering pain pierced her chest as her heart split wide open, leaving her gasping for air. All the hopes and dreams she'd built up over the months of starting a family with Phillip vanished.

"This doesn't prove Phillip is the f-father." Her voice was weak as she made a final desperate attempt to tell the redhead she was wrong.

She no longer wanted anything to do with Phillip, but the soul-crushing disappointment that the man she thought she'd be planning a future with was nothing more than a lying cheat hurt more than anything she'd ever experienced.

"You're right." Avery pulled her phone from her purse and tapped the screen a few times. "This is the two of us at the doctor's office earlier this week." She turned her phone screen so Paige could see a selfie that could only have been taken by the blond-haired, hazel-eyed man she was in love with. He crouched next to Avery, who lay on an exam table, stomach exposed. An ultrasound machine stood in the background.

"He knows you're p-pregnant?" She blinked back the tears that screamed for release.

"Yes, and we finally set a wedding date for April second." Avery's smile looked anything but happy. "I didn't want to have a huge belly in my wedding photos." She gave a small shrug as she pressed her hand to her flat stomach. "We were going make wedding plans over dinner later tonight."

Later.

Of course, Phillip doesn't have a late meeting on Valentine's Day. And he's getting married in six weeks.

What else had he lied about?

Did he lie every time he told me he loved me? That he couldn't imagine his future without me in it.

A collision of some sort behind Paige caused plates to clatter to the floor. She jerked, shooting to her feet. A sudden dizziness hit her as her brain scrambled to process what she'd just learned and searched for an escape from this nightmare.

Phillip said he had something important to discuss with her tonight. She thought he was going to propose. But he probably planned to break up with her. Or did he intend to continue to string her along while he lived a double life?

The thought sickened her.

She blinked away hot tears and looked at Avery. The woman had been incredibly nice under the circumstances. She could have come in and made a huge scene with ugly accusations, blaming Paige for everything. But she didn't.

"I'm so sorry. I swear I had no idea Phillip was enga—" Paige's voice caught. She darted for the door.

Tears blurred her vision, obscuring the surprised and pitying looks from other diners. Thank goodness she didn't know any of them. By the time she made it out the front door of the now-crowded restaurant, she was in full-on ugly cry mode.

He lied to me. Cheated on me. Made me the other *woman. I'm a home wrecker.*

She pushed through the small crowd gathered near the entrance and turned left, intent on leaving before Phillip arrived.

"Paige!" Right on cue, his voice came from down the sidewalk.

She looked over her shoulder to see him hurrying toward her, a large bouquet of red roses in his hand. He didn't look like he intended to break up with her. Her gaze darted to the corner where the light had just turned green for traffic. If she waited to cross, he would catch up to her.

Talking to him now while she was so angry and hurting so badly would only cause a scene that would further humiliate and infuriate her. She couldn't bear to hear more of his lies.

She rounded the corner and darted down the street.

"Paige! Where are you going?"

She needed to get away from him. Fast. With one final look over her shoulder, she darted between two parked cars. She just needed to get to her own car on the other side of the street.

A horn blared.

Tires squealed.

Paige looked up to see a silver crossover bearing down on her. She jerked her arms up in front of her face as if that would somehow protect her from the inevitable.

Pain, sharp and piercing, ricocheted through her left hip and back at the impact. She went down hard, landing on her right shoulder and slamming her head into the pavement.

Through a hazy blur, she registered the sounds of additional tires screeching and more horns honking, mingled with screams, and Phillip yelling her name. Above the cacophony, excruciating pain radiated throughout her body.

Her breaths came in sharp gasps that felt disconnected from her lungs. Phillip's handsome face dropped into her line of sight as her vision rapidly dimmed, plunging her into darkness.

THE DOOR to Summit Physical Therapy opened as Gabe finished rubbing Evan Miller's low back. He hurried over to hold the door for Gladys Fuller, the seventy-five-year-old woman who still used a walker three weeks after knee replacement surgery.

"Ah, thank you, Gabe."

"How are you today, young lady?"

"Terrible, but I made it here for my bi-weekly torture, so I must be alive and kicking still." She waved to the assistants and Dr. Stoker, Gabe's mentor and colleague, as she passed.

"How's the knee feeling?" Gabe followed her as she continued her shuffle to the far side of the room.

"Sore and achy. It kept me up most of the night."

He helped Gladys up onto one of the five tables that lined the south wall. "Let's see how straight you can get your knee this afternoon."

He noted the grimace on Gladys' face as she did her best to straighten her leg. The effort was paltry with less range of motion than earlier this week.

"Looks like it's tight today."

"Yes, and so sore." She rubbed her thigh.

"I'm sure the car ride here gave it plenty of time to stiffen up. Let's start by heating it. Then we'll get you moving."

Gladys' daughter drove her from the small town of Providence to the Tri-Cities twice a week for physical therapy on her knee. The elderly woman would make a full recovery if she kept her appointments and did her exercises, unlike some of their patients from Providence who weren't willing to make the forty-five-minute drive week after week.

Gabe continued to visit with Gladys and other patients throughout the afternoon while he stretched strained muscles and worked out painful knots. The place was always busy, and he loved it.

Shortly before five, he worked with another resident of Providence—a young man with a torn rotator cuff who was the quarterback of the high school football team—when a tall, distinguished gentleman in business attire walked through the door and paused at the receptionist's desk.

Dr. Stoker stood and crossed the room to greet the man. "James, it's good to see you."

"How are you, Paul?" James shook Dr. Stoker's outstretched hand.

Dr. Stoker insisted everyone call him Paul, but Gabe respected the man too much to address him in such a casual manner.

"What brings you to our neck of the woods?" Dr. Stoker asked.

"I have something I'd like to discuss with you. Do you have a few minutes?"

"Sure." Dr. Stoker motioned him to the back of the gym.

James' gaze landed on Travis as they passed. He stopped. "Hey Travis, how's that shoulder coming?"

"Slow." Travis' bored expression said he'd rather be anywhere but here.

"That's to be expected. You do what the therapists tell you and you'll be leading us to another state championship next year." James patted Travis' good shoulder before following Dr. Stoker to the small office the therapists rarely used. They preferred to spend their time on the gym floor with their patients.

Gabe's gaze followed them, his curiosity piqued. He turned back to Travis. "I assume that's Dr. James Young from Providence?" There were only a couple family practitioners in Providence and no specialists that Gabe was aware of.

"Yeah. He's cool, I guess."

"You guess?"

Travis shrugged. "You know, for an old dude."

"Old?" Gabe gaped at Travis. Because of his silver temples, he figured Dr. Young was in his early sixties, but he hardly looked old.

Gabe didn't dare ask Travis how old he thought he was. If the kid thought Dr. Young looked old, he'd call Gabe, who was only thirty, middle aged.

Several minutes later, both men stood at the glass window of the office looking out over the gym. Gabe could have sworn he saw Dr. Stoker point in his direction before he lowered his hand.

"Gabe, will you come here for a minute, please?" Dr. Stoker summoned Gabe into the small office after he finished with Travis. He made introductions. "This is Dr. James Young from Providence Medical Center. And James, I'd like you to meet Dr. Gabriel Rivera. He worked here for three years as an assistant before going to PT school. Then he returned after completing his Doctor of Physical Therapy degree two years ago. He's a skilled therapist and the perfect man to take on your project."

Gabe's chest swelled with pride at Dr. Stoker's words. He gave Dr. Young a questioning look. "Project?"

"Have a seat, Gabe," Dr. Stoker said. "Dr. Young has an interesting proposition. He wants us to open a...satellite office, if you will, in Providence."

"A PT office in Providence?" Gabe gave Dr. Young a sharp look as he settled into a chair. "I know you often send patients our way, but is there that big of need for a full-fledged office in your small town?" Gabe couldn't recall ever stepping foot in the town that was little more than a dot on the map.

"Not full time, no. That's why I feel it would be best to make it an extension of this facility."

And Dr. Stoker wants me to take on the project?

Gabe's heart raced in anticipation. The prospect of an hour-long commute was not appealing, but he'd have his own office. He'd been ready to branch out on his own for some time now, but office space and equipment were expensive, and he was still paying off student loans.

He looked at Dr. Young again. "What kind of space and resources are available?"

"A few years ago, Providence's medical center received a generous donation. We used the funds to add onto the hospital and have been working to bring in specialty clinics like optometry, orthodontia, chiropractic, and counseling, so our citizens don't have to travel so far for their medical needs."

Gabe found himself nodding. Those were all important services but not necessarily on a full-time basis. Was there a big enough need for physical therapy in Providence to make even a part-time clinic sustainable?

Dr. Young went on. "We have a thousand-square-foot space intended for a PT office. I've got personnel and a legal team standing by to complete the necessary paperwork regarding insurance contracts and such. All I need is a list of equipment and supplies from you." The older man's posture exuded confidence, and even though Gabe had just met the man, he read a hint of challenge in Dr. Young's intense blue eyes.

Another surge of excitement filled Gabe, but he tamped it down.

Did he want an office that only saw three to five patients a day? He struggled to see the value in the deal for him professionally and financially.

He narrowed his gaze on Dr. Young and shook his head. "Other than having a vacant space you want to fill, why are you so keen on opening a PT office?"

Dr. Young exchanged a look with Dr. Stoker, who shrugged and nodded. "Your call, James."

Dr. Young stared out the window behind Gabe for a long moment before speaking again. "My daughter was nearly killed in an auto-pedestrian accident two months ago. She suffered multiple fractures to her pelvis, femur, and shoulder."

Gabe couldn't help wincing as the doctor listed his daughter's injuries.

"She's been in a rehabilitation center for eight weeks, but she'll be coming home soon and will need extensive physical therapy. Making the trip to Pasco three times a week will be more than she's capable of for some time."

So, this is personal to the doctor.

Extensive therapy meant Gabe would have job security for a time, but then what? Would he end up having to close the office, because they didn't have enough clients to warrant keeping it open? That wouldn't look good on his resume.

Dr. Young must have sensed his concerns. "Providence is growing. Initially, we'd only require you to have the office open three days a week with extended hours to accommodate patients' work schedules, but if the need grows great enough, we'd welcome a full-time PT office."

Extended hours would mean long days for him, but it'd be worth it for his own space. He knew better than to get his hopes up for a full-time office though.

"You'd finally have your own office," Dr. Stoker said, reading Gabe's thoughts. "And of course, I can always use you here on the other two days of the week. Your leaving will put me in a bind, but I think you should take advantage of this opportunity."

Gabe let out a deep breath and studied the industrial carpet in front of him. The whole thing sounded almost too good to be true.

It's not like he had a social life that would suffer. He'd hardly dated since Harper left him standing at the altar six years ago. And he'd still be able to spend time with his mom and sister on the weekends.

Mom.

All he'd ever wanted was to make her proud. Opening his own PT office would do that.

Dr. Young cleared his throat. "I'm prepared to offer a 'sign-on bonus.'"

Gabe lifted his head to find the older man making air quotes.

"As an incentive, or whatever you want to call it, to sweeten the deal."

"I'm listening."

Dr. Young threw out a figure that was more than Gabe made in a year. He could pay off his student loans and his car.

Dr. Stoker let out a long, low whistle. "If Gabe doesn't want the position in Providence, I'll take it." He chuckled and gave Gabe a look that said he'd be crazy to turn this down. And he was right.

"I'll do it." Gabe locked gazes with Dr. Young's intense blue ones, hoping he didn't end up regretting this down the road.

CHAPTER 2

*G*abe took a final look around the office that smelled like new carpet and vinyl furniture to make sure everything was ready for patients. He let out a sigh. It had been a busy two weeks. The gym wasn't as large as the one in Pasco, but it had all the latest and greatest equipment.

He opened his laptop and clicked on the email Dr. Young sent a few days ago. He'd been so busy getting the new office set up while still logging hours at the office in Pasco that he hadn't had time to look over Paige Young's medical information.

The more he read, the more he realized Paige was lucky to be alive. She'd suffered internal bleeding with multiple pelvic and femoral fractures, in addition to wrecking her right shoulder. The girl had more metal plates, rods, and screws in her body than the weight sets mounted to the wall. Sympathy filled him for a patient he had yet to meet.

The door opened behind Gabe, and a rush of air swept through the room.

"Hey, Gabe. This is a change, huh?" Luke Morrell, one of the assistants from the Pasco office, set his backpack and helmet down behind the receptionist's desk in the corner and peeled off his leather bike jacket before turning on the computer.

"Tell me about it. I can't recall the last time I stood in an empty PT office." Gabe looked around again, feeling a sense of pride laced with a side of panic. The emotions simultaneously took his breath away and made him want to throw up. Could he really make this a profitable office? "Did you complete all the training you were supposed to do?"

"Yes, but that doesn't mean I won't still have questions or find a way to screw things up. I'm a PT assistant, not a receptionist."

"Me either. But we get to do double duty for a while until we're busy enough to require our own receptionist."

"Come on. You know that's never going to happen." Luke tapped a few keys on the computer. "We have a total of six people on the schedule today."

That's three more than I expected.

"I know." Gabe shook his head. "Which means we are going to take very good care of them. At least you get paid whether we have patients or not."

Gabe had done a little finagling with Dr. Young to make sure he and Luke received salaries that compensated them for their time spent in the office and not merely the number of patients they treated each day. And thankfully, Valerie, the receptionist down the hall at the chiropractor's office, was on hand in case they had computer problems.

"Yeah, man. Thanks for that." Luke's head bobbed. "Knowing I'm getting paid a dollar more an hour while I'm here, makes the drive from the Tri-Cities pass a lot quicker."

"The way you drive your bullet bike, you probably got here in half the time it took me."

Luke grinned. "Yeah, but it still takes me three times longer to get to work now than it used to."

It took Gabe four times longer, but he hoped the sacrifice would be worth it in the long run.

"Seriously, man, what am I supposed to do all day?" Luke waved his arms, motioning to the empty room.

Gabe pointed at the backpack behind the younger man. "Homework. You keep your nose to the grindstone, and you'll get your pick of PT schools next year."

He took his laptop to the consultation room at the back of the gym. He wasn't sure how mobile Paige was, but he wanted his hands free in case he needed to help her.

A petite middle-aged woman entered the office as he walked back out onto the gym floor. She held the door open for a pretty young blond who walked slowly with the aid of crutches, favoring her left leg. Shadows framed the young woman's eyes, and despite feminine curves, her slender frame looked like it might blow over in a strong wind.

Knowing the effort Dr. Young went through to get this office up and running before his daughter came home from rehab, Gabe had anticipated working with a spoiled teenage girl, who expected everyone to cater to her. He should have taken note of Paige's age in her file because he was completely unprepared for the beautiful woman with striking blue eyes, who looked to be in her mid-twenties.

"Are you sure you're okay from here?" the older woman asked. "I can stay if you want me to. I'm sure Mr. Harris won't mind filling in for me again in my meeting with the superintendent."

"I'll be fine, Mom. Thanks for the ride and your help this morning."

The older woman hovered as though reluctant to leave. "Call me when you're ready for a ride home. If I can't break away from school, I'll send Faith."

"Okay."

"I'll try to make it home to fix you lunch. If I can't, I'll have Faith do that too."

"Mom." Impatience filled the blonde's voice as she put a hand on her mother's shoulder. "I'm a big girl. I can fix myself a sandwich."

"I just don't want you to overdo it." The older woman tucked a lock of damp hair behind her daughter's shoulder.

Judging by Paige's grimace, she didn't appreciate her mother's hovering. Or maybe she was just tired of being coddled. Either way, she was more independent and less spoiled than Gabe expected.

He approached the women, eager to kick off his practice.

"Tell *him* that." The young woman motioned to Gabe. "He looks eager to torture me."

Her mother spun and faced him. "You must be the new physical therapist. James said you came highly recommended by Paul Stoker." She held out her hand. "I'm Hope Young, Paige's mother."

"It's nice to meet you Mrs. Young. Yes, I'm the new therapist, Dr. Gabriel Rivera." He shook hands with Hope before turning to the younger woman. "You must be Paige."

"Last time I checked." She leaned on the left crutch and smiled as she shook his hand.

Behind the smile that showcased perfect white teeth, Gabe detected an air of exhaustion. It was only ten in the morning, but considering she was still on crutches, the effort it took to shower and dress—even in yoga pants and a t-shirt—must have been taxing.

Paige eyed him skeptically. "You don't look old enough to be a doctor."

"I don't feel it most days. Other days?" He shrugged. "Well...you know how it is when life runs you ragged."

"Yes, I do," she said without hesitation.

"I'm not your typical medical doctor, so I usually insist people call me just Gabe."

"Just Gabe, huh?" This time Paige's smile was big enough to expose a small dimple in her left cheek, but he still sensed reservation behind the emotion.

Considering all she'd been through since the accident, Gabe had a feeling this woman hadn't smiled much over the past few months. Hopefully, he could help her find a reason to smile again. A real smile. Not the exhausted, polite one he'd seen twice now.

I bet she's stunning when she really smiles.

Shaking that thought from his head, he motioned behind the receptionist's desk. "This is Luke, he'll be assisting with your exercises and scheduling your appointments."

Paige acknowledged Luke with a nod and another small upturn of her lips.

"I've got you all checked in, Ms. Young." Luke's right eye twitched in an almost imperceptible wink as he grinned at Paige. The kid was an incorrigible flirt.

"Call me Paige, please." She gave her mother an apologetic look before grimacing. "I'm sure I'll turn into my mother soon enough, no need to rush it."

Hope gave a little chuckle. "I'll take that as my cue to leave. See you later, honey." She turned to Gabe. "How long do you think PT will take?"

"It's hard to say, but Paige has a lot of rehabilitating to do." Gabe made a face that was a mixture of a grimace and a smile. "Best guess? About two hours. Maybe a little longer."

Both women's eyes widened, and Paige's jaw dropped.

Hope stepped closer to him, lowering her brows and voice. "I assume you're aware of the full extent of her injuries?"

"I am."

"Don't you think two hours of physical therapy is kind of long considering all she's been through?"

"It *is* a long time. It'll feel like a lot longer than that to Paige, I'm sure. She's got a lot of down time to make up for, and we'll be working on multiple parts of the body. It's important she get back full range of motion soon."

"But—"

"Mom. I'll be fine." Despite the determined lift of Paige's chin, she didn't look convinced.

"Don't worry, Mrs. Young, your daughter is stronger than you think. Stronger than even she realizes." He gave Paige an encouraging smile. "The therapists did multiple sessions of therapy with her each day at the rehab center, helping her work up to what she has to do now."

"You've got this, honey." Hope patted Paige's shoulder. "Give me a call when you're done."

Gabe motioned to the back of the gym after the door closed behind Hope. "If you'd like to follow me to the consultation room,

we'll do an evaluation and set up a plan for your continued rehabilitation."

"Sure thing, Just Gabe." Her dimple stood out again when she
smiled, but it still didn't reach her eyes.

Chuckling, he walked beside Paige as she slowly made her way
across the room. "Are the crutches for stability or to avoid weight
bearing?"

"Both. My pelvic fractures were unstable, so weight bearing was
delayed by a few weeks. I'm only supposed to put about fifty percent
of my weight on my left leg. Next week, I can bump it up to seventy-
five percent."

"You've only been mobile for two weeks now?" Gabe ventured a
guess. The last person he worked with that had pelvic fractures
couldn't bear weight for eight weeks.

"Depends on your definition of mobile." She gave him another hint
of a smile. "One therapist at the rehabilitation center thought if I
could get myself into a wheelchair then I was considered mobile."

"With limited use of your right arm, I'm sure even that was difficult since you couldn't use it to propel the wheelchair."

"Yes." She let out a sigh. "It's been a long road. Most days I wonder
if I'll ever get back to normal."

"It will take some time, but don't worry, you'll get there," he said
with confidence.

They were almost to the door of the consultation room when
Paige's left crutch caught on the leg of a nearby chair. Her body
lurched forward, but her crutch didn't budge.

A rush of adrenaline surged through Gabe, sending his heart into
his throat, as he watched her pitch forward.

Her right crutch swung wildly, hitting his leg. Then she released
the left one and flailed her arm. Her momentum shifted, and she
suddenly teetered backward as her crutch clattered to the floor. She
let out a cry of alarm.

Gabe threw an arm behind her back. When he was certain he'd
stopped her fall, he wrapped his other arm around her waist to steady

and balance them both. He froze, half bent over with her in his arms, her right crutch sandwiched between them.

She grabbed the front of his shirt in a tight fist and squeezed her eyes shut. She inhaled sharply then seemed to hold her breath.

Gabe did too. He often had to get up close and personal with his patients, but not this personal. He slowly brought them both upright and forced himself to inhale.

"Are you okay?"

Paige's eyes popped open; wide and alarmed. Her head jerked in a nod. "Thanks for catching me. Falling would have hurt so bad."

A spark of attraction shot through Gabe at the intensity of her icy blue eyes. "Are you sure you're okay?" When she nodded, he asked, "Do you feel steady?"

She took a deep breath and slowly let it out. "Yes."

"Good. Then will you loosen the death grip you have on my shirt?" Gabe didn't have much hair on his chest but what little he had was firmly clenched in her fist.

"Sorry." She relaxed her hold on his shirt then patted his chest before pulling her hand away.

He waited for her to get her right crutch under her before removing his hand from her waist. Keeping a hand at her back, he bent to pick up her other crutch.

A surge of protectiveness tightened his chest as he watched her make her way into the room. The emotion surprised him. Only his mother and sister had ever evoked that feeling in him.

Gabe opted to leave the door open. There was no need for privacy since the gym was empty and leaving it open felt like a good safety measure, because he was very attracted to Paige.

He'd worked with plenty of pretty women over the years, and he had no problem staying professional. Paige felt different somehow. Maybe it was the distress in her eyes that spoke of emotional pain as well as physical.

He stayed close to her until she'd settled into a chair, then he opened his computer. "Your father sent me some information concerning your injuries, but I'd like to hear from you how you sustained them."

"I ran in front of a car." The matter-of-fact way she said the words surprised him.

"You *ran* in front of a car?" Gabe's jaw dropped, and he felt his eyebrows hike up. He snapped his mouth closed. "Like you were out jogging and forgot to check both ways before crossing the street?"

"I wasn't jogging." Shadows flitted through Paige's eyes. She rubbed her right arm as though trying to ward off a chill. Her eyes bounced around the room, looking everywhere but at him. "I checked the traffic. I knew there were cars coming, but I decided to cross anyway."

"Why?" Again, Gabe struggled to hide his surprise.

"Are you always so nosy?" She lifted her chin, a defiant glint in her eyes.

He gave her a patient smile. "It's important for me to understand your mental and emotional state as we work together to heal your body."

She rolled her eyes. "If you're asking if I was suicidal, the answer is no."

"Glad to hear it." He continued to study her face, trying to figure out why she'd risked her life like that.

She let out a little huff. "It was a stupid thing to do. I know that." Her eyes darted away again. "It's just... I had received some upsetting news and wasn't thinking clearly, okay?"

There were things Paige wasn't telling him. Things that could affect her healing. He didn't blame her for not wanting to confide in him, but he couldn't help being concerned about her psychological wellbeing.

As though reading his thoughts, she said, "You don't need to worry about my mental state." She motioned over her shoulder toward the wall. "Emily Winters, our local psychologist, has already made a house call to check on me."

"House call? Dr. Young has even more sway in this town than I thought." He spoke the words under his breath, but she heard them.

"What's that supposed to mean?" Her brow furrowed.

Warmth crept up Gabe's neck. "Nothing."

"Emily is family." Paige made a rolling motion with her hand. "She's married to my cousin, so that makes her *my* cousin, I guess."

He nodded in understanding, glad Paige was working with a psychologist. Ninety percent of healing the body was mental.

He glanced at the notes on his computer then back to her. "We're going to be working closely together for the next few months. It's important you understand I have your best interests at heart and trust me, even when I ask you to do hard things." When she nodded, he continued. "Healing the body can sometimes trigger emotional trauma. I'm not a psychologist, but I am a good listener, if you ever need to talk something out." Then he gave a light-hearted smile. "PT can feel like torture if you can't relax and be yourself."

"I don't even know who that is anymore." Her shoulders drooped, and she shook her head as she stared at the floor in front of her.

Gabe feared she had as much emotional trauma associated with her accident as she did physical trauma. "Does your current identity crisis have something to do with your accident and your limited mobility?"

Paige studied her hands for a moment, then she raised her gaze to the ceiling.

He spotted the sheen of tears in her eyes before she blinked them away. When he said he was a good listener, he didn't expect to have to employ that talent so soon. He waited, giving her ample opportunity to answer his question.

When she lowered her gaze again, she pinned him with a hard stare. "Have you ever found yourself in a situation you never thought you'd be in?"

Memories from the darkest times in Gabe's life flooded his mind, intermingling until he couldn't separate the events and the pain they'd caused him; his mom crying at the breakfast table because his dad didn't come home last night; watching her battle breast cancer a short time later; his sister's rebellion and unexpected pregnancy; Harper's mother handing him a handwritten note on pink paper while he stood in front of a chapel full of people.

"More times than I care to count," he said.

"No, I mean a situation that is...morally wrong. One you'd never intentionally choose to be in."

He hadn't made the morally gray choices that some of his loved ones did, but they'd affected his life nonetheless.

"Yes, unfortunately." His answer was barely audible.

"Well, I hadn't." She lowered her gaze to her hands again. "Not until two months ago. It has left me questioning all my life choices."

He'd been there, done that. For years.

Each time the bottom fell out of his world, he'd spent months questioning every choice he'd ever made. Was it his fault his father left? If he'd been more obedient would his dad have stayed? If he'd played baseball like his dad, instead of wrestling, would his father have come to his games? And if he hadn't been so focused on getting into PT school, would he have been able to give Harper the attention she needed?

Instead of letting the disappointments derail his life, he'd become more intentional about everything he did. More focused. More dedicated. More cautious.

Gabe couldn't help wondering what situation Paige found herself in that caused such introspection. What happened prior to her accident to make her question every aspect of her life? He remained quiet for a moment, waiting to see if she'd say more, but she reined in her emotions and shot him an apologetic look before staring at the floor again.

"Questioning all your life choices at once is rarely a good idea." He kept his tone light. "How about we take life one day at a time. We'll set small, achievable goals and before long, I'm sure you'll find things have worked themselves out."

They had for him, but it had taken a lot of hard work. Okay, so he was still waiting for some things to work out. But he knew he wasn't responsible for his dad's desertion, and he didn't need his father's approval to be successful. And deep down, he knew it wasn't his fault Harper left him at the altar only to elope with his best friend two weeks later.

Paige's gaze met his, and her lips lifted in what looked like a forced smile. "You're right. My mom keeps reminding me everything happens for a reason. I know I brought this on myself with my own dumb actions..." She made a sweeping motion with her hand, motioning to her body. "Now, I need to make sure I learn the lesson God wants me to learn."

Did I learn the lessons God wanted me to learn?

"DON'T PUSH your right shoulder farther than is comfortable," Dr. Rivera's gentle voice reminded Paige of her father, who was well known for his excellent bedside manner.

After heating her back, hip, and shoulder, Dr. Rivera had her do a series of gentle stretches, leading into exercises that required more movement. Paige now sat in a chair slowly rolling a large pink yoga ball away from her body with her hands, then back in again. She winced every time she reached the limit of her ability in both her right arm and low back.

It was such a simple stretch, but it pulled at muscles she'd used very little over the past two months. Everything the good-looking therapist with killer eyelashes had asked her to do so far—pelvic tilts, clamshells, using a pulley to lift her injured arm—had been easy. Well, they used to be before her accident. Now, even the slightest activity exhausted her.

"Breathe in when you come upright, then slowly let out all the air as you sink into the stretch. Just until it becomes uncomfortable. The point is not to cause more pain." He stood nearby, making Paige self-conscious of her every move.

She was the only patient in the whole office, so she had his undivided attention. Even Luke had his head down in what looked like a large textbook.

Dr. Rivera—Just Gabe, Paige corrected herself—was a lot better looking than Agnes, the full-figured, middle-aged therapist she'd worked with at the rehab center. Paige had repeatedly found herself distracted by the three long hairs sticking out of the mole on Agnes' chin. Now, she found herself jealous of her therapist's eyelashes.

It should be illegal for men to have eyelashes that thick and long.

She couldn't believe how young Dr. Rivera was. He was probably older than he looked, which was late twenties, but he sure didn't look it. He also had a great sense of style. His charcoal gray slacks hugged his trim waist and muscular thighs in an attractive way. And his light blue button-down shirt not only accentuated the muscles in his broad shoulders, it also provided a striking contrast to his dark hair. His Star Wars socks sporting Yoda's face stood out from the business casual ensemble.

She couldn't help letting her gaze drift to his left hand. No ring.

Is he single? Or is he one of those men who doesn't bother to wear a ring?

Her thoughts turned to Phillip. Did he wear a ring now that he was married? Or did he have another woman on the side already?

Nope. Not going there.

She forced thoughts of Phillip from her mind.

When she finished her stretches with the yoga ball, Gabe guided her to a stationary bike. "Have you ridden a recumbent bike since your accident?"

"Yes, in the rehab center, but not until the last two weeks."

"How did it feel?"

"Painful. My muscles loosened up after a bit and it wasn't so bad, but I was sore and achy afterward."

"That's understandable, considering the kind of hardware you're sporting now and how much down time you've had." He motioned for her to start pedaling. "Our bodies are meant to move, so when we restrict movement after injuries, it shuts down to an extent to protect itself from further damage." Gabe pressed buttons on the bike's console. "It's time to wake your body up and remind it what it's supposed to be doing." He watched her pedal for a moment. "Nice and easy. Go as fast or as slow as you're comfortable with."

She relaxed a little when he walked away to talk to Luke. She did her best to distract her mind from the uncomfortable twinges in her back by letting her eyes roam the room, noticing the inspirational quotes hanging on the walls. She read the one closest to her. *All things are difficult before they are easy.*

Boy, isn't that the truth.

Until two months ago, life had never been truly difficult for Paige. But since waking up in the hospital, she had faced both physical and emotional challenges that often felt insurmountable.

She'd quickly decided being confined to a bed for weeks was a special kind of torture. Especially when she still experienced nerve pain, despite the narcotics they gave her. Drugs that did little to soothe the ache in her heart or keep her from thinking about Phillip's duplicity.

She took only over-the-counter pain relievers now, and her pain had settled into a dull ache, both in her heart and body, but no way would she open herself up to that kind of pain again. It wasn't worth it. She'd be the best aunt ever and spoil her nieces and nephew rotten, but she'd resigned herself to a life of being single.

When her five minutes on the bike were up, Paige was ready for a nap. However, Gabe motioned for her to follow him to another piece of equipment with a slanted, padded board, and Paige wanted to cry.

He stayed close as she crossed the room with the help of her crutches. Tension hunched his shoulders as though prepared to catch her again at any moment.

Warmth crept up her cheeks. She couldn't believe she caught her crutch on a stupid chair and practically threw herself at him. The warmth grew to full-on heat at the memory of him having to ask her to let go of his shirt and the way she'd patted his chest before removing her hand. The surprising sense of security she'd felt in his arms made her reluctant to let go.

Just Gabe is every bit as strong as he looks.

"Did they ever put you on a Total Gym in the rehabilitation center?"

"What?" Paige pulled her thoughts from the firmness of his chest.

"The Total Gym." He motioned to the contraption in front of them. "It's for squats."

"No. Because I was so limited in my mobility and weight bearing, my PT consisted mostly of aqua therapy after my incisions healed. That and things that would help me be able to dress and care for myself."

"Aquatic therapy is excellent for patients who can't bear full weight. Did you do well in the pool?"

"I liked it. Moving was easier and less painful, but if I stirred the water too much, I lost my balance."

"I can imagine." Gabe pinched his bottom lip as though deep in thought. "I can tell these exercises are still painful for you. Would you like to continue to do some aquatic therapy? I assume Providence has a city pool?"

"Yes, they have a nice one." Paige nodded. "Are you saying you want to work with me there instead of here?"

"Don't get your hopes up too fast." He pointed a finger at her. "You need to do more exercises than we can do in the water, but if I'm able to make arrangements with the manager, we can do one of your three PT sessions each week at the pool." He took out his phone and made a note. "Luke or I will call or text you when I have more details."

"Okay."

Being the only patient in the office, she already felt self-conscious of the one-on-one attention. Working alone with him at the pool would be awkward, but she loved the idea of getting back in the water.

Gabe dropped his phone into his pocket and clapped his hands. "Time to do squats."

"Easy for you to say." Paige let sarcasm fill her voice. "You're not the one doing them."

He grinned at her. "We have the board slanted to a thirty-degree angle, so you won't be bearing full weight." He held his hands out. "Let me help you get settled on the Total Gym."

She surrendered one crutch at a time and took Gabe's hands to slowly lower herself onto the slanted board that wasn't as padded as she thought. The calluses on his strong hands proved he was as active outside the office as he was inside.

He tapped the metal plate at the end of the bench. "Place your feet here." He gave her a few more instructions, helping her get properly situated. "Good, now push up."

He released a strap above her head. "Okay, you're good to go. Bend your knees and sink down until they're at ninety degrees. If ninety feels too easy, squat a little lower."

She did as he instructed, again feeling the pull in her low back and the tightness in her right thigh.

"How does that feel?"

"It's tight, but it's doable."

"Good. Remember, we want to stretch your limits but not push them so far we cause more injury. Discomfort from tight muscles is okay, pain is not." He pushed buttons on a timer, making it beep repeatedly. "Let's go for five minutes."

Five minutes!

While Paige had lain in a hospital bed day after day, she'd dreamed of being able to get up and move. She longed to go jogging or swing dancing. She'd even visualized working up a sweat in Zumba class. However, now that she was becoming more mobile, she longed to spend more time in her bed. She had never been so exhausted in her life.

This time when Gabe walked away, he didn't talk to Luke but rather sat at a small portable desk and began typing on his laptop.

Luke lifted his head and scanned the room. "Hey Gabe, can we put on some music?" He nodded toward a shelf that held a portable speaker.

"Sure, but I get to pick the music." Gabe pulled his phone from his pocket.

"Come on, that's not fair."

"Get used to the disappointment. Because when it comes to choosing the music for the office, you won't ever be assigned that task."

Luke's chin jutted out. "Dr. Stoker let me pick. Once."

"Once. You blew it by playing that rap garbage."

"I won't play rap. I'll put on something else, I promise."

"You can't fool me." Gabe pointed at Luke now. "I've seen your playlists. Your second choice is always hard rock."

"It's better than the stuff that puts everyone to sleep."

The longer the debate went on, the more Paige recognized the teasing tone in the two men's voices. They had obviously worked together before and had a good relationship. Despite giving him a hard time, Luke seemed to respect Dr. Rivera.

"How about we let Paige decide?" Gabe said.

She lifted her head. "Decide what?"

"What kind of music should we listen to?" Gabe gave her an expectant look.

Was this some kind of test? Gabe and Luke obviously preferred wildly different kinds of music which they were very vocal about. Depending on how she responded, would she make an enemy of one or the other?

"Please no country," Luke said under his breath.

Paige was tempted to say just that to see how the tall, lanky PT assistant responded, but she wasn't a big fan of country music, unless she was swing or line dancing. That was one area where she and her cousin Riley differed. In fact, they'd had many conversations similar to Gabe and Luke's argument.

"How about soft pop?" She said it with hesitation for fear of how both men might react.

"Yes!" Gabe pumped an arm in the air while Luke groaned and dropped his head onto his textbook. "A woman after my own heart."

Paige froze, mid squat. It was a common saying, but to have her physical therapist say it about her was...odd.

Luke must have thought so too, because his head jerked up, his right brow arching. The broad grin on his face said he didn't intend to let Gabe live the comment down.

Gabe's own eyes widened, and ruddy spots colored his tan cheeks. "I uh..." He coughed. "I didn't mean that like it sounded." He gave a small shake of his head and hunched one shoulder. "I just meant that you have excellent taste in music."

Luke snickered behind the reception desk, but Paige didn't tear her gaze away from Gabe until he busied himself on his computer again.

Needing something to focus on besides Just Gabe's slip-up, she read the quote on the opposite wall. *A positive attitude leads to positive outcomes.* Emily, her cousin who was a psychologist, had reminded her that having a positive attitude would speed up her healing.

But healing was painful. She'd only been doing squats for a few minutes, and her butt and thighs were on fire. Her lungs weren't doing much better.

Being positive had never been a problem for Paige. In fact, her family used to call her Lil' Miss Sunshine when she was young because she was always so cheerful. But knowing Phillip lied to her and strung her along for eight months while he was engaged to another woman, made her think she was too naive and trusting. If she was more pessimistic and cynical, maybe she wouldn't have fallen for a man who ended up breaking her heart.

Paige was halfway through her five minutes of squats when the door to the PT office opened and Gladys Fuller, her fourth-grade teacher, walked into the office, supporting herself with a cane.

"Awe, there's my favorite tyrant." A gleam filled Gladys' eyes as she clapped a hand to her mouth in feigned shock. "I mean that handsome therapist." She waved at Luke behind the receptionist's desk. "And you brought the charming assistant with you. I couldn't believe my ears when the receptionist in Pasco told me we were getting our own physical therapy office here in Providence. How did you swing this, Gabe?"

"You can thank Paige." Gabe motioned to her.

Paige stopped deep in a squat. "What's that supposed to mean?"

Those small ruddy spots returned to his cheeks.

"Nothing. Sorry." When she continued to scowl at him, he went on. "It's just that your dad went to great lengths to get a PT office set up in Providence, so you wouldn't have to travel to Pasco for physical therapy." He turned his attention back to Gladys and grinned. "You could say Dr. Young made me a deal I couldn't refuse."

Gladys made her way over to Paige. "I'm so glad you're doing better. I think all of Providence has been praying for you and your family ever since we heard about your accident. It was such a shock to hear you'd been hit by a car, especially after what happened to Ben's wife and daughter a few years ago."

Paige gave Gladys a tight smile. "I appreciate everyone's prayers."

She could hardly compare her accident with the anguish her brother, Ben, went through four years ago. What happened to her was her own fault, but Ben had no control over the car accident that killed his wife. Having his infant daughter kidnapped from the car had almost destroyed her brother.

Paige was good at finding the silver lining in every situation, but she had been unable to find a silver lining for Ben. Not until single mother Amy Lawson's car broke down in Providence, and Ben stepped up and came to Amy and her daughter's rescue.

Where's my silver lining?

Learning the truth about Phillip before he married Avery didn't feel like much of a silver lining.

Paige watched Gabe tease Gladys about using her cane to fight off the men. She seemed to enjoy joking with him as much as Luke did. Was he this jovial with all his patients?

Did he really think of her as some sort of pampered princess? He hadn't called her that, but he'd insinuated it when he said her father went to great lengths to get this office set up.

Who am I kidding? I am.

She'd been surrounded by family ever since her accident. As soon as they were able, her parents had transferred her to a rehabilitation center in the Tri-Cities area, so her family could visit more often without having to make the four-hour drive to Seattle. Her dad had been adamant about bringing her home to recuperate as soon as possible, promising her the best in physical therapy care.

She looked at Just Gabe. It was too early to know if her father had delivered or not, but she wanted her life back. Well, her life pre-Phillip, that is. And there was only one way that was going to happen.

Hard work and determination.

Fighting a grimace, she sank deeper into her squat.

CHAPTER 3

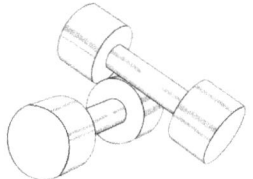

"*H*ow did PT go today?"

Paige and her parents had barely settled around the dinner table when her dad started with the questions.

"It was exhausting, but good." Paige gave a thoughtful nod.

"You should have seen her when I picked her up." Mom served herself green beans. "She was wiped out."

"Gee thanks, Mom." Paige didn't need her mother confirming she'd looked as exhausted as she felt by the time she'd finished PT.

"You know what I mean, dear." Mom patted Paige's arm. "You're as beautiful as ever, but you looked like a limp rag this afternoon. I'm glad you took a good nap."

"Me too." The three-hour nap had restored her energy. "I only hope it doesn't keep me from sleeping tonight."

She was stuck in a vicious cycle. Physical exertion wore her out, so she napped. But napping made it hard to sleep at night, which only left her more tired the next day.

"That's what your sleeping pills are for." Dad gave her a stern look.

"I know, but they make me more sluggish the next day."

Dad nodded in understanding as he buttered a roll. "What did you think of Dr. Rivera?"

Gorgeous. Charming. Kind. Killer eyelashes.

So many words came to mind but voicing them felt inappropriate.

"He's handsome," Mom said when Paige didn't answer right away.

Took the words right out of my mouth.

Not that she'd ever admit to her father that she found her physical therapist attractive.

"And young," Mom added.

"Good thing he's not thirty years older, huh?" Paige's dad winked at her mom. "Or I might have some competition."

"No." Mom waved a hand in dismissal then she wiggled her eyebrows at Paige. "But when you finish PT, we should arrange for you to get to know Dr. Rivera on a personal level."

"Oh please, Mom, no." Paige was done with men.

Dad's gaze shifted back to Paige just as she shoved a bite of chicken in her mouth. "Well, now I know what your mom thinks of the new physical therapist, but what do you think of him, Paige?"

She took her time chewing as she debated how to respond. She was tempted to echo her mom's words, because Gabe was definitely young and handsome. And strong too. He had the kind of thick, wavy hair that made her want to plunge her fingers in and mess it up. But she doubted that's what her father wanted to hear. He was interested in Gabe's professional abilities.

"He seems to know his stuff," Paige finally said after swallowing. "He had me do a much broader range of exercises than the therapists at the rehab center."

He also rolled up his sleeves, exposing muscular forearms, and spent nearly twenty minutes helping her stretch at the end of her session and massaging her tight muscles. The therapists at the rehab center had never done that.

"You'll feel each and every one of those exercises tomorrow, I'm sure." Dad chuckled. "But you'll start seeing real progress soon in your ability to get around and do things."

"I hope so." Paige was tired of being an invalid, and even more tired of being treated like one.

Gabe was right. She was stronger than she thought. Surprisingly, she'd made it through two and a half hours of PT. Most of the exercises caused some discomfort, but it felt amazing to move again.

"Now that you're on your way to full recovery, what are your plans?" Dad asked as he cut a piece of chicken.

The question took Paige by surprise, because for over two months all she'd thought about was making it through each day.

Dad gave her an apologetic look. "Sorry, I didn't mean to make it sound like we're trying to get rid of you already."

"You should be," Paige said. "You've been sitting by my hospital bed and visiting me in the rehabilitation center for over two months. I'm as ready to get on with my life as you are, believe me." She took a bite of her mashed potatoes and let them melt in her mouth before she spoke again. "I'm just not sure what that looks like right now."

"It's okay, honey." Mom put a hand on her arm. "Emotional healing can take as long—sometimes even longer—than physical healing."

To avoid questions concerning her accident and Phillip's absence at the hospital, she'd told her parents she and Phillip had broken up. She'd led them to believe he'd dumped her, which was essentially true, since he'd set a wedding date with another woman.

"The school year is almost over. You have the whole summer to decide on your next steps." Mom changed the subject. "I assume you still have a position at your school to return to next year?"

When Principal Stevens heard Paige had been hit by a car and nearly died, he hadn't balked at giving her all the time off she needed, even when she ran out of PTO. He'd found an excellent long-term substitute to fill in for her, and the other second-grade teachers had rallied around the sub, helping with lesson plans and providing support.

Paige had been miffed about being replaced so easily, but when she realized what a long recovery she had ahead of her, the disappointment turned into gratitude.

"Yes, I got an email from Principal Stevens this morning." Paige fiddled with her fork. "He assured me he'd hold my job for me."

But he also wanted to know if she intended to return next school year. Paige had wanted to respond, telling him of course, she planned to return, because she loved her job. But for some reason, she'd hesitated.

Was it because she still wasn't fully healed? Or because she'd enjoyed being close to family and didn't want to lose that? Returning to Seattle was one of the life choices she was currently questioning.

Something had been missing from her life ever since her cousin Riley moved back home to Providence last year. She'd thought it was because she was eager to get married and start a family. Something she'd hoped to do with Phillip.

Her grip on her fork tightened with the familiar twinge that seized her chest every time she thought about him. She forced thoughts of Phillip from her mind.

"I'm glad you still have a job to go back to after all these months," Mom said, "but I'll be sad to see you leave when school starts again. Seattle is just too far away."

"I know." Paige's gaze dropped to her plate.

Other than her job, there wasn't anything left for her in Seattle. Her hopes of marrying and starting a family with Phillip had been crushed.

Gah. Stop thinking about Phillip already.

Dad turned his attention to her mom. "And how was your day, dear?"

Grateful the conversation had shifted away from her, Paige tuned out while her mother, who was the high school principal, talked about how busy this time of year was and how she'd finally secured a guest speaker for graduation.

There's nothing waiting for me in Seattle except my job. But the only thing here for me is my family.

Would it be enough? With only one elementary school, she'd be hard pressed to find a job teaching in this sleepy little town.

I suppose I could try the Tri-Cities area.

She was still mulling around the idea of searching for a job closer to home when her parents shooed her from the kitchen while they cleaned up. Helpless and hopeless. That was her life now.

The front door opened as she settled on the couch. Her nieces,

Kallie and Cassey, ran into the family room followed by their much-slower, little brother James whose toddling run looked like a drunk football player zigzagging toward the end zone.

"Aunt Paige!" Kallie, the outgoing one, ran full bore toward her.

"Kallie!" Paige's brother, Ben, darted forward to stop his daughter. "Remember you have to be careful around Aunt Paige."

Kallie skidded to a stop, and Cassey, who always followed her sister, ran into her. "Is she still broken?"

Paige's sister-in-law, Amy, crouched down by the four-year-old girls who weren't related by blood but could almost be twins with their blond hair and blue eyes. "She's not broken anymore, but she's still healing."

"Like my booboo?" Cassey asked, angling her elbow that sported a Band-Aid up in the air.

Paige laughed. "Exactly like your booboo, Cass."

"Do you need Mommy to kiss your booboo better?" Kallie asked. "My owies always feel better after Mommy kisses them."

Paige laughed. This was why she wanted to stay in Providence. She loved being surrounded by family.

AN HOUR LATER, Paige was ready for a little less family and some fresh air. She heaved a sigh of relief when her phone chimed with a text from her cousin.

Riley: *Want to go for a drive?*

Paige: *YES.*

Paige loved her nieces, but they both kept insisting she help them color their picture. And Kallie's pointy, little elbow had been digging into her good thigh for the last fifteen minutes.

When Riley arrived, Paige hobbled outside and breathed in the fresh air.

Riley frowned, concern filling her face as she held the passenger door of her Jeep open for Paige. "Um...I didn't think about how we were going to get you up inside."

"We got this." After being cooped up in the hospital then a rehab center for over two months, Paige refused to let this little setback keep her from going for a ride. "Give me a minute. I'll figure it out."

She shifted this way and that before leaning back against the seat, handing over a crutch, and grabbing a hold of the handlebar with her good arm. She pulled herself up as much as her strength allowed. "Help me lift my left leg in."

Riley obliged, being careful not to jostle Paige more than necessary.

"Okay, now give me a boost up with the right leg." Paige's voice was strained from the effort.

Riley clasped her hands together and put them under Paige's foot when it came off the ground and lifted so Paige could pull herself onto the seat.

"Yay, we did it!" Riley gave her a high five before closing the door.

Paige sucked in a deep breath and wiped the beads of perspiration from her brow before Riley climbed in the driver's side.

Just Gabe had said she was stronger than she thought, but Paige wasn't so sure. No yet, anyway.

Thinking about her therapist brought to mind the strange dream she had this afternoon. Gabe had twisted her up like a pretzel then demanded she confess. She wasn't sure what he wanted her to confess, nor how her body contorted like that, so the whole thing left her feeling confused.

She'd read somewhere the brain processed emotions and consolidated memories while dreaming. What emotions and memories did she need to process from her PT session?

She recalled the way Gabe caught and held her secure in his strong arms. His concern and tenderness made her want to tell him exactly what drove her to dart in front of a car. She hadn't told anyone the full truth about Phillip, and apparently it was eating at her so badly it affected her dreams now.

She'd cried so many tears while in the hospital she thought she'd processed all the emotions from his deceit, but maybe she still had some unresolved issues.

"Paige?" Judging by the look on Riley's face, she'd said her name more than once.

"Sorry." She gave Riley a sheepish look. "What did you say?"

"Where do you want to go?"

"Anywhere. I don't care." She waved her hand in a circular motion, ending with pointing out the window. "Let's drive up to the bluff."

"Are you okay?" Worry lines creased Riley's forehead.

"Of course, I'm fine." Paige pasted on a smile then changed the subject. "Where's Daniel tonight?"

"At his AA meeting."

"That's right. I'm glad he's still going."

"Me too." Riley put the Jeep into gear and backed out of the driveway. "He just started mentoring a guy who is ten years older than him."

"That's great."

They talked as Riley drove north of town, then turned to the east before hitting the Double Diamond Ranch that had been Paige's second home growing up. Even though it felt like old times, Paige's chest grew tighter with each mile. She didn't want everyone to know what happened with Phillip, but she needed to talk to someone. And Riley was her person. She talked to Riley about everything.

Riley had barely put the Jeep into park on top of the bluff before she grinned at Paige. "I've got a secret I've been dying to tell someone."

Paige smiled back at her best friend. She loved that she was Riley's person too. "What kind of secret?" She suspected she already knew, but she played along.

"I'm pregnant!" Riley said with a squeal. "But you can't tell anyone yet. We're trying to decide how to announce it to our families."

"Congratulations!" Paige carefully leaned over and hugged Riley with feigned enthusiasm. No, not feigned. She was truly happy for her cousin, but her own secret put a massive damper on her ability to be cheerful.

They chatted for several minutes about Riley's morning sickness, her due date, and whether they were going to find out the gender, then Paige couldn't fight it anymore. "There's something I need to tell you," she blurted out. "Phillip was cheating on me."

"What?" Riley's smile disappeared as she turned wide eyes on Paige. "Are you serious?"

"Dead serious." Paige held her gaze. "Actually, he was using me..." She jabbed a finger into her chest. "To cheat on his fiancée."

"He's engaged?" Riley's eyes grew even wider, and her jaw dropped. She looked so comical Paige would have laughed if she wasn't so miserable.

"Well, he's married now, and she's—" Paige's voice broke as the emotions of that terrible Valentine's Day rushed to the surface all over again. "Sh-she was very pretty and nice, c-considering the circumstances."

"Wait, you met her?" Riley unbuckled her seat belt and shifted to face Paige. "Like actually talked to her?"

"She showed up at Tulio's on Val-Valentine's Day before Phillip did." Snot and tears ran down Paige's face now, but she didn't care.

She thought she'd worked through Phillip's deceit, but apparently, she hadn't even started. All the tears she'd shed in the hospital had simply been her grieving the loss of what could have been.

"She ambushed you and told you she was dating Phillip too? And you believed her just like that?" Riley grabbed napkins from the glove compartment and handed them to Paige.

"No, not just like that." Paige mopped at her face. "She said she'd been engaged to Phillip for almost a year, but I didn't believe her— even though she had an engagement ring—until she showed me a picture on her phone of her and Phillip at her ultrasound appointment."

"Ultrasound?" Riley's mouth dropped open again. "She's pregnant?"

A new rush of tears filled Paige's eyes as she nodded. "They got m-married last month."

"That lying, cheating louse!" Riley smacked the steering with the palm of her hand. "How could he do that to you?"

"And why?" Paige sniffled. "Why did he ask me out when he was already engaged?"

"I always knew there was something I didn't like about that man." Anger filled Riley's voice.

"You should have told me." Then before Riley could speak, Paige waved her hand and went on. "I had a feeling you didn't like him. At first, I thought you were just jealous of the time I spent with him. Then later, I got the impression you didn't think he was good enough for me because he traveled so much."

Except he didn't really travel.

"He *wasn't* good enough for you." Riley's brows tilted downward as remorse filled her face. "I'm sorry I wasn't around for you to talk to last year. Maybe if I'd told you something felt off about him, you would have thought twice about getting involved with him." She leaned over the center console to slide her arm around Paige's shoulders and pulled her close until Paige's head rested on her shoulder.

"Maybe, but none of it was your fault. You were dealing with so much after being assaulted last year." Paige shook her head. "No, this is all on me. We had so many friends getting married, I decided I wanted that too. When Phillip paid attention to me, I jumped in with both feet."

"So, when you left the restaurant and got hit by the car it was after meeting Phillip's pregnant fiancée? Not because Phillip dumped you?"

Paige dabbed at her eyes as she nodded. "I was in shock and utterly humiliated, but then I spotted Phillip coming down the sidewalk with a bouquet of roses. I just couldn't face him, so I..." Paige's voice died off as she acknowledged yet again how stupid she'd been.

She should have had the courage to face Phillip and tell him to take a hike. She was just so certain she'd been hearing wedding bells that finding out they weren't for her left her reeling.

Riley brushed a lock of hair back from Paige's face. "Why didn't you tell everyone what really happened?"

"I just couldn't." Paige lifted her head and pointed a finger at her cousin. "And you can't either."

"Why not?"

"I'm ashamed. I-I...was the *other woman*," she said the words with disgust. "I'm practically a homewrecker." Paige shifted her gaze to stare out her window. "I'm such an idiot."

"It's not like you did it on purpose. It's not your fault he was living a double life."

"Maybe not, but I should have realized something wasn't right." Paige shook her head again as she straightened in her seat.

"Hey," Riley massaged Paige's shoulder. "I know it's been a rough road, and you still have a ways to go, but you're going to be okay."

Paige wanted desperately to believe Riley, so she nodded. "But why did things have to turn out like this? Why couldn't God just tell me with a neon sign or something that Phillip was wrong for me. I would have listened. Eventually."

Paige's mind raced over the past year. Had God tried to warn her? She couldn't think of any signs she might have missed. Sure, Phillip was gone a lot, but he was very devoted when he was around. Had she been so sure he was "the one" that she'd overlooked the warning signs?

"Maybe you just needed a love reset," Riley said.

"A what?" Paige's full attention was on her cousin now.

"It's something Daniel and I joke about. A year ago, I was content with my life in Seattle. No way would I have considered coming back home if Collin hadn't attacked me. And Daniel would never have come back home if he wasn't struggling with his sobriety." Riley grinned as she shrugged. "God needed to break us down to build us up again, and He needed to put us where we could find the one we were meant to be with."

Did God break me down, so He can build me up again? The way He wants me to be.

For the first time since they parked, Paige took a moment to appreciate the beautiful view that lay before her. Green pastures with grazing cattle, circular hay fields, and a golden sunset took her breath away.

Did God mean for her to find love in Providence? Paige almost burst out laughing. The prospects in this small town were seriously limited.

No, she couldn't trust a man with her heart again. Not for a very long time. Besides, she had other more pressing matters to worry about.

"Do you think I should go back to Seattle?"

"Why wouldn't you go back?" Riley's brows knit together. "You love your job there."

"I do, but it's so far away from family."

"I know what you mean. When I first came back last year, the last thing I wanted was my mom and my brothers nosing around in my life, but they were all there for me when I needed them most." Only a hint of dark shadows flitted through Riley's eyes at the mention of needing her family.

Paige was glad her friend had been able to work through the trauma of being drugged and abducted last spring. "Exactly. I didn't realize how much I missed my family until I came home."

Riley rested a hand on the steering wheel as she watched the sun set. "It's funny how when we were young, we couldn't wait to get out of this small town. But after living in the city for years, we realized it's not so bad."

"Oh, it's still bad." Paige laughed. "With it's quirky citizens, gossip mill, and slow pace, but I've decided I don't mind those things so much anymore."

"Are you thinking about moving back then?" Riley's face turned hopeful.

"Other than my job, it doesn't feel like there's anything left for me in Seattle." Paige ticked items off on her fingers. "First you left, then Jen got engaged, and Shaylee accepted that job on the east coast. Come August, I'll need to find new roommates." That prospect made it even harder to want to return to Seattle. "Besides, if I go back to Seattle, I risk running into Phillip—at the gym or the grocery store."

Riley grimaced. "That's reason enough alone not to go back, if you ask me."

"So, you think I should stay here?" Hope flickered in Paige's chest.

"Will you be able to find a job?" Riley pointed a finger at Paige. "I know you. You won't be content sitting around doing nothing."

No, I won't.

Being laid up over the last few months had taught her that.

"I doubt they'd have an opening in the elementary here in Providence, but maybe I could find one in the Tri-Cities area."

"I think you should go for it!" Riley slapped her palm on the console. "I mean, what have you got to lose?"

"Nothing, I suppose. Principal Stevens has been hounding me, wanting to know if I plan to return next year."

"Then you'd better stop dragging your feet and see if there are options for you here."

Paige's phone dinged with a text notification, distracting her from thoughts of finding a new job. She pulled it from her pocket. An unfamiliar number showed on the screen, and below it the words: *This is Gabe Rivera.*

Surprised to be getting a text from her therapist, she tapped the screen to read the full message.

Gabe: *Just checking in to see how you're doing after today's PT session. Hope I wasn't too hard on you.*

Warm brown eyes surrounded by long, thick lashes and a charming smile filled Paige's mind followed by her strange dream this afternoon.

"What is it, Paige?" Concern filled Riley's voice.

Paige's head jerked up. "Oh, it's just my physical therapist."

"Your physical therapist is texting you?"

"He's just checking in with me to see how I'm doing after today's session of PT." Paige's lips turned up. "I think he's afraid he pushed me too hard."

"Did he?"

"At the time, I felt like he expected a lot of me, but I actually feel pretty good."

She typed a response: *I'm fine.*

Gabe: *Good. Meet me at the pool at 8 Wednesday morning for aqua therapy.*

CHAPTER 4

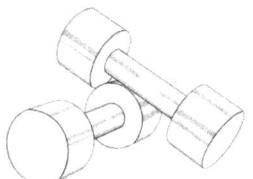

*P*aige grimaced at her reflection in the mirror after taking off her swimsuit cover-up. The pink-floral tankini she'd worn as a teenager didn't fit like she remembered.

Was I really that late of a bloomer?

She leaned on one crutch and tugged the top of the tankini up to minimize the amount of exposed cleavage, but that only widened the swatch of skin visible on her midriff. And the bottoms... She wished the boy short bottoms had been popular ten years ago, instead of the bikini cut ones.

She either needed to make a trip to Seattle soon to pack up some clothing or go shopping. She was tired of wearing the clothes she left behind when she moved out ten years ago. Clothes her mother was supposed to have donated to charity.

She frowned as she surveyed the scars on her shoulder and upper thigh. They looked much better than they did two months ago, but they were still purple and slightly puckered.

Reminding herself there was nothing she could do about them, she followed the smell of chlorine from the dressing room to the pool. She stepped out just in time to see Gabe pull his t-shirt off over his head.

Holy cow!

Paige could tell by the way his button-down hugged his shoulders on Monday that the man was built, but she hadn't expected chiseled pecs and six-pack abs. His blue swim trunks hugged equally muscular thighs.

Paige's stomach flipped then flopped. As if she wasn't already self-conscious of her scars, she had to work with a Greek god.

"Are you ready for this?" Gabe clapped his hands, then rubbed them together with too much enthusiasm for so early in the morning. The noise echoed through the large open area with high glass ceilings.

Paige scowled at him. "Are you always this eager to torture your patients?"

"Torture?" He put a hand to his chest. "I'm offended. I like to think of myself as a gentle yet ruthless taskmaster."

"Ruthless, huh?" Paige couldn't help cracking a smile as she gave him an exaggerated eye roll. "Is that why we're doing this so early?"

"It's not that early." Gabe quirked an eyebrow and looked at the clock on the wall. "Besides, the pool opens for lap swimming at nine-thirty. I figured you'd rather not have other people stirring the water while you do your exercises."

"You figured right." Still, it felt strange to be alone with him. Technically, they weren't alone, because the manager was here somewhere, but Paige would have Just Gabe's undivided attention again.

He motioned to the water. "Shall we?"

"How do I get in?" She crutched to the edge of the pool near the steps then stopped. "At the rehab center they lowered me into the water with a special chair."

"Unfortunately, they don't have one of those here." Gabe glanced around. "Looks like you have two choices. Crutch down the steps—"

"Won't water get into my crutches?"

"Yes, but it should drain out fine."

"What's my other choice?"

"I carry you."

Paige's gaze—which she'd tried to keep on his face—dropped to his bare chest. The last time he held her against all that muscle, she hadn't wanted to let go, and he was fully clothed then. Having her physical therapist hold her in his arms while he was shirtless felt all kinds of wrong. Besides, going into the pool was one thing, him carrying her out when they were both wet... That was another accident waiting to happen.

"A little water won't hurt my crutches." She plunged them into the pool, placing them on the first of three wide steps.

"Wait a second." He stepped around her. "Let me get in first, so I can catch you if you slip."

The water was colder than she expected, and goosebumps covered her skin. Her whole body shivered by the time the water reached her waist. Whether from the cold or the anxiety of trying to keep her feet under her with the movement of the water she wasn't sure. Or maybe it was knowing she'd be working closely with Gabe.

"Are you okay?" Concern lined Gabe's face.

"Yeah, just cold," she lied.

"It is a little chilly, isn't it? I'm sure we'll warm up once we get moving." He guided her to the side of the pool. "Hand me your crutches and I'll get the water out of them."

She did as he asked, and he raised each in the air to drain out the water before laying them on the side.

"They shouldn't be any worse for wear." He rubbed his hands together again, a sign—she was learning—that meant he wanted *her* to get to work. "Are you feeling steady?"

She let go of the side of the pool. Her body swayed with the gentle rocking of the water, but she was able to keep her feet under her. She shook her hand in a so-so motion.

"Let's give walking a try. I'll stay close in case you find yourself off balance." He motioned for her to walk farther into the pool. When the water reached her shoulders, he stopped her. "This is deep enough. Now let's walk across the pool." He placed himself between her and the deep end where the floor of the pool sloped. He stayed by her side as they walked.

"It's crazy how much effort it takes to walk with the resistance of the water." Paige focused on keeping her balance as she moved. The caress of the water against her skin—now that her body was mostly submerged and no longer cold—invigorated her. "It feels so good to move though. Especially without crutches."

"Your muscles have atrophied over the past couple months. That makes even simple exercises challenging. It's going to take hard work to rebuild the muscle. Movement is important. It lubricates our joints and muscles." Gabe pointed a finger in the air as though lecturing someone. "'Motion is lotion.' That's what my physical therapist used to always say."

"You did physical therapy?" When he nodded, she asked, "When? And for what?"

"I suffered a cervical spine injury back in high school while wrestling."

Wrestling? No wonder he's so muscular. He certainly hasn't let himself go.
Paige grimaced. "A neck injury?"

"I had a dislocation and hairline fracture of the C5 vertebrae. Inflammation and a bulged disc caused temporary paralysis." He grimaced. "I had to wear a halo for three months."

"A halo? Is that some sort of neck brace?"

He motioned to his chest. "It strapped around my chest, over my shoulders, came up under my chin, and up the back of my neck. It also strapped around my forehead."

"That sounds torturous." Paige shuddered. "You had to wear that for three months? I thought I had it bad. I can't even imagine the kind of restrictions you must have had." The feeling of near weightlessness lessened as she considered how painful and difficult that must have been for Gabe.

"It was a nightmare. Getting comfortable to sleep was almost impossible. Even after the inflammation went down and I was able to walk and use my arms, all variations of physical activity were banned." When they reached the other side of the pool, he turned. "Let's go back now a little faster. If you're able to keep your balance, we'll add more movement."

Paige started walking back. "I bet you were sick of lying around and watching Netflix after the first week."

A shadow flickered through his eyes. "Streaming services were still new at the time, and we couldn't afford them. So, my mom borrowed every possible DVD and audiobook from our city library."

"I bet even that got old real fast."

"It did. The worst was not being able to play soccer or hike and bike with my friends."

"I know the feeling. I never thought I'd miss Zumba class so much."

"Zumba? Are you a dancer?"

"Not really. I just enjoy moving." She shrugged one shoulder. "Did your accident end your wrestling career?"

"Yes, it came to a screeching halt my senior year right when I had college scouts looking at me."

"I'm guessing it cost you a scholarship."

More dark shadows filled his eyes as he nodded.

"How long did you have to do PT?"

"Six months." A small smile lifted his lips. "You think I'm a tyrant, you should have seen my mom."

Her brows arched. "Your mom was your physical therapist?"

"No, but she went to every appointment with me. Then she made sure I did all my exercises at home every day."

He understands that recovery is difficult and painful. He isn't pushing me for the fun of it.

When they reached the edge of the pool, Gabe turned again. "Okay, let's go back, but this time lengthen your stride and swing your arms under the water like big scissors." He demonstrated. "Exaggerate your movements."

She followed him, mimicking his actions. The additional movement of the water pulled at her, threatening to throw her off balance, but with concentration, she managed to keep her feet under her.

"Tell me about your family," Gabe said as they walked. "I've met your parents, obviously. Do you have siblings?"

Paige told him about her brother Ben and his family, who lived across the cul de sac from her parents. She talked about her cute nieces and nephew before asking him about his family.

"What about you? Do you have siblings?"

"A younger sister. She and my mom live in Richland, about thirty minutes from my apartment in Pasco."

Paige noticed he didn't mention his dad. Was he still in the picture? Curbing her curiosity, she asked, "Is your sister married?"

"No, we're both still single, much to my mom's dismay."

Well, I guess that answers that question.

Not that it mattered. Gabe might be single, but as her physical therapist, he was off limits. Besides, she wasn't looking for another relationship. She was better off single and lonely than getting her heart broken again.

They continued to talk about their families, interests, and hobbies as they made multiple laps across the pool. First walking, then marching and sidestepping. They followed the laps with a combination of resistance and low-impact exercises designed to strengthen and elevate the heart rate.

Paige had to repeatedly grab a hold of the edge to regain her balance, but she was surprised at how many of the exercises she was able to do with relatively little pain. Eventually, she sagged against the side.

"Wait." She gasped for air. "I need a break."

"That's fine. Take a minute to catch your breath." Gabe nodded as he stopped moving. "You're doing great."

"You covered everything they did with me at rehab in the first five minutes."

"With an injury like yours, it's important to break back into the exercise slowly." He gave a mischievous grin. "But you're almost healed now, so it's time to get your life back."

"I wish it was that easy." Paige lowered her gaze as her thoughts turned to the eight months she'd wasted on Phillip. She'd never get those back.

She felt a little lighter after telling Riley the truth about Phillip the other night. The tears had been cathartic, but now that she'd opened the gates on her heartbreak, she couldn't seem to close them again. Phillip kept creeping into her thoughts, bringing a myriad of emotions from sorrow to anger and everything in between.

She couldn't believe he'd had the audacity to visit her at the hospital after her accident. Fortunately, her mother had been getting lunch, so Paige was able to tell Phillip exactly what she thought of him, but that hadn't kept him from trying to make her empty promises, including leaving a pregnant Avery for her.

Like I'd want a man who would do that.

He hadn't said as much, but from the way he talked, it didn't sound like Phillip planned to tell her on Valentine's Day that he was marrying another woman.

Gabe ducked his head to meet her gaze. "Hey, we agreed to take things one day at a time, remember? Your only focus right now is getting stronger. You work on building yourself up physically, the rest will come."

"Maybe." Paige forced a smile. "If my physical therapist doesn't kill me first."

"Speaking of that, are you ready for a core exercise that will leave your abs burning?" The teasing glint was back in his eyes as he rubbed his hands together.

She groaned. "Now I know why Gladys called you a tyrant."

He winked. "I'm only a tyrant with my favorite patients."

Did he mean Gladys was one of his favorite patients? Surely, he didn't mean her. This was only their second session together. So why did he wink?

A brief grimace crossed Gabe's face before he cleared his throat. "Shall we get back to work? Put both hands on the edge of the pool a little more than shoulder width apart. Like this." She followed his instructions, and he continued. "Let your body float out behind you like you're Superman."

She let her legs rise to the surface.

"How does your right shoulder feel?"

"It's okay as long as I don't have to push or pull with my arms."

"Nope, just hold on. If at any time this hurts your shoulder, tell me and we'll stop." He waited for her to nod before demonstrating the exercise. "Now, engage your core and pull your knees into your chest."

After only a handful of repetitions, Paige's stomach muscles protested. "I see what you mean about burning abs. I'll definitely feel this tomorrow."

"Four more of these then we'll shift to a harder variation." He grinned at her over his muscular shoulder.

"Harder?" Paige huffed, exaggerating her breaths.

"Yes, harder." Gabe's grin turned devilish, making her heart skip a beat. "Doesn't it *feel so good to move?*"

Paige couldn't resist any longer; she splashed water in his face.

"Hey!" He splashed her back, but she'd anticipated retaliation and turned her back to him.

She made her way to the shallow end of the pool.

"Where are you going, Miss Young? We're not done."

"The water is too active, I don't feel very stable."

In more ways than one.

His long lashes and charming smile were disarming. Not only was he built like a Greek god, but he was also empathetic and easy to talk to. A deadly combination that made her want to rethink her resolve to stay single.

"Besides, it's time for lap swim." She pointed at the clock as two women walked out of the dressing room.

Gabe walked up beside her. "Time sure flies when you're having fun."

Paige scowled. "You have a twisted view of fun." She resisted the urge to splash him again. He was too close to avoid retaliation.

"My mom would agree with you."

"That means you either lead a very boring life, or you're demented."

He grinned again. "Probably a little of both." He handed her the crutches.

"Thank you." She made her way out of the pool with him hovering close by. The higher she climbed, the heavier she felt. No wonder she liked aqua therapy so much.

Gabe swiped his hands over his chest then down his muscular arms, wiping off the water. "Change your clothes and meet me in the first aid room. The manager said I could use the table in there to help you stretch and roll you out."

Paige froze in the process of squeezing the water from her hair. "Um…I didn't bring a change of clothes. Only a cover-up."

Now Gabe froze too. His gaze raked over her wet body, and she was all too aware of the amount of skin her swimsuit left exposed. "Okay…well…we'll make do the best we can." His voice lacked its usual conviction as he scratched his neck.

She recalled how he worked her low back, buttocks, and IT band the other day. Having him touch her like that while she wore only a swimsuit would be a whole new level of awkward.

He's a doctor. Doctors do things like this all the time. It's not a big deal.

So why did it feel like one?

GABE BREATHED a sigh of relief when he spotted a stack of white towels on the shelf in the first aid room. He grabbed one to cover Paige with while he worked on her, because her hot-pink cover-up didn't hide a whole lot.

He motioned to the table. "Lay on your stomach. We'll work on your back first."

She slid onto the table and handed him her crutches. As she carefully rolled to her stomach, he caught a glimpse of the scar on her hip. He'd tried to break up the scar tissue on Monday through her yoga pants, but the AISTM tool was more effective on bare skin.

"Actually, I think I should work on your scars before rolling you out." Instead of covering her with the towel, he tucked it into the edge of her swimsuit so he wouldn't get massage cream on her clothing. "We need to break up the scar tissue, surrounding your scars, so it doesn't hamper your healing. I'll try to be gentle, but I'll have to use a fair amount of pressure to break it up. So this will likely be painful."

It wasn't the first time he'd worked on a patient who needed to undress to an extent for him to do AISTM, dry needling, or cupping, but because of his attraction to Paige, it felt different.

Knock it off. She's just like any other patient.

When Paige winced and sucked in a sharp breath, he searched for something to distract them both. "So, what do you do when you aren't lounging around in rehab centers?"

"Lounging around?" She gave a short laugh that sounded like a snort. "I guess that's technically what I did, but it certainly wasn't by choice." She looked at him over her shoulder and rolled her eyes. "Pre-lounge era, I was an elementary school teacher."

"Was?" Gabe noted her use of the past tense. "Don't you plan on returning to teaching after you're healed?"

"Yes." She drew out the word with a lengthy sigh.

"You don't sound sure about that."

"I want to teach again. I'm just not sure I want to do it in Seattle."

"Seattle?" He vaguely remembered seeing the name of a Seattle hospital in her file but hadn't given it much thought.

"That's where I went to college, and I've lived there ever since. But I'm not sure I want to go back to the city."

"You considering getting a teaching job here then?"

"I'm thinking about it, but small towns have fewer students, so there isn't as big of a demand for teachers."

"That makes it difficult, doesn't it?" He shifted the conversation. "You're looking at six months of PT. If you do end up returning to Seattle, we'll have to find you a therapist there." For some ridiculous reason that thought depressed him.

"Six months? I knew I'd have to do therapy for a while, but I didn't realize it would take so long."

"You can't rush rehabilitation without causing further damage."

"I know. I'm just impatient." She sucked in another deep breath as he scraped at the knotted muscles.

"Sorry, I know this hurts."

"It's okay." She slowly let out her next breath through her nose. "I'm just being dramatic."

But Gabe knew that wasn't the case. AISTM scraping often brought his patients to tears. Paige was tolerating the worst part of PT better than most.

They continued to talk about their jobs and compared city life to small town living as he scraped and massaged the scar on her hip. Then he worked on her shoulder. He enjoyed getting to know his patients while he worked on them, and Paige Young was no exception.

Nine hours later, Gabe scrubbed a hand over his face as he got on the freeway headed home. It had been a long day.

Feeling guilty that he hadn't spent much time with his mom and sister over the past two weeks while getting the new office set up, he pressed the button for the speaker phone on his steering wheel.

"Call Mom."

"Hi, Gabe." His sister's voice came through his car speakers after three rings.

"Hey, Grace, how was your day?"

"Good. Busy."

"Isn't it always?"

"Yes, unless I'm working the night shift. Even then, it can be crazy sometimes."

Grace worked as a lab tech in the radiology department at Eden Medical Center in Richland. Gabe was grateful that despite being financially stable, she was content to live at home with their mother. He hated the idea of their mom being alone, and Grace was introverted and slow to trust thanks to a traumatic experience as a teenager. Knowing she and Mom had each other gave him peace of mind.

"Is Mom busy?"

"She's asleep on the couch." Concern filled Grace's voice.

Gabe's stomach clenched. "Again?"

"I'm telling you; I think aliens abducted our mom and replaced her with a woman who suddenly likes to sleep. She went to bed at eight o'clock last night."

Over the past month, Marisol Rivera, the most energetic woman he knew, had started sleeping in on the weekends and taking naps after work. Something she'd never done while Gabe was growing up.

After his dad walked out on them, Mom cried and moped for a month, but then she snapped out of it and started building a new life for herself and her children.

"Has she had any cold or flu symptoms?"

"Not since she had that cold two months ago."

His gut twisted as he recalled the fatigue his mom experienced twelve years ago while she battled breast cancer. Was something wrong with her again? Anemia maybe? Thyroid problems? He considered her age; fifty-three. Could be hormone changes. All of those were much easier to accept and treat than cancer.

"Is that Gabe?" He heard his mom's voice in the background.

"Yes," Grace said. "You're on speaker now, Gabe."

"Hi, Mom. How are you?"

"I'm great." Despite the positive response, her voice lacked its usual liveliness. "How are things at your new clinic, Mijo?"

"Slow but good."

"You expected that. It will take time to build up a clientèle." The clank of dishes and silverware sounded in the background. "Before long, you'll have a reputation as the best physical therapist in town."

Grace snickered in the background.

"I'm the only physical therapist in town."

"So it shouldn't take long for word to spread," Mom's tone was optimistic.

If she knew how truly small Providence was, she'd worry—like he did—that there weren't enough people who needed rehabilitation. At least he saw a new patient this afternoon and had another scheduled for Friday.

"Do you have any challenging patients?"

"If by challenging, you mean patients who need long-term and specialized therapy? Then yes, I have one at the moment."

The real challenge, however, was keeping his attraction to said patient in check. He'd never been so drawn to a client before, and it rattled him, making him say and do crazy things. Calling Paige one of his favorite patients was one thing—he often did that—but he never winked at them, like he did Paige.

Luke had teased him incessantly on Monday after he made that *woman after my own heart* slip.

Good thing he wasn't there to hear my faux pas this morning.

Gabe was captivated by more than Paige's pretty face. He admired her grit and determination. She persevered even when the exercises were hard, and she was exhausted.

"What makes this patient so challenging?" Mom's voice pulled him from his thoughts of Paige.

He was careful to never share the name of a patient, but he often told her some of the challenges they faced. "She's recovering from multiple fractures to her pelvis, femur, and shoulder. She can't bear full weight yet."

"Are you doing aqua therapy with her then?"

Gabe smiled. As usual, Mom was spot on.

"We did our first session of aquatic therapy today. I work with her at the office twice a week as well."

Grace broke in. "Do you want to join us for dinner tonight? I have lasagna in the oven."

His stomach growled, reminding him all he had at home were TV dinners and frozen pizza. "Not tonight. I just left Providence, so I wouldn't get there until after nine."

"Why so late?" Mom asked.

Gabe changed lanes to pass a semi. "I had a client who couldn't come in until after he got off work at five-thirty."

"And tomorrow is your early morning at the clinic in Pasco." Mom's voice was full of sympathy.

"Yes." Gabe already regretted agreeing to the early morning shift in Pasco on Tuesday and Thursday mornings. Six a.m. rolled around way too early when he didn't get home from Providence until almost nine.

"We'll save some lasagna for you to take home this weekend," Grace said.

"Thanks, Hermana."

"You're coming over on Saturday, aren't you?" Mom asked.

"Yes, I'll be over around noon."

He always went home on the weekends. Partly to help with the upkeep of the house and yard, but mostly to spend time with his mom and sister. They were the only family he had. He would always be there for them.

"Good, because I need your help."

CHAPTER 5

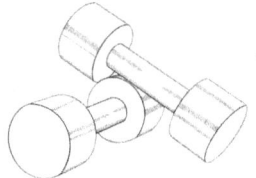

"So, what do you think of Paige Young?" Luke's out-of-the blue question did more to spike Gabe's blood pressure than the exercises he'd been doing for the past thirty minutes.

Paige had pushed back her appointment, so he and Luke had been killing time by lifting weights. It wasn't the first time this week they'd used the PT office as their personal gym.

"What do you mean?" Gabe's attempt to keep his voice casual failed. He had been thinking about Paige way too often since their aqua therapy session two days ago.

"She's a hottie, don't you think?"

Gabe bit his tongue to keep from snapping at Luke. He doubted the kid meant for his words to sound derogatory, but they did. Or maybe Gabe took them that way because he felt protective of Paige, and he had no idea why.

Instead of snapping at Luke and telling him to stay away from her, he chose his words carefully. "Paige is determined and hard-working when it comes to her recovery. Which is good, because she has a long way to go."

Luke snorted. "That's such a clinical thing to say."

"Well, I *am* her physical therapist."

"You can't fool me, *Dr. Rivera.* I know she's a *woman after your own heart."* A teasing tone filled Luke's voice.

Gabe clamped his jaw shut, willing himself not to react. It would only make it worse.

Even though Gabe dressed down in jeans and a polo on Fridays, instead of slacks and a dress shirt, he avoided exercises that made him work up too much of a sweat. It wouldn't look professional to be covered in sweat stains when the patients arrived.

Yet that's exactly what happened thirty minutes later when Paige walked through the door, fifteen minutes earlier than expected. Like an idiot, he'd let Luke talk him into a push-up contest. He regretted it the moment he spotted her crutches and tennis-shoe clad feet.

Gabe froze in plank position.

"No, keep going, man," Luke said with a grunt. "I'm going to beat you this time."

Gabe glanced up at Paige.

"Don't mind me." An amused grin filled her face as she made a rolling motion with her hand. "Carry on."

It was the most genuine smile he'd seen on her face since he met her five days ago, and it made her look radiant. Against his better judgment, he let his pride take over and lowered himself to the floor again.

After five more push-ups, his arms trembled, but he kept going, because Luke's grunts had grown deeper and more frequent. The kid was ready to collapse. So was Gabe, but pride wouldn't let him quit. If there was one thing he'd learned after his dad walked out, it was to push himself. Recovering from his neck injury, helping support his family while his mom battled breast cancer, and putting himself through college taught him he could do anything he put his mind to.

"Gah!" After three more push-ups Luke finally dropped and didn't get up.

Gabe struggled through one more for good measure then flopped on the floor too. Panting, he rolled over on his back and stared at the ceiling. He refused to look at Paige as heat rushed up his neck to his ears.

"You're a beast!" Luke gave Gabe's shoulder a weak smack from his prone position on the floor. "Every single time, man. I don't know how you do it." He pushed to a sitting position and propped his elbows on his knees.

Gabe would never admit how close Luke had come to beating him this time. Nor would he tell anyone Paige was the only reason he'd persevered. His pride couldn't handle it if his assistant beat him in front of a patient.

"No wonder you both look like Greek gods." Humor filled Paige's voice.

"Hardly." Luke's face beamed from the compliment. "Well, Gabe does, but I've got a long way to go to get arms like his. He's so ripped!" A teasing glint filled Luke's eyes.

Gabe would have smacked him if his arms didn't feel like jelly.

"Are all men so competitive?"

Gabe lifted his gaze to see Paige with one brow cocked. She wore a hint of makeup today which made her pretty blue eyes stand out.

"I used to think my brother's and cousins' competitiveness was just a stubborn family trait, but now, I'm not so sure."

"Oh no, pretty much every man hates to lose," Luke said in a disgusted tone. He shot Gabe a scowl as he got to his feet. "It's all about pride and bragging rights." Then he jokingly pounded his fists on his chest. "We must conquer."

"Conquer?" Paige's head jerked back. Dark shadows flitted though her eyes as she narrowed her gaze on Luke.

"Yeah, you know, we have to brave the elements, be the victor *and* the bread winner, all to convince women we're worth having around." Luke's joke fell flat with Paige, but he didn't seem to notice. "Have a seat on the middle table and I'll get your heat packs."

Gabe's gaze followed her as he rose from the floor. If he had to guess, he'd bet there was a man in Paige's past who took the need to prevail too far where she was concerned.

Her expression returned to normal, but her posture remained stiff as she settled on the table.

He stepped to the foot of Paige's table. "How did you fare after aqua therapy on Wednesday?"

"I felt good. Not as exhausted as I was on Monday." She smiled as she nodded. "I think I'm getting stronger every day."

The smile was still small, but it looked sincere. They were making progress.

"You are. And you'll keep getting stronger if you stick with your exercises." Gabe gave her an encouraging nod. "You'll be back to normal in no time."

Her smile dimmed, and shadows filled her eyes again. Every time he mentioned getting back to normal or getting her life back, her demeanor changed. There was something in her past—recent past, he guessed—that she was mourning or didn't want to return to. She suffered more than just physical pain.

He hated to think that someone had hurt Paige.

There was that protective surge again. The one that tightened his chest and warmed his blood. He curled his hand into a fist to keep from resting it on her leg in an effort to comfort her.

He locked gazes with her. "Things will work out. Trust me."

The corner of her lips lifted in a hint of a smile as she nodded.

The door swung open, and Gladys shuffled in. "Another day, another round of torture."

"Gladys, my favorite patient." Grateful for the distraction, he focused his attention on the older woman. He caught Luke's eye and nodded toward Paige, letting his assistant know he wanted him to work through Paige's exercises with her.

It was much safer for Gabe to work with the seventy-two-year-old retired schoolteacher than the attractive young one who kept triggering his protective side.

"Isn't he the hottest doctor you've ever seen?" Nikki Dalton, a new patient with a hamstring injury, lay on the table beside Paige doing IT band stretches. Still a senior in high school,

Nikki was skipping out of school during her dance class to do PT.

"What?" Paige turned to find Nikki leaning so far off her table she feared the girl might fall off.

"Dr. Gabe. Isn't he hot?" Nikki jerked her head toward the reception desk where Gabe spoke with a man named Ernie, who was inquiring about what Gabe charged for self-pay, since his insurance refused to pay for more PT for his Achille's tendon problems.

"I'll say." Gladys, who sat on the table to Paige's left with ice and electric stimulation patches on her knee, fanned herself. "I'd call dibs if I was forty years younger."

Paige bit back a grin as her gaze returned to Gabe. Apparently, she wasn't the only one who thought he was good looking.

"What about you, Paige?" Nikki asked.

"What about me?"

"Are you going to speak dibs?"

"What? No way." Paige frowned as she shook her head. "I'm done with men."

It didn't matter that the handsome therapist, who liked quirky socks, was easy to talk to and upbeat. Or that he treated each patient like they were his favorite. Paige refused to get involved with him or any other man right now.

"But just look at all those muscles." Nikki's voice was full of admiration. "And his eyes. Aren't they gorgeous?"

They were, but Paige didn't feel it appropriate to say so out loud. "He's our physical therapist. There shouldn't be any calling dibs."

"Pshaw." Gladys waved a hand. "Don't mind her, Nikki. I think she's still trying to find her sense of humor since her accident."

Paige scowled at Gladys. Sure, she'd been moody and out of sorts since getting her heart and body broken, but who wouldn't be?

Before she could contemplate Gladys' words further, she overheard Ernie say, "Are you sure, Gabe? I know that's not fair to you."

"The important thing is to get you better." Gabe clapped a hand on Ernie's shoulder. "Luke will get you scheduled. I want to see you twice a week initially."

Paige wasn't looking for more reasons to be attracted to Gabe, but she'd found one. There was nothing more admirable than a man who showed compassion to others.

But she didn't need more reasons to like him. She needed the opposite. Despite what she told Nikki, there was something about Just Gabe that made her wish she'd met him eight months ago instead of lying, cheating Phillip.

Before long, Paige had finished her exercises, and Gabe was rolling out her left quad. Thanks to Nikki, she couldn't keep her gaze off his eyes and his impossibly long lashes.

"I'd kill for your eyelashes." The words slipped out before Paige could stop them. She wished she could take them back when a series of snickers surrounded her.

Gabe jerked back with a wide-eyed look. "What?"

"Well, not literally. But you know what I mean."

"No, I don't." His expression was dead pan, but she spotted a twinkle in his eyes.

"I'd die to have lashes as thick and long as yours." She explained even though embarrassment already warmed her cheeks.

"Me too," Nikki said.

Despite Nikki chiming in, Gabe's gaze remained focused on Paige. "You came close to dying once already this year, and now you want to do it again for my eyelashes?"

"I didn't mean it literally." Paige let out an exasperated huff.

"What if I died tonight? Everyone here heard you say you'd kill for my eyelashes." He looked at Luke, Nicole, and Gladys for confirmation. When they all grinned and nodded, he went on. "You would become the number one suspect."

Paige rolled her eyes. "Don't worry, your lashes are safe. You're right, I've come too close to dying once already this year. So, I guess I'll just have to make do with my own pale, thin lashes."

He looked closely at her eyes. "Your lashes look nice."

"That's because they're fake, or most of them anyway. Mine are so thin and pale that I look sick if I don't add lash extensions." It was the first thing she did after leaving the rehabilitation center last week. She needed the confidence boost.

He leaned a little closer and studied her face, his gaze bouncing from one eye to the other. He was so close, she spotted little specks of gold in his brown irises. The hint of mint gum on his breath caused a shiver of awareness to shoot through her.

"They look so natural, I can hardly tell." The low timber of his voice caused goosebumps to break out on her arms. "Your eyes are such a striking blue. Like your father's."

Warmth crept over her cheeks under his intense scrutiny. "Thank you. My mom's eyes are blue too. And so are my brother's."

"A strong family trait, huh?" He grinned as he straightened. "At least it's a good one. I got my grandpa's big ears that poke out." He pulled both ears out from his head and made a funny face, making his eyes bulge.

Everyone burst out laughing.

"Your ears do not poke out," Paige said when he stopped being silly.

"They used to. When I was a kid, I wore a baseball hat all the time and I tucked my ears into it to hide them."

"No, you didn't." She'd learned Gabe liked to joke.

"I did. I swear." He pulled his phone from his pocket and tapped a few times before turning his phone for her to see. "My sister sent me this gem last month. I was about six years old."

A photograph of a young boy with long eyelashes and missing two front teeth filled the screen. He wore a baseball cap tugged low on his head; ears tucked under the rim.

She chuckled. "They don't stick out now." She studied his ears skeptically. "Did tucking them in the hat help with that?"

"It doesn't work like that," Gladys said as she got off her table. "I bet he had plastic surgery."

"I would never." Gabe let out a bark of laughter. He turned back to Paige and grinned. "Fortunately, I grew into my ears. Now, I just have a big head."

"I'll say." Luke threw a small towel at Gabe, hitting him square in the face.

Laughter filled the room again.

Fifteen minutes later, Paige was reluctant to leave after scheduling next week's appointments. She'd laughed more over the past three hours than she had for months. Lingering would be awkward though, so she headed for the door.

It opened before she grabbed the handle. A teenage boy, who looked like he could be Brent Butler's younger brother, walked in carrying a sub sandwich. The red and white checkered paper around the sandwich was a dead giveaway that he'd just come from Charity's Diner—the diner—originally owned by Paige's Aunt Charity but recently been purchased by Paige's sister-in-law Amy.

He held the door open for Paige.

She thanked him and was almost through the door when Gabe's boisterous voice filled the room. "Where's *my* sandwich, Travis? I'd *kill* for a good turkey bacon club."

Paige whirled around and glared at Gabe.

He'd teased her about using that figure of speech, yet here he was saying it to Travis. He made eye contact with her and gave her a devilish grin that made her heart skip a beat. The handsome therapist was still smiling when the door closed.

CHAPTER 6

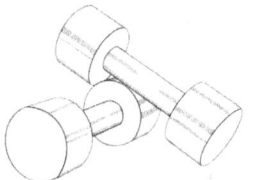

*G*abe stored the gardening tools in the shed and latched the door. He wiped the perspiration from his forehead as he and surveyed the yard.

Mom and Grace helped him clean out the garden plot and plant tomatoes, jalapeños, peppers, and onions. Then Mom disappeared inside, saying she needed to do laundry.

Grace stuck around to help him clean out the flower beds and plant the new annual flowers mom bought every spring, until she received a phone call a few minutes ago.

There was a certain satisfaction to seeing all they'd accomplished, but his concern for his mother had intensified over the course of the afternoon. She'd rested twice in the shade of the birch tree on a lawn chair, but by the time she went inside, she looked exhausted.

When he walked into the house he was not surprised to see his mom napping on the couch, yet the sight alarmed him, tightening his chest. He washed up then sat on the loveseat beside Grace, who had a book in her hand.

Gabe studied his mother's sleeping figure. More strands of gray streaked her black hair than a year ago, and even with her face relaxed, the fine lines around her eyes were more prominent than ever. So were the shadows under her eyes. He noted the protrusion of her cheek bones.

Has she lost weight?

"Do you think there's something wrong with her?"

He startled at Grace's quiet question. "I don't know. She certainly hasn't been herself lately. How's her appetite been?"

Grace shrugged one shoulder. "It's dropped a little, I guess."

"Her exhaustion could be any number of things from stress at work to hormone changes."

"Yeah, maybe." Grace didn't sound convinced.

He wasn't either. He couldn't help remembering that difficult time when his mother battled breast cancer. He hated to think she might have to face something like that again.

He and Grace tried to be quiet as they fixed dinner together an hour later, but their noise must have woken Mom, because she joined them in the kitchen. However, instead of helping chop vegetables and sauté chicken, she sat on a bar stool and watched them work.

Gabe waited until they were seated around the dinner table, before bringing up her health. "Grace said you've been tired a lot lately."

Her head popped up. She shot Grace a surprised look, and his sister in turn scowled at him.

Mom waved a hand, dismissing his concern. "We all get run down sometimes. You know how it is."

"Yes, we do, but I haven't seen you nap since..." Gabe stopped, not wanting to bring up that dark time in their lives.

"Since I went through chemo, I know." Mom patted his arm. "I'm fine, don't you two worry about me." She picked up her fork again and continued to push the food around her plate.

"I just want to make sure you're taking care of yourself. When was your last physical?"

"I saw Dr. Marcum earlier this week."

"Good. What did he say about your exhaustion."

"Nothing."

"What do you mean nothing?" Frustration built in Gabe's chest.

"They drew blood. He's running some tests." She gave him the same look she often gave him as a child; a mixture of scolding and forced patience. "These things take time. You're a doctor, you know that."

Gabe wanted to remind her he wasn't that kind of doctor, but she was right. A good doctor didn't give a diagnosis without running tests first, and it took time to get results back from labs.

"What other symptoms have you had besides exhaus—"

"Basta!" She held up a hand. "That's enough. I'll let you know what Dr. Marcum says when the lab results come back. Until then, there's no point worrying about it." She pointed her fork at him. "Now tell me, Mijo, when are you going to start dating again?"

All signs of exhaustion disappeared from Mom's face, and her pointed stare looked exactly like the woman who never let him get away with anything as a child.

Gabe nearly choked on the bite of fajita he'd just taken. Grace snickered across the table, and it was his turn to scowl at her. "What do you mean? I date."

"Oh, you do?" Disbelief filled Mom's face. "When was the last time you went on a date?"

Gabe froze like a deer in headlights as he racked his brain trying to remember the last time he took a woman out. He couldn't even remember the last time he met someone he was interested in dating.

That's not true.

He met someone this week who interested him a great deal, but Paige Young was a client and off limits. So he shouldn't be flirting with her and complimenting her on her striking blue eyes.

That's not me. I don't flirt with patients.

Luke did it all the time, but that was just his way. Besides, he was only an assistant. Gabe was *the* physical therapist. He was a doctor for Pete's sake. He should be held to a higher standard.

"Well, I've been...really busy with work lately, setting up the new office and all."

"Perhaps it would be easier for you to remember the name of the last woman you took out." Grace prompted with wide, innocent eyes.

That *was* easier to remember, but Mom wouldn't like the answer. It had been almost six months since he decided he and Giselle, Dr. Stoker's niece, didn't have enough in common.

He shot Grace another scowl, telling her to mind her own business. He was about to make another lame excuse when Mom pointed a finger at Grace.

"You're no better, Mija." Mom shook her head in disgust. "I'm never going to be a grandma if you two don't get busy?"

Grandma?

Gabe fell into a coughing fit after choking again. This time on his own saliva.

CHAPTER 7

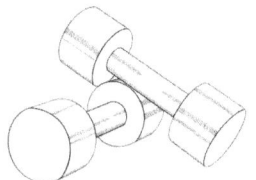

*P*aige surveyed her reflection in the dressing room mirror at the pool. The new tankini with a higher neckline and boy shorts fit her much better than her old one. She'd also brought a change of clothes, which would be unnecessary if Gabe decided to do that scraping thing on her scars again.

Grateful to be able to put a little more weight on her left leg, she made her way out to the pool, arriving at the same time as Gabe.

"Good morning, how are you today?" He pulled his shirt off over his head as he spoke.

He wore the same blue swim trunks as last week, but somehow, he looked even more amazing in them than Paige remembered. She'd forgotten how sculpted he was.

She'd decided being attracted to Gabe was a good thing. Finding other men good looking meant she was getting over Phillip. Crushing on her physical therapist was safe, because nothing would ever come of it, which meant he couldn't break her heart.

They exchanged pleasantries as they made their way to the water. Like last week, Gabe preceded her down the steps into the pool, staying close in case she slipped.

"Okay, let's do some warm-up laps before we stretch." He rubbed his hands together. "We'll start with the same strides as last week. Let's try to keep a little faster pace this time." They'd barely done half a lap when Gabe asked, "What did you do this weekend?"

"I went shopping on Saturday." She motioned to her new swimsuit. She almost told him about the Marvel-character socks she bought for him. They practically screamed Gabe's name.

She'd justified the impulse purchase by convincing herself that giving her therapist socks as a thank you gift when she finished therapy wouldn't be considered inappropriate. Now she just had to hang onto them until she finished therapy or until the end of summer. Because if she didn't find a job, she'd have to return to Seattle. And the whole job thing wasn't looking very promising yet.

"We had a big family dinner on Sunday with all the cousins on my mom's side of the family who live close." Paige continued to talk, telling Gabe a little about her aunts and cousins who also lived in Providence. "Oh, and the best part was talking to my cousin Damon. I don't get to see him very often, but he's been good at checking in on me since my accident. He's two years older than me, but we were really close growing up." She swung her arms in wide arcs under the water as she talked. "Damon joined the army after high school and has been stationed all over the country."

She caught a grin on Gabe's face as they reached the edge and started another lap with a different stride. "What's so funny?"

"Nothing." He schooled his features. "I just don't think I've ever heard you talk so much."

Warmth filled Paige's face. "I've been monopolizing the conversation, haven't I?"

"A little, but I don't mind." He grinned again. "You're so animated, it's fun to listen to you."

"I'm starting to feel more like my old self, and I'm noticing my gift to gab has returned."

"Gift to gab, huh?" He raised an eyebrow, his expression curious.

Paige changed the subject. "So, what did *you* do this weekend?"

"My weekend wasn't nearly as exciting as yours. On Saturday, I helped my mom and sister plant a hundred tomatoes."

"A hundred!"

"It was actually only twenty, but it felt like a hundred. When it comes time to harvest the tomatoes, it's going to feel like a million." He turned when they reached the edge again and started a sideways lunge, swinging his arms out to the side. "We also planted a bunch of onions, peppers, and jalapeños."

Paige once again noticed Gabe didn't mention his dad. Tamping down her curiosity, she focused on what he *had* said. "Do you make your own salsa?"

"Not just our own. My mom makes enough to feed an army. For Christmas, all her neighbors and coworkers get a jar or two—made exactly the way they like it, from mild to hot, to extra hot."

"I wish I lived in your neighborhood. Chips and salsa are my favorite snack, although I hate to admit I'm a wimp when it comes to spice."

"There's no shame in admitting you can't handle the heat." The smirk he gave her said otherwise.

When they reached the edge of the pool again Gabe clapped his hands and rubbed them together. "Okay, I want us to do one more lap before we stretch. This time, lift your knee in front of you then rotate it out to the side before lowering it." He demonstrated, and Paige followed his example. "Lift the right knee every time, then we'll focus on the left leg when we make our way back." He continued to talk as they made their way across the pool. "This exercise stretches the inner thigh and works the outer thigh and glutes. It'll help with the weakness in the hip and low back."

They hadn't even made it halfway across the pool before Paige felt the tightness in every muscle Gabe mentioned. She appreciated that he explained the purpose of the exercises and how they would benefit her.

He did the same thing on Monday with Sam Hipwell, who had suffered a stroke that affected his speech and the left side of his body. Gabe's patience and knowledge left her in awe. Every exercise he did with Sam was meant to help him get his life back.

Just like he's trying to do with me.

The problem was, she didn't want her old life back. However, her desire for a fresh start in Providence didn't seem to be panning out.

They were halfway back across the pool, focusing on the left leg, when a sharp, stabbing pain seized Paige's hamstring.

"Ow!" She jerked her leg up and bent to rub the back of her thigh.

The rocking of the water tugged at her as she tried to balance on one foot. She hopped, trying to steady herself and ease the Charlie horse. After landing on Gabe's foot, she jerked sideways. Her heel hit the slope of the floor leading to the deep end and slid out from under her.

She plunged into the water. Releasing her still spasming leg, she flailed her arms, fighting to get her feet under her. But she couldn't find her footing in the deeper water.

Gabe's strong arms dragged her up and pulled her against his firm chest. "Are you okay? What happened?"

"Cramp," Paige gasped and wriggled, desperate to ease the pain. "My left leg."

"In the hamstring?" Without waiting for an answer, his hand reached down and brought her left leg up to his side. "Flex your foot. Keep your leg as straight as possible." He widened his stance and braced her leg against his hip, then he reached around her thigh to rub her hamstring with his strong fingers. His other arm remained clamped around her waist, holding her secure against him.

Despite his grip on her, she clung to him; one arm around his neck, the other hand digging into the back of his arm.

"Is it letting up?"

"Not quite." The painful spasm had spread to her buttock, but she wasn't about to tell him that.

He hitched her leg a little higher. "Take deep breaths and let them out as slowly as possible."

She tried to do as he instructed, but being pressed against his wet, bare chest made it almost impossible to breathe. By the time the Charlie horse subsided, her heart raced like she'd just run a marathon. Gabe's embrace made her feel safe and very alive.

She couldn't help comparing him to Phillip. Physically, they were complete opposites, but they were both charismatic and friendly, always making others feel special. But Phillip had lied to her the whole time he'd showered her with compliments and affection.

Would Gabe do that?

She thought of all the sides she'd seen of Gabe over the past week and a half; compassionate and jovial, strong and caring. She assumed he was the same in his personal life if he spent his weekends helping his mom plant a garden. He wasn't the type to mislead a woman and cheat on her. Was he?

"How does it feel now?" Gabe's voice was much huskier than a moment ago.

It sent a surge of warmth shooting through her. Her eyes darted to his face. When she locked gazes with his hooded yet intense stare, a thrum of excitement coursed through her.

"It's relaxing." She was so breathless, little sound came out.

His eyes narrowed as his head drifted toward hers. "Slowly lower your leg. Let's make sure the cramp doesn't return." Despite his words, it was another long moment before he released her leg and shifted his hand to her waist.

Goosebumps covered her thigh where his fingers grazed her skin. A pleasant shiver rippled through her, and she had to fight the urge to lean into him. She forced herself to loosen the hold she had on his arm and around his neck, but she felt so unsteady she didn't dare let go entirely. Her left hand came to a stop on his chest where his heart raced beneath her palm. It matched the rapid staccato of hers, which only ramped up the attraction coursing through her, stealing her breath.

"How does it feel?"

Paige didn't think it was possible for his voice to go any deeper, but it had, and it made her warm all over despite the cool water that surrounded them.

"Feels amaz—"

Wait. He's referring to my leg, not the warm fuzzies swarming me.

"It's good." Her words came out a hoarse whisper.

"But you're still shaking." It was a statement, not a question.

She nodded anyway as a sudden desire to kiss him hit her. Would his lips be as firm as his embrace or would they be gentle and teasing?

Stop it! You can't kiss your physical therapist. You're done with men, remember?

His gaze dropped to her lips as though he read her mind. His breathing sounded as ragged as hers.

She was wrong. There was nothing safe about crushing on her therapist. He should have been untouchable, but she was touching an awful lot of him right now. And it felt so good. She leaned into him.

He sucked in a deep breath, and his whole body tensed. "I hope you're steady, because I need to let go now."

Then he was gone, and she missed the contact immediately. Not just his touch or the feel of his arms around her but his presence too, because he didn't stop moving until he reached the side of the pool.

He propped his elbows on the edge and shoved his hands into his hair. His shoulders rose and fell as he took deep breaths.

She sucked in a deep breath of her own. Thank goodness, he was disciplined enough to walk away when she'd been ready to kiss her physical therapist.

Talk about inappropriate.

That wasn't her. She didn't kiss men unless there was long-term relationship potential. And she definitely wasn't ready for another relationship yet; long-term or otherwise. Especially not with her physical therapist.

This is all Mom's fault.

Paige hadn't been able to forget her mother's suggestion that she *get to know Dr. Rivera on a personal level* after she finished PT. It didn't help that he was so personable and easy on the eyes.

She watched the water lap at his broad shoulders. Was Gabe as good of a man as he seemed? Or did he have a hidden duplicitous side like Phillip? Had she learned anything after all she'd been through? Or would she always overlook personality flaws because of physical attraction?

Considering what almost happened, she should give Gabe some space, but she needed to know who he really was.

THE MOVEMENT of the water alerted Gabe to Paige's approach, but he refused to look at her. He couldn't. Not while the overwhelming urge to kiss her still coursed through him.

Stupid. Stupid. Stupid.

He'd almost ruined everything. He finally had his own practice, and he almost threw it away by giving into a temptation that could result in a sexual harassment lawsuit.

Talking to Paige felt so effortless. She was so animated and entertaining, that it was easy to forget he was her physical therapist. It didn't help that despite the modest cut of her new swimsuit she was stunning. Her eyes look bigger and bluer than ever, thanks to the vibrant cobalt blue swim top. The way it swooped to the side accentuated Paige's hour-glass figure.

She'd clung to him with complete trust and what felt like longing, making him want to hold her forever. And the water droplets clinging to her rosy lips...

Enough!

Sucking in a deep breath, he steeled himself and turned to face Paige, who stood little more than arm's length away. He wasn't sure what he expected to see in her face, but it wasn't the puzzled expression that furrowed her brow and turned her lips down in a slight frown.

"What?" he asked. "Why are you looking at me like that?"

Was she trying to decide whether to call him out for almost kissing her? With her dad being his boss—sort of—she could easily get him fired, if she wanted to.

The twin creases between her brows deepened as she chewed on her lip for a long moment. "Have you ever been unfaithful in a relationship?"

"What?" His head jerked back.

Where on earth did that come from?

"Have you ever cheated on a woman?" Her expression grew pensive.

"No, of course not."

"Never ever?" Skepticism filled her face.

He felt his brows hike up as he studied her. What was going on in her head right now? He could have sworn she'd felt the sizzling chemistry between them a moment ago, so how did she go from that to this?

"Never ever." He locked gazes with her until the doubt disappeared from her face. "That was random. Where did that come from?"

Was she asking because she was interested in a relationship with him? His heart skipped a few beats at the possibility. Would she be willing to wait six months until she finished physical therapy?

He shook the thought from his head. He couldn't think about that. She was his patient and nothing more.

"My ex—" Paige cut herself off and shifted to lean her back against the wall of the pool before continuing. "Someone once told me all men cheat at one point or another in their life."

"That's not true," Gabe said without hesitation. His body tensed as heat rushed through him. The nerve of the man.

His jaw clenched as he thought about his dad and his former best friend. The two people he'd trusted most in his life—three if he counted Harper, his former fiancée—had disappointed and hurt him deeply with their infidelity. He rubbed his neck to combat the sudden headache the memories triggered.

Paige's eyes narrowed as she watched him. "You say it's not true, but something about that statement makes you uncomfortable. Why?"

"Men aren't the only ones who cheat." He shook his head in disgust. "For every man out there who cheats, there's another woman he's doing it with." His life had been wrecked twice by such individuals.

Paige reeled back as if he'd slapped her. Her cheeks flushed, and tears flooded her eyes before she turned away.

He'd struck a nerve. Frowning, he wondered why she reacted like that. Did her ex cheat on her?

"Sometimes..." Paige's voice was defensive, "the *other woman* has no idea." She shot him a glare before looking away again.

Gabe made a sound that was a combination of a scoff and a snort. His dad's secretary knew he was married when they started their two-year-long affair that resulted in Gabe's dad walking out on his family. And Harper—despite being engaged to Gabe—knew Dirk, his best friend, was in a committed relationship when she made a play for him.

"It's true," Paige's voice remained defensive, but she didn't make eye contact.

"Is that what happened to you?" he asked gently.

She simply stared into the water and didn't respond.

"Did he find someone else while you were together?" When she still didn't respond, he tried again. "Or was he already in a relationship when he started dating you?"

Paige flinched and wrapped her arms across her abdomen in a protective gesture.

Gabe's chest tightened at the thought of a man using and hurting Paige like that. His fists doubled at his side as his protective instincts kicked in. Did her accident have something to do with her ex?

No wonder she wasn't thinking clearly. He knew that kind of betrayal, and it had left him reeling for a long time.

"I swear..." Her unfocused gaze shifted to a spot at the other side of the pool. "I didn't know Phillip was engaged the whole time we dated."

"Engaged?" The word came out sharper than Gabe intended as past wounds ripped open.

She flinched again then gave him a weak smile as she pushed away from the edge of the pool. "I'm sorry I brought the whole thing up. We should probably get back to the exercises."

"Wait." He held out a hand to stop her from moving away but decided it best not to touch her again. "Do I get to know why *my* fidelity is in question?"

She looked at him with a furrowed brow. "I didn't question *your* fidelity."

"Didn't you?"

A flash of guilt crossed her face as she huffed and folded her arms across her chest. She averted her gaze again.

"What triggered this questioning?" He pressed when she didn't answer.

"I find you—" She stopped herself and seemed to weigh her words carefully. "I'm trying to figure out if you're really as nice of a guy as you seem."

A spark of warmth lit in his chest. "You think I'm a nice guy?" He did his best to keep his voice neutral as he tamped down the thrill of excitement that shot through him.

"You're good at your job." She ticked things off on her fingers. "You're great with your patients. You're humorous and fun to be around." She pinned him with a piercing gaze before continuing. "I'm trying to figure out if you're hiding something that makes you someone other than who you claim to be."

Hiding something?

"I haven't claimed to be anything other than a physical therapist."

"I know." She propped her hands on her hips and let out another huff. "I'm just afraid I'm not a good judge of character anymore, so I need to know..." Her words trailed off.

He bit back a smile at her expressive behavior. "What do you need to know?"

"Nothing. Never mind." She shook her head, but the motion was jerky and sharp.

"I would never cheat on a woman, Paige." He pressed a hand to his chest as he met her gaze. "I'm sorry about what happened with your ex, but not all men are unfaithful." He squared his shoulders. "We don't deserve to be labeled as such just because you had a bad experience with one man."

A twisting sensation hit his gut. Hadn't he done the same thing with women after Harper cheated on him? There was a reason he was still single six years later. After being burned so badly, it was hard to go near the fire again.

"You're right. I'm sorry." A look of contrition filled her face. "I never should have accused or doubted you."

"Why are you concerned about my character?"

A rosy tint colored her cheeks as she cupped water in her hands. "No reason."

He was tempted to press her for an answer, but if she felt even a fraction of the desire he did a few minutes ago—and he suspected she did—it was best to leave it alone. He'd already flirted with danger once today when it came to Paige Young and nearly jeopardized his job.

Once was enough.

CHAPTER 8

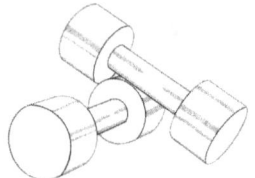

"*A*re you mad at me?"

Gabe pulled his gaze away from Sam who shuffled sideways with Luke's help and looked at Paige. "No, why do you ask?"

"You've hardly talked to me since last Wednesday at the pool. I'm sorry if I offended you when I asked—"

"You didn't offend me."

It was easy to overhear others' conversations in the small gym, and Gabe didn't need everyone wondering why Paige asked him if he'd ever cheated on a woman. He was still trying to figure it out himself, but every time he thought about the events leading up to her questioning, he decided it was best to let it go.

Yes, he'd kept his distance on Friday—and again today—until it was time to help her stretch and massage her. It seemed like the best way to keep his attraction to her in check. It didn't seem to be working though.

"I'm relieved to hear that. I had no right to question you like that, and I'm sorry for assuming you would ever—"

"So, how does it feel to be able to bear full weight on your left leg?"

His phone vibrated on his small desk by his computer for the second time as he changed the subject. Whoever it was would have to wait, because he didn't answer personal calls and texts while he worked with patients.

"It feels good," Paige said. "I've been waiting for this day forever, but I'm leery of ditching the crutches altogether. I still feel unstable sometimes."

"Understandable. It might help you adjust if you use only one. Like this..." He grabbed one of her crutches from where they leaned against the wall and demonstrated. "It will give you support until you learn to trust yourself again."

"Learn to trust myself." Paige made a scoffing sound then gave a small grin. "Do they make crutches for life?"

He replaced the crutch and resumed rubbing her shoulder. "They're called therapists."

"Well, aren't you cocky." She quirked an eyebrow at him.

"I don't mean physical therapists." He smirked back at her. "I mean psychologists."

"Are you saying I need mental help?"

Gabe feared he'd offended her until he spotted the teasing gleam in her eyes. "*I'm* not saying anything. You're the one who admitted to having trust and judgment issues."

"I did, didn't I?" Paige grimaced.

"Aren't you seeing Dr. Emily Anderson...uh Winters?" Gabe had learned that despite the door plate saying Dr. Anderson, the psychologist went by her married name of Winters in her personal life.

"After Emily realized I wasn't suicidal, she told me her door was always open if I wanted to talk, but I haven't taken her up on it." She shrugged. "I'm not sure why, other than...I don't want to talk about what really happened with Phillip."

Gabe didn't blame her. However, he was curious how she'd found out the truth about her ex. Was it a humiliating, public scene? Had she overlooked the same red flags he did with Harper? He bit his tongue. Such a conversation was too personal for the physical therapy office.

"I'm not sure you need to talk to a licensed professional, but it might be good to talk to someone you trust and feel comfortable with. A friend or parent perhaps."

He considered her father's efforts to set up this office and her mother's hovering. Paige might find their concern overbearing. Even though he was close to his mom, he wouldn't blame Paige if she didn't want to go to her parents with her problems.

A thoughtful look filled her face as she nodded. "I suppose the important thing is to talk to *someone,* even if it's not Emily."

Gabe clamped his jaw shut to keep from volunteering to be that someone. There was so much he wanted to know about Paige, but he was having a hard enough time remaining professional as it was. Being her confidant would only make it harder.

"I'll have to see if my cousin is busy this weekend." The grin that filled Paige's face made her look radiant. It was the kind of smile that lit up the room.

To distract himself from her hundred-watt smile, Gabe turned his attention back to Sam, who now did a seated march. His phone vibrated on the desk again as he finished up with Paige. Longer this time, signifying a call. Someone sure wanted to get a hold of him.

As curious as he was about the call and texts, he resisted the urge to check his phone until Paige was gone, and he'd finished working with Sam. It buzzed with yet another text before the office was empty and Gabe was able to check his messages.

All the texts were from Grace.

Call me ASAP.

You need to come home tonight.

Seriously, Gabe, answer your phone.

Gabe's gut twisted with the urgency of each message. Something was wrong. Grace was rarely this impatient and prone to melodrama. He was about to hit the phone icon to call his sister when he noticed a voicemail, also from Grace.

With tightness gripping his chest, he tapped the voicemail and raised the phone to his ear.

"Darn it, Gabe. Pick up your phone. Mom got her test results back —" Grace's voice broke. "And they aren't good."

Gabe's stomach plummeted. His already tight chest hardened to stone, trapping the air in his lungs. The results must be really bad to make Grace cry like that.

"Luke, cancel my afternoon appointments." Thank goodness there were only three. Gabe was halfway out the door before Luke called his name.

"Gabe, wait! What's going on?"

He turned to find Luke on his feet; his face filled with concern and confusion.

"I have a family emergency. Clean up and lock up please." He wished he could give Luke more information, but he couldn't. Even if he had more information, he wasn't sure he'd be able to articulate words around the lump forming in his throat. That's why he waited until he was in the privacy of his car to call Grace.

PAIGE WALKED out of the dressing room on Wednesday with the aid of a single crutch, like Gabe had shown her, and stopped short. Her stomach sank as disappointment swamped her.

Gabe wasn't waiting for her near the pool. Instead, she found a large, barrel-chested, dark-haired man with bronzed skin, who looked to be in his late thirties.

"Hi, you must be Paige." He held out a massive hand that engulfed hers. His gaze raked over her before his lips turned up in a smile that looked both appreciative and predatory.

A shudder of revulsion rippled through her, causing her skin to break out in goosebumps. "Yes, and you are...?"

"I'm Kelekolio Tuatagaloa, but everyone calls me Toa. Gabe couldn't make it today, so he asked me to fill in."

Couldn't make it? Or didn't want to?

He said he wasn't offended when she questioned his fidelity last week, but maybe he'd decided she was out of line with her questioning. Or maybe he realized she'd been ready to kiss him and decided it was safer not to be alone with her.

"Gabe told me a little about your accident and your subsequent surgeries." Toa's thick eyebrows dipped as he grimaced. "Sounds like you've had a tough recovery. He said you only started bearing full weight this week."

He didn't phrase it as a question, but Paige nodded anyway as she lifted her crutch. "Yes, but I still feel a little unsteady sometimes, so I'm weaning myself off the crutches one at a time."

"How's your balance in the water?" He stepped to the stairs and motioned for her to precede him into the pool.

Paige couldn't help comparing Toa's lack of concern for her well-being with the way Gabe always preceded her into the water so he could catch her if she slipped.

"It's been a little rocky." She laid her crutch on the cement and used the handrail to steady herself as she stepped into the pool. "But I'm improving with each session."

As the chilly water enveloped her body, she prayed she didn't get a cramp in her hamstring again. Toa was certainly strong enough to catch her and support her until it subsided but talk about awkward.

Her mind jumped to last week's Charlie horse. The way Gabe held her secure in his arms while he rubbed out her hamstring hadn't felt uncomfortable at all. It felt amazing and somehow right, even though it should have been wrong.

Funny how a little over two weeks ago, Gabe's one-on-one attention made her self-conscious, but now she missed it. From day one, she'd felt comfortable and safe with him.

"Let's warm-up with a high knees jog in place, then we'll stretch before we start your exercises." Toa started pumping his legs up and down.

Gabe never started with a jog. His warm-ups were more gradual and catered to her limited abilities.

As she started to jog, Paige immediately felt the pinch in her low back and hip. It took every ounce of her concentration to stay on her feet while jogging, especially with Toa's bulk creating extra movement in the water.

Gabe should have canceled this morning's session. Or at the very least, give me a heads up.

The pang of disappointment tightened her chest. Where was he anyway? Had he taken the whole day off? Or was he just avoiding her?

She was breathless by the time Toa stopped jogging and shifted to underwater jumping jacks. Paige only moved half the speed he did and was careful not to lift her right arm too high, but their up-and-down motion rocked the water so much it knocked her off her feet. She caught herself easily enough, but a sense of panic consumed her for a moment before she was stable again.

"I can't keep my balance when the water is so active," she gasped out after righting herself.

Toa stopped bouncing. "Gabe mentioned that, but I figured we'd give it a try anyway."

She glared at him. "Give it a try? You realize I have two metal plates holding my pelvis together, a rod in my femur, and screws and pins in my shoulder. After nearly dying and spending two and a half months in a rehabilitation center, I'm not interested in *trying* things that might cause a setback."

"Okay." Toa gave an exasperated sigh as he raised his hands in surrender. "Let's go ahead and stretch."

Paige bit her tongue to keep from telling Toa he was doing it wrong every time he asked her to stretch beyond her limits. She silently cursed Gabe for putting her in this position.

Is a simple call or text too much to ask for?

Her heart rate spiked as her disappointment turned to anger. How many times had she asked herself that exact question while she dated Phillip. He treated her like a queen when he was with her, but he'd always been slow to return her calls and texts. And he'd canceled their plans more time than she could count when work interfered.

Except it wasn't work.

It wasn't fair to compare Gabe to Phillip, but she couldn't help it. She wasn't in a relationship with her therapist, but she felt let down just the same. Despite the conversations they'd had and the things she'd learned about him and his family, there was a lot about Dr. Gabriel Rivera she didn't know. Add his lack of communication about being gone today, and it felt like he was hiding something.

"Gabe is one lucky duck." Toa said as they transitioned into his version of her exercises.

"How so?"

"He gets all the breaks." He raised a hand. "Don't get me wrong, he's a good therapist. One of the best at Summit in fact, but getting this gig in Providence..." He whistled. "The commute's not great, but I'd give my right arm for a sweet gig like this."

Toa's actions slowed when he talked, so Paige was determined to keep him talking. "What makes this *gig* so sweet?"

"Are you kidding me?" He gave her an incredulous look. "He's got his own office already. Only two years after finishing PT school. And he only sees six to eight patients a day?" He motioned to her with both hands. "Plus, he gets to work one on one with sexy women like you."

Paige's skin crawled, and once again she hated Gabe for standing her up.

"Do you work in the same office as Gabe in Pasco?"

"Only on Tuesdays and Thursdays. He works the early shift, and I work the late one, but our afternoons overlap. I also work in the Richland office on Mondays and Fridays."

That explains why he's able to be here in Providence on a Wednesday.

"Gabe and I went to PT school together." His voice grew critical as he continued. "Talk about an over-achiever. He always got near perfect scores and raised the curve for all of us. He made those grueling three years look easy, but some of us actually had a social life."

Paige assumed Gabe was either very intelligent or hard-working. Knowing how good he was at his job and that he spent his weekends helping his mom and sister, she had a feeling he was both.

Toa continued to talk as they worked their way through her exercises, frequently speaking negatively about Gabe and other therapists in the offices where he worked and always painting himself as either a victim or a hero. Recognizing him for the narcissist he was, Paige did her best to tune him out.

Her irritation with the substitute physical therapist grew each time he tried to change her exercises to a more "challenging version that would make her stronger."

She didn't hesitate to give him a piece of her mind when the new exercises hurt her. Finally, deciding she'd had enough, she told Toa she needed to use the restroom.

Just before stepping into the dressing room, she looked at the clock then at Toa. "Lap swim will be starting soon, so I won't bother coming back out. And I have a dentist appointment, so I don't have time for you to work on me."

It was a lie, but she was glad she'd fibbed when a look of disappointment crossed his face.

And boy, was she going to give Gabe a piece of her mind on Friday.

CHAPTER 9

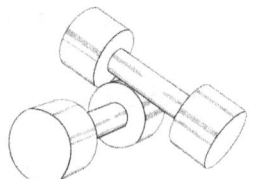

"*What* do you mean it's inoperable?" Gabe pitched forward in his chair, itching to crawl across Dr. Sumner's desk and wrap his hands around the man's neck until he changed his diagnosis. He felt betrayed by the man he'd known and trusted for over a decade.

"I'm sorry. I know this is difficult to hear." The oncologist's gaze shifted to Gabe's mom who sat between him and Grace. Except for the slight quiver of her bottom lip, her face was stoic. "Marisol, you know I hate to be the bearer of this kind of news. But your pancreas is riddled with tumors. As well as—"

"Then remove the pancreas and give her insulin injections." Gabe's voice was sharper than he intended, but he didn't care. The news they'd waited on pins and needles for all week was unacceptable.

"It's not that easy. Your mother also has sizable tumors in her right lung, stomach, and liver." His voice turned even more serious. "It's in her lymph nodes, Gabe."

Tightness seized Gabe's chest as his stomach turned to lead. Each beat of his heart thudded in his ears, sounding slow and sluggish. He struggled to find his voice around the sudden thickness in his throat. "How soon can she start...chemo?"

The words felt like sandpaper on his tongue. He hated the thought of his mom going through that again. The nausea and vomiting, the sleeping all day, being unable to care for herself because she was too weak. But she'd have to in order to beat this.

And he'd do whatever was necessary to take care of her and Grace. Just like he did last time. He'd move home, even though it would add thirty minutes to his commute. He'd hire a maid and a chef, if need be. Not that Mom would be able to keep anything down.

"No chemo." Mom's words were quiet but filled with determination.

Gabe reeled back as though she'd struck him. His eyes burned. "Mom, it's the only way—"

"She has stage-four pancreatic cancer, Gabe." Dr. Sumner's blunt words packed a powerful punch right to Gabe's gut, stealing his breath and making him want to vomit. "Chemotherapy wouldn't be effective. It would only make her weaker and more miserable."

Gabe shook his head so violently it started to pound. He couldn't accept that answer. There had to be something they could do.

I can't lose my mom.

He pounded his fist on Dr. Sumner's desk. "How did this happen? It's only been eight months since her last set of scans. They were clear. How did this get so advanced in such a short period of time?"

"Gabe, that's enough." Mom put a hand on his arm.

He would have considered her grip firm if he couldn't feel the tremor in her hand. Letting out a heavy sigh, he slumped back in his seat. As terrifying as this was for him and Grace, it was much worse for his mom, and his anger and denial weren't helping. He rotated his wrist and clasped her hand in his.

Grace, pale faced and eyes brimming with tears, held her other hand.

Dr. Sumner lifted a paper from his desk and studied it. "Eight months ago, her white blood cell count was elevated. Not severely, but enough that I felt it necessary to do some scans. And you're right, those scans showed nothing, but this very aggressive cancer was likely in its beginning stages back then."

"How long do I have?" Mom's voice was so quiet Gabe almost didn't hear her, but his chest constricted at the resignation in her tone.

Dr. Sumner gave them each a sympathetic look before answering. "It's hard to say. Three to six months maybe. Although I've seen people with stage four pancreatic cancer live twelve to fifteen months."

Three months?

Gabe struggled to draw in a full breath under the weight of the elephant that sat on his chest.

"No." Sobbing, Grace spoke for the first time since they entered Dr. Sumner's office. "There has to be something we can do. Aren't there drugs that slow the growth of cancer cells?"

"There are. I don't know how effective they'll be when the cancer is this aggressive, but I'd like Marisol to take them." Another sympathetic look accompanied his next words. "They might buy you a little time, which I encourage you to make the most of. Make lasting memories and..." his gaze returned to Gabe's mom, "get your affairs in order."

A little more time is not enough!

Mom let out a heavy sigh as she slowly nodded.

Grace's sobs intensified.

Gabe felt his face crumble as pain, sharp and swift, pierced his chest. He sucked in a deep breath and schooled his features. Mom and Grace needed him to be strong. He could let out all these horrible emotions that threatened to suffocate him later. When he was alone.

The three of them were quiet, their footsteps slow and heavy as they left the oncologist's office. Mom carried the card of a trained professional who could help them navigate this horrible nightmare they'd been thrust into. Why anyone would choose to go into such a line of work was beyond Gabe.

He'd planned to take them out for a celebratory lunch after they got the news that his mom's latest scans didn't show anything to be concerned about. But that didn't happen, and now, he didn't think he could eat if his life depended on it.

The twenty-minute drive home felt like an eternity as they each processed the shell-shocking news. The silence in the car grew heavier with each mile and so did the ache in his throat and burning behind his eyes. Grace's soft sniffles drifted from the backseat occasionally, but Gabe couldn't bring himself to look at her in the rearview mirror. If he did, he would lose it. He was barely keeping it together as it was. Seeing his mom wipe away silent tears every couple of miles didn't help.

When they walked through the front door of the small home Mom rented—and eventually purchased—after the divorce, she gave them a weak smile. "I'm not hungry, but you kids make sure you get some lunch. I'd like to rest for a bit, then we'll talk about what needs to be done over dinner." Her soft footfalls shuffled down the hall. The click of her bedroom door sounded as lethal as the cocking of a gun.

What needs to be done.

The ache in his chest expanded, creating a massive void. How did he help his mom get her affairs in order? And how was he supposed to be strong for her and Grace when all he wanted to do was curl up in a ball and cry?

"Why?" Grace dropped onto the couch, huddled into the corner with her knees hugged to her chest. "Why Mom? Why does it have to be cancer again?" Anger and resentment deepened her voice.

Gabe didn't even try to answer as he sank down beside her, because his own angry thoughts echoed hers. Despite everything she'd been through in her life, his mom had always taught them to put their faith and trust in God. But Gabe wasn't sure he could do that anymore.

Why had God allowed this to happen? This time there wouldn't be a remission. A cold chill swept over him as the beat of his heart slowed to an agonizingly painful drumming. How were he and Grace ever going to cope without their mother?

The pain in Grace's big brown eyes tore at his heart. He wrapped his arms around her and rested his chin on top of her head.

Great wracking sobs shook her shoulders, and her tears soon soaked his shirt. Her pain magnified his own, and he let go of the control he'd been fighting to keep on his own emotions.

At first his tears were silent, then before long, his angry sobs rivaled Grace's.

～

"WE SHOULD MAKE a list of things that need to be done." Mom's quiet voice sounded like a thunderclap around the silent kitchen table.

Grace's fork clattered to her plate as she clapped a hand to her mouth to stifle yet another sob.

Gabe's stomach clenched. He set down his own fork. He'd only taken a few bites of his enchiladas—their favorite comfort food—but his appetite dissipated with his mom's words.

Mom had yet to touch her food.

"I talked to Mr. Henessy this afternoon and told him about...my diagnosis. He was shocked and quite upset, of course."

Welcome to the club.

She had worked for the family-owned furniture company for over a decade, serving as Mr. Henessy's personal assistant for the past six years. He'd been good to her, to their family.

"He wants me to work as long as I feel I'm able," Mom continued, "and he'll make sure I have insurance until the end. We'll hire my replacement soon, so I have plenty of time to train them."

Plenty of time? Replacement?

Mom didn't have plenty of time left. He and Grace wouldn't get a replacement mother. Not that he wanted one. No one could measure up to his mom, who'd probably spent very little of her afternoon resting, but seemed to be weathering this terrible storm—this category five hurricane—with a queen's grace.

"I don't want a lot of fuss or anything fancy, but we should contact a mortuary soon—"

"Mom, stop." Gabe held up a hand. "I can't—" He swallowed hard to force the lump from his throat. "I can't do this yet."

"But you heard Dr. Sumner, we don't know how long I have."

"I know, but I need a little time. *Please?*" He felt like a child begging to stay up past his bedtime.

"Okay." Mom slowly nodded. "But we can't wait too long, Mijo."

"I know." He doubted he'd be ready anytime soon, but he wouldn't let his mom down. It would kill him, but he'd help her plan her funeral and make the necessary arrangements. He couldn't bear to let anyone else do it.

Mom finally picked up her fork and took a bite of enchilada.

Gabe forced himself to do the same.

"I've had a good life," she said after a single bite. "I've raised two wonderful kids who have turned out to be amazing adults." Mom held her head high, but her chin lacked its usual determined tilt. "I don't have any regrets, and I'm not afraid to die."

Grace dabbed at her eyes with her napkin, and Gabe had to once again force down the emotion that clogged his throat.

In truth, Marisol Rivera had had a difficult life; orphaned at the age of eight, then raised by her grandmother who died shortly after Marisol turned nineteen. She'd had a happy life with his dad—or so Gabe had thought—until he walked out on them, leaving her practically destitute with two teenagers to finish raising on her own. But she'd never complained. Instead, she rolled up her sleeves and went to work.

"My only regret is that I didn't get to see you both married with families of your own." She put her hand on Gabe's where it rested on the table. "I'm sorry you were dealt such a difficult hand. Your father left just when you needed him most in your life. I tried to make up for his absence, but I failed miserably."

"Come on, I don't think I turned out so bad." Gabe's attempt to ease the somber tension earned him an eye roll from Mom and a scowl from his sister. "Mom, you didn't fail us." He covered her hand with his. When had hers become so frail? "You did everything you possibly could for Grace and me. I attribute the man I am today to you."

Tears gathered in her eyes as she smiled. "You did most of that on your own. You had such an unbreakable spirit. Until Harper jilted you, that is." Her smile faded. "I kept expecting you to bounce back eventually, but her betrayal left you bitter." Her lips pressed into a thin line as she slowly shook her head.

"I'm not bitter," Gabe said defensively.

He had been for a long time, but he'd eventually come to realize he was much better off without Harper. Especially when she and Dirk divorced only eighteen months after eloping.

"Then why haven't you moved on? I know PT school was stressful, but that's behind you now." Mom squeezed his hand again, giving it a little shake. "My experience with your father probably left a bad taste in your mouth when it comes to marriage, but it's time for you to settle down, Mijo." Tears filled her eyes, and she dabbed at them with her napkin before taking Grace's hand as well. "All I've ever wanted was to see you both in happy, fulfilling relationships."

Regret weighed heavily in his stomach. Yes, PT school was grueling, but he graduated two years ago, and he had yet to make a real effort to form any lasting relationships, let alone get married.

"Don't worry about us, Mom." He cleared his throat to loosen the perpetual lump of emotion that had taken up residence there. "Gracie and I will be oka—" His voice broke on the last word, because how could they possibly be okay without their mother?

Across the table, Grace's sniffles grew louder.

"Oh, I know you will. You've both got my stubborn streak. But there's a big difference between being *okay* and being happy. I'm not saying you need to be married to be happy, but..." Her voice turned tearful again, and it broke Gabe's heart. "I always thought I'd get to meet your spouses." She released his hand and brought her napkin to her eyes again. "And hold my grand babies."

He wanted so badly to fix this for his mother, like he'd done with everything else that had broken over the last twelve years. He hated that he'd let her down in this regard.

If only I could alleviate her concerns...

"I'm seeing someone." The lie was out of his mouth before he could think about how stupid it was. He grabbed his water glass and chugged it to alleviate his suddenly dry mouth and to hide behind.

"You are?" Mom pressed a hand to her chest. Her eyes lit up, all sadness and worry gone. "Since when?"

Grace's head popped up, eyes narrowed, her face full of questions.

Trying to ignore the trembling deep in his core, he gave a noncommittal shrug. "For a while now."

"Who is she?" Mom leaned forward in her seat, elbows on the table. "What does she look like? Where did you meet her?" Excitement filled her voice.

So many questions, and he didn't have an answer for a single one of them. But making his mother's final days happy justified a few lies. Didn't it?

"I uh...met her through work." It seemed like the safest answer, since school and work had consumed his life for the past ten years.

"A colleague or a former patient?" Mom's attention remained on him as she picked up her fork and started eating again.

Most of his colleagues were men or young college-aged girls who worked as assistants, so dating a patient was a more believable option.

"Patient." His stomach rolled as he forced out the lie. If he hadn't already lost his appetite earlier, it was long gone now. He tightened his grip on his fork to keep from fidgeting.

"Why didn't you tell me sooner?" Except for the slight redness around her eyes, all signs of Mom's tears were now gone as she put additional small bites in her mouth.

Perpetuating his lies to keep her eating was wrong, but he couldn't back down now. "I...um... I wanted to make sure it was going to work out first."

"Why wouldn't it work out?"

"Well...she...got hurt pretty badly by an ex...who cheated on her. So she was hesitant to get into another relationship." The lies rolled off his tongue now, and he realized his fictional girlfriend suddenly had a name and face, complete with a tragic backstory.

"And you're sure it's going to last?" Mom's next question pulled him from his thoughts.

"I hope so." Warmth filled his chest as he realized this wasn't a lie.

Was it possible for him and Paige to have a future? Would she say yes if he asked her out after she finished her therapy? His stomach sank as he remembered she might return to Seattle at the end of the summer if she didn't find a job locally.

"Tell me about her. What's her name?"

Gabe's heart stalled. This is where Mom caught him in his lies.

Throwing Paige's name out felt like he was deceiving her as well as his mom. But for the life of him, he couldn't think of the name of any other former female patient he'd found attractive. Not that attraction mattered. It didn't, but he drew a blank on a name at all.

"Well…" He gave a big grin. The grin that had gotten him out of many a lecture when he was young. Hoping it still worked, he winked. "I usually call her *mi amor* or *mi corazón*." He prayed the Spanish endearments would distract her from wanting a name. "Or sometimes sweetheart or darling." Then he sighed. "She has the prettiest blue eyes and an amazing smile that lights up the whole room."

"So, when do I get to meet her?"

Gabe choked on the bite of enchilada he'd just shoved in his mouth. The acid in his stomach bubbled and churned, giving him indigestion.

"I uh…I'm not sure we're at the meet-the-parent's stage just yet." He shifted in his seat that had suddenly grown hot. Fabricating a girl-friend was one thing, making one materialize to bring home to meet his mom was another thing entirely.

Idiot, of course she wants to meet your girlfriend.

"But you said you're sure it's going to last. If you're that serious, why don't you want me to meet her?" Mom's face fell, and so did Gabe's hopes of making her final days happy.

"It's not that I don't want you to meet her. I just…don't want to scare her away by coming on too strong after everything she's been through." And asking Paige to come home with him to meet his mom would definitely scare her away. It could also cost him his job. "I'll…uh…I'll talk to her and see what her schedule is like." Each lie Gabe told sat in his stomach like sharp shards of glass, ripping his gut to shreds.

"Perfecto." Mom patted his arm before pushing away her plate that still contained more than half her food. "I'm going to rest on the couch for a bit while you kids clean up dinner, then we'll see if there is a new movie available to stream."

All too eager to end this discussion and escape the lies he'd told, Gabe grabbed his plate in one hand and his mom's in the other and headed to the sink.

Grace followed him, carrying what was left of the enchiladas. She set the casserole dish on the counter and smacked his shoulder. "What are you doing?" She kept her voice low, but her whispered words were loaded with disapproval.

"Ouch!" He flinched even though it hadn't hurt that bad. "What was that for?" He kept his own voice low to avoid being overheard by their mom who was just around the corner.

"Why did you lie to mom?" Grace folded her arms and glared at him. "You and I both know you've hardly dated since Harper left you standing at the altar."

He sank back against the counter and sighed. "I don't know. I just..."

"Just what?" Her tone softened.

"I don't want Mom to..." He couldn't say it—the word that meant she'd soon be gone. "I don't want Mom to have regrets." Tears stung his eyes. He still couldn't wrap his head around the horrible news they'd received today. "I don't want her to feel like she let us down somehow."

"Of course she didn't." Grace's voice grew husky. "She was the best mom ever. Especially under the circumstances."

"Yes, she was." Gabe's own words were fervent as he scraped the uneaten food from the plates into the garbage. He reminded himself to lower his voice. "But I think she's afraid that because her and dad's marriage failed, and she chose not to remarry, that we believe marriage isn't worth it."

Grace's brow creased as a puzzled look filled her face. "I don't think that. Do you think that?" When he shook his head, she asked. "Why would *she* think that?"

"Because neither of us are married. I'm pushing thirty-one and you just turned twenty-seven. Most people are married by the time they hit their mid-twenties."

"Yeah, but many aren't." She gave him a look that said "duh" as she pulled plastic wrap from the drawer to cover the still half-full pan of enchiladas.

Gabe folded his arms and looked down at his feet as he recalled Mom's subtle hints over the years about seeing a therapist. "She thinks I have a fear of commitment."

"Well, do you?" Grace mimicked his posture. "I wouldn't blame you if you do after what Harper did to you."

"No, I don't." He scowled at her. "I just haven't found the right person."

Now that I think I have, she's off limits. I may never get a chance to see if she feels the same way.

Grace rolled her eyes at him. "I'm not sure you've been looking all that hard."

"I'm not the only one who hasn't been looking." He pinned her with a glare, daring her to argue.

It was Grace's turn to study her feet. "Mom has mentioned many times how much she looks forward to having grandkids. She often apologizes for being sick when I…you know."

Gabe nodded. He knew exactly what she referred to but didn't want to say out loud. They'd agreed many years ago not to talk about what happened to Grace when she was fifteen because it was a painful reminder of a dark and difficult time in their lives.

Marisol Rivera had a granddaughter that she'd only been able to hold briefly for a few minutes before the newborn infant was handed over to Social Services. And they hadn't seen her since.

"I think she worries I'll never get married because I have trust issues. Or that I'll always punish myself for the mistakes I made."

Gabe could have questioned Grace like she did him by asking if she *had* trust issues or if she *was* still punishing herself, but he didn't. That wasn't the point here. The point was they were going to lose their mom and neither of them were ready for that.

They were silent for a long moment; each lost in their own thoughts as they loaded their plates into the dishwasher and cleaned the kitchen. Then Gabe broke the silence. "Did you see how dejected she looked when she realized she'd never get to meet our future spouses?"

"She says she has no regrets, but she does." Grace's words were quiet. Then her expression changed, and she pinned him with a glare. "It was still wrong of you to lie to her."

"I know." He let out a heavy sigh and shoved his fingers into his hair. "We don't know how much time we're going to have with her though, and I just want her to be happy and at peace."

"Me too, but making up a girlfriend? Seriously?" She shook her head in disbelief. "Did you really believe her '*thinking*' you had a girlfriend would be enough to make her happy?" Grace made air quotes when she said thinking. "Of course, Mom wants to meet her." She propped a hand on her hip. "What are you going to do?"

"I don't know." Gabe poured a glass of milk and took a long swig, trying to calm the acids having a heyday in his stomach. "Do you have any friends or coworkers who'd be willing to play the part of my fake girlfriend?"

Grace snorted. "Most of my female coworkers at the radiology lab are married or are considerably older than you. And I'm sure both Natasha and Miley would be all too eager to pretend to be your girlfriend, but mom knows them too well. She would have known if you were dating one of them. Besides, neither of them has blue eyes."

Gabe grimaced. Why did he have to be so specific in his description of his fake girlfriend?

"You really dug yourself a hole, Hermano." Grace patted his shoulder before turning to the sink and wetting a washcloth. "From the way you described this woman, it sounded like you had someone in mind. You almost had me convinced."

For a moment there, he'd almost had himself convinced Paige could be his girlfriend. That they had a future together. Too bad it was all a pack of big fat lies.

Not only was he losing his mom, but he might also miss his chance with the only woman to interest him in a long time because she was a patient.

CHAPTER 10

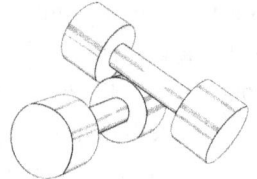

"*D*o you think I'm crazy for considering moving back to Providence?" Paige stared into her phone at her cousin Damon.

He'd called to video chat just as she picked up her phone to see if Riley wanted to hang out.

"That depends. If you want to move home for the exciting night life, then yes, you're crazy."

Paige snorted. "What night life?"

"Exactly." Damon laughed. "Now, if there was a man in Providence that you've fallen for, then I'd think you're only mildly crazy." He pointed at his phone before she could speak. "And I'm not talking about Zack Hastings. I hope you're smarter than that after all these years."

"Zack Hastings?" Paige scowled. "Why would you bring him up?"

"You crushed on him all through high school, and I heard he recently got divorced."

"Eew. No." Paige made a face. "I stopped liking him my senior year when I realized what a womanizer he was." She'd seen Zack's true colors easily enough, so why hadn't she seen through Phillip's deceptions?

"There must be a man though. Why else would you want to move back home?"

Paige's mind jumped to her handsome physical therapist and their near kiss at the pool last week.

Nope, not going there.

She shrugged then picked up her phone and started to pace her room. She was tempted to tell Damon the truth about what happened with Phillip and her fear of running into him if she returned to Seattle, but she didn't want her cousin to think she was an idiot for letting herself be duped for so long.

"I miss being around family. Ben's kids are growing up so fast, and I feel like I've missed so much."

"Tell me about it. I hardly recognized my nieces and nephews when I came home for Riley and Daniel's wedding."

"Do you plan to settle down?" Paige asked. "Will you ever come back to Providence for good?"

"Whoa! Those are heavy questions." Damon's face turned thoughtful. "Settle down? Yes, someday, but not while I'm still enlisted."

"Why not?"

"Two reasons." He held up a finger. "One, I don't want to have to worry about leaving a possibly pregnant wife behind when I deploy, and she shouldn't have to worry about whether I'll come back in one piece." He held up a second finger. "And I don't want the distraction of wondering if she'll stay faithful while I'm deployed."

Paige figured he probably had plenty of buddies who had been in each of those situations. "Those are valid reasons, but how much longer do you plan to stay in the military? You want to have a family, don't you?"

"Yes, I want a family." He shook his head. "I don't know how much longer I'll stay in. Some days, I love that the military is my life."

"And other days?"

"Other days, I miss my family and long for the slower pace and simpler, safer life of a small town like Providence."

"So, are you thinking about getting out soon?"

"I'm not sure I'm ready to get out just yet. I'm due to re-up next spring though." He grinned as he shrugged one shoulder. "So, unless I meet a woman who changes my mind between now and then, I'll probably re-enlist for another three to five years."

"I hope you meet someone," Paige said, giving him an intense look. "Wives aren't the only ones who worry when their loved ones are deployed."

"Yeah, my mom keeps reminding me of that." Damon shifted to lay back on his bunk. "Are you serious about moving home then?"

"I am, if I can find a job." They spent several minutes discussing the lack of teaching positions in southeastern Washington until Paige's phone signaled an incoming call from Riley. "Hey Damon, I gotta go. Riley's calling me."

"Okay. Take care. Tell Riley I said hi."

"Will do. Love you, bye." Paige ended her video call with Damon and held the phone to her ear. "Hi, Riley."

"Why didn't you tell me how good looking the new physical therapist is?" Riley's voice sounded like she'd just found out a juicy secret.

"Hello to you too."

"Hi, now stop trying to change the subject. Why didn't you tell me the physical therapist was tall, dark, and handsome?"

"He's not all that tall. I don't think he's even six feet."

"You're right, but two out of three isn't bad." Humor filled Riley's voice. "Seriously, Paige, how did you forget to mention how gorgeous he was?"

Paige sighed. "Because I didn't want you to act like my mom."

"Why would I act like your mom?"

"She thinks I need to get to know Gabe on a personal level after I'm done with PT." Full of restless energy, Paige continued to pace around her room.

"You absolutely should."

"No way. I've sworn off men."

"I don't blame you for being gun-shy." Riley's tone was full of empathy. "But by swearing off men you might miss *the one*."

"The one?" Paige felt her brows draw together as she paused to look out the window.

"Yeah, you know, your soulmate. The one you're meant to be with."

Paige believed in love, but she'd never believed everyone had a soulmate. That there was only one person in the whole world you could be happy with. Only one person you could ever love. As long as there was mutual attraction, respect, and *fidelity*, Paige figured she could be happy with any number of men. There should probably be more than just those three attributes, but Paige was confident love could grow from any relationship that was properly nurtured.

She paused at her own thoughts.

Phillip isn't the only man I can be happy with.

The thought was freeing, but that didn't mean she was ready to open herself up to the possibility of being hurt again.

"I know Phillip hurt you terribly, but that just means he wasn't the right guy for you." Riley's voice interrupted Paige's thoughts. "You'll see, the right guy will come along when you least expect it and sweep you off your feet."

Sweep me off my feet? Didn't Gabe do that last week at the pool?

No. Technically, he'd put her back on her feet and made her feel safe and secure.

A part of her wanted to tell Riley Gabe almost kissed her, but she wasn't certain she hadn't imagined that heated look in his eyes. The almost kiss could have been wishful thinking on her part.

She'd felt a keen disappointment when he wasn't there for aqua therapy on Wednesday, and that feeling was amplified this morning when she showed up for PT to find another fill-in therapist.

She asked Gary, the stoic substitute therapist, where Gabe was, but all she got was a shrug. When Luke informed her Gabe left early on Monday for a family emergency, she peppered him with questions. But he didn't have the answers.

Missing four days of work after leaving for a family emergency meant it was something serious. Knowing how close Gabe was to his mom and sister, Paige had prayed for both of them. Again, she wondered if his dad was in the picture.

"Hello? Paige are you still there?" Riley's voice jerked her back to the present.

"Yes, I'm here." Paige let out a heavy sigh. Her attraction to Gabe was as confusing as feeling she should stay in Providence with no prospects of a job.

"Sorry, I didn't mean to get preachy and sound like your mom. I just don't want you to lock your heart so tightly you miss what's right in front of you." Her voice dropped to a reverent tone. "Every day, I think about the pain and trauma Daniel and I could have avoided if I didn't walk away from him years ago."

"You guys were meant to be together. It was only a matter of time before you found your way back to each other."

Maybe I do believe in soulmates.

"You're meant to be with someone special too, Paige." Riley's tone was adamant. "There's a reason God brought you home, and there's a reason He brought a good-looking physical therapist to our little town. Who knows, maybe those reasons are supposed to intersect for more than just PT."

"Now you really do sound like my mom." Paige let out a chuckle. "Fine, I admit I find Gabe attractive, but he's my physical therapist, Ri. I can't fall for him. That's like totally opening myself up to more heartache, because doctors don't date their patients."

"It's frowned upon, yes, but you won't be in PT forever."

She still had months of physical therapy ahead of her, but Paige doubted she'd be ready for a relationship even then. Besides, what if Gabe wasn't interested in pursuing a personal relationship when their professional one ended? What happened at the pool could have just been a heat of the moment thing.

No. Regardless of what Riley thought, Paige was better off not getting her hopes up.

CHAPTER 11

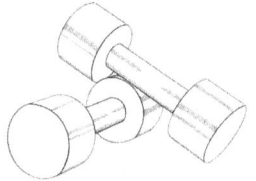

Fake it 'til you make it.

Gabe drew in a deep breath as he unlocked the door to the PT office Monday morning. For the next ten hours he had to pretend his world hadn't fallen apart.

He settled at the small desk and checked his patients' exercise logs then opened the case notes for each. Just as he suspected, Toa had changed several of the patients' exercises on Wednesday, then made notes in their file about their complaints at the end of the session. And Gary... Well, Gary hardly made any notes at all. He never did. And it drove Gabe crazy.

"Boy, am I glad to see you back." Luke had barely cracked the door open before speaking. "Last week was the longest week of my life. I thought listening to Toa drone on about how awesome he is was bad, but then I had to work a whole day with Gloomy Gary on Friday. Have you ever spent a whole day with that man?" After depositing his backpack and helmet behind the desk, Luke stood in front of Gabe with his hands on his hips. "Making conversation with him between patients was painful. And I swear he has no idea what he's doing when it comes to stretching and rubbing them out."

"Sorry about that."

Gabe hated asking either of the men to fill in for him while he was gone, but finding a replacement on short notice was difficult. There was a reason each of the men were available. They only worked part-time at their clinics, because they weren't competent enough to run their own.

Gabe was tempted to ask Luke how Paige did during PT last week, but he stifled the urge. He'd never missed a patient when taking a few days off, but he'd thought about her several times over the course of the week while they waited for the results of his mom's scans. And ever since he told his mom that ridiculous lie, he'd been unable to get her off his mind.

"No, wait. I'm sorry." Luke slapped a palm to his forehead. "I forgot to ask how things are with your family. Everything okay?"

Gabe clamped his jaw shut and drew in a deep breath through his nose as a sudden rush of emotion hit him. After giving in to the tears again last night, he thought he'd be fine, but he just couldn't wrap his head around the fact that he didn't have much time left with his mother.

Luke's brow furrowed as he pulled a chair over to sit in front of Gabe. "What's going on, man?"

Gabe swallowed hard and took another fortifying breath before speaking. "My mom is…sick. Very sick."

"Wow, I'm sorry." Luke shook his head in disbelief. "Do they know what it is? What's her recovery look like?"

"Pancreatic cancer. Stage four." Gabe forced another lump from his throat. "She's…terminal." He forced the word out. It grated even more painfully than the word chemo."

"Oh man, I'm so sorry." Luke hung his head for a moment before looking at Gabe again. "I only met her a few times, but she was— I mean *is* a classy lady. She makes the best empanadas and flan."

"Yes, she does." Gabe tapped the side of his thumb on his small desk. "Listen, don't um…say anything to anyone, please. I'm not ready to talk about it yet."

But I need to talk to Dr. Stoker soon.

Gabe would eventually need to cut back on his hours at the clinic in Pasco and condense his time here in Providence.

"No problem, man." Luke nodded. "I'm a vault. And seriously, whenever you need to take a day off, I promise I won't complain about having to work with Toa and Gary."

Gabe smiled. "Barring emergencies, I promise to try get more reliable replacements when I need to be gone."

Luke stood then paused. "Let me know if there is anything I can do for you and your family." Luke gave him an earnest look. "I mean it. Anything you need, I'm here for you."

"Thanks, I appreciate that."

Relief filled Gabe when Luke walked away, leaving him to his thoughts. Thoughts that immediately turned to his mother and the lie he'd told her.

He stood and cleared his throat. "Actually, there *is* something I could use your help with."

Luke looked up from the computer he'd just booted up. "Name it."

I can't believe I'm asking my twenty-two-year-old assistant to find me a girlfriend. How humiliating!

"I was...um...wondering if you knew a woman who would be interested in...pretending to be my girlfriend." The final words came out in a rush.

Luke burst out laughing. "Good one, man." When Gabe didn't join in the laughter, he sobered. "You're serious?"

"Dead serious." Gabe shoved his hands into his pockets, fighting the urge to fidget.

"You want *me* to line you up with one of my lady friends?" Luke's brows rose in disbelief.

Gabe grimaced and shook his head. "Not line me up per se but help me find someone willing to play a part."

"Yeah, 'cuz that would go over well. Instead of saying 'Hey, would you like to go on a blind date with my boss?' I'm supposed to say, 'My boss needs a fake girlfriend. Are you a good actress?'"

Luke was right. This whole idea was stupid.

Why couldn't I have just convinced Mom I'm happy and will get married someday?

That kind of non-committal promise wouldn't have brought her the peace he wanted her to have in her final days.

Day? Weeks? Months?

Not knowing how long he had left with her killed him. The thought of losing her made it difficult to breathe. He felt like he hadn't drawn a deep breath since Grace called last Monday.

"One of my mom's biggest regrets is that she didn't get to see me or my sister married."

"Married? I thought you wanted a fake girlfriend, not a wife."

"I don't want either." Gabe ground his teeth and rolled his shoulders. "But I'm hoping if she sees me with a girlfriend and thinks it's serious, then she can...die without regrets." He nearly choked on his final words.

"You plan to lie to your mom, hoping to convince her you're on the road to matrimony?" Luke's expression said Gabe was crazy.

Gabe dropped his gaze then scratched the back of his neck. "I already have."

"You've already..." Luke's eyes widened, and his mouth dropped open. "You told your mom what exactly?"

"That I have a girlfriend...and it's serious." Gabe left out the part about blue eyes and a hundred-watt smile.

"So, you need someone mature enough to convince your mom the two of you have a future." Luke's brows furrowed now as he shook his head. "I hate to admit it, but most of my female friends are too immature to pull off something like that."

That's what Gabe was afraid of. He should have known better than to ask Luke for help. His friends were a whole decade younger than Gabe. And he should have known better than to tell his mom such an outrageous lie in the first place.

"Why don't you just ask Paige to do it?"

"What?" Gabe jerked back as though he'd been shocked by an electric current. "No way!"

"Why not? It's obvious you're into her, and I'm pretty sure she's attracted to you too."

Despite wanting to hear why Luke thought Paige was into him, he focused on the first thing Luke said. "I'm not interested in Paige."

"That's a bunch of bull, and you know it." Luke scoffed. "She's a *woman after your own heart*, remember? And she has *such striking blue eyes*."

Blue eyes. Why did I tell Mom my girlfriend has blue eyes?

"You know what Dr. Stoker always says about fishing off the company bridge," Gabe said in an attempt to derail Luke from his train of thought. If he ever hoped to have a chance to date Paige after she completed physical therapy, he couldn't screw it up by asking her to lie to his mom.

"I never really understood that saying, but I figured it meant we're not supposed to date patients." Luke shrugged one shoulder. "But you're the boss now. You get to make the rules here."

"This office is an extension of the one in Pasco, so I still answer to Dr. Stoker...and Dr. Young. Besides, it's a universal rule that doctors don't date their patients."

"Well..." A gleam entered Luke's eyes. "If Paige only *pretended* to be your girlfriend, you wouldn't technically be dating. You'd just *pretend to date*."

"That's stupid."

"Yes, it is." Luke quirked a brow. "And so is telling your mom you have a girlfriend when you don't."

"I know." Gabe raked his fingers through his hair then laced them together behind his head and stared at the ceiling. "I shouldn't have lied to her. The words just slipped out, and suddenly she was so happy. Then it became one of those things where I feel like if I tell the truth now, she'll be more disappointed in me for lying than for not being married. I'm just adding to her regrets."

"Seeing that look of disappointment on your mom's face is the worst, isn't it?"

Luke was raised by a single mom too. He understood the discomfort of disappointing the only parent who cared.

The door opened with Paige's arrival, and Luke reached across the desk to smack his shoulder. "Don't worry, man. We'll figure something out."

Gabe turned to greet Paige. "How was your weekend?"

"It was good. I'm glad to see you back." Concern creased her brow. "Is everything okay with your family?"

"They're fine," he lied, then deflected. "You've ditched the crutches completely. You must be feeling steady."

"I'm getting there." She smirked. "I just have to be careful not to move too fast or do too much."

"It's easy to forget you can't do everything you used to."

"Do me a favor?" She propped her hands on her hips. "Next time you can't make it to aqua therapy, shoot me a text and cancel."

"That bad, huh?"

Paige's hands moved through the air emphasizing her words as she explained the new exercises Toa made her do and how she hated them.

Gabe felt bad about subjecting her to that, but he was so distracted by the way she used her hands to talk that he couldn't help chuckling.

Her hands landed on her hips again. "What's so funny?"

"You talk with your hands. The more passionate you are, the faster they move."

She gasped. "I do not."

He gave her a sideways grin as he motioned for her to sit on the first table. "Tell me again about that last exercise Toa made you do. Did you use something to provide additional resistance besides the water?"

Paige had barely settled on the table before her hand sliced through the air, demonstrating the exercise.

Gabe grinned and made a show of watching her hands as she continued to talk.

Realizing what she was doing, she clasped them together, but they didn't stay clasped for long. When she changed subjects to talk about how cocky Toa was, they started moving again.

Gabe and Luke stayed busy assisting Paige and Nikki with their exercises. Gladys had bumped her appointment until later that afternoon.

"I'm telling you, man," Luke looked over his shoulder at Gabe as he bent to put a band around Paige's knees before she started her squats on the total gym. "All you have to do is walk out on the street and ask any woman."

Gabe glared at his assistant. He should have known Luke's solution would somehow humiliate him.

Paige and Nikki looked at each other with raised eyebrows, curiosity filling their faces. Understandable, since Luke acted like he was picking up an earlier conversation. Technically, he was, but Gabe wished he'd keep his big mouth shut.

"Ask any woman what?" Curiosity shone in Nikki's hazel eyes.

"Nothing," Gabe said with finality, shooting Luke a warning glare.

Luke gave a casual shrug. "Gabe needs a fake girlfriend, like yesterday."

Nikki gasped. "Seriously? That's totally my favorite romance trope."

Gabe bit back a groan. Just when he thought it was impossible for this situation to get any worse, he discovered he was wrong. Resisting the urge to hide his face in his palm, Gabe busied himself setting up Nikki's next exercise. He angled his head enough to look at Paige out of the corner of his eye. What did she think of Luke's announcement?

She'd stopped mid squat to stare at him, a puzzled look on her face.

She's probably trying to decide if I'm still a nice guy. Because what nice guy needs a fake girlfriend?

"Why do you need a fake girlfriend?" Nikki asked as if it was the most natural thing in the world. "To impress the CEOs and get a promotion or get an inheritance from your controlling grandpa?"

"Nah, nothing like that. It's just that his mom—"

"Luke!" Heat rushed through Gabe's body. He had never spoken with such sharpness, especially in front of patients.

Luke stepped closer to him and lowered his voice. "Relax, man. I know what I'm doing."

I doubt that.

Gabe couldn't see how this could go any direction but south.

"His mom is always harping on him about dating, insisting he needs to find himself a girlfriend. But he works so much, he doesn't have time to date. He just needs someone to help get his mom off his case for a while."

Gabe chanced a glance at Paige again. She stared at him, her brow creased, and lips pressed into a thin line. Her eyes held a questioning look, but Gabe couldn't interpret the question.

"I'll be your girlfriend." Nikki gave him a broad smile, then she giggled. "I mean I'll be your *fake* girlfriend."

Is she batting her eyelashes at me?

Nikki was cute and all, but she was way too young for him to take home to his mother.

"Thanks, but no thanks." He gave Nikki as nice of a smile as he could muster. "I don't want to get arrested."

"Hey, I turned eighteen last month."

"Yes, but you're still in high school."

"Only for two more weeks." Nikki's features transformed into a pout.

"Gabe doesn't want his mom to think he robbed the cradle," Luke said with a wink at Nikki to soften the blow.

Instead of feeling relieved Luke stepped in, Gabe shot the kid another annoyed look.

"You should do it, Paige." Nikki pointed across the room.

Paige's head popped up. "Do what?"

"You should pretend to be Gabe's girlfriend," Nikki insisted.

"Me?" Wide-eyed, Paige pointed at her chest. Then she jerked her head side to side before shooting Gabe an apologetic look. "No way. Sorry, but I'm done with men."

A myriad of emotions flitted across her face including what looked like regret, distrust, and a hint of confusion.

"That's a pity," Luke said. "You and Gabe would make an attractive couple."

Nikki giggled again. "The cutest."

Paige's brows shot up as her mouth dropped open. Color reddened her cheeks as she again shook her head.

A surge of relief filled Gabe. If Paige had offered to be his girl-friend—like Nikki did—he'd feel obligated to accept. But getting involved with Paige outside the office could cost him his job and possibly his heart.

Disappointment chased away the relief. Paige had rejected him. He assumed it was because of how badly she'd been hurt by her ex, but it was hard not to take her rejection personally, especially after the chemistry between them at the pool last week.

All this humiliation, and I still need to find a woman to take home to meet my mom.

He had no idea where or how to do that.

CHAPTER 12

*T*hursday evening, Paige had just settled on the couch with her laptop to look for jobs in the neighboring school districts—yet again—when the doorbell rang.

"I'll get it," Mom said, exiting the kitchen.

Paige had been hesitant to tell her parents she was looking for a local teaching position, because she didn't want to get their hopes up in case she didn't find anything. But as the high school principal, her mom might be privy to openings Paige wouldn't see posted. Needless to say, her parents—especially her mom—had been thrilled that she wanted to stick around.

Paige only hoped she didn't disappoint them.

Mom returned less than a minute later, a hesitant smile on her face. "Someone's at the door for you."

"Who is it?" Paige wasn't expecting a visitor.

"Phillip."

Paige's heart lurched, sending a jolt of pain through her chest.

Why is he here? Did he come to rub his happiness in my face?

"I don't want to talk to him."

Mom sat next to Paige and put a hand on her knee. "I know you said he broke up with you, but you never told us why. You were so happy with him. You've really struggled since your accident, and I think it might be good for you to at least talk to Phillip."

Paige couldn't bring herself to tell her mom he was the reason she got in the accident in the first place. She wanted to tell Phillip to take a hike, but she also needed some answers and closure. She needed to know why he'd targeted her.

Is it possible he's come to apologize for what he put me through?

Doubtful.

A sense of dread filled her as she pushed up from the sofa, making her feel heavy and her movements laborious. Slowly and cautiously, she made her way to the door. She no longer used the crutches to walk, which was unfortunate, because Phillip could use the visual reminder of how he'd broken her.

Her heart jerked again when she opened the door and saw the tall, lean, blond man she'd fallen in love with. He was as handsome as ever in his red short-sleeved Henley and faded denim jeans, but knowing the duplicitous man he was, she no longer found him attractive.

"Paige, it's so good to see you." Phillip's face lit up. "I'm glad you're all healed." He leaned in to hug her, but she held out a hand to stop him.

Her palm pressed against his chest. The muscle behind the fabric wasn't nearly as firm and sculpted as Gabe's. She used to think Phillip had a nice body, but he looked skinny and gangly compared to her physical therapist.

"I'm not *fully healed* yet. I still have months of physical therapy ahead of me."

"Right." A guilty look crossed his face as he lowered his gaze. "You didn't answer any of my texts or emails."

"Hello! I blocked you as soon as I regained consciousness in the hospital."

"I figured that was the case." He dipped his head in a nod. "I was afraid you'd refuse to talk to me today."

"I did, but then I decided I needed some answers." She eased herself down into one of the two rocking chairs on the porch. "The first of which is what are you doing here, Phillip?"

He sat in the other rocking chair. "Avery lost the baby."

A twinge of sadness hit her chest for the pretty redhead who had been cheated on by the liar who deceived them both.

"I'm sorry to hear that, but it doesn't explain why you're here."

"I broke up with her."

He said the words so casually another twinge hit Paige for Avery's sake. It was probably the best thing that could ever happen to Avery, but Paige felt bad for the woman who had suffered so much heartbreak. Although after everything Phillip put her through, maybe his leaving didn't break Avery's heart. It was probably a welcome relief.

"You *broke up* with her? Don't you mean you're divorcing her?"

"No. Avery called off the wedding in February. Said I had to prove I could be faithful before she would marry me."

Smart woman.

Paige snorted. "Why would you walk away from a woman like Avery?"

"Because I want to be with you." Phillip leaned toward her, an expression somewhere between pleading and a smolder on his face.

A sharp pain pricked her heart. Three months ago, those words would have brought tears of joy to her eyes, but now, they made her want to vomit. She felt so broken and damaged that hearing Phillip still found her desirable and wanted to be with her boosted her self-esteem. But no way would she get mixed up with him again.

"Not interested." She held up a hand, palm out.

Phillip grabbed her hand and slid to one knee beside her chair. He pressed his lips to her knuckles. "Come on, Paige, honey, I know you still love me."

She jerked her hand away. "No, I don't."

"You told me a few months ago that you loved me more than you ever thought possible." His voice took on a low, seductive quality as he rested his hand on her knee and caressed little half circles with his thumb. "I don't believe you stopped loving me just like that."

"Yeah, well turns out the man I thought I was in love with doesn't exist, so it wasn't all that hard." She shoved his hand away from her leg. "I can't believe you were living a double life the whole time we were together."

He lowered his gaze to his hands, but his face didn't look contrite.

She couldn't get rid of him fast enough, but she also needed to know why he'd led her on.

"Why me?"

"What do you mean?"

"Why did you target me?" She folded her arms and glared at him.

"I didn't *target* you."

"What was all that stuff at the gym? You flirted incessantly with me. Then when you ran into me at the grocery store, you followed me around like a puppy dog, talking about your grandma's favorite recipes. You kept asking me out until I caved. Why did you do that when you were already engaged?"

"Because you were beautiful, spunky and fun. I loved your positive attitude and your zeal for life. I felt so alive after every interaction with you that I had to get to know you better. And the better I got to know you, the more I wanted to be with you. I fell in love with—"

"Don't say it." Paige cut him off. "Don't you dare tell me you fell in love with me when you were supposed to be in love with another woman." She shook her head and scoffed. "You were planning to marry her for Pete's sake."

"I insisted we put off the wedding after I met you. I thought maybe I'd made a mistake in proposing to Avery."

Yet you continued to sleep with her, so she ended up pregnant.

Paige didn't bother voicing the words, because he would only tell more lies to justify his actions. She couldn't believe anything that came out of Phillip's mouth anymore.

"No, your mistake was flirting with me when you were engaged to another woman." She sliced her hand through the air then jabbed it in his direction. "You strung us both along for eight months. Eight months, Phillip!" She poked him in the chest. "I wasted the better part of a year with you, thinking our relationship could lead to a happily ever after."

"It can now, sweetheart." Still down on one knee, he pulled a small black box from his pocket.

Paige's stomach clenched and every muscle in her body tensed. She shook her head so hard it throbbed.

"I want to spend the rest of my life with you, Paige." He popped the box open to reveal a large square-cut diamond.

Paige couldn't be sure it was the same one Avery had worn, but it looked similar.

The proposal she'd anticipated three months ago was finally happening, but it brought Paige no joy. It sickened her that Phillip considered her Plan B. He trampled all over Avery's heart. There was nothing to keep him from doing the same to her. The moment another woman turned his head, he wouldn't hesitate to go after her, like he did Paige, and she would be the one with her heart in tatters. Again.

Was that why Noelle, his crazy ex, was out to get him? Had he done the same thing to her?

"It's time for you to leave, Phillip." She pushed to her feet. "And don't ever come back."

"Paige, wait." He got to his feet and caught her hand. "I know it's going to take time to earn back your trust, but I plan to convince you that you're the only woman for me."

"Even if we both live to be a hundred, you'll never be able to earn my trust again." Paige jerked her hand from his and made her way to the door, eager to get away from him.

"I'm not giving up on us." He stepped between her and the door, his face and posture full of confidence. "I took the weekend off, and I rented a motel room here in town. Let me take you to lunch tomorrow. I'll prove I can be faithful to you."

Like you did to Avery? Only to dump her after she lost the baby.

Paige shuddered. The last thing she wanted was Phillip constantly hanging around, trying to wear her down. If he kept showing up, she'd have to tell her parents the truth about why she broke up with him. She'd have to admit she'd been the *other woman.*

She spun around, nearly losing her balance. "It doesn't matter whether you can be faithful or not, because I'm seeing someone else."

It was a big fat lie, but she had to sell it.

Gabe's laughing brown eyes with long, thick lashes filled her mind. Technically, she *was* seeing another man. Three times a week as a matter of fact. For hours each day. He got up close and personal with her when he stretched and rolled out her tight muscles. No one would ever confuse PT with dating, but it was really just semantics.

"He's everything you're not. He's kind, compassionate, and *honest*."

Except with his mom.

That was a huge red flag, but maybe if she knew his mom, she'd understand why he felt the need to lie to her.

Squaring her shoulders, she went on. "He would never cheat on a woman."

Phillip's confident expression faltered. "I don't believe you. You're just saying that because I hurt you. But I'm ready to make amends for all of my indiscretions."

"I don't want you to *make amends*. I want you to leave me alone." She shouldered past him and opened the door.

"I meant it when I said I'm not giving up on us, Paige."

She closed the door on him and pressed her back against it. Phillip was persistent. She'd learned that last year when he kept flirting with her at the gym. And even after she'd learned he was engaged to Avery, he still hadn't wanted to end things with Paige.

The thought of having to fend him off for the whole weekend made her stomach roll. She'd cared deeply for him. More than she had any other man. But he'd hurt her terribly. No way would she give him the chance to do it again.

She had to convince Phillip she was not available. Physically or emotionally. Would Gabe help her?

A fake relationship was safer than a real one, because if Gabe needed a fake girlfriend, it meant he didn't have another woman on the side.

He wouldn't cheat on her.

~

RELIEF FLOODED OVER PAIGE, making her feel almost light-headed when she walked into an empty PT office Friday morning. Gabe, the only one in the room, sat at his small desk making notes on his computer. She glanced around a second time to make sure they were alone.

The door to the closet where the laundry facilities were stood open. She caught a glimpse of Luke's shoulder as he folded a towel.

Maybe I should wait.

Recalling Phillip's vow to not give up, she decided it was now or never. She hurried over to Gabe.

"Good morn—"

"I'll do it." She spat out the words before she lost her nerve.

He looked up in surprise. "Do what?"

"I'll be your girlfriend." She tried to whisper but the urgency in her voice made it sound like a growl.

"What?" He sprang to his feet, making her to fall back a step.

"I said I'll pretend to be your girlfriend." She kept her voice low and forced herself to speak slowly. Which wasn't easy, because her heart raced a hundred miles an hour, despite feeling like it had the tightest of the resistance bands wrapped around it.

Gabe's brows jerked up. "Why?"

"It turns out I need your help." She held her breath, willing him to say, *"No problem, what do you need?"*

He stepped back. "What kind of help?" Caution filled his voice.

"I need a fake boyfriend for a while." Paige ground out the words, hating having to make the admission.

Whistling came from the laundry closet.

Gabe motioned her toward the table farthest from the closet. He quickly grabbed heat packs and brought them to the table. "Why do you need a fake boyfriend?"

"Because Phillip, my jerk of an ex, showed up last night, trying to get me to take him back." Despite trying to keep her words quiet, the disdain in her voice made it raise.

"The guy who cheated on you?" Gabe whispered as he tucked a heat pack behind her back.

"Yes."

He studied her face for a long moment. "You really had no clue he was cheating on you?"

"No. It's scary how duplicitous some people can be."

"Tell me about it." The hardness in his voice made her look closely at him. The muscle in his jaw jumped, and his eyes narrowed as a steely determination filled his face.

"Why do I get the feeling you know what I'm talking about?"

"Because I do." He looked up at the ceiling for a long moment and mumbled something in Spanish.

Paige heard the word *loco* which she recalled from her high school Spanish class as meaning crazy. Was he talking about her or himself?

Either way, he's right. This is crazy.

When he looked at her again, his gaze was hard and penetrating. "You don't plan to ever go back to this guy?"

"Absolutely not." Paige spat out the words.

"And you're not seeing anyone else?"

"If I was, I wouldn't need your help." She jabbed a finger in his direction.

"Right." Skepticism lingered on his face.

"I meant it when I said I was done with men. I'm still recovering from my last relationship. Believe me, the last thing I want is to jump into another one—not a real one, anyway." Fear that he might turn her down made her defensive. "I'm not an idiot."

"No, but I might be." He said the words under his breath, but Paige heard them.

"What do you mean by that?" Her brows pulled together.

"Nothing."

"Hey, Paige," Luke said as he walked out of the small closet, carrying a stack of small towels. "I thought I heard your voice."

Gabe locked gazes with Paige as he adjusted the heat pack against her hip. "Can we talk after I get off work today?"

She nodded.

The longer she spent at PT the more tense she became, but it had little to do with the exercises. Every time she caught Gabe looking at her with that pensive expression, her muscles bunched. It didn't help that a small crease furrowed his brow, and he frequently chewed on the side of his lip.

Each time they locked gazes, her heart rate spiked. She wasn't sure if it was the prospect of playing the role of his girlfriend or because she feared he might change his mind.

He didn't actually agree to be my fake boyfriend.

He asked if they could talk after work. Was he waiting until then to tell her he wasn't interested or that he'd already found someone?

"Hey Gabe, did you find a fake girlfriend yet?" Luke's out-of-the-blue question snapped Paige out of her musings.

Warmth flooded her cheeks. Had the assistant overheard Paige's offer this morning or did he bring it up again, hoping to get her to volunteer?

"Not yet." Gabe shot Paige a brief glance before turning a murderous glare on Luke. "But we are *not* discussing it here."

"What's this about a fake girlfriend?" Gladys asked.

Nikki propped up on her elbow on the table beside Gladys. "Gabe's mom is on his case about dating. So, he's trying to find someone to *pretend* to be his girlfriend." She continued despite Gabe's audible groan. "I offered, but he thinks I'm too young."

Paige almost burst out laughing at the stricken look on Gabe's face. He closed his computer and propped his elbows on it to scrub his hands over his face.

"Good grief. Of course you're too young." Gladys' expression was full of disapproval. "Paige is much better suited to be Gabe's girlfriend than you are."

"What!" Paige exclaimed. Never mind that she'd offered to play the part a little over an hour ago, she couldn't help being shocked by Gladys' bluntness.

Gabe must have been equally as surprised, because his head flew up, and he turned wide eyes first on Paige then on Gladys.

"That's what I said," Nikki said with glee. "And Luke even agreed they'd make a cute couple."

"They would." Gladys gave Paige then Gabe an appraising look. "They'd have cute kids too."

"That's enough!" Gabe burst to his feet, and Paige froze mid-squat. "From now on, there will be no more discussions of my love life—or lack thereof—" He held up a finger for emphasis. "Real or fake in this office." One by one, he gave everyone except Paige a hard glare.

Her eyes darted around the room. Luke wore a guilty expression. Nikki looked like her idol had just toppled off his pedestal. And Gladys grinned like she had a secret.

"Methinks the man protests too much." Gladys met Gabe's glare with a raised eyebrow. When he continued to stare her down, she relented. "Oh, you're no fun." She made a shooing motion with her hand. "If we can't talk about your fake love life, let me tell you about mine."

CHAPTER 13

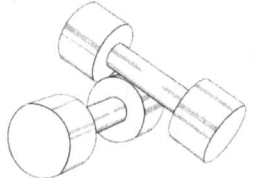

*I*t took forever for the heat to leave Gabe's face and his pulse to return to normal after everyone turned their attention to Gladys. His outburst was unprofessional. He could handle the ribbing and teasing, but when they drew Paige into the middle of it, his protective side reared its head and brought out the worst in him.

What was I thinking?

He should never have asked Luke to help him find a girlfriend. Except, thanks to Luke broadcasting his private life, Paige had volunteered to play the role. He didn't dare so much as glance in her direction as he returned to his computer to review the intake information for this afternoon's new patient.

Luke had said it was obvious Gabe was attracted to Paige. Could everyone else see it too?

He still wasn't sure how he felt about Paige's offer to be his girlfriend. Relieved? Yes. Especially since he'd contacted three former patients he thought might be willing to help him out only to find out the first one was getting married in two weeks; the second was single but expecting a baby any day; and the third had just reconciled with her wife. Gabe shook his head again, wondering how he'd managed to misread the signals from Lena two years ago. He never would have guessed she was into women.

He was also concerned. Could he keep a fake relationship with Paige under wraps? If it got back to Dr. Stoker—not likely, but possible—or worse, Dr. Young, would they fire him? Or at the very least force him to resign?

His chest tightened at the thought. He loved his job, and he didn't want to lose it. But he loved his mother more and making her happy was what mattered most.

What concerned him the most, however, was how easily he could see himself falling for Paige—as manifested by his outburst. But she'd made it clear the other day that she was done with men. After what her ex did to her, he didn't blame her.

Would he find himself in love with her only to have her decide she wasn't ready to move on?

"Are you serious?" At Nikki's outburst, Gabe tuned into Gladys' story.

His eyes grew wide as she talked about pretending to be her brother's best friend's girlfriend to make another girl jealous. She'd been secretly in love with her brother's friend for years, but it wasn't until she threw herself into her role that Harold finally noticed her.

"And the rest is history, so they say." Gladys beamed. "We were married six months later and celebrated our fifty-sixth wedding anniversary shortly before he passed away three years ago."

"That is such a sweet story." Nikki pressed a hand to her chest. "Does that mean if I get one of my guy friends to act interested in me, I could get my best friend's older brother to notice me?"

"No, silly. Then you'd end up falling for your guy friend." Luke smirked as he put a band around Nikki's knees for her to do clamshells. "If you're interested in your best friend's older brother, you need to ask *him* to help you make your guy friend jealous."

Nikki's face blanched. "That would mean actually *talking* to him."

Gabe rolled his eyes as Luke gave Nikki pointers on how to talk to guys.

Thirty minutes later, he was in the process of rolling Nikki out when the door opened, and a man he didn't recognize walked in carrying a bouquet of red roses. He shot Luke a questioning look.

Luke paused in the process of adjusting the weight set on the wall for Paige. He looked as surprised as Gabe.

Paige gasped and hurried toward the door. "Phillip, what are you doing here?"

Phillip? Her ex?

The man with sandy-blond hair winked and grinned at Paige. "I came to take you to lunch, like I promised."

Paige took a small step back. "How did you find me?" Despite whispering, her voice carried through the room.

A quick glance around told Gabe he wasn't the only one eavesdropping. Every eye was on Paige and her ex.

"I happened to catch your mom at home, and she told me you were here." Phillip gave a smug grin.

Paige's fists balled by her sides as her shoulders bunched. "I told you I don't want to see you again. Why won't you leave me alone?"

"Because, Paige, sweetheart, we're meant to be together." He took her hand and gave her an intense look Gabe suspected he'd used on Paige—and other women—many times. "You need to give me a chance to make everything right."

Gabe's grip on the roller tightened. He must have pressed too hard, because Nikki jerked away from him. "Ow."

"Sorry." He stopped rolling.

Both of their gazes returned to the drama playing out near the door.

"No, I don't." Paige jerked her hand away. "There is no way you can make right what you've done."

"Come on, babe." Phillip pressed a hand to his chest in a pleading gesture. "I realize I came on too strong last night with the ring and all."

Ring? No wonder Paige is so desperate for a fake boyfriend.

"We can rebuild our relationship." Phillip went on. "I want to hear all about your recovery over lunch."

"I'm not interested in rebuilding a relationship with you, Phillip. Please leave me alone." Despite backing up a step, Paige's voice wasn't as firm as a moment ago. Certainly not firm enough to convince the jerk to leave.

"You and I belong together, Paige. I'm going to make you see that." Phillip put a hand on Paige's shoulder.

Gabe dropped his roller and was halfway across the room before he realized what he was doing. He hesitated only a moment before walking up behind Paige. He had hoped to keep their fake relationship a secret, but Paige needed him to play his part.

Right here.

Right now.

"Is there a problem here?" Gabe asked with the same firm tone he'd used to forbid the discussion of his love life thirty minutes ago.

"No problem." Phillip sized him up then squared his shoulders and puffed out his chest. "I'm just here to take my girlfriend to lunch."

Phillip was a few inches taller than him, but Gabe wasn't at all intimidated.

He looked over his shoulder. "Gladys, you cougar, your lunch date is here."

Snickers from Luke, Gladys, and Nikki floated through the room.

"No, I'm here to take Paige to lunch." Phillip stepped closer to her.

"I don't think so, pal." Gabe laid his arm across Paige's shoulders. "Paige is *my* girlfriend now."

She flinched as a chorus of gasps sounded behind them. After several long seconds, she leaned into his side and wrapped her arm around his waist, but her body remained tense. "That's right."

The look Phillip gave her was a mixture of disbelief and disgust. "You're dating your physical therapist?"

"Look at him." Paige smiled at Gabe as she made a sweeping motion with her hand. "Can you blame me?"

Her smile looked as stiff as her body, and Gabe didn't blame Phillip for not buying their act.

Her shoulder jerked in a shrug. "You know how it is...when you spend a lot of time...with someone. Feelings...develop." Paige's words were stilted.

Gabe cringed inwardly.

"Yes, feelings like the love you and I shared." Phillip pointed to his chest. "A love like ours doesn't just die overnight."

"They do when one of the partners is unfaithful." Gabe's voice turned hard as he channeled the anger he'd felt toward Harper years ago.

Phillip's expression turned stony, but Gabe held his gaze, unflinching.

"You're making a big mistake, Paige," Phillip said, then he turned and stormed out the door, swinging it open so hard it bounced back and nearly hit him in the face.

"Bravo." Gladys clapped, and Luke and Nikki quickly joined in.

Feeling a sudden headache coming on, Gabe removed his arm from Paige's shoulders and turned to face the group.

Time for damage control.

The applause had barely died down before everyone spoke at once.

"I knew you'd step up to the plate and be the hero Paige needed." Gladys beamed.

"Looks like you've found yourself a girlfriend." Luke grinned and nodded.

"That was so brave of you." The look of adoration on Nikki's face made Gabe uncomfortable.

He rolled his eyes. He was hardly a hero or brave. He only did what needed to be done.

"Listen everyone…" he spoke in his sternest voice. "You can't tell anyone what happened here today. And you can't tell anyone Paige is going to pretend to be my girlfriend."

"Why not?" Nikki asked.

"Because it could cost me my job. Doctors are not supposed to fraternize with their patients."

"Fraternize huh?" Gladys gave him a sly grin. "Do *fake* relationships call for fraternizing?"

Ignoring the heat creeping up his neck, Gabe quirked a brow at Gladys. "You tell me. Did you fraternize with Harold while you were trying to make that other girl jealous?"

"Oh, we fraternized alright." Gladys winked then her face grew serious as she looked at Nikki then Luke. "While most people won't care, Gabe is right. It could jeopardize his job if the wrong people find out he's dating a patient. Especially here in a small town where people can be quite judgmental."

"*Fake* dating," Paige said. "It's not like we'll actually be going out on dates together."

"That's right," Gabe agreed. Although if he took Paige out a time to two, he wouldn't technically be lying to his mom anymore. "So please, don't mention this to anyone." He met each person's gaze in turn, waiting for them to agree.

Luke gave a curt nod.

Gladys' grin returned as she nodded.

Nikki, however, got a calculating look in her eyes. "If we agree, will you promise to keep us posted on how things go when Paige meets your mom?"

Gabe locked gazes with Paige whose face was filled with apprehension. Finally, she nodded and shrugged one shoulder. He didn't want to talk about his mom with these people, but if it was the only way to keep Nikki quiet, he had to agree.

"We'll keep you posted." He clapped his hands then rubbed them together, putting an end to this ridiculous conversation. "Now why are you all sitting around? You've got exercises to do."

Thirty minutes later, Gabe rubbed Paige out. Nikki and Gladys had both left and Luke was busy helping Sam with his exercises.

"Thank you for standing up to Phillip like that." Paige's words were quiet, but the sincerity in her eyes spoke volumes.

He shrugged. "It was the perfect opportunity to play my role. I'm only sorry we had an audience."

"Me too." Paige chewed on her bottom lip. "Do you think they'll all keep their mouths shut?"

"Luke will. Even though Gladys finds the whole thing amusing, I think she understands that this could have serious repercussions for us, or rather me."

"What about Nikki?"

"I don't know." Gabe shook his head. "She's immature and flighty enough that she might let something slip."

"That's my fear too."

"We need to talk." He glanced at Luke and Sam. "Somewhere we don't have an audience. Can we meet after I get off work?"

"Sure. Where?"

"Charity's Diner?" He could kill two birds with one stone. They could talk, and he could buy Paige dinner and call it a date, so he'd no longer be lying to his mom in that regard.

Paige grimaced. "If we're trying to keep this on the down-low, that's the worst place to meet. It's always crazy busy there. Besides, my sister-in-law owns Charity's. She's not likely to be there in the evening, but word would definitely get back to her."

"Hmm…maybe we should just meet at the park next to the swimming pool."

"That's as good a place as any." Paige slowly nodded her head. "Unless there are baseball games tonight."

PAIGE LET out a sigh of relief as she put her car into park and used the rear-view mirror to check her hair and make-up. Then she stopped herself and rubbed her clammy hands on her jeans. It didn't matter how she looked. Like it or not, Gabe was stuck with her as his fake girlfriend.

I can't believe I'm doing this.

It felt good to drive again, especially today of all days. The last thing she wanted to do was ask her mom to drive her to the park for a secret meeting with her physical therapist.

She tapped her fingers against the steering wheel as she surveyed the empty parking lot. Thank goodness there were no baseball games tonight.

Paige had no idea how this thing with Gabe would play out, but she didn't look forward to lying to her parents. She may be an adult, but they liked to know where she was going, who she'd be with, and when she'd be home. Honesty had always been important to her, but it was even more so now after being lied to for eight months.

She didn't feel one bit guilty for lying to Phillip, however. Not after all the lies he'd told her.

Her chest tightened when a dark blue car parked beside hers. It squeezed even tighter, pushing the air from her lungs, when Gabe—despite a long day at work—stepped out of his car looking like he'd just walked off the cover of a magazine in his fitted jeans and blue polo that hugged his biceps. Even the way he pulled off his sunglasses as he looked her direction was sexy.

What am I doing?

How did she pretend to be a girlfriend to all that and not fall for the guy?

Why couldn't my therapist have been some old man? Or even someone like boring Gary?

She climbed from her car and gave Gabe a weak smile.

"Hey." He rubbed his palms down his jeans.

Was he as nervous about this as she was?

"Hey."

Despite the empty parking lot, Gabe looked around nervously. "Do you...uh...want to sit in my car to talk?"

"Can we walk?" She pointed to a path that circled the park. "I can't walk very fast yet, but I need to move, if you know what I mean." Sitting close to him in a car that probably smelled like the woodsy cologne she'd caught whiffs of over the past three weeks wouldn't help her rapidly growing crush.

"Walking is a great idea." He motioned for her to precede him to the path.

They'd walked a good twenty yards before either of them spoke.

"Thanks for backing me up—"

"I know you were pushed—"

They both spoke at once.

Gabe chuckled. "Go ahead."

"I just wanted to thank you again for bailing me out with Phillip."

"It seemed like the right thing to do at the time. Especially since you'd already agreed to be my girlfriend." He rushed on. "I mean my fake girlfriend. I know you were pressured into it by Phillip and everyone at PT, but I appreciate it."

"I still think this is crazy." Paige looked sideways at him. "Are you sure you don't want to just tell your mom the truth?"

"No, I can't. Not right now." Gabe balled one fist at his side and shoved the other hand into his hair. "I need her to believe I'm in a happy relationship."

"But won't she see right through this—I mean—us?"

She mentally chided herself again for the way she flinched when Gabe put his arm around her that morning. How would she react when he touched her in front of his mom?

"I swear moms have a way of knowing when their kids are lying." Paige's voice came out strained thanks to her anxious thoughts.

"While I agree that's true, I also believe people see what they want to see."

Was that why Phillip had been able to deceive her for so long? Because she'd *wanted* to believe he was the one she'd spend the rest of her life with.

"My mom wants to see that I've moved on, so I'm hoping when she meets you, she'll be so happy, she won't question our relationship too carefully."

"Moved on from what?"

The muscle in Gabe's jaw twitched. "Nothing."

Paige stopped walking and propped her hands on her hips. "Fake or not, keeping secrets from each other will only make our relationship harder to sell."

A cold sweat broke out between Paige's shoulder blades. Meeting the parents was always nerve wracking but meeting the mom of a man you hardly knew was downright terrifying.

"You're right." He let out a heavy sigh. "Six years ago, I went through a bad break-up." He shrugged and started walking again. "I haven't dated much since, and my mom thinks I have a fear of commitment."

"Do you?" Paige fell into step beside him.

"Why does everyone keep asking that?"

"Who is *everyone*?" Paige fired back.

"My sister asked the same question when I told her our mom thinks I'm afraid to commit."

"Well, your sister knows you better than I do, so there must be cause for doubt." She raised a questioning eyebrow. When he shook his head, she went on. "So, why haven't you dated?"

"I have. Just not a lot." His admission was quiet.

"Why?"

Gabe gave a tense chuckle. "When did this become twenty questions?"

"When you asked me to lie to your mom for you."

He winced. "Do you have to phrase it like that? Can't we just think of it as putting on a performance for my mom?"

"I should probably warn you that I dropped out of my high school drama class because I'm a horrible actress."

"I'm not much of an actor either, but this is important to me, so you'd better believe I'm going to give the performance of a lifetime."

Performance of a lifetime in a fake relationship?

That thought both thrilled and terrified Paige. How was she supposed to keep her growing interest in her therapist in check if they made their fake relationship that convincing?

"You never answered my question." She changed the subject back to him.

"Which one? You've asked several."

"Why haven't you dated much?"

He shoved his hands into his pockets and shrugged. "For the same reason you've sworn off men."

"She cheated on you?" Paige's heart went out to Gabe. She recalled his reaction last week when she asked him if he had ever cheated on a woman. No wonder he was offended. It must have been incredibly painful for him if he still avoided dating after all these years.

"With my best friend."

"Ouch." Paige grimaced as she resisted the urge to reach out to him. She folded her arms instead.

"You can say that again." He kicked a small rock off the paved path. "I'm over it. Have been for a while, but that doesn't mean I'm eager to jump into another relationship that has the potential…to fail."

"Amen."

"What exactly happened with Phillip?" He looked sideways at her.

Paige didn't want to talk about Phillip any more than he wanted to talk about his ex, but there needed to be honesty between them. She gave him a brief rundown of meeting Phillip at the gym, his persistent flirting, and their months of dating. "I learned the truth on Valentine's Day. From his pregnant fiancée with whom he'd finally set a wedding date."

Gabe let out a low whistle. "No wonder you were so eager to get away from that—" He cut himself off and cleared his throat. "You *were* trying to get away from him when you were hit by the car, weren't you?"

"Yes." Grateful for the lack of judgment on Gabe's face, Paige sucked in a relieved breath as she nodded. "Can you believe he had the nerve to show up at the hospital after my accident to ask me to keep seeing him on the side?"

Gabe stopped walking. "You're kidding."

"I wish." Paige rolled her eyes. "And then last night he showed up, saying Avery, his fiancée—I mean, former fiancée—lost the baby. So he broke up with her, because he wants me back."

"Wow." Gabe shook his head in disbelief. "Just…wow. I can't believe his arrogance. Do you think he bought our act this afternoon? Have we seen the last of him?"

"I don't know. He can be persistent when he wants to be. I mean, he strung me along for eight months." Paige resumed walking.

"I'd rather not stage a public display if we can help it but let me know if he keeps bothering you."

She nodded, hoping that wouldn't be necessary. "How long will I need to play the part of your girlfriend?"

Gabe's posture stiffened and the muscle in his jaw jumped again. "I'm not sure. A few months maybe." The words sounded tense and forced.

"Months?" Paige's stomach sank.

"My mom's not going to believe you're really my girlfriend if you only show up with me once or twice."

"I know, but will she expect us to be together all the time? Because that's going to be difficult to explain to my parents."

He shrugged. "I have a busy schedule, so maybe we can just plan on spending time with my mom and sister on Saturdays or Sundays?"

Paige slowly nodded as she chewed on her lip. "That's doable, but it's going to be tricky to hide from my parents."

"I realize I'm asking you to do a lot more than lie to my mom, and I'm sorry for that, but I could lose my job if your father or Dr. Stoker find out I'm dating—well, sort of dating—a patient."

"I know." Her already slow pace slowed even more. "So, we play our parts and keep this a secret for…a few months. Then what? Do we stage a breakup?"

She thought about Riley's comment that maybe her and Gabe's paths crossed for a reason. What happened if she opened her heart and fell in love with him only to find out he really *was* afraid of commitment?

Gabe's posture stiffened, and his Adam's apple bounced. "That won't be necessary."

"What do you mean?"

He didn't intend to carry this ruse out indefinitely, did he?

He blinked and shook his head as if pulling himself from a stupor. "We'll play it by ear. If necessary, we'll break up." His voice was flat as he stared off into the trees.

"Will that keep your mom off your back for a while?"

He gave a small, sad-looking smile. "I won't have to worry about her after that."

Paige kept glancing at his face as they continued to walk and discuss plans to join his mom and sister for dinner the next evening. For someone who was desperate to find a fake girlfriend, he didn't look very happy to have one.

CHAPTER 14

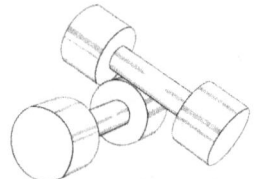

"*H*ow long have we been dating?" Paige released the balled-up fabric from her fist and smoothed the wrinkles from the front of her summer dress for the third time in as many minutes. She still couldn't believe she'd agreed to this hare-brained scheme.

She'd driven to Pasco to meet up with Gabe before driving to his mother's house together. That way, they didn't risk her parents or a member of her extended family spotting her getting into her physical therapist's car.

As it was, she'd almost turned around twice on the drive here. But she didn't, and now she sat in Gabe's car surrounded by the smell of his woodsy cologne, her attraction to him growing by the second as they fabricated a relationship.

"Six months?" Gabe gave her a questioning look. "Does that sound like a plausible amount of time?"

He'd told his mom he was dating a former patient, so they'd decided to tell her—if she asked—that he treated Paige a year ago at the office in Pasco. Otherwise, they figured it was best to stick as close to the truth as possible.

"That's too long, considering I haven't met your mom yet. Three months?" Paige returned his questioning look. "If your mom asks, do I tell her I live and teach school in Seattle? We could say this was a long-distance relationship, and I came home as often as I could to see you. That would explain why you haven't introduced me to her yet."

"I like that." Gabe's lips turned up in a semblance of a smile as he nodded. "Three months it is." His two-handed grip on the steering wheel remained so tight his knuckles turned white.

It was nice to know she wasn't the only one who was nervous. Paige's stomach was so tangled in knots, she wasn't sure she'd be able to eat dinner with Gabe's mom and sister. Knots that formed the moment she told her parents she'd be spending the evening in the Tri-Cities area celebrating the birthday of a former college roommate.

She'd even made a cake—as a front—that she hoped would earn her brownie points with Gabe's family. If anything could help her impress Gabe's mom, it was her sister-in-law, Amy's, triple chocolate cake. If she'd enlisted Amy's help, however, she would have had to lie to yet another person about where she was going and what she was doing, so Paige had made this one. It didn't turn out as pretty as Amy's always did, but hopefully it tasted good.

They continued to make up details for their fake relationship as they drove; concocting dates and activities they enjoyed doing together. Paige was surprised to learn how much they had in common, but she hoped she didn't actually have to remember all the details they discussed.

Dread tightened her knotted stomach as she worried what they would have to do to sell their relationship. How serious did his mom think they were? Would she expect them to hold hands? Or maybe kiss? Paige couldn't make herself ask the questions because she wasn't sure she wanted to hear the answers.

The fabric of her dress bunched in her fists again, and the knots in her stomach tangled tighter the closer they got to the suburbs of Richland.

Searching for a distraction, she let the curiosity that had been eating at her, ever since Gabe first mentioned his mom and sister, push to the front of her mind.

"So...uh...I've only ever heard you talk about your mom and sister. Where's your dad?" Paige didn't think it was possible, but Gabe's grip on the steering wheel grew even tighter. As though it was a snake and his grip on it was the only thing keeping it from striking him.

Obviously, a sensitive subject, but it was a detail a girlfriend should know.

The muscle in his jaw jumped several times before he answered. "He walked out on us just before I turned seventeen."

"That must have been very difficult." Paige put a hand on his arm as an ache filled her chest.

Gabe's gaze jumped to her hand, but his stony expression didn't soften. Neither did the tension in the corded muscles beneath her palm.

She recalled his vehemence that day at the pool when she asked him if he'd ever cheated on a woman. It's possible his reaction had something to do with his dad as well as his ex.

He didn't seem to want her sympathy, so she pulled her hand back. "Have you had any contact with him since?"

"Very little." The muscle in his jaw jumped. "He was supposed to have shared custody, but more often than not, he canceled or flaked out. And now that Grace and I are adults, we make about as much effort as he does to stay in contact. Which is very little."

"I'm sorry."

Gabe shrugged as he slowed the car to turn into the driveway of a small ranch-style home with light blue siding, a sunny yellow door, and a small but well-kept yard.

Paige's chest constricted. Her heart hurt for Gabe, but it was what lay behind that cheerful yellow door that tightened her chest to the point of nearly squeezing off her air supply. She had to convince Gabe's mother she'd been dating him for months and was...in love with him.

Was she the critical, demanding type who wanted nothing but the best for her son? Perhaps she had a woman in mind for Gabe to whom no one else could measure up.

What if we aren't convincing enough?

She recalled the way she tensed up yesterday when Gabe put his arm around her and told Phillip she was *his* girlfriend now. She would blow the whole thing, if she wasn't careful. The moisture in her mouth suddenly vanished, reappearing on the palms of her hands as her anxiety spiked.

"Stay there and let me get your door. If my mom happens to be watching, I don't want her to think I'm not a gentleman."

She stifled a scream when he got out of the car and smoothed out her dress.

This is crazy!

She forced a small smile when he opened her door. Her heart raced so fast she couldn't seem to draw in a full breath as she climbed from the car. She wasn't prone to panic attacks, but she feared she might have one right here in Gabe's mother's driveway.

Not the kind of first impression I want to make.

He grabbed the cake from the back seat and started toward the house.

"Wait." The single word squeaked out of her tight throat.

Gabe turned back. "What's the matter?" He stepped closer and studied her face. "Are you okay?"

"What if your mom doesn't like me?"

He chuckled. "Of course, she'll like you. Just be yourself."

"But what if I say or do something to give away that this isn't real?"

"It'll be fine. Just pretend *you* like *me*."

No problem there.

She did like him. More than she should, considering he was her physical therapist.

He started to turn away then turned back again. "Just don't flinch when I touch you like you did yesterday in front of Phillip."

"H-how serious does your mom think we are?" She swiped her clammy hands on her dress again. "Will she expect us to hold hands and stuff?"

He shrugged. "Probably."

"Probably?" Paige's voice squeaked as she repeated the word.

He scratched his neck as a combination of a grimace and a smirk crossed his face. "She thinks were pretty serious."

Paige's stomach plummeted. "So she's going to expect us to act all lovey dovey?"

She knew this was a possibility, so she shouldn't be freaking out. But ever since their near kiss at the pool last week, she wanted Gabe to be more than her physical therapist.

He set the cake on the roof of the car and planted himself in front of her.

Instinctively, she fell back a step, pressing her back against the car.

"We don't need to act *lovey dovey*, but she'll expect us to show *some* affection toward each other. You are my girlfriend after all."

Fake girlfriend!

She wanted to scream the words but couldn't find her voice thanks to the tightness in her chest. For appearance's sake, even a fake relationship would have physical aspects. That thought had kept her awake half the night. She thought she'd come to terms with the show they would have to put on, but she had a feeling even fake affection from Gabe would affect her in a very real way.

He must have noticed her hand clenching the fabric of her dress again, because he stepped closer, closing the gap between them. "Do we need to practice so you don't recoil every time I touch you?" Without waiting for a response, he took her hand.

She uncurled her fist as his fingertips slid over her wrist and across her palm in a slow caress until his fingers laced through hers. Warmth shot up her arm followed by a tingling sensation as a rush of butterflies swarmed her stomach. He stood close enough for her to smell his woodsy cologne, and it wreaked havoc on her senses.

"See, this isn't so bad, is it?" The intensity of his gaze and his deep voice only added to the flood of sensations assaulting her.

He seemed to be completely unfazed by their proximity. In fact, he looked calm, composed, and...guarded.

"No." Did her voice sound as breathless as she felt?

Meeting his mom was terrifying but having him shower her with affection that took her breath away and left her wanting more scared her to death. Her body didn't understand that it wasn't real. That Gabe was only pretending.

How do I keep my heart from getting involved when the simple touch of his hand sends sparks ricocheting through me?

The breeze blew a lock of hair across her face, but before she could swipe it away, Gabe's fingers were on her cheek, gently tucking her hair behind ear. His fingertips lingered on her jaw as his eyes searched hers.

"This is important to me, Paige. I need to know I can count on you." His warm breath feathered across her face, sending a whole new wave of awareness shooting through her.

"You can count on me. I'm just…nervous." She couldn't concentrate with his gorgeous brown eyes boring into hers and his fingers still touching her face. She lifted her free hand to his chest to nudge him away, but she stilled when she met the firm muscle behind the fabric of his t-shirt. It was all she could do to keep from caressing the sculpted muscles.

His lips quirked as he looked down at her hand. He inched a little closer, trapping her hand between them. "I'm beginning to think you have a fascination with my chest, Miss Young."

He was right, but she'd never admit it. Her mind was too muddled to come up with a light-hearted comeback, so she simply held his gaze.

The desire to kiss him cascaded over her as though she'd just stepped into a warm shower. The sudden moisture in her mouth made her lips feel incredibly dry. She flicked her tongue out to moisten them.

He sucked in a sharp breath, and his grip on her hand tightened. The guarded look in his eyes vanished, replaced by something intense and primal. His composure slipped as he leaned toward her.

"Paige?" The raspy quality of his voice sent shivers ricocheting through her. He angled his head toward hers then paused mere inches from her lips; a questioning look in his heated gaze.

He's going to kiss me.

There was no doubt in Paige's mind this time.

And she wanted his kiss. More than anything. Even though it would catapult her attraction to him from a schoolgirl crush into full-blown infatuation.

But it would change everything. How did she go to PT after kissing him and pretend he was only her physical therapist?

The pull between them was more than she could withstand. Her heart raced in anticipation, stealing her breath, as she leaned into him and lifted her chin.

Kissing Just Gabe is a bad idea. A very bad idea.

KISSING PAIGE IS A TERRIBLE IDEA.

Gabe would never be able to maintain his professionalism around her if he did.

That thought didn't stop him from closing the gap between his lips and Paige's, however. The warm softness of her full lips sparked the dry kindling of attraction that had been building in him since the first time he saw her.

He slid one hand into her hair to cup her head and wrapped his other arm around her. She fit so perfectly in his arms. When she gathered a fist full of his shirt, he pressed his lips more firmly to hers. The surge of adrenaline he felt each time he'd caught her in his arms at PT was nothing compared to the raging river of emotions that now threatened to pull him under.

When he took her hand in his, he only meant to calm her anxiety, but the contact melted away the tension he'd carried since learning of his mom's diagnosis. It filled the empty spots inside him, causing him to let down his guard.

She slid her arms around his neck, her lips parting with a sigh. He couldn't resist; he deepened the kiss for several long delicious moments. A rush of energy swept through him. He knew kissing Paige would be amazing, but he hadn't expected it to make him feel so alive.

This was why he hadn't dated much since Harper left him at the altar. He hadn't found a woman who ignited this kind of excitement in him. And now that he'd found her, he didn't want to let her go, even though it could cost him his job.

Reluctantly, he pulled his lips from hers. He looked down at her, wondering how badly he'd screwed up, but she tucked her face against his neck.

He held her there, grateful for the chance to catch his breath. Except her warm breath against his neck kept the desire humming through him.

"You okay?" The words came out gruffer than he intended. When she nodded, he cleared his throat. "I uh...I didn't mean for that to happen."

She lifted her head, a frown marring her features. "Are you saying you're sorry you kissed me?"

"Not at all." He let go of her and took a small step back. "But I am concerned that I may have jeopardized my career."

"Jeopardized? No." She arched a brow as a small smile lifted her lips. "Complicated? Yes."

He bit back a smile of his own. "We seriously muddied the waters of our professional relationship, didn't we?"

She snorted. "As if me pretending to be your girlfriend didn't already do that."

His smile faded.

Pretending. Right.

The moment his lips met hers, he forgot this whole thing wasn't real.

"It's going to be fine." He said the words to himself as much as to her. Hopefully, she believed them more than he did. "We're in this together, right?"

She didn't look convinced, but she nodded.

He picked up the cake then took her hand. Paige's limp was almost imperceptible, but he kept their pace slow as they made their way to the house. Despite reassuring Paige, his gut churned. He hated lying to his mom, but more than that, he didn't want to let her down. And that's what would happen if he told her the truth and took away the one thing she'd looked forward to all week.

The door opened as they stepped onto the porch. Grace held the door, but it was his mom who greeted them with a smile so big it almost masked the shadows under her eyes. "Ah Mijo, I'm so glad you're home."

Gabe chuckled. She made it sound like he hadn't been home for months, even though he spent Thursday evening with her. He had a feeling she was more excited to see Paige than him.

"Paige brought dessert." Gabe gave Grace a brief one-armed hug then handed her the cake.

As soon as his hands were empty, he gathered his mother in his arms and inhaled deeply. He held her longer than usual, trying to memorize her gardenia scent—the smell of his childhood; of warm hugs, bedtime stories, walks in the park, and unconditional love. After learning of her diagnosis last week, he'd vowed to never miss a chance to hug his mother.

When he finally released her, he took Paige's hand and tugged her forward. "Mom, I'd like you to meet Paige Young. Paige, this is my mom, Marisol Rivera."

Paige smiled and held out her hand. "It's so nice to me—"

Mom pulled Paige into her usual hug, no doubt squeezing the air from her lungs. It was the kind of hug most people reserved for close family and friends they hadn't seen for years. The kind that let the receiver know Marisol Rivera cared.

Paige's eyes widened then squeezed shut as she returned the embrace.

"It's so good to finally meet you," Mom said as she let Paige go. "I can't believe Gabe kept you a secret for so long. But I can see why he fell for you; you're very pretty *and* you know your way around the kitchen." She winked at him as she motioned to the cake. "Muy bonita."

Her wink let him know she was calling Paige beautiful, not the cake, although it looked delicious too. He took a moment to admire Paige, seeing her in a different light after that amazing kiss. The pink and yellow sun dress she'd been mangling on the car ride accentuated her curves that were filling out nicely now that she was mostly recovered. Her hair hung in loose curls, as opposed to the ponytail she often sported at PT, and she wore just enough make up to add color to her cheeks and make her beautiful blue eyes stand out.

He'd been so worried she wouldn't show up, then anxious about how things would play out with his mom that he hadn't taken time to appreciate how pretty his girlfriend was.

Fake girlfriend. This isn't real.

He had a feeling he was going to have to keep reminding himself of that after that incredible kiss.

"You were right, Mijo, she has the most striking blue eyes."

Paige's brows shot up as she gave him a questioning look. No doubt wondering what else he'd told his mom about her since she only agreed to play the part of his girlfriend yesterday. He didn't dare confess he told his mom about Paige's striking blue eyes and radiant smile a week ago.

He gave her a quick wink and introduced her to his sister. "Paige, this is my sister Graciela. We call her Grace for short or Gracie."

"Grace." His sister glared at him before offering her hand to Paige. "Not Gracie. I outgrew that name years ago." Though her tone was friendly, the look she gave Paige was as frosty as a December morning in Antarctica.

"What a pretty name. It's nice to meet you, Grace." Paige's smile was stiff, no doubt sensing the lack of warmth in Grace's greeting.

Grace gave an eye roll as she released Paige's hand and walked toward the kitchen.

His gaze followed his sister.

What's up with her?

She wasn't happy about him lying to their mom, but she was the one who'd pointed out that Mom had been like a new person all week.

"You have perfect timing." Mom stepped behind them to close the door, then she put an arm around each of them. "We just pulled the carne asada off the grill a few minutes ago."

Gabe sensed the tension in Paige but was powerless to do anything about it with his mother between them. They made their way to the kitchen and were soon seated around the table. He asked Mom a question about her work to distract her from how slowly and carefully Paige moved as she took her seat. She had few restrictions anymore, but she was still cautious about everything she did, because some movements still caused her discomfort.

They'd barely said a blessing on the food before Mom started with the questions. "So, Paige, Gabe tells me you're a former patient of his. What kind of injury did you have?"

Gabe tensed. They'd decided to stick as close to the truth as possible, but he couldn't help worrying Paige might let something slip that would tell his mom she was a current patient, not a former one.

"I was…hit by a car while crossing the street." Paige's hands shook as she spread her napkin across her lap. "I suffered multiple pelvic fractures, broke the neck of my left femur, and needed re-constructive surgery on my right shoulder due to multiple fractures."

A sinking feeling hit Gabe's gut as he recalled telling his mom about one of his most challenging patients. He hadn't shared Paige's name, but he'd told his mom the nature of Paige's injuries. The same injuries she just mentioned. He prayed his mom didn't make the connection.

"Oh my." Mom gasped and brought a hand to her chest. "That must have been a long and difficult recovery."

"Too long."

On Paige's right, Grace held out the platter of carne asada. Paige lifted her arm to take it then winced and quickly lowered her arm again. Hoping no one else saw her pained expression, Gabe quickly reached across her to take the platter. He put a few pieces of meat on Paige's plate before serving himself.

Her smile of gratitude didn't come close to meeting her eyes. She looked as tense as he felt.

"She had to do physical therapy for months." Gabe said as he put the platter down.

"I imagine." A knowing grin filled Mom's face. "I hope you waited for her to finish therapy before you asked her out." She quirked a brow at him. "You certainly wouldn't want to chance losing your job."

Paige tensed beside him.

Gabe's gut clenched, and the air whooshed from his lungs, leaving him feeling like he'd been sucker punched. He forced a laugh as he served himself then Paige some black beans. "No, of course not."

"So, when *did* you two start dating?" Grace asked, eyes on Paige.

Gabe shot her a wide-eyed glare that said what-are-you-doing? But she ignored him.

"Our first official date was March sixth," Paige said.

Surprised by the confidence in her response, Gabe's gaze jumped to her face. She said she wasn't much of an actress, but her quick response sounded true. Although he didn't recall them discussing the date their fake relationship started.

She smiled as she met his gaze and laid her hand over his where it rested on the table. He rotated his wrist and clasped her fingers in his. Her skin was so soft, and her hand felt small and delicate. He told himself he was only playing a part and not taking advantage of the situation, but he couldn't deny he liked the feel of Paige's hand in his.

"I spent President's Day weekend in Providence with my family, and while my cousin and I were shopping in Pasco, I ran into Gabe. He got my number, and we talked and texted almost every day over the next two weeks. Then when I came home in March for my mom's birthday, he took me out."

While they'd talked on the drive about their interests and fabricated dates they'd been on, Paige must have been working out in her head exactly when and how their relationship started.

"You're from Providence?" His mom gave him a sly grin when Paige nodded. "No wonder you were so eager to open the clinic there."

He was about to respond when Grace pitched forward in her seat. "You *came* home? From where?"

Gabe itched to kick his sister under the table. She was going to blow everything.

"I live in Seattle."

Grace's brows arched. Her eyes darted to Gabe before returning to Paige. "This is a long-distance thing?"

"Yes, and it's been hard." Paige looked at him with such an adoring look that he almost believed she was in love with him. "That's why I moved home for the summer. To see where this leads."

Gabe's chest expanded at her words. Oh, how he wished they were true. He'd give anything to have her look at him like that every day for the rest of his life. The thought surprised him, kicking his heart rate up a notch, but it felt oh, so right. Holding her gaze, he brought their clasped hands to his lips and pressed a kiss to her knuckles.

"I'm so glad you did," he murmured.

Mom's audible sigh pulled his attention away from Paige. The broad smile on her face was exactly what he'd hoped to achieve. Now to keep it there.

Grace's expression, on the other hand, was anything but happy. She continued to stare at Paige with narrowed eyes, watching her every move. Judging by the tight grip Paige kept on his hand, she felt every ounce of his sister's scrutiny.

He glared at Grace, willing her to knock it off. He didn't understand where her animosity was coming from. When he texted her last night to tell her he'd found a fake girlfriend, he didn't share many details. He figured the less she knew, the less she could accidentally let slip, but maybe he should have given her more information.

"What do you do in Seattle?" Mom asked Paige.

Much to Gabe's disappointment, Paige pulled her hand from his and took a tortilla from the center of the table. "I teach second grade."

"That explains how you're able to spend the summer in Providence." Mom put a small bite of beans and rice in her mouth and chewed before continuing. "It takes a special kind of person to be a teacher. I considered becoming a teacher many years ago, but keeping up with these two hooligans when they were young was enough to convince me I wasn't meant to be with kids all day."

"I'm offended." Gabe brought a hand to his chest. "We were angels."

"Hardly." Mom scoffed. "Has Gabe told you about the time he and Grace decided they wanted to be Smurfs?"

Paige laughed. "No, but I definitely need to hear this story."

"Mom, no." Grace's attention finally left Paige as she scowled at their mom.

Mom set down her fork as she launched into her story. "It was nap time for Grace, so I put a quiet movie on for Gabe—Smurfs, of course —and headed out to the garden. I gave Gabe strict instructions to come get me when Grace woke up." Mom shook her head. "Apparently, she never went to sleep, and they…"

Gabe groaned and leaned his forehead into his hand as mom told Paige every sordid detail of how he and Grace had stripped down to their undies—well, in Grace's case, her diaper—and colored their bodies with blue finger paint. When that ran out, they switched to markers. That proved too slow, so he'd gotten the blue food coloring out of the cupboard. He was old enough to understand he needed to mix it into something, so he chose his mom's face cream, which allowed for triple the coverage while still effectively staining the skin. For days. Not to mention the stains they'd left on the kitchen and bathroom counters. Those had lasted for years.

Despite his embarrassment, he loved seeing the joy on his mom's face as she reminisced. This was exactly how he wanted to remember her. The vibrant, healthy woman who took them to story time at the library, picnics at the park, and on nature walks through the botanical gardens. If reminiscing made her this happy, he'd endure the humiliation. She deserved to relive all the happy memories. He prayed she could see that she was a good mother, and that he and Grace felt loved. She had nothing to regret.

Paige's laughter made his heart rate kick up a notch. He recalled wishing the first day he met her that he could help her find a reason to smile again. Who knew it would only cost him his pride?

"These two were always making messes." Mom launched into another story about the time they got the rice and oatmeal bins out of the pantry and proceeded to divide them among every bowl and pan they could get their hands on. "When they ran out of rice and oatmeal, they started using the cereal." Mom rolled her eyes. "I swear, I was only in the shower for five minutes!"

Gabe piped up. "At least I wasn't as bad as Grace." He shot his sister an apologetic look. "She used to hide her healthy snacks in her shoes, so she could have a treat."

Grace glowered at him. "Well at least I didn't go around asking total strangers if they were pregnant."

Shock filled Paige's face as she looked at him. "You didn't."

"Oh yes, he did," Mom chimed in. "After we first told him there was a baby in my tummy, he started asking everyone he met if they had a baby in their tummy too, even men. As my pregnancy progressed, and my stomach got bigger, he continued to ask anyone with a bit of a belly if they had a baby in their tummy. He was particularly adamant with one older gentleman at the grocery store that he must be pregnant because his tummy was so big."

They all burst into laughter, including Gabe.

Paige patted his knee, sparking the desire he'd felt when he kissed her. "It's nice to know you learned some social skills as you grew up."

He was both relieved and disappointed when she moved her hand away. Now that he'd given in to temptation and kissed her, he had a feeling any physical contact between them would always make him crave more.

They continued to share stories about one another for some time before Mom brought the conversation back to Paige. "Tell us about your family, Paige."

Even though Gabe knew most of what Paige shared about her parents and her older brother and his family, he enjoyed listening to her talk. He loved the fondness that filled her voice as she talked about her nieces and nephew. His eyes grew wide when she told them about her brother, Ben, losing his first wife in a car accident.

The man must have been beside himself with grief to have his daughter kidnapped from the car the same night his wife died. Gabe recalled Gladys mentioning something about Ben's wife and daughter to Paige on her first day of PT, but he had no idea it was such a tragic story.

"That poor, poor man." Mom pressed her hand to her chest. "Did they ever find his daughter?"

"Yes, but not for a whole year."

Thankfully, Mom continued to ask questions that had Paige sharing a story that Gabe—as her boyfriend—should already know but was dying to hear. He loved learning more about Paige's family and wished he could get to know them better.

But for that to happen, this thing between him and Paige would have to be real. Openly dating Paige could cost him his job though. It'd be difficult, but after that kiss, waiting until she was done with PT would be worth it.

But if she doesn't find a teaching job in Providence, she'll return to Seattle. Would she be willing to give a long-distance relationship a try?

Was *he*?

CHAPTER 15

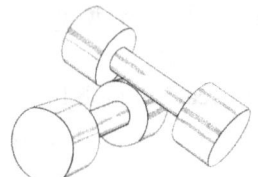

$\mathscr{D}$eciding to save dessert until later, they all helped clean up the kitchen, then Marisol dragged them outside to see her vegetable garden.

Paige took great delight in the flush that covered Gabe's cheeks as his mom sang his praises. Marisol repeatedly mentioned what a dutiful son he was as she pointed out all the things he helped her with. Gabe became the man of the house after his father left, which couldn't have been easy, considering he was still a teenager.

She recalled the way Toa talked about what an easy life Gabe must have had to be able to excel at his studies the way he did. However, Gabe's life had been anything but easy. He'd succeeded because he worked hard and took his job seriously. So why was he jeopardizing it by trying to pass a patient off as his fake girlfriend?

And that kiss!

They'd definitely crossed a line that couldn't be uncrossed, but Paige didn't regret it. She'd never felt such a strong pull toward a man. Kissing Phillip had been enjoyable and pleasant with plenty of warm, fuzzy feelings, but when Gabe kissed her, Paige's whole body came alive. She'd read about women having that kind of toe-curling, knee-buckling reaction in romance novels, but she'd never experienced the all-consuming chemistry that assaulted all her senses in the very best way.

"...don't you think Paige?"

With a start, Paige pulled herself from her thoughts. Her cheeks flamed as she took in the three faces staring at her. Marisol's was expectant, waiting for an answer. Grace's brow remained furrowed, her disapproval palpable. Gabe's right eyebrow arched. He wore a knowing grin as if he knew exactly where her thoughts had been.

"I uh... I'm sorry," Paige stammered. "I'm afraid I let my mind wander and didn't hear your question, Mrs. Rivera."

"Oh please, call me Marisol." Gabe's mom waved a hand. "I mean we're practically family after all. You'll be calling me Mom soon."

Paige froze. How did she respond to that?

Gabe started coughing as though choking on something that had the ability to do him in.

Even Grace's eyes widened as panic filled her face.

Paige was torn between bolting out the side gate of the backyard and pounding Gabe on the back. And not just because he was choking. Her recent injuries prevented her from running, so she chuckled awkwardly.

"It's only a matter of time, right?" Marisol gave her an innocent look. "Isn't that why you came home for the summer?"

Drat!

Had she oversold their relationship during dinner? She was only trying to act like a devoted girlfriend, but maybe she'd taken it too far.

"It is." Paige stifled her laughter before it became hysterical and turned to Gabe. "Are you okay, honey?"

He pounded his chest and coughed one final time. "Uh...yeah, I'm fine." He took her hand in his, and like each time he touched her during dinner, the tension in her body drained away.

She bit her tongue, waiting for him to say something to ease the sudden awkwardness that surrounded them.

"Are you sure you don't want me to replace this old trellis, Mom?" He put a hand on the aged trellis covered in climbing roses.

It was probably white originally but was now gray and fuzzy. It looked like attempts had been made to shore up the broken diamond pattern with additional pieces of wood and twine, but the effects were unattractive and not fully successful.

"Don't even think about it." Marisol held up a hand. "You'll damage my roses if you try to replace it. But I do want you to take a look at the bottom step on the deck. It's loose."

Paige quickly zoned out again as they discussed whether more than one board needed to be replaced. Gabe had effectively diverted his mom's attention, but he hadn't set her straight concerning the seriousness of their relationship. What exactly had he told his mom to make her think they were "pretty serious."

They eventually made their way inside again, and Paige found herself sitting between Gabe and his mom, looking at family photo albums. Gabe's presence beside her on the worn yet comfortable sofa both calmed her and filled her with an intense awareness. With his solid thigh pressed against hers and his muscular arm around her shoulders, curtailing her attraction was impossible.

As they made their way through the photo albums, Marisol shared more stories about Gabe and Grace, some embarrassing and some endearing, but always, her voice was filled with affection. Paige felt privileged to have this glimpse into Gabe's life.

She found herself laughing at one picture of the cute little boy with impossibly long eyelashes. The angle of the photo made his ears look abnormally large. "You weren't kidding when you said your ears stuck out."

"I wasn't kidding," Gabe said. "Thank goodness I grew into them."

Paige turned the page to find the picture he showed them at PT of his ears tucked under the brim of his hat.

"He was like his dad in that regard." Marisol grabbed another scrapbook and showed Paige pictures of Gabe's dad, Manuel, when he was young. His ears stuck out too. "Manuel grew into his ears during his teen years and was a handsome man."

Looking at Gabe's father, it was easy to see where he got his good looks. Paige was surprised to learn that even though Manuel's family immigrated from Mexico when he was a young boy, his mother was as blond and fair skinned as Paige's own mom. Marisol's parents immigrated from Argentina before she was born.

She'd seen pictures of Gabe's father in the other scrapbook. Marisol's lack of animosity when she spoke of her ex-husband surprised Paige. In fact, her voice was tinged with fondness and respect. The resentment radiating off Gabe and Grace, however, was palpable. Their father walking out on them had obviously hurt them, but she had to wonder what had happened for them to still be so bitter over a decade later.

Paige admired Marisol's ability to forgive. She also struggled to reconcile the angel of a woman beside her with the picture Luke painted at PT of Gabe's mom. Paige had expected her to be critical and demanding, but she wasn't. Fondness filled her voice whenever she talked about Gabe and Grace. Marisol Rivera was one of the sweetest women Paige had ever met.

And that hug she gave me...

Marisol had embraced her with the ferocity of a bear and the kindness of a saint. Paige had never felt so special and like a bigger fraud. She hated lying to this sweet woman.

"Paige, would you like to help me cut and serve your cake?" Grace stood from the loveseat.

"Sure." Paige shoved the scrapbook onto Gabe's lap and pushed to her feet. Despite Grace's animosity toward her, she was eager to put some distance between her and the woman she was deceiving as well as the man who drove her more than a little crazy.

She tried to think of a way to win Grace over as she followed her to the kitchen.

They'd barely rounded the corner when Gabe's sister whirled on her. "How much is he paying you?" Her voice was low, but it was every bit as sharp as the daggers she'd been shooting at Paige all evening.

Paige fell back a step. "Excuse me?"

Grace stepped closer, her scrutiny growing more intense. "How much is my brother paying you to pretend to be his girlfriend?"

Paige's stomach clenched, threatening to make her dinner reappear. They hadn't fooled Gabe's sister.

"I don't know what you're talking about." She forced as much bravado into her words as she could while keeping her voice down. The last thing she wanted was for Gabe's mom to hear Grace calling her out.

Grace rolled her eyes as she stepped away. "I know you're not really Gabe's girlfriend. He's hardly dated for years. We considered having one of my friends play the part, but Mom knows all of my friends and would have seen right through it." She took small plates from the cupboard and a large butcher knife from a drawer.

She knows Gabe brought home a fake girlfriend.

Paige's shoulders relaxed, and she let out a sigh. Something still felt off about the whole thing though. Why would Gabe's sister try to help him find a fake girlfriend? Marisol was a sweet, loving mother. Why were they lying to her?

"So how much is he paying you?" Grace stood with the knife poised over the cake but pointed in Paige's direction.

Alarm bells sounded in Paige's head. Grace may be in on Gabe's ruse, but that didn't mean she trusted Paige. "He isn't paying me anything."

Grace's eyes narrowed again. "What's your angle then?" She kept her voice low but no longer whispered, apparently confident the low rumble of conversation coming from the living room would mask their own.

"What do you mean?" Paige squared her shoulders and met the other woman's gaze.

This time Grace's eye roll was accompanied by a sigh of impatience. "What do *you* get out of this whole thing?" She motioned to Paige with the knife.

Paige would be all too happy to confide in Grace, but not while she held a knife and kept glaring at her like she was an intruder. She didn't want to betray Gabe's trust, but she had a feeling Grace wouldn't let it go.

"I'm just returning a favor." Paige shrugged like it was no big deal.

"What kind of favor?"

Grace was relentless. She'd make a great interrogator.

"Gabe pretended to be my boyfriend when my ex showed up, begging me to take him back."

Her eyebrows arched. "That's it?"

"That's it."

"You're not after him for money?" Grace finally pushed the knife into the cake. "Because I'll be honest with you, he doesn't have much. Despite his title of doctor, physical therapists don't make the kind of money medical doctors do. Besides, he has a bunch of student loan debt."

"I'm not after his money."

Grace didn't look entirely convinced. "And you don't have a hidden agenda?"

"Like what?" Paige gave her a confused look.

What was Grace getting at? Gabe's sister obviously didn't like her, but she couldn't understand why. Well, other than the fact that Paige was lying to their mom.

The other woman stared at her for another long moment before speaking again. "My brother has been hurt enough to last a lifetime. I won't let it happen again." Her words were clipped and hard. "He's dealing with too much right now to have to worry about someone manipulating him or taking advantage of his compassionate nature."

Paige jerked back. "I would never."

Was Grace referring to their father walking out on them or the break-up that left Gabe gun-shy when it came to dating? Or maybe both? Paige agreed with Grace; Gabe had had more than his share of heartache. But what was he dealing with right now? And why did she get the feeling there was something Gabe and his sister weren't telling her?

"I'm glad to hear it." Grace's expression suddenly softened, and she dropped the knife and reached across the counter to cover Paige's hand with hers. "Thank you for pretending to be his girlfriend." The sheen of tears filled her eyes.

Paige was so surprised by Grace's one-eighty, she almost jerked her hand away. Why was she thanking Paige for deceiving her mother?

Before Paige could ask the question, Gabe and his mother walked into the kitchen. "What's taking you ladies so long? I can't wait to try Paige's baking." He winked at her, but Paige was too confused by her conversation with Grace to enjoy his flirting.

"Surely Paige has baked for you before," Marisol said, a questioning look on her face.

Gabe tensed, his shoulders stiffening to the point it looked like he was flexing. "Well, yeah...of course." His words were stilted. "But she's never...made this cake for me before."

"I'm not much of a chef." Paige grimaced then chuckled. "Thank goodness Gabe's a good sport." She forced a smile she hoped didn't look as stiff as it felt as she patted Gabe's shoulder. "Sorry, honey, I didn't make this cake for *you*. I made it for your mom and sister."

"I see where I rank." Gabe pressed a hand to his chest, feigning offense.

Their words, meant to sound flirty, came across stiff and stilted. Cringing inwardly, Paige glanced around the room.

Marisol wore a smile as she took a saucer with a slice of cake on it.

Grace's gaze jumped back and forth between Gabe and Paige. Her brow furrowed again, but instead of the disapproval she wore earlier, her look said they were idiots.

And she was right. Pretending would be easier if Paige understood why Gabe was so adamant about lying to his mom. Even then, she was certain she'd still feel guilty.

"Do you cook often, Paige?" Marisol asked as they settled around the table.

"Not really. I don't mind cooking, but I don't enjoy being in the kitchen all the time, like some people. When I do cook, it's usually simple stuff."

"Well, I'll have to teach you how to make some of Gabe's favorite foods." Marisol winked and grinned. "You know what they say, the quickest way to a man's heart is through his stomach."

"Mmm..." Gabe and Grace said in unison as they took their first bite of cake.

"And a woman's too apparently." Marisol laughed. "You've already captured my son's heart, but now you know you can woo him with your cake, if need be."

Paige forced a smile. She liked the idea of winning Gabe's heart, but not under false pretenses. Her stomach was so tangled with shame, she had a hard time forcing down the rich chocolate cake that tasted almost as good as Amy's.

She remained quiet as Gabe and his mom and sister talked about their favorite foods and the work that went into making them. Apparently, they cooked together often.

Gabe repeatedly met her gaze, a questioning look on his face. He even took her hand at one point. She didn't pull away because she enjoyed the contact too much, but she hated that he only did it to convince his mom they were something they weren't.

They finally said their goodbyes, and once again, Marisol hugged Paige like a long-lost daughter. A heavy sinking feeling weighed Paige down. What she and Gabe were doing was wrong.

His hand fell to the small of her back as they made their way out the door, but Paige couldn't enjoy the contact. She stepped away from him the moment the door closed behind them and hurried as fast as she could to the car. She yanked her door open before Gabe could do it.

He blocked her path before she could climb in. "What's wrong?"

Paige was tempted to deny anything was wrong, but it ate at her too much to let it go.

"Why are you lying to your mom?" She motioned toward the house. "She hugged me so tight. Like she was welcoming me into the family."

"She's like that with everyone."

"But she thinks we're going to get married. Someday soon, from the sound of it." Her voice took on an accusing tone.

Gabe shoved his hands into his pockets and stared down at the driveway. "Last week when I told her I was seeing someone, I led her to believe it was quite serious."

"Why would you lie to your mother like that?"

Gabe's posture stiffened. "I told you I have my reasons."

Heat built in Paige's chest. "So you keep saying, but you won't share them with me. How am I supposed to keep playing the part of your girlfriend in this ridiculous charade, when I know next to nothing about you and feel like you're keeping secrets from me?" She folded her arms across her chest and gave him an expectant look. When he didn't even bother to look up, she threw a hand in the air. "And then there's your sister."

His head popped up. "What about Grace?" Defensiveness filled his voice.

"She practically gave me the third degree, warning me not to hurt you. Then she turned around and thanked me for lying to your mom. Why is your sister encouraging this whole thing?" She propped a hand on her hip, waiting for him to respond. When he didn't, she went on. "When you said your mom has been on your case about dating, I expected her to be critical and conniving. But she's not. She's the sweetest woman I've ever met. And she loves you."

"I've never doubted that she loves me." Conviction filled Gabe's voice.

"So tell her the truth."

"I can't!" His expression was as fierce as his shouted words.

"Why not? If you're still hurting over what happened with your ex, then tell her. I think she'd understand." Paige was about to suggest he also go to counseling, when he interrupted her.

"She's dying, Paige." Anguish deepened Gabe's voice, and pain lined every feature of his handsome face.

A jolt shot through her. "What?"

He let out a heavy sigh as he looked toward the house. "Last week, my mom was diagnosed with...stage-four pancreatic cancer." Shoulders sagging, he propped his elbows on the car and shoved his hands into his hair.

"Oh, Gabe." Paige stroked his back and leaned her cheek against his shoulder. Her heart ached just thinking about what he must be going through. "I'm so sorry."

He sucked in and released several shuddering breaths. His voice was gravelly when he spoke again. "Ever since my dad walked out on us, I've done my best to take care of her and Grace, but I can't fix this." He pounded a fist on the top of the car. "There isn't a single thing I can do to help her through it this time. So I lied, hoping to bring her a little peace and happiness. I know that makes me a horrible pers—"

"What do you mean *this time?*"

~

GABE STUDIED Paige for a moment then looked at the house again where his mother was probably already getting ready for bed. Despite her excitement over meeting Paige, the evening had taken a toll on her, and she looked exhausted by the time they walked out the door.

"Can we go somewhere and talk?" He gave Paige an imploring look. "I'll answer all your questions and tell you anything you want to know." Talking about how little time his mother had left was the last thing he wanted to do, but Paige deserved to know everything if she was going to continue to pretend to be his girlfriend.

"Sure," Paige agreed.

Silence filled the car as Gabe drove. Thankfully, Paige held her questions and didn't push for conversation before he was ready. He was still debating what to tell her when they arrived at the neighborhood park.

He shut off the engine but didn't speak. Where did he begin? The things he'd told Paige about himself had been minimal. After having both his dad and Harper leave him, he found it difficult to confide in others.

"Do you want to get out and walk?" Paige asked in a quiet voice.

"Yes." He had his door open before the word left his mouth. Would he find it easier to talk about things he'd discussed with few people if he was moving?

He looked around the almost deserted park as he stepped onto the walking path that meandered through it. The sun would be setting soon.

Paige fell into step beside him. He sensed a tension in her and expected her to start asking questions any second. But she remained silent, waiting for him to do the talking.

He cleared his throat. "One month before walking out on us, my dad drained his and my mom's savings accounts to help his secretary, whom he'd been having an affair with for two years, put a down payment on a condo. Then he moved in with her and filed for divorce." Gabe balled his fists at his side as heat that had little to do with the warm May evening filled him. "He had a better lawyer than my mom could afford, so he got the house and most of their assets. Mom ended up with the car that kept breaking down and barely enough furnishings to fill a small rental home."

"Wow. Now I understand why you reacted so strongly that day at the pool. Between your dad having an affair and your ex cheating on you, I don't blame you for being relationship adverse."

"It's a little more involved than that, but I'll come back to that in a minute." He rolled his shoulders as he launched into a subject that after all these years still managed to cause his shoulders to bunch with stress. "After the divorce, we struggled financially. Even though my dad paid child support and a pitifully small alimony, it wasn't enough to live on. My mom got a job, but after being a stay-at-home mom for so many years, she didn't have the earning potential my dad did. Then when our car died for good, Mom had to buy a new one. It was used, but the payments were more than she could afford, so she got a second job. I felt bad that she had to work so hard to support us, so I got a part-time job working at a car wash to help with the bills and cover things like my wrestling fees."

"Wait. Didn't you injure your neck during your senior year of high school?"

"Yes." He clasped his hands behind his back and studied his shoes as he walked. "Between school, wrestling, work, and homework I was exhausted all the time. That may have contributed to my injury. I wasn't in peak physical condition."

"I can't imagine having that kind of stress and responsibility as a teenager." Sympathy filled Paige's voice.

Gabe wasn't the only teenager forced to grow up before he was ready. He'd learned—like so many others—that feeling sorry for himself wouldn't change anything.

He shrugged. "I went back to work as soon as I could after recovering. I graduated high school and busted my butt all summer, working two jobs, to come up with enough money to pay tuition and rent an apartment. Then I moved across the city to attend college." His steps slowed. "Halfway through my first semester, my mom was diagnosed with breast cancer the same day Grace—" He cut himself off and stopped walking.

Staring across the park at three teenage boys, who played Frisbee, he relived that horrible night. He hadn't planned to go home for the weekend because he had a ton of homework and was running low on money. But when his mom called, saying she needed to talk to him, the emotion that choked her voice had him rushing to the bus stop.

He arrived home to find his mom and Grace in a heated argument about a party. Mom didn't want her hanging out with that crowd. But Grace was adamant. He could still hear her yelling about how horrible her life was and how much she hated her family before slamming the front door as she stormed out.

Gabe had held his mom and assured her she was doing the best she could. Then he comforted her all over again when she told him she'd been diagnosed with breast cancer. Shortly before midnight, he'd convinced her to go to bed, promising to wait up for Grace. Thirty minutes later, he answered a call from the police station.

The party Grace was at got busted and several kids had been arrested for underage drinking and two adults for possession of cocaine. Grace swore she'd only had a few drinks and didn't touch the drugs.

Going to court with her—because his mom was too sick from her chemo treatments—was stressful, but that was nothing compared to the bomb she dropped on them a few weeks later.

She'd made out with some guy at the party, who took advantage of her in her inebriated state. And now she was pregnant.

Gabe's chest grew tight, restricting his breathing, as he recalled the stress he was under that year.

"It's okay." Paige slipped her hand into his, bringing him back to the present. "Whatever it is, you can tell me."

He gripped her hand, drawing strength from her presence. If he was going to share the most difficult parts of his life with someone, he wanted it to be Paige. He led her to a nearby bench.

She sat beside him, her hand still in his.

"It's not my story to tell, but..." He shook his head and tightened his grip on Paige's hand. "Grace went off the deep end after my dad left. She started hanging out with a bad crowd, skipping school, and partying. Mom was doing the best she could, but she wasn't home much, especially after my injury and she had to take me to PT all the time."

"I'm sure your dad's leaving was hard on her."

"It was hard on all of us, but Grace took it especially hard. She did things she shouldn't have and ended up...in a bad situation...that had some serious consequences. She needed a lot of help and support while my mom was going through chemotherapy." He scrubbed his free hand over his face. "I barely managed to pass my classes that first semester after I moved home to take care of them. Then I dropped out of school for the next year to work full-time and take care of Grace and my mom until she was in remission and Grace's...issues were resolved."

For weeks, he'd sat beside Grace, pouring over applications from prospective adoptive parents and praying they were making the right decision. Grace had been full of remorse and had done a one-eighty. It had been a turning point in their relationship. They'd bonded during those difficult months and had been close ever since despite their almost four-year age gap.

Paige leaned into him, pressing her shoulder against his. "What about you?"

Warmth flooded through him at the contact. The sympathy in her blue eyes eased the tension inside him. "What about me?"

"Who took care of you while you were taking care of everybody else?" Compassion and concern filled her face.

He could have used a friend like Paige twelve years ago when his world was in chaos. Someone who could help carry his burden or at least listen when he needed to vent. But then he would have fallen in love with her, and he didn't have time back then to foster a relationship. It wouldn't have been fair to Paige.

What about now?

Never mind that she was his patient and should be off limits. He had even less time now than he did back then. He needed to devote every minute possible to his job and his mom for the foreseeable future.

"I didn't really have anyone, but my boss at the grocery store where I worked at the time was very understanding."

"I'm sorry you had to go through that."

"When our lives returned to normal, I threw myself into my studies again while working part-time at a physical therapy office. I took courses through the summers to make up for the lost time. I eventually got a couple scholarships, but they weren't enough to pay my full tuition, so I had to take out student loans. I was determined to succeed."

"And you did."

He smirked and shrugged. "I'm not sure I'm truly successful yet, but I'm getting there."

That is if I don't screw it up by dating a patient.

Except, he wasn't really dating Paige. This was all fake.

So why did I kiss her? And why am I still holding her hand?

Stomach tight, he pulled his hand from hers to scratch his other shoulder. He continued before he lost his nerve. "I didn't have much of a social life at college because I was so focused on my studies, but at the beginning of my final year of undergrad studies, one of the girls in my physiology class invited me to join a study group. I ended up being the only one to show up. We talked for hours and studied very little. Then we got together again the next evening. The rest, as they say, was history." Gabe rubbed the back of his neck as the old familiar tension filled him. "Except it wasn't."

"Was this the woman who cheated on you with your best friend?" Sympathy again filled Paige's voice.

He nodded. "Except Dirk wasn't just my best friend, he was my *best man*. And Harper was my *fiancée*."

Paige gasped. "Seriously?"

"Harper left me standing at the altar. Literally." He kept his voice as neutral as possible, not wanting to admit how much pain still accompanied memories of that humiliating day. "Her mother handed me a note while I stood in front of a hundred of our closest friends and family members. It said she was sorry, but she'd realized she didn't love me enough to marry me." He gave a rueful laugh as he shook his head. "Then she ran off and eloped with my best man two weeks later."

"Ouch." Paige drew out the word dramatically. "I thought finding out about Phillip's double life the way I did was bad. I couldn't imagine learning the truth in front of all my family and friends."

"I should have seen what was happening." Gabe berated himself. "Should have known she wasn't content. I was so focused on getting into PT school that I neglected her."

"If she truly loved you, she should have been supportive of you. Not running around behind your back." She lowered her gaze. "Except for my cousin, who is my best friend, I haven't told anyone what happened with Phillip and the real cause of my accident."

"Why not?"

She gave him an incredulous look as she poked herself in the chest. "Hello. I was the *other woman*. I didn't want everyone judging me for the part I played in Phillip breaking up with Avery."

"No. Phillip is the reason his relationship with Avery fell apart. He should never have asked you out when he was engaged to someone else."

"I keep playing every interaction over in my mind, wondering how I missed the signs." She shook her head in disgust. "I'm so gullible, I believed him every time he canceled our plans because something came up with a client in London or India. And I should have known he didn't need to travel so often on weekends for his business trips."

"Some people can be very convincing," Gabe said to make her feel better, but his words made his gut tighten. Had they been convincing enough with his mom?

"You said your mom has stage-four pancreatic cancer." Paige changed the subject. "Do they have a treatment plan? Or is it too far...?" Her voice died off, but Gabe felt to his core the words she didn't voice.

His chest tightened just as it did a week ago when he first learned about his mother's diagnosis and as it did every time he considered how little time he had left with her. Despite Paige's willingness to help him, he still struggled to draw in a full breath every time he thought about losing his mom.

"It's too advanced." Gabe swallowed the lump in his throat before continuing. "The doctor couldn't tell us how much time she has left, but he said probably three to six months. Maybe longer, maybe—" Emotion clogged his throat, making it impossible to finish his sentence.

"I'm so sorry." Paige leaned into him again, and Gabe couldn't help himself; he wrapped his arm around her and pulled her close.

He buried his face in her sweet, floral-scented hair. He shouldn't encourage what was supposed to be a fake relationship, but he needed this. He needed to know he wasn't alone. Sure, he had Grace, but he felt like he needed to be strong for her even though she was an adult now. Sometimes though, he needed someone to comfort him.

He held Paige until the tightness in his chest eased. With her in his arms, he felt like he would somehow survive this nightmare. He kept his arm around her when he finally relaxed his hold.

For several long minutes, they watched the sunset in silence, enjoying the way the golden rays of sunlight pierced the scattered clouds. The sounds of the city surrounding them grew gradually quieter.

"I know I shouldn't have lied to my mom about having a girlfriend, but her biggest regret is that she never got to meet our spouses and see us married."

"Married?" Paige's voice squeaked as she pulled away.

"Don't worry, I don't plan to carry the ruse that far. I just wanted to bring her a little peace and happiness. I want her to see that Grace and I are going to be okay." That was a bigger lie than telling his mom he had a girlfriend.

"Is Grace bringing home a fake boyfriend too?"

"No." Gabe laughed. "Like me, Grace doesn't date much. She has trust issues. If we both suddenly announced that we were dating someone, Mom would have seen right through that."

"Do you think she bought our act today?"

"I think so. She sure looked happy. Happier than I've seen her in a long time. I know you hate lying to your family and mine, but I need you." He turned imploring eyes on her. "At the risk of sounding like a teenage boy, will you please be my girlfriend a while longer?" He rushed to correct himself. "I mean fake girlfriend."

He needed to remember their relationship wasn't real, no matter how much he wanted it to be.

Indecision filled Paige's face, and Gabe's lungs burned from the breath he held there. Finally, she nodded. "I do hate lying to your mom and my parents, but at least now I understand why this is so important to you."

"We can't let the truth get out, not just with my mom, but at the office." Gabe shifted on the bench. "The only reason I got a full-time position as a therapist as quickly as I did after graduating was because the doctor I replaced was caught with a patient."

He'd reportedly slept with his patient, which Gabe had no intention of doing with Paige, but after that amazing kiss this afternoon, he was reminded how strong temptation could be. Besides, rumors had a way of convoluting and polluting the truth. His career might not survive scandalous rumors.

Nor did Paige deserve that kind of scrutiny.

CHAPTER 16

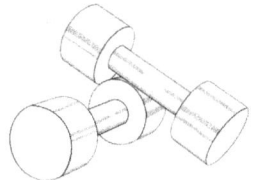

"*S*o, how did it go?" Nikki asked as she walked through the door to PT on Monday.

Paige winced. Nikki needed to learn some decorum. That and to lower her voice.

Thankfully, Gladys wasn't here today, but Sam was. Not that he was able to communicate well enough since his stroke to gossip about Paige being Gabe's fake girlfriend.

Gabe looked up from where he propped Sam's feet on the stepper. "How did what go?"

He acted as though he had no idea what Nikki meant.

Paige knew exactly what Nikki was talking about, and it twisted her stomach into a knot. She hated lying—to her parents, who asked how the birthday party went, and to Gabe's mom, who hugged Paige like she was her own daughter.

"You promised you'd tell us how it went when Paige met your mom." Giddiness filled Nikki's voice as she plopped down on the middle table.

"That's right," Luke said over his shoulder as he prepared a heat pack for Nikki. "I forgot to ask about that."

Paige exchanged a quick glance with Gabe. Surely, they didn't need to tell them *everything*. She'd like to keep the knee-buckling kiss and heart to heart with Gabe between just the two of them.

She'd done well pretending nothing had changed between her and Gabe since arriving today. It helped that he was busy with Sam. But after that kiss, and knowing what he was going through, she'd never be able to see him as just her physical therapist again.

"Who said she met my mom?" Gabe's expression remained neutral.

Paige didn't know how he did that. One minute he was joking, the next he looked dead serious even though he was teasing. Although Paige didn't think he was in a joking mood at the moment.

"No one." Nikki's expression said she saw right through his act. "But you were anxious to find a girlfriend to take home to your mom, and Paige volunteered, so I assumed you took her home over the weekend." Nikki now gave Gabe a look that said duh. "So how did it go?"

"It went fine." The tone of Gabe's clipped words would have told most people he didn't want to discuss it, but Nikki wasn't great at reading social cues.

She turned her attention to Paige. "So is his mom like totally crazy?"

"No, she's very nice." When the expectant look on Nikki's face didn't change, Paige added, "We had a nice visit over dinner."

"Did you have to hold hands and all that stuff?" Nikki's gaze darted between Paige and Gabe.

Paige had no idea what Nikki meant by *all that stuff*, but she didn't want to disclose any more than was necessary.

"Yes, I held Paige's hand." Gabe's tone was dull, sounding almost bored. "It was expected, since she's supposed to be my girlfriend."

A gleam filled Nikki's eyes as she grinned. "Did she make you guys kiss?"

Paige's heart rate spiked, and warmth swept over her as she recalled their kiss. Gentle at first, then more demanding and highly intoxicating.

Gabe's brows furrowed as he stared at Nikki. "Why would my mother make us kiss?"

"You know, to make sure your relationship is really legit." She giggled. "That's what always happens in romance novels."

"Oh brother." Gabe shook his head then scowled at Nikki. "My mother *did not* make us kiss." A tone of finality filled Gabe voice, and Paige hoped Nikki would let it go.

The younger woman would laugh her head off if she knew Paige and Gabe had stumbled over that particular hurdle before she even met Gabe's mom. She'd relived that kiss many times, and every time, she concluded that it was one of the best kisses she'd ever had.

"Bummer." Nikki's face fell. "Your mom was supposed to make you kiss. And that's when you realize you're soulmates who were meant to be together."

Gabe locked gazes with Paige. She couldn't decipher the message in his eyes because she was too busy wondering if their amazing kiss meant something, never mind that she didn't believe in that kind of stuff. He gave an almost imperceptible shake of his head before he looked away.

"You've been reading too many romance books, Nikki." Gabe looked over his shoulder at the nosy girl as he strapped Sam's left hand to the handle of the stepper. "If you believe all the nonsense you read in those books, you'll be sorely disappointed in real life."

Nonsense?

A sharp twinge pricked Paige's chest. She'd read her share of romances, and yes, when it came to her experience with Phillip, she'd been bitterly disappointed. But to hear Gabe so easily dismiss what every woman longed for stung, especially after the breathtaking kiss they'd shared.

"You're probably right." Nikki shrugged, not at all offended. "Because real men can never live up to our book boyfriends." She grinned at Paige. "Am I right?"

The twinge expanded to a dull ache in Paige's chest. Until a moment ago, Gabe had totally exceeded any book boyfriend she'd ever had. Why did he have to go and crush her illusion?

Because this isn't real, remember. You're only his fake *girlfriend.*

Paige gave Nikki a tight smile. "They never do."

She'd prefer to believe Gabe only meant to distract Nikki and protect his image in front of Luke and his patients, than to think he was oblivious to what happened between them last weekend.

"That's because men are clueless to everything that's important to women," Luke said as he set up the weight machine for Paige's next series of exercises.

Paige tuned out Luke and Nikki as they argued about whether men should naturally know that women liked romantic gestures like flowers and chocolate.

She focused on a quote on the wall above Gabe and Sam. *Sometimes you win, sometimes you learn.* She frowned as a sinking sensation hit her stomach.

She'd read all the quotes in this office multiple times, but today, she couldn't help wondering if she was in for another learning experience. A heart-breaking one. Because her heart had apparently missed the memo that she was taking a hiatus from men.

Forty minutes later, Gabe was in the process of rubbing out Nikki's hamstring on the table next to Paige when she propped up on her elbows. "So, Paige, tell me about Gabe's mom."

Gabe's expression instantly turned into a scowl. His posture stiffened as he gave Paige a look that was a mixture of warning and pleading.

"Did she totally give you the third degree?" Nikki pressed.

Paige shrugged. "She asked me a lot of questions about myself to get to know me." Gabe struggled to talk about his mom's diagnosis, so Paige figured it was best to divert Nikki's attention. She shot Gabe an apologetic look before continuing. "His sister, on the other hand, was a different story. She totally gave me the third degree and threatened me with a knife."

"A knife?" Gabe's head popped up. "You didn't tell me that."

"Seriously?" Nikki's mouth dropped open.

"Well, she didn't actually *threaten* me with the knife, but she was holding one and pointing it in my direction when she warned me..." Paige paused to choose her words carefully. "Not to take advantage of Gabe."

174

"Awe that's sweet, but also kind of terrifying." Nikki grimaced. "Is she older or younger than Gabe?"

A crease formed between Gabe's brows as he watched Paige, making her wish she could read his mind.

"Younger by...three years?" She looked to Gabe for confirmation.

He nodded. "Almost four."

"Why does she feel the need to protect Gabe? And how brave is that? I'd never dare give my brother's girlfriend the third degree, especially not while holding a knife. Mostly because if it ever got back to him, he'd kill me." Then she launched into a story of how her brother mixed peroxide into her shampoo to get back at her for telling their parents he'd sneaked out one night.

Thankfully, Paige didn't have to answer any more questions.

Eventually, it was her turn to have Gabe work on her. While she lay on her stomach with his hands on her low back, she couldn't help remembering how those hands had held her while he kissed her senseless. This was probably all clinical to him, but after the intimate moments they'd shared, she had a hard time not reacting to his touch.

It was a good thing he talked football with Luke and Travis, who arrived ten minutes ago, because she couldn't think of a single thing to say that wouldn't give away how often she'd replayed Saturday evening's events in her mind. Especially that kiss.

It wasn't until after he'd rubbed her back and hip, and she now sat up for him to work on her shoulder that he turned his full attention on her. "Thanks for shutting Nikki down. I'm sorry Grace gave you such a hard time."

Paige shrugged. "She was convinced I was after you for your money."

"What money?" Gabe snorted. "Student loans, remember?"

"Grace made it a point to point out that physical therapists don't make as much money as medical doctors. So, she wanted to know what my angle was."

"Your angle?" Gabe smirked as he sat on the edge of her table to scrape her shoulder.

Paige's breath caught when his thigh pressed against hers, proving an effective distraction from the discomfort of the scraping. She'd seen him sit on Gladys' table when they were deep in conversation while he rolled out her leg. But he'd never sat beside her while working on her. Until now.

Was it a familiarity thing? Did that mean he was comfortable with her?

She forced herself to focus on the conversation. "Grace couldn't figure out why I agreed to go along with your hair-brained scheme."

He glanced briefly at her face then returned his gaze to her shoulder. "Did you tell her?"

"I told her I was returning a favor. So naturally, she wanted to know what kind of favor, and I had to admit you bailed me out when my ex showed up." Paige realized the faster she talked the louder her voice became. She glanced across the room to where Luke and Travis now discussed colleges, before lowering her voice. "After she realized I didn't have a hidden agenda, her attitude changed."

"I'm glad. Thanks again for going with me last weekend." He gave her a hesitant look. "Will you come again this weekend? My mom wants to get to know you better."

A knot formed in Paige's stomach. It was only a matter of time until Marisol figured out Gabe and Paige were lying. She hated the idea of hurting that sweet woman, especially considering what she was going through. She also dreaded having to lie to her parents again.

Despite her trepidation, she nodded. "When?"

"I'll see what Mom and Grace have planned and let you know." He ducked his head and lowered his voice. "I'm not supposed to use information from your file to contact you for personal reasons, but is it okay if I text you?"

Just another reminder that they shouldn't be doing what they were doing.

Trying to ignore the knot growing in her stomach, she nodded again.

"I've been thinking..." Gabe cleared his throat but kept his voice low. "Considering what almost happened a couple of weeks ago at the pool...I think it best if we stop doing aqua therapy. Especially since you're fully weight bearing and mobile now."

Disappointment hit Paige, swift and sharp. Initially, she'd been self-conscious under Gabe's close tutelage, but now, she loved the one-on-one time with him. Was he canceling their aqua therapy sessions because he could tell Paige was falling for him?

Taking a page from his playbook, she kept a straight face as she feigned ignorance. "What do you mean? What almost happened at the pool a couple weeks ago?"

"You know very well what I mean." He cast a quick glance over his shoulder at Luke and Travis before his gaze met hers, his stare intense. "The same thing that *actually* happened in front of my mom's house. Against my car."

His voice was low before, but that was nothing compared to the raw huskiness of it now. The deep, sexy tone sent shivers of awareness coursing down Paige's spine. A flush of warmth surged through her body, gathering in her chest, where it ignited a spark.

"I can't lie and pretend both incidents didn't faze me." Gabe's fingers stilled on her shoulder.

The spark flamed, sending a thrill of excitement shooting through Paige. What did that mean for them?

"So..." She chose her words carefully, considering their setting and the other occupants in the room. "Does that change anything?" When his brow creased, she rushed to add, "I mean in our...fake relationship?"

"No." His answer was so quick it doused the fire in her chest. "It can't. My job is on the line here." He gave what looked like a frustrated shake of his head. "Besides, I don't have the time or energy for a real relationship right now. Outside of work, my mom is my only focus until..." He stopped talking, and despite it being inappropriate, Paige put her hand on Gabe's knee next to her thigh.

"I need you, Paige." His voice was gruff. "I mean, I need your help convincing my mother I'm in a happy relationship. But other than backing you up where Phillip is concerned, I can't promise you anything."

Message received.

Her spirits sank. She wasted eight months on her last relationship that failed miserably. Even if she waited until after Gabe's mother passed—Paige's heart hurt at the thought—he'd need time to grieve, and there was no timeline for that. There was no guarantee he would still want a relationship with her down the road.

She understood where Gabe was coming from, but she hated to admit how much his words saddened her. She patted his knee before withdrawing her hand. "I understand."

CHAPTER 17

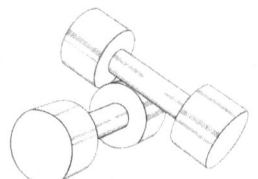

*P*aige set her steaming plate of spaghetti and meatballs on the kitchen table next to her laptop. She said a quick blessing on the leftovers then opened her computer to check for job listings in the local school districts while it cooled.

It had only been a few days since she'd last checked, but she kept hoping something would open up. There was supposedly a teacher shortage, but you'd never guess it by the lack of elementary job listings. There were, however, plenty of part-time jobs like bus drivers, custodians, and cooks.

She'd nearly had a panic attack last Saturday when she finally emailed Principal Stevens, informing him she wouldn't be returning to Seattle and asked for a letter of reference. She had no doubt he would give her a great reference, but she hated letting him down. She was committed now, though, and it was giving her more than a little anxiety.

The ringing of the doorbell kept her from spiraling into full-on panic.

She pushed to her feet, wondering who was at the door. Her parents were out for the evening, and she wasn't expecting anyone. A quick glance out the window of the sitting room made her skid to a stop. Phillip's red Nissan sat in the driveway.

Instead of opening the door, she hurried back to the kitchen on bare feet and grabbed her phone. She rocked from foot to foot as she scrolled through her texts.

Come on. Where is it?

Finally, she found the text Gabe sent, checking on her after her first day of PT. She opened it and jabbed the call icon at the top. "Please pick up. And please still be in Providence."

She didn't know what time he left the office on Mondays, but she knew they stayed late a couple nights a week. She sent up a little prayer, fully aware that what she and Gabe were doing was wrong, and she didn't deserve to have it answered.

The doorbell rang again, followed by Phillip shouting, "Come on, Paige, open up. I know you're home."

She needed Gabe's help to convince Phillip she was over him. He wasn't likely to leave her alone otherwise.

"Hello?"

Relief surged through her at the sound of Gabe's deep voice. "Oh, thank goodness you answered. Please tell me you're still in Providence."

"I'm still in Providence, but only for a few more minutes."

She looked up at the ceiling. *Thank you, God.* She didn't deserve to have her prayer answered, but she was grateful it was.

"Phillip's at my front door." Urgency filled her voice. "Can you come to my house and pretend you're picking me up for a date or something?"

"Uh...sure." Gabe's voice held too much hesitation, and his pause made her stomach drop. "I need your address."

Phillip knocked long and loud on the door.

"It's okay, you have my permission to get it from my file."

"I just left the office, it would be quicker for you to give it to me, so I don't have to go back inside."

"Oh right, okay." She rattled off her address as she hurried down the hall to her bedroom.

"Thanks, I'll be there in a few minutes. Stall him the best you can."

Ending the call, she tossed her phone on the bed then stripped off her shirt and yoga pants before grabbing her ratty old bathrobe from the closet. Maybe she could make Phillip think she'd been in the shower. She darted to the bathroom, wrapped her hair in a towel, then dabbed some water on her neck. She finished tying her robe as she reached the front door.

"Alright, alright." She swung open the door. "Hold your hors—" She feigned surprise. "Phillip? What are you doing here?"

His gaze rake over her, lips lifting in an appreciative grin that she used to find flattering but now looked too much like a leer. He folded his arms and leaned against the door frame as though he had all the time in the world. "Well, hello, darling."

She used to get goosebumps when his voice took on that seductive quality, but now, it made her skin crawl. She tugged the neck of her robe closed.

"Why are you here?" Ice filled her voice.

"I tried to leave Providence, but I just couldn't." He shoved his hands into his pockets, making himself look insecure. "I need you in my life, babe."

The action didn't look nearly as endearing on Phillip as it did on Gabe. When Gabe did it, Paige saw it as a protective shield, not a ploy for attention.

"You were gone when I stopped by Saturday evening, but your mom assured me you'd be home alone tonight." He pulled his hands from his pockets and clasped them in a pleading gesture. "Spend the evening with me. Please. Let me prove that we belong together."

My mom set me up?

Heat flared in Paige's chest, and she promised herself she'd tell her parents the truth about Phillip tonight. She'd even wait up late for them if she needed to.

"I have plans this evening. With my *boyfriend*." She put emphasis on that last word.

"Your therapist? You honestly think that will last?" His face filled with skepticism.

"Of course it will," she said ignoring the doubts that filled her head and heart earlier that afternoon. "He's not cheating on me, like you did."

Although he is lying to his mom.

Even though she understood why, it still bothered her.

Phillip cocked a brow. "Are you sure about that?"

She growled in disgust and started to push the door closed, but he stuck his foot over the threshold, stopping it.

"I'm sorry. That was out of line." His expression grew more earnest. "Paige, honey. I refuse to give up on us."

"There is no *us*," she insisted, frustration raising her voice. "There never should have been any form of us, because you were engaged to someone else, remember?"

Gabe's car came to a stop in front of the house, lifting a weight from her shoulders and weakening her knees.

Phillip barely glanced over his shoulder before trying again. "I need you in my life, Paige." He looked down for a moment and shuffled his feet. "I'm willing to play second fiddle until you realize we're meant to be together."

Revulsion ricocheted through her. "What?"

"If you come back to me, you can keep seeing your therapist on the side."

Paige's mouth dropped open. Why would Phillip think she'd be interested in such a disgusting proposition? Did he think it only fair, since he'd seen someone else the entire time he was with her?

"And if her *therapist* isn't okay with that?" Gabe's voice bordered on a growl.

Phillip looked only mildly surprised. He gave Gabe a quick once over before turning back to Paige. "I'm confident, if given the chance, I can win you back." Cockiness filled his voice.

Paige was in the process of vigorously shaking her head when Gabe shouldered past Phillip who blocked the doorway.

He wrapped his arms around Paige. "Hola, mi amor." He planted a brief kiss on her lips then looked down at her robe and quirked an eyebrow. "You said you'd be ready by seven."

"I am." The words popped out of her mouth before taking the time to remember she wore a bathrobe. She was so flustered by Phillip's audacity and Gabe's nearness she couldn't think straight.

"Are you now?" His gaze swept over her again. "Not exactly what I had in mind for tonight. But I'm open to a change of plans." He brought his mouth close to her ear and whispered, "If we ignore him in favor of a PDA will he go away?"

His warm breath tickled her neck, sending shivers of awareness coursing down her spine. It took every ounce of her focus to play her role.

She giggled and wrapped her arms around his neck. "Sounds fun. I'm game."

"Paige." Phillip's voice sounded almost tortured, but she couldn't find an ounce of sympathy.

How could she care about Phillip when she felt so alive in Gabe's arms? Safe and treasured. Then suddenly those strong arms released her.

Gabe spun and addressed Phillip. "Why are you still here?"

"I-I need to...talk to Paige." Phillip's voice was whiny now.

"She's done talking to you, pal." Gabe turned back to her. "Do you have anything else you'd like to say to him?"

"Other than get lost?" She shook her head and folded her arms, bolstered by Gabe's presence.

"Are you even remotely interested in his repulsive offer?"

"Absolutely not!"

"Good answer." Gabe smiled and pressed a kiss to her temple. Then his grin broadened, looking almost maniacal, as he turned to face Phillip. "Because I'm the possessive type and have been known to give into bouts of violence when I'm challenged."

Paige could no longer see Gabe's expression, but something in it made Phillip fall back a step. Or maybe it was the way Gabe effortlessly flexed his muscles. She bit back a giggle.

"It's time for you to leave." Gabe's voice was hard as stone. "If you come back, we'll call the police and have you arrested for harassment."

He wrapped an arm around Paige, pulled her further into the house, and slammed the door.

Paige wanted to sink against the wall in relief, but that would distance her from Gabe, and she wasn't ready to do that yet. She considered playing the fragile female and sinking into him instead, but then she recalled his words that afternoon.

I can't promise you anything.

Gabe made no move to release her, however. So, she stayed put, enjoying every second of his embrace, knowing it wouldn't last.

"Thank you for coming. That man does not take no for an answer."

"Do you think he'll leave you alone after this?"

His face was so close to hers, it wouldn't take much effort to lean in and press her lips to his. Her heart rate accelerated at the thought of kissing him again. She both loved and hated that Gabe affected her so strongly.

"I hope so." She chided herself for her breathlessness. "You were pretty convincing."

"You weren't so bad yourself. Except…" He touched the edge of her towel. "…the little triangle of hair showing up here is bone dry."

She forgot she even had it on after Gabe arrived. Gasping, she tugged the towel off and shook her head.

Gabe sucked in a sharp breath.

"What?" She patted her hair at his stunned look.

He continued to stare. "That was pretty, the way your hair cascaded down around your face like that." The low baritone of his voice sent a shiver coursing down her spine. "I like your hair down."

Her breath caught in her throat as he reached up to brush back a lock. Then his fingertips created a trail of fire from her temple to her jaw.

"But you're pretty with a ponytail too." His gaze roamed over her face as his fingers drifted closer to her lips. "You're a beautiful woman, Paige."

The sincerity in his voice made her knees go weak. A warm flush enveloped her as moisture filled her mouth. Those few words from Gabe sounded more sincere than all the flattering words Phillip had ever spoken. It was a good thing he held her—otherwise, she might have melted to the floor.

"Thank you," she whispered. Paige couldn't resist anymore. She leaned into him.

His gaze settled on her lips as his arm tightened around her. Then suddenly, his whole body stiffened as though someone flipped a switch. The hand that had been caressing her face balled into a fist, and he let out a low growl of frustration.

"I'm sorry. I can't." Gabe released her and stepped away. One hand raked through his hair while the other gripped the doorknob.

Paige fell back a step at his sudden absence. A weight pressed against her chest, so tight it stole her breath and pricked her heart.

"I don't want to hurt you, Paige." The raspy tone of his voice matched the pained look in his eyes. "But I've worked too hard to get where I am. I can't—"

"I know." She held up her hand to stop him. "You can't risk losing your job."

It was easier to curtail his apology than to have to bear full-on rejection. Having him choose his job over her hurt, but they'd only known each other for barely a month. It was ridiculous—and selfish— of her to think he would.

"And with everything going on with my mom, I'm not..." He didn't meet her gaze this time. Instead, he stared at the wall behind her as his Adam's apple bobbed. His fingers plowed through his hair again, agitated and jerky.

"I understand." She stepped in front of him, so he'd have to look her in the eye. "I'm truly sorry for everything you're going through with your mom. I recognize that, emotionally, you are unavailable."

He snorted and cracked a smile. "You make me sound like the tortured hero in some romance novel."

Grateful for the lightened mood, even though that hadn't been her intent. She laughed and shrugged. "I call 'em like I see 'em."

Now he scowled at her.

She chuckled again as she raised her hands in surrender. "All I'm saying is, you sure seem to know a lot about romance novels for someone who hates them so much."

His brows lowered, making his scowl more intense.

"I appreciate your honesty, Gabe. The last thing I want is to be strung along and used again in a relationship that doesn't have a future." She sucked in a deep breath and rushed on. "Don't worry, I don't have any expectations. Outside of convincing your mom we're together, we'll make it a point to avoid situations like this." She drew a circle in the air with her hand. "Acknowledging the chemistry between us will help us combat—"

"Stop." Gabe was the one with his hand up now.

"I'm rambling, aren't I?" Warmth flooded her cheeks.

"Yes, and you're talking with your hands, which I find adorable." He shook his head. "I'm not sure there is any way to combat this... magnetic pull between us." He motioned back and forth between them.

"Now whose talking with their hands?" She quirked a brow at him.

He caught himself and grinned. "We managed to diffuse the... tension, but this feels too much like flirting, and it's building again." He grabbed the doorknob.

Disappointment swamped Paige. "Wait. I feel like I should at least offer you some dinner after making you come to my rescue." She jerked a thumb over her shoulder toward the kitchen. "I've got some leftover spaghetti and meatballs."

"Sounds delicious, but..." His gaze roamed beyond the entryway, deeper into the house. "It's probably best I don't cross paths with your parents."

"They're not home. They're in Spokane at some gala that kicks off a medical conference."

"You're here alone?" His eyes jump back to her, a series of emotions racing through them. He cleared his throat. "In that case, I'd better leave, because my self-control is waning when it comes to that chemistry we just discussed." He opened the door and stepped out so fast, she didn't even have time to move from behind it. "Good night, Paige."

Then he was gone, and Paige slumped against the wall. If it wasn't for her bare feet sticking on the hardwood, she would have slid down to the floor. She had sworn off men, so how was she so effortlessly falling for her physical therapist?

Could Riley be right? Was her life meant to converge with Gabe's for more than just PT? And if that was the case, how did she get Gabe to see that?

~

GABE PULLED his car over to the side of the road before getting on the freeway. It wasn't safe for him to drive with his mind racing like it was.

He smacked the steering wheel with the palm of his hand. Why did the perfect woman have to come along at such a complicated time of his life? Why couldn't he have met Paige somewhere other than PT? So he could ask her out and freely spend time with her?

Like I ever go anywhere else.

And this stupid ruse he'd involved her in to make his mom happy had him crossing boundaries he'd never considered crossing with a patient before. Of course, he'd never had a patient like Paige before.

Just the sight of her kicked up his heart rate. Every. Single. Time. He found her incredibly attractive whether she wore a swimsuit, summer dress, or a ratty old bathrobe. Her smile truly lit up whatever room she was in, and he could stare into her gorgeous blue eyes all day.

Her sense of humor meshed well with his. She was full of grit and determination. He admired the way she stood up to her ex as much as he appreciated the effort she put into healing and get stronger. She hadn't needed him to get rid of Phillip, but he was glad she'd turned to him. Considering all the times his protective instincts had kicked in concerning her, he was glad to finally put them to use.

Then he got caught up in the electricity that always sizzled between them. Kissing her in the privacy of her home wouldn't have jeopardized his job any more than anything else they'd done, but it would have made him want things he couldn't have right now. He already wanted those things, so kissing her would make it unbearable.

She'd wanted that kiss as badly as he did, he was certain of it. The fact she understood and excused his behavior made him feel like a jerk.

Emotionally unavailable.

Maybe Paige was right, but as long as his time with his mother was limited, that wouldn't change.

He picked up his phone and tapped it against his thigh, debating. He owed her an explanation.

He typed out a text. *I don't hate romance books. But you have to admit they aren't realistic.*

He hit send then tossed his phone onto the passenger seat and put his car into gear. He didn't anticipate a response any time soon, since Paige was probably mad at him for leaving so abruptly.

His phone buzzed before he could pull out into traffic. When her name flashed across the screen, he put his car back into park.

Paige: *Duh. That's the point. It's called escapism.*

Before he could decide how to respond, another message came through.

Paige: *Reading about the same garbage we experience in real life is boring. No one wants to read about men or women who are cheated on by their significant others.*

She had a point.

Gabe: *True. For your information, I've read my share of romance novels.*

Paige: *You read romance books?!*

Multiple emoticons followed her text, including a surprised face and the rolling on the floor laughing emoji.

His lips turned up as he typed a response.

Gabe: *Past tense. Remember me telling you about my neck injury and how my mom borrowed every DVD and audiobook possible from the library? Our library was small, but it had a large collection of romance books on audio. More than any other genre.*

Paige: *That must have been torture for a teenage boy.*

More emojis accompanied her response, and he could almost hear Paige's laughter.

Gabe: *You have no idea.*

Paige: *Protest all you want, you're still a tortured hero.*

Gabe: *Whatever.*

He paused before adding his next thoughts.

Gabe: *Does that make you a damsel in distress?*

Paige: *I was distressing pretty hard before you showed up tonight.*

Gabe: *Nah. You and your bathrobe had everything under control.*

He sent another text before she could respond.

Gabe: *I think our current situation makes us...star crossed lovers.*

He held his breath after hitting send. He'd told Paige at PT that he couldn't promise her anything, but his rebellious heart wanted to make her all kinds of promises. He watched the little dots dance as she typed a response, then they disappeared.

She'd decided not to respond right now. Or maybe ever.

He didn't blame her. She probably felt like he'd dropped a bomb on her. He was about to set his phone down when the dots returned. His chest tightened and so did his grip on his phone as he waited.

The dots disappeared again.

Stomach sinking, he tucked his phone into the cup holder and put his car into gear again. This time there was no traffic to prevent him from pulling out and getting on the freeway. His grip remained tight on the steering wheel.

Stupid move, man.

He was a mile down the freeway when the screen lit up again. Ignoring the dangers of texting and driving, he snatched it up. He checked the road before letting his gaze dart to his phone. A gif of a female actress—whose name he couldn't recall—sighing and blowing her hair out of her face filled his screen.

No wonder it took her so long to respond. Finding a gif to adequately depict this kind of frustration and disappointment wasn't easy. He couldn't devote the attention necessary to finding a gif of his own while driving, so he decided to leave it be. Which was probably for the best.

He put his phone face-down on the passenger seat and pressed the button on his steering wheel. "Call Mom."

CHAPTER 18

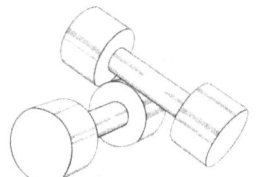

*P*aige poked at her Belgian waffle, wishing she had an appetite. The constant twisting of her stomach in knots was going to give her an ulcer. She'd kept so many things bottled up all week, she feared she'd explode at any moment.

Her dad was almost finished with his breakfast, but Paige had hardly touched hers.

"Is something wrong, dear?" Mom eyed her from across the kitchen table.

"Um...there's something I need to tell you and dad." Though hesitant, her voice must have sounded serious, because her dad who was in the process of standing dropped back into his chair.

Her plans to tell her parents the truth about Phillip Monday evening fell apart when Mom texted, saying she'd decided to spend the night in Spokane rather than make the late-night drive home. Then the week had been busy for everyone. Between high school graduation activities that her mom, as the principal, was involved in, and her dad spending a couple extra days at the medical conference, Paige hadn't had an opportunity to talk to them.

She'd even been enlisted to help her sister-in-law Amy with redecorating Aunt Charity's diner. Then because she could see Amy was stressed, she'd volunteered to babysit last night so Ben could take Amy out on a date. The diversions had been welcomed, but they'd allowed her to remain a coward.

"What is it, honey?" Concern deepened the lines around her mother's eyes.

She hoped she'd finally seen the last of Phillip, but her parents needed to know the truth in case she was wrong. She sucked in a fortifying breath. "I need to tell you the truth behind my accident and what really happened with Phillip."

Mom leaned forward, a puzzled look on her face. "What do you mean?"

"Right before my accident on Valentine's Day, I found out from Phillip's *fiancée* that he'd been cheating on her with me." She forced out the words she'd rehearsed Monday night.

"What?" Mom gasped, her eyes wide.

Dad's brows lowered until they became a single unit, and the muscle in his jaw jerked, much like Gabe's did when he was upset.

She gave them a play by play of what happened before she darted in front of the car, including Avery breaking the news that she was pregnant and that she and Phillip had set a wedding date.

Her mother's eyes grew wider, while her father's hands balled into tight fists.

"That miscreant! I'm so sorry, honey. I can't believe he lied to you all this time." Mom's nostrils flared in her red face. "And he has the gall to show up here wanting you back when he's married?"

"He's not married. He broke up with Avery after she lost the baby." Paige's tone was full of disgust.

"That poor woman." Sympathy filled Mom's voice.

"I feel bad she lost the baby, but she's better off without him, believe me."

"He stopped by again Saturday night while you were at your friend's birthday party. I told him to come back on Monday." Mom's hand flew to her mouth. "Did he show up here?"

"Yes. It wasn't easy, because he's very persistent, but I think I finally convinced him to leave me alone." She resisted the urge to fan herself as she recalled Gabe's part in persuading Phillip to leave and how he'd almost kissed her again. "But I wanted you to know the truth, so if he ever shows up here again, you can support me in getting rid of him."

"Of course we support you, honey." Mom put a hand on Paige's arm. "Why didn't you tell us sooner? I would have handled things much differently if I'd known."

Paige looked down at her now soggy waffle. "I was humiliated and ashamed for my part in breaking up his and Avery's relationship."

"No." Dad spoke for the first time. He pointed a finger at her. "Phillip is the one who destroyed that relationship. Not you. Do you understand?"

Her father's passionate defense of her brought tears to her eyes. Gabe had said the same thing, and it meant the world to her that the most important men in her life agreed. She shouldn't think of Gabe that way, but she couldn't help herself. She'd noticed other similarities between Gabe and her father lately, but it was best not to dwell on them.

"Your father is right." Mom circled the table and sat in the chair beside her. She wrapped an arm around Paige's shoulder. "You have nothing to be ashamed of."

Now the tears came in full force. "I just feel so stupid for not seeing through his lies. I let his attention and words of flattery suck me in. I hate that I let him use me for eight months."

"How exactly did he use you?" Tension deepened Dad's voice, and his fists balled again. His expression looked downright murderous now, and Paige could guess what might be going through his mind.

"Not like that, Dad, I promise." She held up a hand. "He wanted an intimate relationship, but I refused to give in."

"Good for you, honey." Mom squeezed her tighter. "I'm proud of you for sticking to your morals."

It was a miracle that she'd been able to withstand him, considering how persuasive and persistent Phillip was.

"You're a strong young woman, Paige." Dad's voice turned gentle as he gave her an earnest look across the table. It was the bedside manner that he was so well known for. "I'm proud of how hard you've worked to recover, both physically and emotionally."

"Me too." Mom patted her shoulder before removing her arm away. "I know it hasn't been easy."

Even though breakfast no longer looked appetizing, Paige speared a strawberry and stuck it in her mouth.

"How is your physical therapy going?" Dad asked as he stood from the table and picked up his breakfast plate.

The strawberry stuck in her throat, and she had to swallow hard to force it down. "It's going good."

It was the highlight of her day every Monday, Wednesday, and Friday. She looked forward to seeing Gabe even though he continued to add more difficult exercises to her routine. She enjoyed the cama-raderie between him and Luke and the entertaining discussions that often included everyone in the office, including two new patients that had recently started PT.

It had been busy enough this week that there hadn't been a chance for things to get too personal between her and Gabe, but they always found something interesting to talk about while he massaged and stretched her.

"How is Dr. Rivera working out?" Dad turned from the dishwasher and looked at her.

Images of Gabe and Luke's push-up contest filled her mind, and her lips turned up. "He's working out great. He's an excellent therapist."

"Good." Dad nodded. "I'd hoped he'd be a good addition to our community."

Addition to our community?

Did Dad expect Gabe to eventually run a full-time office here in Providence? It was certainly busier this week than it was four weeks ago, but even if there were enough patients here for a full-time office, Gabe would never consider moving here permanently. Not while his mother was so sick.

Gabe's mother.

And that brought Paige to the second thing that kept her stomach twisted in knots all week.

Mom now loaded her dishes into the dishwasher and would soon leave the kitchen, so Paige blurted out. "By the way, I'm planning on going to the Tri-Cities this afternoon to hang out with Angie and some of her friends again."

Angie was the former college roommate whose birthday party she'd told her parents she was going to last weekend. If she kept her lies consistent, maybe she'd find them easier to remember.

"Good for you." Mom came back to the table and patted her shoulder again. "I'm glad to see you getting out. You've been stuck at home with us old fogies for too long."

Well, that went better than I thought, on both accounts.

Her parents hadn't judged her for what happened with Phillip, and they *wanted* her to go to the Tri-Cities on the weekends for a social life.

Unfortunately, she didn't feel any less guilty about lying to them.

CHAPTER 19

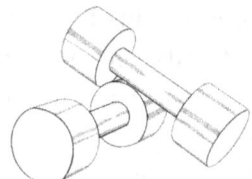

*S*ilence filled the car as Gabe drove Paige to his mom's house again. He and Paige had found no shortage of things to talk about during PT this week, but now, alone in his car—with her only a foot away—everything that came to mind felt too intimate.

As usual, the air between them fairly crackled with electricity, and he couldn't help remembering their kiss last Saturday as well as their near kiss earlier this week. His grip on the steering wheel tightened as he fought the urge to take her hand.

He'd have plenty of opportunities to do that later, while they were with his mother. He shouldn't be so excited about that, considering it only made it harder to fight his developing feelings for her, but he was.

"I told my parents the truth about Phillip this morning," Paige said, studying her hands in her lap.

"How did they take it?"

"About like you'd expect. My dad was quiet, but got that murderous look in his eyes, and my mom was appalled." Paige's hand started moving through the air as she talked, and Gabe had to bite back a smile.

"What made you decide to tell them now?"

"That whole thing with Phillip on Monday could have been avoided if I'd told them sooner." She went on when he gave her a questioning look. "Apparently, he showed up last Saturday while I was with you, and she told him to come back on Monday when she knew I'd be home alone."

Last Saturday.

And he was right back to thinking about their kiss again. He forced his thoughts back to the topic at hand.

Gabe nodded. "I'm sure if she'd known the truth she would have sent him packing."

"I feel like a coward for not telling everyone what he did. What *I* did."

"You are not at fault. Phillip is. He deceived you." Gabe grabbed her hand and gave it a squeeze. "You need to stop blaming yourself."

"My dad said the same thing." She looked up at him then. "It's just that... Well, you know how hard it is to admit you were wrong about someone. That the relationship you've devoted so much time to was all a mistake."

"I do. It's easy to blame yourself, but you can't take responsibility for something that isn't your fault. You'll never be able to move forward if you keep looking back at your mistakes."

"Are you still looking back?" The question was quiet, but it struck him to his core.

Am I?

He was so focused on his studies during PT school that he'd hardly dated. Yes, he'd been afraid he'd end up neglecting any woman he dated, like he had Harper.

School was behind him now, so he had no excuse. Except that he hadn't met anyone he was interested in dating.

Until now.

Enjoying the feel of Paige's hand in his more than he should, he let go and returned his hand to the steering wheel. Instead of answering her question, he changed the subject. "Has Phillip bothered you anymore since Monday?"

"No, thank goodness."

Silence again settled between them.

Gabe cleared his throat. "Are we okay?"

She cocked one brow giving him a questioning look.

"I feel bad about how we— I mean, the way *I* left things on Monday."

Paige burst out laughing.

He wasn't sure how he'd expected her to respond, but it wasn't like that.

"What's so funny?"

"You are." Paige chuckled again. "I think you've read—or listened to —too many romance novels."

"What do you mean?" Confused, he scowled at her. He never should have admitted to reading romances.

"The woman is usually the one concerned about defining the relationship."

"I'm not trying to define the relationship." His defensive tone made the words sound like a growl. "There isn't a relationship." But he wished there was.

"I know. There can't be, because there's too much at stake." Her voice was a combination of sarcasm and boredom. Then she grinned as she pointed a finger at him. "Except there is. It's fake, but there's a relationship."

"That's not what I meant."

"I know." Her eyes flashed as her voice turned defensive. "But unless you've changed your mind about being able to make promises, this fake relationship..." she circled her hand in the air, "is all there is. And as far as I'm concerned, it doesn't need to be defined."

Meaning she didn't want to discuss it anymore. She'd put him firmly in his lane, which was where he needed to stay. He couldn't have a real relationship with her if he wasn't willing to tell his mom the truth and risk his job.

Would Mom be glad he'd finally moved on if he lost his job because of it?

Arrival at their destination prevented further conversation, but Gabe couldn't help wondering why he had to meet Paige now when his life was so complicated? Why couldn't they have met years ago, before he became her therapist? And why did the only relationship he could have with her have to be based on lies?

When Gabe opened Paige's door for her, he was tempted to pin her up against his car again and steal a kiss, but that was out of line in light of their recent conversation.

Neither Mom nor Grace met them at the front door this time, but Gabe took Paige's hand in his before walking into the house. The scent of savory meats and spices combined with hot oil greeted them. His stomach rumbled. He'd been too keyed up to eat much today.

Gabe guided Paige toward the kitchen, where they found his mom and sister up to their elbows in flour and dough.

"What? No welcome committee today?"

"Ah Mijo," Mom threw her flour-dusted hands in the air. "We got caught up in our preparations and lost track of time." She quickly cleaned her hands and greeted them with hugs.

Gabe hadn't always welcomed his mom's hugs, especially as a teenager, but nowadays, he cherished every single one.

Mom wrapped Paige in an equally tight hug, and like last week, Paige's eyes squeezed shut. Her expression looked both pleased and pained.

She hates lying to my mom.

He did too, but he couldn't recall the last time he'd seen her look so happy. He couldn't bear to take that away from her. Even though the shadows of fatigue under her eyes were ever-present, excitement filled her face on Saturdays when he brought Paige over.

"Okay, you two wash your hands." She pushed them toward the sink then clapped her hands twice. "It's time to get cooking."

Paige laughed as they bumped elbows at the sink. "Is that where you get it from?"

Gabe looked at her beside him. Eyes alight with laughter, she looked radiant. His heart stuttered. He regretted not stealing that kiss when he had the chance.

"Get what from?" His voice was gruffer than a moment ago.

"When you want your patients to get to work you always clap your hands like your mom does. Except you've added your own flair by rubbing your palms together afterward."

Gabe had never thought about how closely his desire to be upbeat and encouraging mimicked his mom's habit. He couldn't think of a better person to model his life after.

"He doesn't only do that with his patients." Grace piped up behind them. "He does it every time he takes charge and gets bossy."

Gabe turned and pulled a face at her as he dried his hands. "We all have our quirks." He pointed at Grace but looked at Paige. "For example, Grace often makes humming and moaning noises while she eats." Ignoring his sister's scowl, he wrapped his arm around Paige's shoulders. "And Paige here likes to talk with her hands. The more excited she gets the faster they move." Paige gasped and started to pull away, shooting him a scowl of her own, but he kept his arm around her. "It's very cute."

Her outrage morphed into an adorable grin. "Not as cute as you having push-up contests with Luke at work." She poked his stomach.

Gabe tensed, fearing Mom would remember that Luke was his current assistant and pick up on the fact that Paige was a current patient, not a former one. Paige must have realized her mistake, because her eyes widened, and she went as still as a statue. Even Grace gave them a wide-eyed look.

"Are you boys still doing silly stuff like that?" Mom tsked as she attacked the dough in her bowl again. "May as well be walking around like a couple preening peacocks." Thankfully, her head was down so she didn't see the panic on their faces.

Paige grimaced then gave him a tight smile. "Do you still make that face when you rub out your patients?"

"What face?" Gabe was too surprised by her question to appreciate the save.

"You know, the one where your lips are half-pursed to the side. Sometimes you push your tongue into your cheek."

"Yes!" Grace pointed at him and laughed. "He does that all the time when he's concentrating or deep in thought."

"Concentrating, huh?" A pensive look covered Paige's face as she stared up at him with those expressive blue eyes. "What are you thinking so hard about all the time?" Her voice suddenly sounded seductive.

Or maybe it was just his imagination. Regardless, a curl of desire flickered in his stomach.

"In your case, I was *totally* not letting my mind wander in inappropriate directions while I massaged your backside." He wiggled his eyebrows at her.

When her eyes widened, he couldn't resist any longer. He brought a hand up under her chin and dipped his head until his lips met hers. Even though he desperately wanted to thoroughly explore her mouth, he kept the kiss brief and mostly chaste, which wasn't easy considering the desire that surged through him the moment Paige responded. And when her hand found its way to his chest, it was all he could do to not crush her in his arms.

After he ended the kiss, he looked pointedly down at her hand. "You really do have a fascination with my chest, don't you, mi amor?" He kept his voice quiet, but not so quiet Mom and Grace couldn't hear.

A rosy tint colored her cheeks as her eyes widened again. Then she poked him in the side. He wasn't ticklish, but the pressure was firm enough to make him squirm away.

"Okay, you love birds," Mom said in an amused tone, "it's time to get to work."

They joined Mom and Grace around the counter and before long had dough spread across its surface. Mom monopolized Paige's attention, as she explained the art of making empanadas.

When she took Paige to the stove to show her the assortment of fillings—both sweet and savory—and to demonstrate how to fold a spoonful into the little pockets, Grace turned to him and whispered, "That was a pretty convincing show."

He didn't like the way that sounded. It made it sound like he was using Paige. Technically, he was, but that kiss had been purely for his selfish benefit. Which meant he was an even bigger heel than Grace intoned.

"It wasn't a show." The words ground out through his clenched jaw as his stomach tightened.

Grace's expression remained skeptical for a moment before her lips lifted in a grin. "Careful, Hermano, you keep that up, I'm going to think you're really in love with her." She smacked his shoulder then walked over to the stove to join Paige and Mom.

Grace had cornered him last Sunday while their mom rested and demanded to know how he'd talked Paige into going along with his ruse. He hadn't intended to tell her how attracted he'd been to Paige since he first met her, but Grace saw right through his attempts to downplay his interest. She still thought Gabe was crazy for lying to their mom, but even she admitted Mom was much happier lately.

Gabe's chest expanded to a point of being almost painful as he watched the three women he cared deeply about laugh at Paige's attempts to pinch her empanada closed without pushing out the filling.

Grace was right. He was in love with Paige.

Gripping the table, he swore under his breath. He'd tried to keep his attraction to her in check, because besides being beautiful, she had so many charming qualities that he knew he was at risk of falling for her. But the moment she agreed to be his fake girlfriend, he started losing that battle, and somewhere along the way, he'd lost his footing on a slippery slope that had him careening out of control faster than a skier with no poles on a Black Diamond run.

The problem was he didn't know what to do about it.

He couldn't handle a repeat of what happened with Harper, who felt so neglected that she'd gone elsewhere looking for love. With everything going on with his mom, he feared he'd end up doing the same thing to Paige.

He didn't want to hurt her like that. Nor could he bear to have her dump him for someone else. He couldn't handle that kind of heartbreak again. Not when he was already losing his mom.

Which meant there was only one thing he could do. Fake or not, he needed to back off and keep their relationship platonic.

No more stealing kisses.

~

"I'm so full." Paige leaned back from the table and put her hand to her stomach. Even her sides hurt. Probably from all the laughing they'd done while they cooked and ate.

"Me too." Gabe and Grace said in unison.

Marisol hadn't eaten more than a few bites, but she seemed to enjoy herself as she kept them entertained with more stories from Gabe's and Grace's childhood mingled with many from her own.

No one made a move to get up from the table and start cleaning the kitchen, so Paige stayed put, content to keep visiting.

Marisol shifted topics as she looked at Gabe. "Evelyn says the physical therapy office in Pasco isn't the same without you there." Then she turned to Paige. "My good friend Evelyn broke her ankle and has been going to physical therapy for months."

"I'm still there two days a week," Gabe said.

"I know, but Evelyn works on Tuesdays and Thursdays." Marisol took a sip of water. "She says Dr. Stoker is great and all, but even he doesn't spend the kind of time you do working on your patients."

"Well, she's welcome to make the drive to Providence," Gabe said in a joking tone. Then he tensed beside Paige and shot her a brief wide-eyed look. Regret filled his face.

Was he worried Evelyn would actually show up in Providence? While Paige was at PT perhaps?

Marisol went on. "Those other guys they've had filling in—Toa and...Gary, I think it was—Evelyn didn't like those guys at all."

Paige leaned forward in her seat about to agree but caught herself. She shouldn't give away that she'd done PT with both men recently in case they hadn't worked with Gabe a year ago when Paige had supposedly done PT.

"Few people do. Unfortunately, at PT school, they don't teach the people skills necessary to truly be a good physical therapist." Gabe grinned at her. "Paige had to work with Toa once, didn't you?"

She jumped at the opportunity to express her opinion of the obnoxious physical therapist. "Ugh. That man is so stuck on himself he can't see beyond the end of his nose. He has no idea what's best for his patients."

Marisol nodded. "That's exactly what Evelyn said. He's always trying to change her exercises from what Dr. Stoker has set." Marisol tutted and shook her head. "And Gary...well it sounds like that man hardly talks."

Paige bit her tongue, waiting for an opening from Gabe. When he gave an almost imperceptible shake of his head, she said, "PT is torturous enough, having a therapist like that would make it even more so."

"Hey, I resent that." Gabe pressed a hand to his chest in feigned offense.

"Don't you give me that." Paige grinned as she nudged his shoulder with hers. "You admitted to being a tyrant and a ruthless taskmaster on my second day of PT."

Grace gave a soft snort across the table.

Gabe pointed as he returned Paige's grin. "A ruthless yet gentle taskmaster. But only with my favorite patients." He reached out as though to take her hand then paused and pulled back.

A sinking sensation swooped through Paige's chest and abdomen. She shouldn't be so disappointed, but she was. She was also confused. Shortly after they arrived, he kissed her in front of his mom and sister, then as they prepared dinner, he'd gradually withdrawn. Even though he sat less than a foot away, he'd hardly touched her all through dinner.

Was he upset she had exchanged phone numbers with his mom and sister? That's what a real girlfriend would do. Besides, Paige and Grace had hit it off.

Maybe the guilt of lying to his mom was getting to him. Would he break down and tell her the truth soon and end their fake relationship?

That thought depressed her more than it should.

"So, Paige, have you made any special plans for Gabe's birthday yet?" Marisol looked at her expectantly as she took a nibble off her half-eaten empanada.

A sense of panic seized Paige, making her hot and cold at the same time. She had no idea when Gabe's birthday was, so of course she hadn't made plans. She didn't even know how old he was.

Gabe cleared his throat. "I have to work next Friday, so we aren't really planning on celebrating."

She shot him a look of gratitude and forced a smile. "I thought we could do something fun on Saturday to celebrate." She took Gabe's hand. Thankfully, he didn't resist. "What would you like to do?"

"I don't want to make a big fuss. A quiet dinner at a restaurant would be nice."

"Oh, we're going to make a fuss alright," Grace said. "You only turn thirty-one once. Besides, this might be the last one you get to celebrate with Mo—" Her works choked off as tears flooded her eyes. She ducked her head.

Tears sprang to Paige's eyes as a somber mood settled over the table. Gabe squeezed her hand with an almost bruising force. She did her best to return the pressure, trying to comfort him.

Thanks to Grace, she now knew how old Gabe was, but her only thought was that he was too young to lose his mom.

"Come now. None of that." Marisol clasped Grace's hand. "We're going to be grateful for the time I have left and make the most of it, remember?" She turned her attention to Gabe. "So yes, we are going to make a big deal of your birthday. Either you can decide what you'd like to do, or we can surprise you."

Gabe studied his mom for a long moment before saying, "Fine. Then I want to spend the day with you all at the Arboretum in Yakima."

"No, let's do what you want to do, not what I would choose."

"That's what I want too, Mom." Gabe gave his mother an earnest look. "I want to spend my birthday at the botanical gardens with you."

Marisol's lips lifted as she nodded. "That's what we'll do then. Should we pack a picnic or—"

"No," Gabe cut her off. "I'll treat you guys to dinner at that steak house we all like."

"We should treat you on your birthday." Although Paige wasn't sure her dwindling savings could afford to pay for dinner for four at an expensive steak house, especially if she didn't get a new job lined up soon.

"You asked what I want to do, and there's my answer. I want to take the most important women in my life to dinner on my birthday." Gabe's gaze lingered on his mom before shifting to Grace.

Paige kept waiting for him to look at her, but he didn't. He simply gave her hand a slight squeeze before releasing it to pick up his water glass. A cold chill swept over her as disappointment rained down on her. Gabe had told her he couldn't make any promises, so why did she keep getting her hopes up?

"So, what are you giving Gabe for his birthday?" Grace asked a gleam in her eyes.

Another surge of panic hit Paige, tightening her full stomach. So much for thinking she and Grace were friends. A true friend would never put her on the spot like that.

Paige recalled the socks she bought that reminded her of Gabe when she was shopping for a new swimsuit. She could give them to him for his birthday, rather than save them until she finished PT. But socks were a lame gift to give to a boyfriend.

"Well...um...I'm still deciding. I bought a little something for him a couple weeks ago, but I was hoping you guys could give me some ideas of what else to get him."

"You already bought me something?" Surprise registered on Gabe's face and in his voice.

She grinned. "I did."

"Seriously?" When she nodded, he asked, "What is it?"

"Nice try." She wagged a finger at him. "You'll have to wait until your birthday to find out." He continued to study her with a perplexed expression as she turned her attention back to his mom and sister. "You know how Gabe is—always taking care of everyone else—but doesn't want anyone to make a fuss over him."

"He's always been like that," Marisol said. "He never wants anything big. He's content with a book or new socks."

Paige grinned, proud of herself for recognizing that part of Gabe's personality before getting to know him. And at his mother's mention of a book, an idea formed in the back of her mind as she recalled the memory book Amy made for Ben after Cassey was found. Maybe she could do something to preserve Gabe's memories of his mother. She didn't have much time though. She'd have to think long and hard about it and enlist Grace's help.

"Grace and I will think about it and see if we can come up with some ideas for you." Marisol picked up her plate and stood from the table.

"Actually, you already gave me one." She darted a glance at Gabe before turning back to Marisol and Grace. "But I'm going to need your help."

"Help with what?" Curiosity filled Gabe's voice.

"It's a surprise, birthday boy." Paige patted his chest before standing. "I'll call or text you ladies tomorrow."

"I hate surprises," Gabe grumbled.

"We know," Grace and Marisol said in unison. Then Grace added, "That's why we like planning them for you."

Considering Gabe's serious nature and how intentional he was in everything he did, Paige didn't doubt he hated surprises. Especially when they came in the form of his dad walking out, his fiancée leaving him at the altar, and his mother receiving a diagnosis of stage-four cancer.

Once the kitchen was clean, they settled in the family room to play games, where Paige found herself repeatedly laughing about one thing or another. Gabe's mom and sister were so easy to get along with.

Even though she and Gabe were partners in some of the games and sat beside each other, Paige couldn't help but feel the emotional distance he'd put between them. One moment he was kissing her in the kitchen, and the next, he was throwing up walls.

She couldn't help thinking about what she went through with Phillip. He'd said he cared about her, but he was slow to text her back or answer her calls? In this case, why didn't Gabe touch her?

It was dusk by the time they left Gabe's mom's house. He'd grown quieter over the course of the evening. So much so, Paige was certain she'd done something wrong.

With the silence in the car growing more oppressive by the mile, the drive back to Gabe's apartment lasted an eternity. Paige wanted to ask him what she'd done wrong, but she feared he'd tell her he'd changed his mind and didn't want her to be his fake girlfriend anymore.

Gabe had been insistent about opening her door, so she waited for him to let her out when they arrived back at this apartment. She walked straight to her own car, then stopped before opening the door.

I can't leave things like this.

It would drive her crazy all week wondering where they stood. The irony that the tables had turned from this morning was not lost on her.

She turned to find him standing closer than she expected. "Did I do something wrong?"

"No, of course not. Why would you think that?" He moved back a step. The dim streetlight cast shadows over his face, and she struggled to read his expression.

She propped a hand on her hip. "You acted like you didn't want anything to do with me all evening."

"That's not true."

"Then why did it feel like you avoided me?"

"I'm sorry." Gabe let out a sigh and studied the ground. "I'm trying not to make this harder on both of us."

"How does you rejecting me in a *fake* relationship make this…" She motioned in a circle with her hand. "…easier?" Anger sharpened her words.

"I didn't reject you."

"Didn't you?" Both hands were on her hips now as she cocked a brow. "One minute you're kissing me in front of your mom and sister, and the next, you're pulling away. I've had enough duplicity and rejection to last me a lifetime. I don't need you playing games with me too." She turned to open her car door, but Gabe put a hand on her shoulder.

"I'm not trying to play games with you, Paige. The last thing I want is to hurt you." He withdrew his hand and raked it through his hair. "You were right when you said this relationship may be fake, but it's still a relationship. Fake or not, it's possible to develop real feelings."

Paige's heart stuttered. Was Gabe saying what she thought he was?

"The closer we get in this fake relationship, the more likely I am to disappoint you when I don't measure up to your expectations." His expression was as grim as his tone.

"What expectations?" She frowned in confusion. "You've already played your role where Phillip is concerned."

"That's not what I meant." He let out a sigh of frustration. "Pretending in front of my mom lets us—I mean me—*act* as if we're in a real relationship." His voice grew husky as he continued. "Every touch, every kiss, makes me fall a little more for you, Paige. But it's wrong of me to lead you on like that."

Paige didn't know it was possible to feel a rush of warmth and cold chills at the same time. Shouldn't it be impossible to feel excited and giddy when her chest was so tight she could hardly breathe?

"So, what are you saying?" She folded her arms. "Are you ready to tell your mom the truth or..." She didn't want to voice the other option, but she needed to know the answer. "Or do you want to stage a break-up?"

"No, neither of those," he said quickly. "I just don't want you to get your hopes up, because I'll end up letting you down when I can't give you the kind of time and attention you deserve."

Too late.

Her hopes were already up, and by distancing himself, he *was* letting her down. Paige schooled her features, trying to hide how much his words hurt.

"Because you need to focus on your mother." She understood what he was saying, and she hated it. But that made her feel selfish and insensitive, considering what he was going through.

His only response was a nod.

He was afraid he'd neglect her like he did Harper. Who knows, maybe he would, but Paige was coming to realize she cared for him too much to walk away. Even though it might break her heart to have to wait for who knows how long for him to come around, she could never set her sight elsewhere.

She didn't understand why God had led her here—to Gabe—but she felt strongly that she was supposed to be with him. She couldn't tell him that though. It wasn't fair to put that kind of pressure on him when he was dealing with so much.

"Thanks for being honest with me." She opened her car door. "I guess we'll just ignore the chemistry in our fake relationship, like we are in our...non-relationship." Forcing an air of casualness into her voice, she climbed into her car. "Easy peasy." She shot one last look his way before closing the door. "Good night, Gabe."

CHAPTER 20

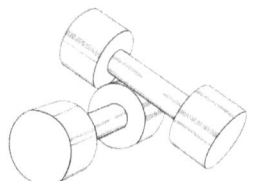

*G*abe was surprised to find Grace alone on the church pew the next morning. He was late, but only by a few minutes. He ended up oversleeping after tossing and turning most of the night, trying to get the hurt on Paige's face out of his mind.

She'd pretended him telling her not to get her hopes up didn't hurt, but he'd seen the pain and disappointment in her eyes. He hated himself for hurting her, but it was best to do it now than wait until she'd fallen in love with him, like he had her.

Keeping his gaze on the pulpit, he leaned toward Grace and whispered, "Where's Mom?"

"She wasn't feeling well this morning."

Had cooking and playing games yesterday been too much for her?

He frowned as he looked at Grace. "What's wrong with her?"

"Nauseous and dizzy. She said she threw up in the middle of the night."

"Does she have a fever?"

"I don't know." When Gabe scowled at her, she said, "I don't think so. She didn't look flushed or anything."

The old lady in front of them shot a dirty look over her shoulder, but Gabe was unfazed. Had Mom been exposed to the flu somewhere?

He leaned toward Grace again. "Why didn't you stay home with her?"

"To watch her sleep?" Sarcasm filled her voice, which only deepened his frown. She let out sigh. "I offered to stay home, but Mom insisted I come to church. She said she planned to rest all day."

"Did you at least make sure she had something to eat?" Gabe hated how helpless he felt.

"Of course I did." It was Grace's turn to scowl at him. "I left some herbal tea and toast by her bed. Not that she'll eat it." Worry lines filled her face. "Yesterday before you and Paige arrived, she complained of pain in her chest and said she felt short of breath."

The lady in front of them turned and shushed them with a finger to her lips as though they were children.

Gabe lapsed into silence. Not because he felt bad about talking during the service, but because his mind raced a hundred miles-per-hour. This was more serious than the flu.

He reviewed in his mind the symptoms of late-stage pancreatic cancer he'd researched after his mom was diagnosed. Sleepiness; check. Mom had been suffering exhaustion for months. Loss of appetite and stomach pain; check. She ate very little nowadays. That's why he was so surprised she'd vomited. But she shouldn't be experiencing dizziness or shortness of breath and chest pains yet.

Unless the cancer is progressing much faster than Dr. Sumner predicted.

Gabe's stomach hardened as a chill swept over him. He propped his elbows on his knees and shoved his fingers into his hair. It had only been three weeks since her diagnosis. Wasn't the medicine she took supposed to slow the growth of the cancer?

I can't lose her yet. I'm not ready.

He spent the rest of the hour-long service praying—no, begging and pleading—for a little more time with his mom. Eventually his prayers turned to asking the Lord to help him accept His plan and being able to cope without his mother.

When the service ended, he shot to his feet. "I'll meet you at home." Grace barely had a chance to say okay before he was out the door, having stepped on a few toes in his haste.

When he reached the house, he hurried inside and down the hall to his mom's room. He knocked softly on the door then opened it a crack without waiting for an answer. Spotting her in bed, he opened it wider and stepped inside. He watched her for a moment.

The rise and fall of the blankets eased his mind, but he took in the dark shadows around her eyes and the hollows of her cheeks that had become more pronounced over the past few weeks.

Please Lord, just a little more time.

More time than what? The thought entered his mind as though spoken aloud behind him.

Gabe spun around, half expecting Grace to be there. But she wasn't.

More time than what?

He repeated the question in his mind as he continued to watch his mom sleep. He'd had an additional twelve years with her after she beat breast cancer. Gabe should be happy for that, but it wasn't enough.

Dr. Sumner had said three to six months, maybe even as long as fifteen. Even if Mom lasted that long, it still wouldn't be enough. As her cancer progressed and her condition worsened, he'd feel guilty begging God to prolong her life for his own selfish purposes. But he couldn't bear to let her go.

He recalled how sick she was when she went through chemo-therapy. He'd often wished he could take that pain and sickness from her for a while. But he couldn't. Just like he couldn't take this from her.

"Gabe," Grace whispered behind him, making him jump. "What are you doing?"

How did he tell his sister that he was grieving the loss of their mom, even though she was still with them?

"Just checking on her," he finally said.

"She looks less flushed now than she did earlier." She paused for a moment before adding, "And peaceful."

Gabe nodded. Mom did look peaceful, but he knew there would come a time when she wouldn't be able to rest unless she was on heavy pain meds.

"What are you two whispering about?" Mom's voice rasped as she lifted her head.

"We're just checking on you." Gabe crouched by her bed. "How are you feeling?"

"Tired, as usual." She tried to clear her gravelly voice. "And thirsty."

She propped up on her elbow and reached for the almost empty glass of water on her bedside table that sat beside her untouched toast and cold tea.

Gabe grabbed it before she could. "Here, let me get you some fresh water." He hurried to the master bath. His gaze wandered over the counter as he filled the glass, spotting multiple prescription bottles. He picked one up, recognizing the common NSAID prescribed for pain. Cold water spilled over his hand as he grabbed the next bottle.

He shut off the water and dried his hand before picking up the second bottle again. It was one of the medicines meant to slow the growth of the cancer. He pulled his phone from his pocket to look up side effects for the drug. Nausea, dizziness, stomach pain, shortness of breath, chest pain, dry mouth, mouth sores, plus a host of others.

Gabe's stomach plummeted. The medicine meant to buy Mom a little more time was making her sicker.

He picked up the glass of water and carried it and the pill bottle to the bedroom. He waited for his mother, who now sat up to take a lengthy drink, before he crouched by the bed again and held out the bottle. "Have you been taking these pills, Mom?"

Confusion filled her face. "Yes, along with the other ones Dr. Sumner prescribed."

"Grace said you experienced some chest pains and shortness of breath yesterday."

"Yes, most of the day."

"Have you developed sores in your mouth?"

She sighed and nodded. "Crunchy and spicy foods have become almost impossible to eat."

Dread twisted in Gabe's gut.

"You didn't tell me you had sores in your mouth." Grace's voice was accusatory.

Gabe wanted to tell her to cool it, but the look he shot her was apologetic instead. He sucked in a deep, steadying breath. "Mom, I think you should stop taking these pills."

"What?" Grace's outburst didn't surprise him. "She can't stop. They're supposed to slow the growth of the cancer and give her more time." Her voice broke on the last word.

"I know, Gracie, but they're making her miserable."

"What do you mean?"

He handed her his phone with the list of side effects. "And that's just this medicine. I haven't looked up the other one yet."

Her frown deepened as she skimmed over the words on the screen. Tears filled her eyes. "But if she doesn't take them..."

Gabe didn't bother to finish her sentence. He didn't need to. They all knew what would happen if mom stopped taking the medicines.

Mom beckoned for Grace to come closer. When she dropped to her knees beside Gabe, Mom took each of their hands. Her gaze jumped back and forth between them. "I would do anything for the two of you. I hope you know that." When they both nodded, she went on. "I don't like the way these medicines make me feel, but if you need that time, I'll take them for you. I don't need more time to know how blessed I've been to be your mother and to remember the wonderful times we've had together, but if you need that time, I'll take them as long as you want me to."

Gabe swallowed several times to force the lump of emotion from his throat. Grace sniffled and wiped at the tears streaming down her cheeks.

Gabe found his voice first, gravelly as it was. "We're not ready to say goodbye yet, Mom. Let me talk to Dr. Sumner to see if there are other options with lesser side effects." He swallowed hard again. "But for now, I think you should stop taking these." He shook the pill bottle.

Mom looked to Grace for agreement. It was several long moments before his sister nodded.

"Okay, I'll stop taking them, but we'll call Dr. Sumner tomorrow." Mom dried Gracie's tears with a tissue from the box on her nightstand. "I'm not giving up. I promise you both, I'm going to fight for as long as I can." Then she stood and stretched. "I think I'm actually hungry for a change. What should we have for lunch?"

"Enchiladas?" Grace suggested, needing the comfort food.

Gabe got to his feet. "No, if she's got sores in her mouth, it needs to be something mild."

Mom's lips turned up. "Mashed potatoes sound good."

"The cheesy, creamy kind?" Grace's own lips quirked.

"With garlic," Gabe added.

"Okay, now I'm really hungry, but I need a shower first." Mom made a shooing motion with her hands. "You guys get started on lunch, and I'll be out in a bit."

He and Grace made their way to the kitchen and set to work peeling potatoes, a somber mood hanging over them.

Grace spoke first. "Do you think there's another medicine that will be effective in slowing down the cancer but won't make her so sick?"

"I don't know." Gabe's voice was grim. "But I'm going to exhaust every avenue before I give up."

"Good." Graced nodded, then her eyes filled with tears again. "I can't bear to see her so sick, like she was last time, but I'm not ready to let her go yet."

"Me either, but at some point..." He cleared his throat. "We're going to have to accept that it's time..."

The tears streamed down Grace's face as she nodded before turning away.

Gabe blinked back tears of his own. "Next time you go shopping, buy some of those nutrition-packed protein drinks. As the tumor in her stomach grows, she's going to find it harder and harder to eat."

It would only prolong the inevitable, but Gabe needed to believe they were doing everything they could for their mom.

LUNCH WAS A QUIET AFFAIR, and Gabe's mother was soon resting on the couch again. As the acceptance he'd tried to force upon himself earlier cycled back around to anger and denial, he couldn't bear to sit still.

When Grace stepped out of the living room to take a phone call, he went to the backyard.

He grabbed a hoe from the shed and made short work of the few weeds in the garden and flower beds. Then he stood in the middle of the yard with his hands on his hips, searching for something to do.

His gaze landed on the rickety trellis with the climbing roses. Mom loved those roses, but the trellis was an eyesore. He walked over and studied the way the roses had woven around each other and the trellis. If he cut the support wires, maybe he could untangle them and replace the trellis. Easier said than done, but a deep-seated need to do this act of service for his mom filled him.

An hour later, Grace came outside. "What on earth are you doing?"

"I'm replacing the trellis." He grunted as he tugged one vine loose from another. His grunt was followed by a hiss as more thorns tore at his skin.

Scrapes and abrasions covered his hands and arms. He cringed at the number of leaves and rose petals littering the ground, fearing he'd undertaken an impossible task.

"Mom said she didn't want you to replace it." Grace planted her hands on her hips in a defensive stance.

"I know, but this old thing is such an eyesore." He flicked a loose section to emphasize his point. It wobbled back and forth, shaking the whole trellis.

"You're going to ruin her roses." Her voice took on a desperate edge.

"If I don't replace the trellis, the whole thing is going to come down with the next stiff wind. Her roses will never survive that." He tore into the depths of the roses again trying to wiggle free the vine he'd been wrestling with for the last twenty minutes.

Another thorn tore into the flesh of his thumb. Swearing, he jerked his hand back and shoved the stinging digit to his lips. He sucked away the blood.

"Why are you torturing yourself?"

"Because I have to do *something!*" The volume of his voice made her flinch. Lowering it, he went on, "I can't just sit around, feeling like I've failed everyone." He threw his arms in the air like Paige often did.

Paige.

He'd failed there too, never mind their relationship was supposed to have been fake. He'd fallen in love with her only to turn around and let her down.

"How have you failed everyone?" Grace's brow furrowed in confusion.

"I'm supposed to take care of you and Mom, and I—"

"Says who?"

Gabe gave a non-committal shrug. "I had to be the man of the house after Dad left. It was my job to take care of—"

"Stop!" She held up a hand. "I know with Mom being diagnosed with breast cancer and me getting…well, you know… You had to take on an awful lot of responsibility, and you did a fabulous job. I don't know what either of us would have done without you during that time." Her voice grew thick with emotion. "But newsflash: I'm an adult now, and Mom's cancer is not your fault. You don't have to fix everything for everyone." She choked up again. "Replacing the trellis won't change Mom's diagnosis, Gabe."

"I know." He ground out the words then punctuated them with another swear word.

"Mom would be so disappointed to hear you talk like that."

His gut clenched. Grace was right, but he felt so helpless. He looked down at the mess he'd made. He'd managed to untangle two vines. He still had several more to go, but he couldn't stop now. Doing so would feel like he had lost hope.

He dug back into the roses, determined to finish what he'd started. There would come a day when he'd need to let go, but he wasn't ready for today to be that day.

More time than what?

The words filled his head again, but he pushed them aside. He couldn't justify why he should be allowed more time with his mom, when others lost loved ones all the time without warning.

Grace sighed. "At least change your clothes and get some gloves."

He surveyed his clothes. Several small tears and specks of blood dotted his white dress shirt. A few drops had even landed on his gray slacks that sported grass and dirt stains. They were already ruined. What was the point in changing now?

She shook her head and walked away, returning a few minutes later with two pairs of gloves. "Stop punishing yourself and put these on."

He doubted the gloves would do much good since he'd already mangled his hands, but he didn't have the energy to argue. In some perverse way, he felt like he deserved the pain he'd inflicted on himself.

Grace pulled on the second pair. "Tell me what to do."

"You don't have to help me." He shook his head as he went after the vine that had been giving him fits. "You should stay close to Mom, in case she needs something."

"She's not a child or an invalid, Gabe. Not yet anyway." She studied her gloved hands. "She reminded me of that this morning. We need to let her be independent for as long as we can."

Grace was right. Again. He acknowledged her words with a grunt. "Hold this vine while I untangle the other one from it."

They worked together for some time; their grunts and hisses the only thing to break the silence. Then out of the blue, Grace said, "I still think it's wrong to lie to Mom, but for what it's worth, I like Paige."

Gabe's head jerked up. "Good, but did you seriously have to give her such a hard time last week?"

"I had to make sure she was good enough for my brother." Grace grinned, unrepentant.

"It's fake, Grace. You don't need to protect me from a fake girlfriend."

She quirked a brow at him. "Are you sure about that?"

"That I don't need your protection?" He scowled at her. "One hundred percent certain."

"No, are you sure it's still fake?" Skepticism filled her face.

"Of course it is. It has to be—" He sucked in a sharp breath when a thorn dug into his arm. "I don't have the time or emotional energy for anything more."

Grace dropped the vine she'd been holding and propped her hands on her hips. "That's nonsense."

"It's not nonsense. It's called being realistic and responsible."

"Responsible?" Grace's face looked like she'd sucked a lemon. "Love isn't supposed to be responsible, or so I've been told." She smacked his arm. "You're supposed to feel a little out of control when you're in love, aren't you? But you don't care, because you love the way you feel when you're with that person. I mean, I've never been in love, so I don't really know."

His life felt out of control alright, and he loved being around Paige and her sunny personality. So much so, he was risking his job.

Grace stared at him, waiting for a response. When he didn't speak, she nudged his shoulder. "Is that how it was with Harper?"

"It was different with Harper." His words were little more than a grunt.

"How?" Grace picked up her vine again.

"Harper pursued me. She bowled me over with her big personality, and I got caught up in the idea of being in love and having a woman in my life." He recalled Paige mentioning how charismatic and persistent Phillip was and imagined she experienced something similar. "I asked Harper to marry me, because she convinced me marriage was the next step." He shrugged one shoulder. "Otherwise, I probably wouldn't have thought about marriage until after PT school."

"And then she cheated on you and left you at the altar." Contempt laced Grace's words.

Gabe studied his Sunday shoes that were now ruined. "Because I didn't give her the attention she needed."

"Stop taking the blame for her actions." She pointed a finger at Gabe. "Sure, you're not perfect. Nobody is. But it's past time for you to stop punishing yourself for her faults."

Didn't he tell Paige something similar yesterday?

Even if he stopped shouldering the blame, it didn't mean he'd changed. He tended to be hyper-focused when he had a goal, and right now, his goals were to ensure the new PT office was a success and make the most of his final days with his mom. He couldn't accomplish both of those *and* make Paige happy. She deserved more than he could give her right now.

"This thing with Paige..." He halted when Grace's curious gaze jumped to his face. "I think I've screwed it up."

"What did you do?" Grace's expression became wary.

"I told her not to get her hopes up. I don't have the time to devote to a real relationship."

"Time?" Grace scoffed. "I know you have a lot going on right now, and our lives have been in upheaval since Mom's diagnosis, but there is no perfect time to fall in love." Her expression was earnest as she gripped his arm. "Love is a gift from God. We don't get to choose when or if it will happen to us. But we *can* choose if we will accept it and let it enrich our lives." Then she shrugged one shoulder as she let go. "Or you know, you can reject it and continue to be miserable."

"You sound like Mom." Gabe found himself smiling.

Grace grinned and lifted her chin in the air. "Well, she *is* a very wise woman."

"For the record, I wasn't miserable before I met Paige."

"Maybe not, but now that you've gotten to know her, do you honestly think you'll be happy if you push her away?"

No.

He was miserable just thinking about how he hurt her last night. But how did he make sure he was there for his mom, succeeded in his job, *and* didn't neglect Paige when just being with her put his job at risk.

She'd have to drive to Pasco for PT if they were ever going to be together, which is exactly what her father wanted to avoid by insisting Gabe open the office in Providence.

"To be honest..." Grace looked down at her gloved hands. "I envy you."

"What?" Gabe gave her a confused look. "Why?"

"You have someone to talk to and share your pain with as we face all of this..." Tears flooded her eyes as she motioned toward the house. "...uncertainty with Mom."

As hard as it was to discuss, talking to Paige about what he was going through made him feel less alone. Twelve years ago, he had no one to talk to when he'd had to be strong for his mom and sister. It didn't have to be that way this time.

He wanted to accept this gift from God.

But that meant truly opening his heart to Paige and possibly losing his job. Was he willing to make that sacrifice?

CHAPTER 21

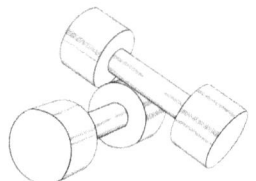

*R*iley set the piping hot pizza on the counter in front of Paige. "Thanks for keeping me company while Daniel is at his AA meeting."

"Any time. Especially if you're cooking." Technically, they had assembled the pizza together, but Riley already had the dough made when Paige arrived. Paige leaned over and inhaled deeply. The sausage, pepperoni, and tomato sauce with Italian spices made her mouth water. "It's been ages since I've had homemade pizza."

"It's been ages since I've made it, so I can't guarantee how it's going to taste." Riley dropped the oven mitts on the counter and pulled two plates from the cupboard. "Proceed with caution."

"Is this Lottie's recipe?"

Riley's mother-in-law, Lottie Hamilton, was one of the best cooks in the county. She'd been the cook and housekeeper at the Double Diamond ranch that Riley's family owned for over thirty years. Lottie's homemade scones with whipped honey butter were always Paige's favorite part of sleepovers at the ranch.

"The crust is Lottie's recipe, but the sauce is from a jar. I'm not that ambitious. I'll never be able to cook like Lottie, so I don't know why I even try. Thank goodness Daniel isn't picky."

"I'm pretty sure Daniel didn't marry you for your culinary skills." Paige wiggled her eyebrows at Riley.

Her cousin laughed. "Thank goodness."

"So how are you feeling? Do you still have morning sickness?"

"Some, but it's not as bad as I expected." Riley cut the pizza then lifted a slice of the gooey cheesy pizza onto her plate.

"Are you planning to find out the baby's gender?" Paige helped herself to a slice. "Will you do a gender reveal?"

"We're still undecided. We both kind of want to know, but we kind of want to be surprised too. If we do find out, we will *not* do a big gender reveal. They're anticlimactic." Riley rolled her eyes. "I mean, it's always either pink or blue, and the parents are always happy about both. And if they're not, they should be."

Too impatient to wait any longer for her pizza to cool, Paige blew on it for several seconds then took a bite. The meat, cheese, tomato and dough concoction melded into a tantalizing burst of flavors in her mouth.

"Mmm...not bad, Ri."

They talked about Riley's work for a while before shifting into the success Daniel was seeing with the architectural firm he was building and how busy he was staying.

Then Riley abruptly changed the subject. "Speaking of jobs, how is *your* job search going?"

"Not great." Paige dropped the last half of her second slice of pizza onto her plate and grimaced. "Unless I want to work part-time as a library aide or a custodian. Or you know, I could get my CDL and become a bus driver."

"Seriously? That's all there is?" Riley reached for her third piece of pizza. "Have you tried applying in the Tri-Cities area?"

"Yes, but all I've found there are a handful of jobs teaching band, French, or woodworking at the high school level."

Riley grimaced. "So, what are you going to do if you don't find a job?"

"I don't know. I keep wondering if I made a mistake by quitting my job before I had something else lined up." But it felt wrong to list Principal Stevens as a reference when he still thought she planned to return to her job in Seattle.

"It's barely the second week of June. I'm sure something will come available soon." Riley attacked her pizza again.

Paige took a bite of her own. "I hope you're right."

"How's physical therapy going?" Riley asked with a pointed look and a grin that hinted at wanting juicy details.

"Fine." Paige refused to take the bait. "I'm getting stronger all the time, but I still have a lot of muscle soreness and weakness. I'm working on getting back my full range of motion in my shoulder."

"And how are things with your physical therapist?"

Wonderful and terrible.

She loved spending time with Gabe and his family, until he pulled away Saturday night. She couldn't even enjoy the fact that he was falling for her because his backing off felt too much like rejection.

Paige couldn't help feeling a sense of deja vu. She'd entangled herself in another relationship—never mind that it was fake—where she was falling for a man who only wanted to use her for his own selfish purposes.

A pain pricked her chest as she recalled Gabe's shortness with her this morning when she asked how he got all the cuts and scrapes on his hands. He shut her down faster than he did Nikki every time she asked about their fake relationship. Paige tried not to take it personally, assuming his mood had something to do with his mom having a difficult day yesterday.

When she called Grace Sunday afternoon, she asked her opinion on enlisting Marisol's help to make a memory book for Gabe. Paige had been completely unprepared for Grace's emotional response. She'd spent half an hour listening to Grace cry and rant, wishing she could comfort her and Gabe in person.

She'd wanted to tell Gabe she was sorry for what he was going through, but Nikki had been too close at the time, and she never got the chance to talk to him without an audience.

"He's not *my* physical therapist."

"Isn't he?" Riley winked. "Sure, he's a lot of other people's physical therapists too, but that doesn't make him any less *your* therapist."

Paige itched to tell her cousin everything. How she'd agreed to be Gabe's fake girlfriend, but she'd fallen in love with him. And how all the enjoyment, excitement, and infatuation she used to feel in Phillip's arms paled in comparison to what she felt in Gabe's.

But Riley would want to tell Daniel, and he might let it slip to his parents or Riley's brothers, and if their mom—Paige's Aunt Faith—got wind of her fake relationship with Gabe, her parents and the whole town would know in no time.

No matter how badly she needed to talk to someone, it couldn't be Riley. Which depressed her, because she told Riley everything. It was another reminder that she shouldn't be lying to her parents and Gabe's mom.

Paige plucked a piece of pepperoni off her pizza. "Gabe has worked hard to get where he's at and takes his job seriously. He wouldn't risk it by openly dating a patient."

"I get it. That kind of thing *is* taboo in the medical field, but that doesn't mean you can't let him know you're interested. That way when you finish PT, the ball is in his court."

"He knows I'm interested." Heaviness hit Paige, constricting her chest and giving her the sensation of a stomach full of lead.

"And...?" Riley's eyes widened as her lips turned up. "What did he say?"

"He said he can't make me any promises." Paige's voice fell flat as she tore the slice of pepperoni into pieces.

"Oh." Riley's face fell. They were quiet for a long moment, then Riley perked up. "You still have a couple months of PT. You'll win him over. Just be your fun, cheerful self, and by the time you finish PT, he'll be half in love with you and begging you to go out with him."

Paige couldn't tell her Gabe was already half in love with her—at least that what he intoned Saturday night—but he still refused to make her any promises. Maybe Riley was on to something, though.

She recalled one of the quotes on the wall at the PT office. **Winners are not people who never fail, but rather people who never quit.**

If Paige threw herself into her role as Gabe's girlfriend every time they were with his mom, maybe he'd fall deep enough in love with her, he'd be willing to take a chance on them.

CHAPTER 22

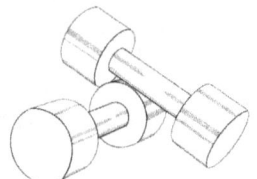

"*N*o way am I riding in that." Marisol stood with folded arms, glaring at Gabe.

Paige shifted from one foot to the other, shooting a concerned look at Grace, who looked equally as uncomfortable to be witnessing the battle of wills between mother and son.

The hour-long drive to the Arboretum in Yakima had been heaven. With Marisol and Grace in the backseat, Gabe held her hand most of the way. The tension that had been present between them at PT this week had drained away, and Paige determined to enjoy every moment of this day.

When they decided to drive to the botanical gardens together, Paige had insisted Marisol take the front seat, but Gabe's mother refused.

"Oh no, Mija, a mother should never come between her son and the future mother of her grandchildren."

Paige was so stunned by the comment and Marisol calling her Mija that Gabe's mother claimed the spot in the back seat before she could.

And now, Gabe stood over the wheelchair he'd pulled from the trunk of his car, insisting his mom get in it.

"I'm not an invalid." Marisol held her ground. "You all need to stop treating me like one."

A look of guilt flitted across Gabe's face, but he didn't back down. "These gardens go on for miles, Mom, you know that. You'll wear yourself out if you try to walk them all."

"I'll feel like a fraud if I ride around in that all day."

"You don't have to ride in it *all day*. Just part of it." He grinned as he winked at Paige. "I'll make Paige take turns with you. She likes being pampered like that."

Paige felt her hackles rising until she locked gazes with Gabe.

His expression held both pleading and affection. "There are a lot of gardens here. I don't want *anyone* to overdo it."

Paige was getting stronger, but walking through the gardens would likely be as exhausting for her as it was on Marisol. A sudden warmth shot through her at Gabe's thoughtfulness, making the warm summer day even hotter.

Despite the distance between them this week, it was nice to know he'd been thinking about her as well as his mother. She loved the glimpse this sweet, caring act gave her into the man she'd fallen for.

"Does that mean I get a turn too?" Grace asked with a grin.

"Sure, right after you push me. I'm the *old man* after all." He pretended to rub his aching back, which made them all chuckle. "Okay ladies, who's riding first?"

Marisol, defiant expression still firmly in place, glared at her son then scowled at Paige and Grace.

Paige was about to volunteer to take the first ride to help smooth things over, when Grace said, "Mom, if you overdo it today, you won't feel good enough to go to church tomorrow. The Allred sisters were worried about you when you weren't there last Sunday."

"Fine. I can't believe you're all ganging up on me." Marisol shook her head before dropping into the chair. "Grace, you push, so Gabe and Paige can walk together."

"No problem." Grace winked at Gabe as she stepped behind the wheelchair. "I'm sure the lovebirds would like to hold hands anyway."

Heat filled Paige's face, but she wasn't about to argue. In fact, she had to bite her tongue to keep from thanking Grace less than a minute later when Gabe laced his fingers through hers.

They fell into step behind Grace and Marisol, strolling slowly, but passed them when the ladies stopped to take pictures of the lavender-colored rhododendrons. Before long, they were twenty yards ahead of the others, but Paige didn't mind.

It almost felt like she and Gabe were on a real date. She was determined to enjoy it for all it was worth, knowing she might still end up with a broken heart.

"I meant it when I said I want you to take a turn in the wheelchair," Gabe said.

"If this place is as big as you say, you won't hear any complaints from me."

Surprise registered on his face. "You've never been here before?"

"No, most of our family outings were spent at my uncle's ranch or at the lake where my mom's family has a cabin."

Gabe asked questions about both the ranch and the lake, and they got caught up in conversation as they walked. He continued to hold her hand, and thanks to the beautiful flowers and greenery surrounding them, Paige felt like she was in paradise.

She didn't realize how self-centered Phillip was until she compared him to Gabe. Phillip hadn't bothered to learn anything about her family. He only met her parents once, because they made the trip to Seattle and insisted on taking them to dinner. Phillip spent the whole time talking about himself, telling what she now realized was lies.

So why did he come back, insisting they belonged together?

And why am I thinking about Phillip while I'm holding Gabe's hand?

She hoped to never see Phillip again, but his reappearance in her life had continued to bug her the past few weeks.

It wasn't about me. It was all about him.

Despite what Phillip said about dumping Avery, Paige was certain it had been the other way around. Any smart woman in Avery's position, would have shown Phillip the door. But he couldn't bear to lose.

The narcissist in him needed to win. He didn't want Paige. He only wanted to conquer.

She looked up at the wispy clouds in the blue, summer sky and sent up a prayer of gratitude.

Thanks for the love reset.

It had been four long, hard months since her accident, but she was grateful God had remodeled her life. She'd dodged a bullet when it came to Phillip. And she'd met a man who was compassionate and thoughtful. Gentle and kind. He was attractive, inside and out.

It still bothered her that he insisted on lying to his mother but being with Gabe felt right. She thought often about what Riley said about God bringing her home and Gabe to Providence. Maybe their paths were always meant to intersect for more than professional reasons.

Here in eastern Washington with Gabe was where she belonged. She'd never felt these powerful, all-consuming emotions with Phillip. What she thought was love four months ago had been nothing but a cheap facade that rusted when the truth came out.

She looked up at Gabe and grinned. Their future was uncertain, but her feelings for him couldn't possibly be stronger. Well, maybe they could after they'd been married a few years.

That thought flooded her with warmth and made her heart dance in her chest.

Gabe caught her staring at him. "What?"

Paige continued to grin as she shrugged. She couldn't help it. She smiled when she was happy, and this was the happiest she'd been in years.

He squeezed her hand. "Why are you looking at me like that?"

"Do I need a reason to look at you?"

"It's your smile. It makes me think you're up to something."

She stopped walking and stepped close to him. Her expression serious as she tried to keep her teasing mood from showing on her face. "Do you want me to be up to something?" Her voice sounded sultrier than she'd intended.

Gabe's eyes widened, and a grin split his face. "It depends." His own voice dropped, sending a ripple of warmth cascading over her as he shifted closer.

"On what?" She searched his warm brown eyes. She could get lost in their depths.

"If it has something to do..." He ran a finger along her jaw, bringing it to a stop near her mouth. "...with your pretty, glossy lips..." Each word sounded like a seduction as he caressed her bottom lip with his thumb. "...wishing me happy birthday."

Paige let out a breathy sigh and leaned into him. She moistened her lips with her tongue and watched his eyes grow wider. "Happy birthday, Gabe!" She threw her arm in the air as she shouted the words. Then she burst into laughter at the shocked look on his face.

She turned to move away from him, but his arms caught her around the waist and pulled her against his body. The heated look in his eyes doused her teasing mood and pushed the air from her lungs. The warm summer day suddenly got a lot hotter.

"You're such a tease." The deep timber of his voice sent goose bumps racing across her skin despite her rising temperature.

"I really am." Her smile returned.

Hope flared in her chest. She didn't know what happened since last Saturday to cause this change in him, but like a sponge, she'd soak up every ounce of attention Gabe gave her. Hopefully, somewhere along the way, she'd convince him he didn't have to choose between her and his mom. Their relationship could survive the storms he faced with his mother. She'd show him she wasn't a flighty woman whose head turned every time she didn't get enough attention.

"I can tease too." His voice dropped even lower as he settled his hands on her hips and tugged her a little closer.

"Is that so?" She took her time sliding one hand up his chest and over his broad shoulder, before finally bringing it to a stop at the back of his neck to play with his thick hair that was due for a trim. The other hand she kept firmly planted on his chest.

He lowered his head, bringing his lips close to her ear. "Teasing is really just..." His warm, minty breath against her ear and cheek sent her pulse racing. "...enjoying another person's discomfort."

She tilted her chin, angling her mouth closer to his ear. "Hmm...I don't think you're very good at it, because I'm quite comfortable at the moment."

A low chuckle rumbled through his chest, and his hands tightened on her hips. "So am I."

"Correct me if I'm wrong..." She leaned back to look him in the eye. "But it sounded like you were begging for a birthday kiss."

His lips quirked. "*Begging* is a strong word."

"Your birthday was yesterday. I brought you cupcakes. If you wanted a birthday kiss, you should have asked for it then."

"In front of Nikki, Gladys, and Luke? No way."

"I'm sure Nikki would have been happy to give you a birthday kiss too." Paige laughed. "And I bet it wouldn't have taken much persuasion to get Gladys to join in."

Gabe growled, pulling her flush against him. "It was your idea to celebrate my birthday today with my mom and sister. So..." He kept one arm clamped around her waist as he lifted the other hand to caress her neck, his thumb lingering on the racing pulse below her jaw. "You should give me a gift *today*."

"I have presents for you back at your mom's house." Paige couldn't hide the breathlessness in her voice. Resisting was getting harder by the second.

"But I want one *now*." His voice dropped to a whisper. His face inched closer to hers as he slid his hand into her hair, sending tingles racing across her scalp. He cupped the back of her head.

She lifted her chin, angling it closer to his. "That sounds a lot like begging to me." Her words were airy; the teasing swallowed up by the anticipation of his lips on hers.

"Aren't we all beggars?" His breath mingled with her own, and the final thread of Paige's self-control evaporated.

"Indeed." He may as well have spoken the word, because his mouth was on hers before it had fully left her lips.

Warmth and contentment swept over Paige as Gabe's mouth claimed hers. The electrifying thrill she experienced the first time they kissed hit her again, amplified this time by a weeks' worth of stubble on his jaw.

She plunged her fingers into the thick hair at the back of his neck as she savored each caress of his lips against hers. Her other hand gripped the t-shirt at his chest. If she didn't somehow ground herself, she feared she'd float away with the exhilarating energy that buzzed through her.

Sheer perfection. Gabe's kiss was what she'd been missing all her life. Here in his arms was where she belonged. Even the birds singing in the trees above her seemed to agree. She would never tire of kissing Gabriel Rivera.

He let out a small moan as the kiss became more urgent and exploratory. She eagerly melted into him, silently giving him her heart and soul. He might regret this later, but she never could.

She enjoyed every stroke of his lips against hers and brush of his fingertips against her scalp. She'd ride this wave for all it was worth, knowing it would come crashing down on the shore all too soon.

She kissed him for several long delicious moments before pulling her lips from his. He held her close in the circle of his arms, where she was content to stay until she'd caught her breath.

"Happy birthday, Gabe," she whispered.

"Mmm… All other gifts will pale in comparison to that."

They locked gazes. A myriad of emotion flitted through his eyes. She struggled to interpret them, but she was certain she saw contentment and desire in the depths of his gorgeous brown irises.

Marisol and Grace's voices drew closer, and disappointment settled over her. Especially when Gabe released her and took her hand.

"Thank you for spending the day with me and my family," he said as they started walking again.

"It's my pleasure. Seriously. I love your mom and sister."

And I'm head over heels in love with you.

If she voiced the words out loud, Paige feared he'd back off, distancing himself from her like he did last week. She couldn't pressure him. But she could pray he would see they were meant to be together.

"They like you too." The contemplative look he gave her before his lips turned up in a smile seemed to hold a promise.

Of what, she wasn't sure, but she'd take whatever he offered.

CHAPTER 23

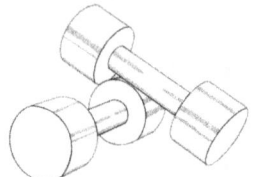

"*H*appy Birthday to you!"

Gabe's gaze darted around the table as his mom, Grace, and Paige sang to him. His attention was torn between his mom and Paige. This could be the last time he heard his mother sing Happy Birthday, so he wanted to savor that, but he was distracted by the sweet soprano of Paige's voice. He had no idea she could sing so well. There were so many things he wanted to know about her.

"Okay, make a wish," Grace said when the song ended, "then blow out the candles."

Gabe stopped making birthday wishes after his father walked out on them, but he'd humor Grace. He looked at the expectant faces surrounding him, his gaze jumped between his mom and Paige again.

Too bad he couldn't *wish* his mom back to health. Turning to the Lord in prayer and supplication was more effective than hoping for a birthday wish to come true. Even if his prayers weren't answered the way he wanted.

His gaze shifted back to Paige. Warmth filled his chest as he watched the way the candlelight danced in her blue eyes.

With his mom and sister sitting in the backseat on the drive to Yakima, he felt like he should hold Paige's hand. That contact had cemented his decision to make their relationship real despite the risks. He didn't know how things would play out, but he'd do whatever was necessary to keep Paige in his life.

"Come on." Grace poked his shoulder. "It's not that hard. Just wish for a kiss from Paige and blow out the candles already. They're dripping on the cake."

He closed his eyes and made his wish which turned out to be more of a prayer. Something he had been doing a lot lately.

Please, God, let me find a way to make this real.

Keeping his eyes on Paige, he blew out the candles on the tres leches cake Grace had made that morning. All thirty-one of them. Paige's smile lit up the room much brighter than the bonfire of candles.

Mom and Grace's cheers pulled his gaze from Paige. Grace wore a knowing, I-told-you-so grin, and the twinkle in Mom's eyes looked like she had a secret she was dying to share.

They chatted as they dug into the cake then moved to the family room, where his sister insisted he open the presents that sat on the coffee table. He made short work of the gifts from Grace; two t-shirts. One said, "The World's Best Big Brother." The other read, "I have the Best Sister in the World. She's also CRAZY and scares me."

Gabe burst out laughing. "So true."

"I want to see you wear it every week," Grace insisted.

"Maybe on Saturdays." He gave her a dubious look. "When I do yard work."

"I dare you to wear it in public." She glared at him.

"I'll wear it in public when you're with me. So people can see who the *crazy* one is."

Her eyes widened, and they all burst into laughter.

He opened his mom's gift next; a new white button-down dress shirt and gray slacks. To replace the ones he ruined last Sunday, wrestling with the roses. Surprisingly, she hadn't gotten upset with him for replacing the trellis, and thankfully, it looked like the roses would survive.

"Thank you, Mom."

"You're welcome, Mijo."

Gabe wasn't sure why he saved Paige's gift for last, but eager antic-ipation filled him as he pulled the gift bag toward him. He was equally curious what gift she had supposedly bought for him weeks ago—and what she picked up this morning that made her late getting here. He found two presents inside; each wrapped in tissue paper and tied with a ribbon. He opened the bulkier one first. A six-pack of Marvel char-acter socks.

"Those are so Gabe," Grace said at the same time Mom said, "They're perfect."

He grinned at Paige. "I love them."

"I saw them when I was shopping for a new swimsuit a few weeks ago, and they just screamed your name."

"I'm touched that you thought of me." He lowered his voice, but his mom and Grace couldn't help overhear. Mom would assume they were already dating at that time, but he knew differently.

"I noticed my first day at PT that you like funky socks."

"Funky?" He grimaced. "I prefer to think of them as fashionable."

She patted his arm. "Call them what you want, honey, they're still funky."

He loved the way the endearment rolled off her tongue in regard to him.

"Thank you, mi corazón." He longed for another kiss like they shared at the Arboretum. Dropping his gaze to her lips, he leaned toward her.

"Open Paige's other gift." Grace's excited voice broke the spell Paige had over him.

"Okay, okay." Hiding his disappointment, he took out the other tissue-paper wrapped present and tugged on the bow.

His brows shot up when he uncovered a square hardcover book with a picture of him and his mom at his high school graduation on the cover. Silence descended on the room as he opened the book.

He found a picture of his mom on the first page. She was just a baby in her mother's arms. The next two pages held more images of her childhood and adolescence. Then he turned another page to find a picture of his mom framing her pregnant belly. Soon pictures of Gabe as an infant in his mother's arms filled the pages.

He kept turning page after page, recognizing many of the images from the family scrapbooks plus a bunch he couldn't recall ever seeing before. Pictures of her pushing him on the swing and reading to him. Pictures of her cheering for him at his wrestling matches and hugging him each time he graduated; first high school, then college, and finally, PT school.

Tears blurred his vision. Paige had documented his relationship with his mom in pictures. Grace and Mom had obviously supplied the pictures, but Paige must have spent hours poring over this book, organizing and determining the perfect placement of each photo.

His heart spasmed when he reached the back page. Script that looked like his mother's handwriting filled the page. In large letters at the top, he read: *A letter to my son.*

His gaze jumped to the first line.

My dear son,

I never thought I'd have to say goodbye to you so soon...

Emotion seized his throat, threatening to cut off his air supply. His eyes burned with hot tears that begged for release. He stopped reading.

"I can't." His voice croaked. "I'm sorry, I can't read this right now." He shot his mother an apologetic look.

"It's okay," Mom said. "Read it when you're ready."

Gabe didn't think he'd ever be ready, but he nodded. "Thank you, Mom." Then he wrapped his arm around Paige and pulled her close. He pressed his lips to her temple. "And thank *you*. You have no idea how much this means to me."

"You're welcome." Her gentle voice was consoling and comforting. She laid her hand on his chest over his heart. "She'll always be with you, Gabe."

He nodded, greedily accepting the small measure of peace that settled over him.

Mom rose from her position on the couch. "I have something else I'd like to give you, Gabe. Well, both of you, I guess. I'll be right back."

Then she walked down the hall to her bedroom with that secretive grin back on her face.

Paige jumped up as well. "I have something for you too, Grace." She hurried to the oversized purse she'd left by the front door when she arrived and took out another book like Gabe's.

"You made a book for me too?" Grace's voice hitched and moisture flooded her eyes as she accepted the book. Then she pulled Paige in for a hug. "If my idiot brother screws this up, promise me we will still be friends." Before Paige could respond, she went on. "A sister would be so much better than a friend, but I'll take friend if Gabe messes this up."

"Hey." Gabe's protest was drowned out by Paige and Grace's laughter.

Paige settled back on the loveseat beside him just as Mom returned carrying a small, palm-sized velvet bag.

She took her seat again and smiled at him and Paige. "Getting to know you, Paige, has brought great joy to our lives during this difficult time. It makes me so happy to see my son fall in love again. I'm glad to know Gabe and Grace will have you after I'm gone."

Gabe's heart constricted as though a giant fist squeezed it. He hated hearing his mom talk like this. She had accepted her imminent departure so much better than he and Grace.

"I don't want you two to feel like I'm rushing you or anything, because as far as I'm concerned, you're already an integral part of this family, Paige, but when you're ready to make it official..." Mom extended the small bag to Gabe. "Maybe you'll consider using this."

What is she talking about?

Confused, Gabe took the bag. As soon as his fingers clasped it, he felt the hard circular object inside, one side much bulkier than the other. He knew exactly what it was, and what his mom was saying.

He sucked in a sharp breath. There was always the risk his lies would come to this, but he felt blindsided, nonetheless. He didn't want to open the velvet bag for fear of how Paige might react.

"Go ahead, Mijo, open it and show Paige."

He chanced a quick glance at Paige. Her face showed all the confusion and curiosity he'd felt a moment ago. Giving her a tight smile, he silently prayed she wouldn't freak out. He untied the silky cords, stretched open the top of the bag, and dumped a ring onto his palm. A wedding ring with a matching band that had been melded together long ago.

Paige's shoulder pressed against his as she leaned in and studied the ring. "It's beautiful."

Gabe gave her a sharp look. That was not the reaction he'd expected.

"I'm glad you think so," Mom said with a satisfied smile. "It was my mother's wedding ring."

Paige picked up the ring to get a closer look, surprising Gabe even more. "That explains the intricate vintage design." She studied the solitaire diamond complimented by a band with a twisty vine pattern that held tiny, leaf-shaped diamonds. "It's such a classy and timeless pattern."

"I'm not saying you have to use it, since it probably isn't the style you would choose, but I want you to have it." A hopeful look filled Mom's face.

"Me?" Paige dropped the ring and jerked her hand back so fast Gabe thought it had shocked her. "No, I couldn't."

"Well, I'm gifting it to Gabe, to give to the woman he marries." Mom's eyes twinkled as her smile grew. "And it looks like that will be you."

"No, no, no." Paige held up both hands, palms out. "They should go to Grace. They will be more meaningful to her." Paige's pleading gaze flew to Grace, begging her to claim the ring.

"Grace has already expressed interest in having my grandmother's wedding ring." Mom said before Grace could open her mouth. "This ring goes to Gabe." She leveled an intense gaze—the kind only a mother can give—on him. "Like I said, I don't want to rush you two, but my time *is* limited, and I would very much like to see you married —or at least engaged—before I die."

"Married?" Paige's voice squeaked.

Gabe didn't even try to speak, because his throat was equally tight.

Overwhelmed by how out of control his lie had become and the ease with which his mom spoke about dying, he couldn't have found the appropriate words if his life depended on it. And judging by the wide-eyed panicked look Paige gave him, his life might very well depend on the next words that came out of his mouth.

"I uh...I don't know...what to say." A cold sweat pricked the back of his neck as he searched for words that would appease his mom and not send Paige packing.

He didn't want to disappoint his mother by telling her he'd been lying to her all along, but he also didn't want to screw things up with Paige. He was certain she cared about him, but getting engaged was a massive jump from a fake relationship.

He licked his suddenly dry lips and turned imploring eyes on Paige, hoping she'd go along with the charade a little longer. Just until they could talk privately and come up with a plan.

She shook her head so violently, he feared she'd give herself whiplash. "I need some air." She bolted off the loveseat. Her hamstring must have spasmed, because she whimpered as she limped to the sliding glass door.

Gabe let out a heavy sigh. He needed to come clean with his mom, but a small part of him wished Paige had held out her hand and let him slip the ring onto her finger.

He'd never felt so conflicted in his life. He wanted desperately to make his mom happy for the short time she had left. Telling her the truth now would turn the joy she'd found in her final days into bitter disappointment.

And despite fearing he'd end up neglecting Paige when he became too caught up in caring for his mom, he wanted nothing more than to make her his fiancée. Knowing she would be a part of his future made the thought of losing his mom bearable.

"Oh dear. I was too pushy, wasn't I?" Remorse filled Mom's face. "I'd better apologize."

"No. I should talk to her." Gabe curled his fist around the ring he still held and pushed to his feet.

This mess was all his fault. It was only right that he be the one to fix it.

~

GABE SLIPPED the ring into his pocket and stepped onto the back deck. Deciding against turning on the back porch light, he stepped to the stairs. It wasn't fully dark yet, but it would be soon. No need to put a spotlight on what was about to go down between him and Paige.

Paige paced a line just beyond the deck, her agitation manifested in her hunched shoulders and the way her hands fidgeted.

"What are we going to do, Gabe?" A hint of hysteria crept into her voice as she turned wide eyes on him. "We can't just pretend to be engaged. The next thing you know your mom will be pushing us to set a wedding date and asking me if I've bought a wedding dress yet." She rubbed her forehead with a shaky hand. "She's going to want to meet my parents."

Gabe's gut clenched at the thought of facing Dr. Young and having to tell him he'd crossed the line with a patient who happened to be his daughter.

I've made such a mess of everything.

"Relax." He held his hands out in a consoling gesture, feigning a calmness he didn't feel. "I didn't come out here to convince you to pretend to be my fiancée."

"You didn't?" She looked at him in surprise. "You're going to tell your mom the truth?"

His stomach tightened again, making him nauseous. He sank onto the new wicker bench he'd purchased when he replaced the trellis.

Mom loved the bench, just like he'd hoped she would. She'd spent time out here every day this week.

Sighing, Paige sat beside him. Her posture remained rigid, but the hysteria had vanished from her expression. Now she just looked sad.

The light that shown through the sliding glass door played across her blond hair and face, creating tiny golden stars in her eyes. Gabe caught his breath at her beauty. He felt like the luckiest man on earth, but he feared that was about to change.

Sitting on the bench put them in full view of the house, but taking Paige out of sight would look suspicious.

"I see you replaced the trellis." She looked up at the roses behind them. "That's how you got all the cuts and scrapes on your hands, isn't it?"

He looked down at his hands, mostly healed now, and nodded. "I needed to let off some steam on Sunday." He propped his elbows on his knees and scrubbed his hands over his face. "The medicine my mom was taking to slow the growth of the cancer was making her sicker, so I asked her to stop taking it."

"I'm so sorry." She rubbed his back in a comforting gesture that soothed the ache in his heart. "I can't imagine how difficult that must have been for you and Grace."

"She started new meds on Thursday, but we have to wait to see how she responds to them." He recalled his mom's unsteadiness as she got out of the car this evening. He hoped it was just exhaustion, despite riding in the wheelchair most of the day. "If they work, they'll buy us a little more time with her. If they don't..."

He couldn't finish his sentence, but he didn't need to for Paige to understand the gravity of the situation. Her hand on his back continued to provide the comfort he so badly needed.

Silence stretched between them as Gabe searched for the words to make right all the things he'd said and done wrong, not just with his mom, but with Paige too.

"You're a good son, Gabe. A good man."

"I sense a 'but' coming." He straightened and shifted to face her.

"But you are not responsible for your mom's—or even your sister's —happiness."

Deep down, he knew that. But it didn't change the fact that he cared about them and wanted them to be happy. If he could make that happen, then he felt compelled to do so.

"What about your happiness?" he asked softly as he took her hand in his.

One side of her mouth quirked up. "You're not responsible for my happiness either. But we seem to have become intrinsically connected. Everything you do affects me."

"I know, and I'm so sorry for this latest turn of events. I had no idea my mom was planning to give me my grandma's wedding rings."

"I'm tired of lying, Gabe." Her eyes glistened with the sheen of tears.

"Me too, but…"

Would he scare her away if he told her the truth? That he wanted her to be his fiancée for real. Not just to make his mom happy, but because he loved her, and he wanted to come home to her every day for the rest of his life.

"Your mom looked so happy today." She shifted her gaze to the house where they had a clear view of Mom and Grace sitting on the couch. "It'll break her heart if we go in there and tell her the truth."

He nodded, hating the idea of destroying his mom's happiness. Happiness that came from seeing him fall in love again. And boy, had he fallen. If they told his mom the truth and ended their fake relationship, would he be able to convince Paige to take a chance on a real one?

He didn't want to wait until she'd finished PT to court her. And what if she couldn't find a job in Providence and decided to return to Seattle? His stomach twisted with the what-ifs.

"I've lied to her long enough though." He sucked in a deep breath, bracing himself for what he needed to do. "Just promise—"

"I wish we could drop the charade and make this real."

His eyes cut to her face. Was she serious?

"Me too." He squeezed her hand as hope exploded in his chest. "Let's do it. Let's make this real."

Her eyes widened and her hand jerked in his as if she meant to pull it away but changed her mind. "Stop kidding around."

"I'm not joking, mi amor." He squeezed her fingers and locked gazes with her. "I know this all started out as a fake relationship, but I started falling for you long before I brought you home to meet my mom." Her breath hitched, but he plowed on. "And then we kissed, and it felt so right that I forgot we were supposed to be pretending." He caressed her cheek with a finger. "Every kiss...every touch after that was because I wanted it. Not because I was trying to convince my mom you were my girlfriend."

Despite her face splitting into a grin, her eyes filled with tears. "But you said you couldn't make me any promises. Just last week, you told me not to get my hopes up."

"I know, and at the time, I thought I was doing what was best for both of us. But Grace reminded me that love is a gift from God, and we don't get to choose when it comes our way. I tried to distance myself from you this week at PT while I decided if I could embrace that gift, and it made me miserable." He inched a little closer to her. "I don't want to pretend anymore, because I'm in love with you, Paige."

Her smile broadened. "You love me?"

"With all my heart." He pressed a hand to his chest that swelled with a feeling of wholeness. "I tried to fight it because you're my patient, but it was a losing battle from that very first day when you threw yourself into my arms."

"I didn't *throw* myself into your arms. I tripped."

Hiding his disappointment that she hadn't returned his declaration of love, he grinned as he shrugged. "You ended up in my arms. The effect was the same."

Her face fell. "But I'm still your patient. You could lose your job if we make this real."

"I know." The sensation of fullness that occupied his chest a moment ago now created a heaviness in the pit of his stomach. "I don't want that to happen, but I don't want to lose you either."

Gabe considered suggesting she start doing PT at the office in Pasco. But it wasn't fair to ask her to make that drive multiple times a week. Especially when it meant she'd have to work with Toa or Gary, since Dr. Stoker's schedule was usually packed.

He studied their clasped hands for a moment. "I need some time to figure out how to broach our relationship with Dr. Stoker..." A hot flash swept over him, making his stomach churn. "...and your father." He gave her an imploring look. "Can you give me that, mi corazón?"

"You keep calling me that. What does it mean?"

"My heart." He squeezed her hand as he pressed his other hand to his chest again.

She sucked in a sharp breath. The dimple he loved flashed in her cheek. "I like that." Now it was her turn to study their hands. "So, we're really going to do this? Instead of being your fake girlfriend, I'm now going to be your *secret* fiancée?"

He cringed. "It sounds horrible when you put it that way. But I just nee—"

"We haven't even dated." She held up a hand. "Don't get me wrong, I want this. I want a relationship with you, Gabe, even if it needs to stay a secret for a while, but…"

"It's not ideal, I know."

"It's just that…after Phillip, I swore I would never fall in love again, but here I am." Now she pressed a hand to her chest. "I'm still trying to figure out how this happened when we haven't even gone on an actual date."

"Me too." He chuckled, delighted to hear her confession of love. Then he sobered and caressed her knuckles. "Do you believe in fate?"

"Not really, but I do believe God has a plan for us. I'm living proof that if we get on the wrong track, He will correct us."

"I agree." He continued to caress the back of her hand. "Despite the obstacles we still need to deal with, I feel good about the path we're on."

"Me too."

"As soon as I talk to Dr. Stoker and your dad, I promise I'm going to start taking you out on dates. And hopefully, we'll get to do a lot more of this."

He pressed his lips to hers in a lingering kiss that made his blood pump a little faster.

Paige jerked back and gasped. "Did we really— Are we engaged now?"

Gabe bit back a smile. "Only if you want to be. My mom's time is limited, but I don't want to rush this, not even to make her happy." He glanced toward the house again, where Mom and Grace's heads suddenly jerked toward each other—a poor attempt to hide that they'd been watching him and Paige. "I don't relish going in there and telling her the truth, though."

She'd be happy he and Paige had fallen in love, but he dreaded seeing the disappointment in her eyes when he admitted he'd lied to her.

"So don't."

His gaze jumped back to Paige. "What?"

"Don't ruin this day for her." She gave a casual shrug. "Yes, you owe her the truth, but if you're serious about everything you just said, it doesn't need to be today." Then she winked. "It'll probably go over better if you wait until our wedding day to tell her."

Gabe burst out laughing. "As much as I like that idea..." He looked at his mom again. "I need to tell her the truth."

He pushed to his feet and tugged Paige's hand to pull her up, but she resisted.

"Aren't you forgetting something?" She raised an eyebrow at him.

He narrowed his at her, giving her a questioning look.

"Correct me if I'm wrong, but I think we just got engaged." Her nose wrinkled as she scrunched her brow. "Did you bring the ring with you? Shouldn't we make this official? Well, unofficially official." She shook her head and frowned. "That doesn't make sense." She tried again. "Secretly official." Her eyes lit up with that one, and he laughed.

He took the ring from his pocket then sat back down beside her. "Are you sure about this?"

"Am I sure I want to be engaged to my physical therapist, who I've only known for two months and have never actually dated because he's not supposed to date his patients?" She paused just long enough to suck in a breath before continuing. "Yes, because not only is he a compassionate and kind man, who always puts others' happiness above his own, he's incredibly handsome, gives great massages, and has a set of six pack abs to die for."

"Abs?" Gabe chuckled. "And here I thought you were checking out my pecs all this time."

She winked. "I was checking out those too."

He reached for her hand, ready to slip the ring on her finger.

"Uh-uh." She wagged a finger at him. "This is the real deal. You're going to do this right." She pointed at the ground in front of her. "Besides, your mom is watching. This is the only proposal she'll get to witness, so you'd better make it good."

Grinning, Gabe slid off the bench and dropped to one knee. He hadn't prepared for this in the slightest, but it didn't take much contemplating to figure out why he wanted to marry Paige.

He sobered as he took her hand. "A crazy anticipation hit me when I woke up this morning, because I looked forward to spending the day with you." He shook his head and gave a rueful smile. "If you'd told me this morning that I'd be proposing tonight, I probably would have canceled our plans. Because I was scared. I was afraid I couldn't give you everything you deserved, or that I wouldn't measure up, and you'd end up walking away." His grip on her hand tightened. "But I can't bear to lose you, Paige."

He caressed her knuckles with his thumb as he continued. "The moment I took your hand in mine on the drive to the Arboretum, your touch filled the gaping hole in my heart and smoothed out the troubled spots. I knew I needed to embrace this gift from God. All day, I kept wishing this day would never end. But when my mom handed me this ring, I realized I had been wishing for the wrong thing. One day with you would never be enough. I want a lifetime."

"That's beautiful." Tears filled Paige's eyes as she pressed her fingers to her lips.

"I know this is asking a lot, but will you marry me—someday, down the road—after I've had a chance to court you properly?" He rushed on when she opened her mouth to speak. "With the stipulation that we need to keep it a secret from everyone except my mom and sister for now?"

"That *is* asking a lot." A grin teased at her lips. "But yes, Just Gabe, I will marry you—someday, down the road. I can't wait for you to court me." She pitched forward, wrapping her arms around his neck, and pressed her lips to his.

It took every ounce of his core strength to keep them from

toppling over onto the grass. After sharing a lengthy kiss, he slipped the ring on her finger.

Paige smiled as she studied her hand. "It fits like it was made for me."

"For some reason, I'm not surprised."

He tucked a lock of hair behind her ear. "I can't promise life won't be a little rocky, or that I'll always put you first as my mom's health fails, but I promise to do my best to make you happy."

CHAPTER 24

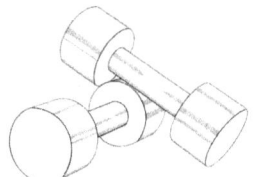

*P*aige's stomach grew tight as she and Gabe walked hand in hand into the house. The euphoria of a few minutes ago swallowed up by the discomfort of facing Marisol and admitting her part in this charade.

Gabe's mother beamed at them, her smile so big her cheeks would likely ache later. Grace's expression was both cheerful and quizzical. She searched first Gabe's face, then Paige's, no doubt trying to decide if what she just witnessed in the backyard was real or not.

Gabe pulled Paige to the loveseat where she sat beside him. "Mom, there's something I need to tell you."

"No need. I saw." Tears glistened in Marisol's eyes as she clapped her hands. "I'm so happy for you both."

"Thank you, but that's not what I need to confess." His grip on Paige's hand tightened as he sucked in a deep breath. "I lied to you. Paige isn't—wasn't..." He shook his head. "My girlfriend."

Marisol's brows dipped. "I don't understand."

"We've been lying to you from the beginning. We never dated prior to him bringing me to meet you two weeks ago." Paige expected Marisol's face to fill with anger or even shock and disappointment, but she almost looked like she fought a smile. "Please don't be upset with Gabe. He really is a good guy. He had the best of intentions when he lied to you about having a girlfriend."

"I know he did, Mija." Marisol leaned over and patted her knee.

Paige's heart stalled as the air whooshed from her lungs. Her surprise over Marisol's use of the endearment was eclipsed by the revelation that Gabe's mother knew all along they'd been lying.

"Wait. You *knew* it was all a lie?" Gabe found his voice before she did.

Marisol gave Gabe a patient smile. "You've always been very open with me, so I knew it wasn't true. The day you told me you had a serious girlfriend was the day I received my diagnosis. It was a very emotional day for us all. You saw how upset I was over not getting to see you and Grace married, which wasn't fair of me." Her remorseful look quickly morphed to a smile. "But you did what you do best. You went into 'fix-it' mode."

Her gaze shifted to Paige. "When he told me he was seeing someone, I peppered him with questions, thinking he'd give in and admit it wasn't true, but..." Marisol pointed a finger in the air. "When he said his girlfriend had the prettiest blue eyes and that her smile lit up the room, I could tell he was interested in someone."

Paige thought back to when Gabe would have told his mom he had a girlfriend. Had he been talking about her the whole time? She quirked an eyebrow at him.

Pinkness infused his tan complexion. "Guilty."

"Was that whole conversation at PT with Luke about you needing a fake girlfriend staged?"

"No way. The kid is lucky I didn't wring his neck." Then he grinned. "But I suppose I should thank him."

"I called Gabe's bluff," Marisol said. "I insisted on meeting you. I'll admit I was surprised when he actually produced a girlfriend. But right off the bat, I could see there was something special between you two. So, I continued to prod."

"Prod?" Paige's mind scrambled to process Marisol's words.

"I figured asking you to call me Mom and referring to you as the mother of my grandchildren would either push you away or bring you closer. Either way, I hoped it would be the wake-up call Gabe needed." Marisol sighed as her gaze returned to Gabe. "Ever since Harper left you at the altar, you've guarded your heart. You needed a push. A big one. That's why I gave you my mother's rings. I figured it would either make you face your feelings or scare Paige away for good." Her lips split into a grin. "I'm glad it wasn't the latter."

Paige was speechless. Gabe's mom had orchestrated her and Gabe's relationship to an extent.

"You apologized for lying to me, but I don't think you did." Marisol's expression turned smug.

"But Gabe and I were just doing each other a favor," Paige said, still reeling from Marisol's revelation.

"It may have started with false pretenses, but the first time I met you, I could see the chemistry there. So, you can't tell me it was all a lie." She leaned forward and locked gazes with Paige. "I don't believe you would have let him put my mother's ring on your finger if you weren't in love with him."

"I am in love with him," Paige said fervently, "but it's not that simple."

"What do you mean?" Marisol's brow furrowed as she frowned.

Grace chewed her bottom lip as her gaze bounced back and forth between them and her mom.

"Paige is not a former patient." The tension in Gabe's words seemed to suck the air from the room. "She's a current one."

Concern lined Marisol's face. "Oh dear. That does complicate things."

PAIGE PACED HER BEDROOM. It was a large room, but it wasn't big enough to absorb the nervous energy coursing through her. She really wanted to ride horses, but she kept forgetting to ask Gabe if he thought it would be okay.

How am I going to keep from slipping up?

She was so exhausted when she finally got home last night that she went straight to bed. She'd totally forgotten to take Gabe's grand-mother's ring off her finger until it glinted in the mirror as she brushed her teeth this morning. It was probably a good thing she'd slept in and skipped breakfast with her parents.

Despite tucking the ring into her purse, she'd fidgeted all through the church service, earning her concerned glances from her parents. To avoid questions, she'd feigned a headache and retreated to her room as soon as she got home. But she was so keyed up all she could do was pace.

She hated having to keep this a secret. That had been her only hesitation to saying yes to Gabe's proposal last night. At least his mother knew the truth, but even she agreed they should keep it under wraps until Gabe had a chance to talk to Dr. Stoker and her dad.

This was one of the happiest days of Paige's life, but she couldn't tell anyone, and it was killing her. As much as she trusted Riley, she couldn't share this secret with her. It was too risky. It could get back to her parents too easily if Riley let it slip.

Maybe I should call Grace.

They'd become good friends in the short time they'd known each other. She snatched up her phone from the bed, but instead of calling Grace, she found her cousin Damon's name. She hesitated only a moment before hitting the video call button. Then she continued to pace around the room as she waited for him to answer.

And waited.

And waited.

With a growl, she hit the end button and tossed her phone back on the bed. Then with a dramatic huff, she threw herself onto the bed as well.

I can't believe I'm engaged.

It still felt surreal how quickly and effortlessly she'd fallen in love with Gabe. She hadn't known him very long, but she felt certain he was the reason God brought her back to Providence. That meant things would all work out, didn't it?

She studied the bumpy texture of her ceiling, as she pondered the roadblocks in their path. She still needed to find a job here, and hopefully Gabe didn't lose his.

Her phone rang beside her, making her jump. She grabbed it and looked at the screen. Spotting Damon's face, she pushed to a sitting position.

"Hi, Damon."

Her cousin's face filled her screen. "Sorry I couldn't answer when you called. I was at the gym, and it was very noisy in there." Trees and a blue sky danced above his head as he walked. "How's my favorite cousin?"

"I'm kind of going crazy."

"Kind of?" Damon's brows hiked up as he looked into the phone. "Didn't that happen a long time ago?"

"Very funny." Paige stuck her tongue out at him before pushing to her feet to resume her pacing. "I seriously need to talk to someone."

Damon's image stopped bobbing on his screen, and the trees froze above his head. "Something happen between you and Riley?"

"No, I just can't talk to her about this."

"Is it Daniel? Did he start drinking again?" Damon's brow furrowed as his image started bobbing again.

"No, Daniel's doing great." Paige waved her arms in frustration. "But I can't talk to Ri about *this*."

Damon started walking again, a comical look on his face. "About what?"

"You have to promise not to tell a soul what I'm about to tell you." Paige pointed at her phone.

"Sounds serious. Are you sure it's something you should be telling me?"

"I need to talk to someone or I'm going to burst, but I can't risk it getting back to my parents."

"Does this have something to do with that jack—" He cleared his throat and changed his wording. "That jerk, Phillip?"

"Who?" Paige was taken back. Phillip couldn't possibly be farther from her mind.

"My mom told me how he played you. I'm sorry, Paige." The phone jostled around with Damon's face bouncing in and out of view, then the inside of his truck appeared. "It's a good thing I'm on the other side of the country, or I'd have driven to Seattle and broken every bone in his body." The movement of his phone settled, showing Damon's face again.

"No, this isn't about Phillip at all." Paige spun around, changing directions, and waved an arm through the air. "Well, I guess it kind of had something to do with him at first, but so much has happened since then, that all feels like ages ago."

"I have no idea what you're talking about. And I still don't understand why you can't talk to Riley about this." He held up a hand. "I mean, I'm glad you called me, but are you sure everything is okay between you two?"

"Yes, they're fine. I just can't risk her telling Daniel, and him letting it slip—to his parents or Jake and Robert." She made a broad circle with her arms. "If Aunt Faith gets wind of this, it'll be all over town in a heartbeat. Then my parents will find out, and that could be disastrous."

"What could be disastrous?" Despite the confusion filling Damon's face, he looked like he was on the verge of laughter.

He and Daniel had often accused her and Riley of being melodramatic. But Paige didn't feel like she was being overly dramatic. She was in love, and she wanted to shout it from the rooftops. Keeping it a secret was killing her.

She sucked in a deep breath, then blurted, "I'm engaged, and I can't tell any—"

"Whoa. Back up. You're engaged? I didn't know you were even dating anyone."

"I'm not. Not technically. I mean, we can't go out in public or anything." Paige couldn't help motioning with her hands.

"How did you get engaged to someone you haven't even dated?" Damon's brow furrowed. "And why can't you go out in public?"

"Because he's my physical therapist, and he could lose his job over this." She threw her hands up.

Now Damon's brows hiked up, his eyes wide. He opened his mouth to speak then closed it again.

"It was supposed to be fake, but then I fell for Gabe."

"I take it Gabe is your physical therapist?" When she nodded, he asked, "Why was it supposed to be fake?"

She was about to explain that Gabe needed a fake girlfriend because his mother had cancer, but Damon stopped her. "Paige, I need you to sit down and prop up your phone. You're talking with your hands while you pace, and you're making me dizzy."

"Fine." Paige dropped into the chair at her desk and propped her phone against the stack of overdue library books she had yet to read.

"Okay. Now start at the beginning." He barely glanced at his phone now, which meant he was driving.

Paige told Damon how she'd been attracted to Gabe from day one, about his mother's diagnosis, and her desire to see her children married. Then she went into Phillip showing up, trying to win her back.

"Let me guess, you had your physical therapist in mind when you told Phillip you were dating someone." Damon shot a lengthy glance toward his phone.

"Well, of course. I'd only been out of the rehabilitation center for a couple weeks by that time. It's not like I'd had a chance to meet anyone else. Especially in this small town."

"Okay, so you agreed to be Gabe's fake girlfriend. How did you go from that to being engaged?"

Paige continued with her story, sharing more personal information than Gabe would have liked, so Damon would understand why she'd fallen head over heels for her therapist.

"So now we're engaged, and I can't tell anyone." She dropped her head into her hands.

"Because it's taboo for doctors to date patients?"

"Yes."

"Your dad did." Damon shrugged.

"Technically, my mom was no longer his patient when he took her out."

"Only because she bailed on what was supposed to be their first date."

"She was vomiting." Paige defended her mom. "Her appendix had ruptured."

Their love story had a unique beginning. Her mom canceled on her blind date because she was throwing up, then two hours later, the doctor called in to remove her ruptured appendix turned out to be the man she'd stood up.

"What I'm saying is everyone in the small town of Providence got over it. Even the pious little old ladies, who like to gossip over everything and nothing at their book clubs and tea parties. They'll get over this too."

"But what if Gabe gets fired?"

"Then you'll weather the big storms early on in your relationship. If you love this guy as much as you say you do, then you'll stick by his side and find a way to make things work."

"I do love him. I've never felt surer about anything in my life. Even when I was hoping Phillip would propose there was always something in the back of my mind that made me question if he was the man for me." She spread her arms wide. "There is none of that with Gabe. I feel complete when I'm with him."

"So, find yourself a different therapist and marry this Gabe guy." Damon made it sound so simple.

"That means driving to the Tri-Cities area multiple times a week." She could get stuck working with Toa. That thought made her shudder.

"So?" Damon gave her a look of annoyance. "Do you want to marry this man? Or would you rather just keep pining after your physical therapist and risking his job?"

Paige dropped her gaze. "His life is really complicated right now. We decided not to rush the wedding for his mother's sake, because we really haven't known each other that long. But we don't know how long she'll be with us, and if she passes soon..." She shrugged one shoulder. "He's going to need time to grieve."

Damon shook his head. "I get that this is an inconvenient time to fall in love, but if it were me, I'd want the woman I love by my side through it all."

Gabe had said something similar last night. She'd agreed to the engagement for her own selfish purposes, knowing it would give her an opportunity to convince Gabe they could weather the loss of his mother together. But it touched her to know he *wanted* her by his side through it all.

A knock sounded on her door before it cracked open. Paige looked over her shoulder as her mom stuck her head into the room.

"Do you have a minute?"

"Uh...sure." She glanced back at her phone. She should let Damon go. She'd been talking to him for over an hour.

He'd given her a lot to think about. Could it be as simple as finding a new therapist?

"Hi, Aunt Hope," Damon called.

"Oh, you're chatting with Damon?" Mom walked into the room and stood behind Paige. "Hi, Damon. How is North Carolina?"

"Hot and muggy." His gaze shifted back. "Think about what I said, Paige, and keep me posted, so I can request leave." He winked at her. "Keep in mind, I'm scheduled to deploy again this fall."

The screen went dark.

"Head's up for what? What does he need to take leave for?" Curiosity filled Mom's voice.

"Nothing." Paige laid her phone face down as if that would make Mom forget what she'd just heard. "I was just wondering when he was going to come home again." She swiveled her chair to face her mom. "What's up?"

"How's your headache?" Concern lined Mom's face.

"It's letting up." Paige hated how accustomed she'd become to lying to her parents.

Mom's face morphed into a smile as she perched on the corner of Paige's bed. "I visited with Principal Jones' wife after church." Her grin grew as she clasped her hands together. "A position teaching fourth grade at the elementary school just opened up. Jenny Langston's husband got a big promotion that requires them to move to San Francisco."

"Are you serious?" Hope flared in Paige's chest, stealing her breath.

Could she really be so lucky to have a teaching job land in her lap just as the rest of her life was falling into place—except the part where she needed to keep her engagement to Gabe a secret, that is.

"I know you love teaching second grade, but if you're interested in making the shift to fourth…" Her mom gave her a hopeful look. "I think Mr. Jones would hire you in a heartbeat."

Paige couldn't believe Mr. Jones was still the principal at the elementary school. The man had to be pushing seventy.

"I do love teaching second grade, but…" Paige suppressed a squeal as she grinned. "I'm open to change."

"It'll be so nice to have you home for good." Mom clasped her hands. "You don't have to live here with me and your dad, of course. I'm sure you'd rather have your own space, but it will be so good to have you back in Providence."

"I want to move home, Mom. For now, anyway. It'll probably take me a while to find a place of my own, what with the housing shortage around here."

"It'll be so nice when Debbie and Austin Reed get those new apartments built." Mom's face grew thoughtful as she studied Paige's face. "You seem so happy lately. Being at home and rebuilding old friendships has been good for you." She put her hand on Paige's knee. "I'm so glad you didn't let what happened with Phillip keep you down."

"I am happy." Paige was dying to tell her mom the reason she was so happy. The fact that she couldn't tell her mother, whom she'd always been close to, about the best thing to ever happen to her put a damper on her day.

She was so tired of keeping secrets.

Her mom's grin widened. "Isn't it wonderful how the Lord guides us to the path we're meant to be on?" She gave Paige a quick hug then pointed a finger at her as she walked to the door. "Call Principal Jones while I tell your dad."

"But it's Sunday."

Mom waved a hand as she tapped on her phone. "I just sent you his number. His Sabbath will be more peaceful if he knows he has a teacher to fill Jenny's position."

Paige's own smile lingered. Yes, it was great how the Lord had guided her and remodeled her life. Now if only she and Gabe could announce their engagement, before it blew up in their faces.

CHAPTER 25

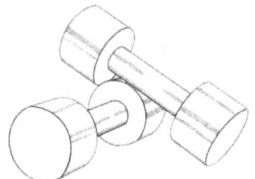

"*L*uke, take over here." Gabe stopped Sam's sideways motion when Paige walked through the door. His heart beat a little faster at the sight of her. "I'll help Paige today."

He'd been eagerly waiting for her arrival for the last hour, full of anxious energy that made it impossible to sit still.

Luke's shrug looked nonchalant, but the question on his face as he took Gabe's place spoke volumes.

The younger man's confusion was understandable since Gabe usually avoided working with Paige until the end of each PT session. He'd thought keeping his distance from her would curb his attraction, but it had only made him jealous every time Paige laughed at one of Luke's corny jokes.

"Hey, Paige, you're late," Nikki said from the middle table where she stretched her IT band.

"I know. I had to push my appointment back because I had a job interview this morning."

Gabe grinned as he prepped her heat packs. When he talked to her on the phone last night, she'd told him she might have an opportunity for a teaching job at the local elementary. He couldn't wait to hear how her interview went.

Things were falling into place.

"Really?" Gladys asked. "Where?"

"At the elementary school."

"Here in Providence? Are you planning on moving home for good?" Surprise lifted Gladys' pencil-drawn brows.

"That's the plan." Paige grinned, brightening the room and his day.

He approached her with heat packs in his hands, a smile of his own on his face until Nikki beat him to the question he was dying to ask Paige.

"So how did the interview go?" Nikki forgot she was supposed to be stretching.

He locked gazes with Paige as he tucked a heat pack around her hip. "I'd like to know too." There were so many things he wanted to say to Paige without an audience.

He rehearsed all day yesterday what he planned to say to Dr. Stoker tomorrow, but he was still unsure how to approach Dr. Young. With him, the conversation would be about more than Gabe dating a patient. It would be asking for his daughter's hand.

"It went great!" Paige's cheerful voice pulled him from his thoughts. "By law, they have to post the job for a certain period of time, but you're essentially looking at the new fourth-grade teacher at Providence Elementary."

A chorus of "that's great" and "congratulations" swept through the room. Gabe wanted to wrap her in a hug, but he refrained, giving her a high five instead. It was another confirmation they were on the path they were supposed to be on.

He wanted to perch on the edge of Paige's table and simply talk to her, but the ladies had other plans. First, Gladys shared tips for teaching fourth graders, then Nikki changed the subject to the latest chick flick to hit the box office. Despite moving around the room as they did their exercises, they kept a string of conversations going for the next hour.

Gabe felt left out, but he loved it. This was exactly the comfortable atmosphere he'd hoped to have in his physical therapy office.

Around noon, he was working on Gladys' knee when the door

opened. He looked up, thinking Travis was early, and froze when he saw Evelyn Tate, his mother's best friend.

What is she doing here?

He vaguely remembered Luke mentioning last week that Evelyn had scheduled an appointment here in Providence. At the time, he hadn't thought anything of it. But he got engaged Saturday night which changed everything.

His mom had promised not to tell anyone about the engagement until he'd had a chance to come clean with Dr. Stoker and Dr. Young. Then she apologized yesterday for telling Evelyn he was engaged. His mom's friend knew she planned to give him his grandmother's wedding rings, and she wanted to hear all about his reaction.

"But I didn't tell her Paige was a current patient. So if by chance it gets back to Dr. Stoker, he won't know that you've been seeing a patient." Mom's effort to smooth things over hadn't been at all reassuring, and with Paige's excitement over the prospect of a new job, he'd forgotten to tell her Evelyn knew of their engagement.

This could be bad.

"Hey, Evelyn," Luke greeted the woman before Gabe found his voice. "I can't believe you drove all the way to Providence for PT."

"It's better than working with that stuffed shirt, Toa. I try to make sure I end up on Dr. Stoker's schedule, but with Gabe here three days a week, he's busier than ever. So I get stuck with Toa way too often." The tall, slender woman's lips turned up when she spotted Gabe. "Congratulations, Gabe. I couldn't believe it when your mother told me the news." She crossed the room with her arms spread wide and wrapped him in a hug "She's so excited you're engaged."

Gabe's stomach plummeted so fast it created a vacuum that squeezed his chest and sucked the air from his lungs. He'd never wished harder for the ground to open up and swallow him than he did at that moment. Bury him alive. He deserved it. It couldn't be any worse than having to claw his way out of the pit his lies had created.

Weights clanked on the other side of the room, and audible gasps filled the space that had gone utterly silent. His gaze jumped to Paige, his eyes full of apology.

Her face registered confusion and panic.

Oblivious to the collective shock of the room's occupants, Evelyn dumped a truck load of dirt into his pit. "Your mom says Paige is perfect for you. She absolutely adores her."

"You and Paige are engaged?" Nikki's voice, full of surprise and excitement, sounded shrill in the quiet room. "Every time I asked how things were going with your fake relationship, you told me there was nothing to report. But now you guys are suddenly engaged?" Her accusing gaze darted between him and Paige, who stood next to the weight set attached to the wall, eyes closed, her head slowly shaking.

Luke's eyes were almost as wide as his grin.

Gladys wore a similar expression.

Even the right side of Sam's lips turned up, the twinkle in his eyes showing his amusement.

"Fake?" Evelyn's jaw dropped as her own gaze darted around the room. "What is she talking about?" Her full focus landed back on Gabe again.

"Do you have something to share with the class, Gabe?" Gladys blinked up at him with innocent eyes. She was giving him a chance to come clean with them, but he wasn't fooled. She wanted the scoop just as much as Nikki.

He looked at Paige again. Posture rigid, her expression was a mixture of shock and desperation. She gave a small shake of her head, but he was tired of lying, so he pasted on a smile.

"Paige and I have an announcement to make." He walked over to where she stood stiff and unmoving and put his arm around her. She didn't reciprocate. "We got engaged on Saturday."

The room erupted.

"Yay!" Nikki cheered. "I can't believe you didn't keep us in the loop like you promised."

"Congratulations!" Gladys smiled like she'd known all along.

"I knew it." Luke pointed at them. "It was so obvious you two had a thing for each other."

Even Sam grunted something that sounded like, "Attaboy."

"Wait a minute." Evelyn's voice rose above the rest as she walked toward him and Paige. "*This* is Paige? A current patient? Not a former one?" Her brows inched up with each question. "And what is this about a fake relationship?"

The rest of the room quieted, and Gabe scrambled for the words that wouldn't cause his world to come crashing down around him.

"Evelyn, I'd like you to meet Paige Young, my fiancée. Paige, this is my mom's best friend Evelyn Tate." He lifted his chin and met Evelyn's gaze. "Yes, she is a current patient."

"But you told your mom—"

"I know what I told my mom, Evelyn. I lied to her to make her final days happy." He recalled his mom's tears of joy when he and Paige returned to the living room hand in hand Saturday night. "And it has." He stared at her, daring her to argue.

Coming clean with his mom and knowing Paige would be by his side through it all had helped him find a measure of peace concerning letting his mother go. He would always wish he had more time with her, but he was trying to focus on gratitude. Gratitude for the last twelve years he'd enjoyed with her.

Evelyn pointed at Nikki. "But she said this was a fake relationship."

"It started out that way, but we fell in love." He tugged Paige, who had yet to soften, a little closer to his side.

"So, you're dating a patient?" Evelyn's expression hardened as she folded her arms. "Isn't that against your code of conduct or something? Does Dr. Stoker know?"

He kept his head high, hoping they wouldn't notice the perspiration forming on his brow. "Yes, it's against the ethical guidelines of the American Medical Association, and I could very well lose my job over it. I will be discussing my engagement with Dr. Stoker tomorrow. I would appreciate it if you'd keep this information to yourself for now." His heart raced, pounding against the tightness of his ribcage. He'd asked so many people to keep his secrets that he was losing track. "At least until I have a chance to talk to Paige's dad and Dr. Stoker." He looked around the room with a pleading expression. "That goes for all of you. Please, give me twenty-four hours before you say anything to anyone."

Evelyn's expression softened a little, but her disapproval was apparent in the lines around her mouth. "And when do you plan to come clean with your mother?"

"I told my mother the truth after Paige and I got engaged. She knows everything." That had taken a huge load off his mind.

"I sure hope you know what you're doing." Evelyn shook her head, disapproval still lingered in her eyes. "You could lose your license for dating a patient."

"I know, but it's a sacrifice I'm willing to make for the woman I love." He turned to Paige, but she stepped away.

She shook her head vigorously and backed away from him. "I'm sorry, Gabe. I can't do this." Tears filled her eyes as she bolted to the door.

For the second time in a matter of minutes, Gabe's stomach plummeted—this time through the floor. His heart followed, leaving a gaping hole in his chest.

"Paige, wait." He stood dumbfounded, trying to figure out what he'd done wrong. He thought he'd handled the whole thing quite well, so he couldn't understand why she'd walked out on him.

Heat filled his face as he looked around the room, spotting the sympathetic faces. There were fewer witnesses to his humiliation this time than when Harper left him at the altar, but that didn't mean it hurt any less.

"Why are you just standing there?" Gladys jerked him from his stupor. "Go after her. You can't work out whatever is wrong if you don't talk to her."

He nodded repeatedly as his feet pulled him toward the door. He shot Luke a desperate look before walking out.

"I got this, man." The younger man waved. "Go after her."

"Thanks." Gabe raced down the short hall to the exit, desperate to catch Paige before she drove away.

$\sim$

Bright sunlight blinded Paige when she stepped outside. Her eyes watered, creating more tears that blurred her vision. She shaded her eyes and hurried to her car.

"Paige, wait!"

She turned to see Gabe coming out the door, shading his own eyes. Part of her wished she'd been able to walk fast enough to get away, the other part was glad he'd come after her.

He jogged over to her. "Talk to me, please."

"I'm sorry." She swiped at her eyes. "I just..." She fanned herself and sucked in a deep breath as she tried to make sense of the overwhelming emotions swirling around inside her. Emotions that tightened her chest and made her feel like she might vomit.

Humiliation for being caught in their lies and the gossip that could trigger. Fear that Gabe might really lose his job. And dread that something would ruin this amazing thing she'd found with Gabe.

"Mi amor." He pulled her into his arms, wrapping her in his calming warmth. "I'm sorry for whatever I said or did that upset you, but I can't fix it if I don't know what's wrong."

She chuckled. "Spoken like a man who has spent his life surrounded by women."

He pulled back and wiped a tear from her cheek. "I learned a long time ago that an apology goes a long way, even if I don't know what I'm apologizing for."

"I just felt so overwhelmed by everything. Everyone was staring at me like a bug under a microscope. And I panicked." She pushed away from him and fanned herself again.

"I'm sorry I forgot to tell you last night that Mom told Evelyn about our engagement. She knew Mom gave me the ring Saturday night and wanted to know how we reacted." He shook his head. "I'm sorry it all came out like that. I had hoped to keep it under wraps until I'd spoken with your dad and Dr. Stoker."

"Eight months, Gabe." She lifted her chin and looked him in the eye. "That's how long Phillip kept his relationship with me hidden. I was his dirty little secret." She sucked in a deep breath. "I don't want the community I grew up in finding out through the rumor mill that

I've been secretly seeing my physical therapist. I can't bear to hear the criticism and see the judgment on their faces." Tears flooded her eyes again.

"I don't want that kind of gossip either. I promise I'm going to make it right."

"I know. I just freaked out at hearing you ask everyone to continue to keep this a secret." She jerked a hand toward the hospital. "I'm caught up in living a lie all over again, and I'm afraid somebody will let something slip, and it's all going to blow up in our faces."

"Me too."

"Do you really think you will lose your job over this? I mean, we've always known that was a possibility, but hearing Evelyn point out that you could lose your license, it hit me at how dire the consequences could be for you."

He let out a heavy sigh as he raked his fingers through his hair. "In the beginning, I tried to distance myself from you during PT, because I knew exactly what the risks were for getting involved with a patient. When you agreed to be my fake girlfriend, I tried to tell myself I wasn't crossing any boundaries, because there wasn't an emotional attachment. But then I made the mistake of holding your hand and kissing you. I fell for you so fast after that." He put his hands on her shoulders. "I never should have lied to my mom in the first place, but I don't regret it, Paige. If I hadn't been so intent on making her happy, I would have kept my emotions locked up. I never would have let my guard down and let myself fall in love with you."

Tears sprang to Paige's eyes. "Falling in love shouldn't cost you your job and your reputation."

"God willing, it won't." He locked gazes with her. "I meant what I said to Evelyn. I don't want to lose my job, but if I need to give it up to have you in my life, I will."

She was touched that Gabe would give up his dream for her. But he shouldn't have to make that kind of sacrifice. She dug in her purse for his grandmother's ring.

"I think we should break off our engagement until we no longer have to keep secrets. Maybe you'll be less likely to lose your job if we aren't involved in any kind of relationship."

His face fell when she held the ring out to him. "Paige, no. I've already requested a meeting with Dr. Stoker tomorrow morning." He shifted from one foot to the other. "And I'm hoping to catch your dad after work today."

Poor guy. Talking to her dad about this whole thing would be doubly difficult.

She pressed the ring into his palm. "I still think it's best if we aren't involved until after everything is cleared up." Which would hopefully only be twenty-four hours. With her heart feeling like it might split in two, she walked the short distance to her car and opened the door.

He followed her. "It won't change anything. The damage is done. I'm going to tell them the truth; that I've fallen in love with one of my patients."

Fresh tears welled up in her eyes. "Good, but I still think it best we take a step back. Just until we can move forward without pretenses and secrets." She put a hand on his arm. "It might help if I talk to my dad before you do."

"No." He squared his shoulders. "It was my lies that got us into this whole mess in the first place. I need to face the music."

"Call me tonight?" When he nodded, she turned to climb into her car then remembered one other thing. "By the way, I called the office in Pasco this morning. Dr. Stoker's schedule is booked solid for the next two weeks. Looks like I'm stuck with Toa."

When they talked on the phone last night about her driving to Pasco for PT, Gabe said he'd make sure Dr. Stoker fit her into his schedule, but that might be easier said than done.

"We'll figure it out." He stepped close and took her into his arms again. "Don't give up on me, Paige. I'm going to do everything I can to fix this."

"I'm not giving up on you. On us." She wrapped her arms around his waist and laid her head against his shoulder. "But I am going pray really hard that this doesn't cost you your job."

"I'd appreciate that."

CHAPTER 26

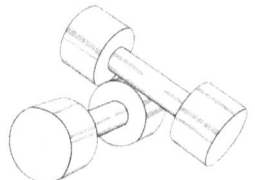

*G*abe's leg bounced as his eyes scanned Dr. Young's office. Other than his undergrad and medical school degrees, a family picture in which Paige was a teenager was the only decor on the walls.

He rolled his shoulders, willing himself to relax. If he acted nervous, Dr. Young would pick up on that and assume he was guilty of more than falling in love with a patient.

I am guilty of more.

It wouldn't surprise him if word had already spread throughout the hospital complex—or worse yet, town—about the fiasco in the PT office this morning. When he'd returned to the gym after Paige drove away, he'd been pelted with questions. His response that everything was fine between him and Paige was yet another lie, but his expression must have been grim enough they hadn't hounded him for details.

He was hopeful if he presented his case to Dr. Stoker in the right manner, he wouldn't lose his job. But he didn't know Dr. Young well enough to know how he'd respond to Gabe dating a patient, who happened to be his daughter.

He still couldn't believe Paige had broken up with him. Sort of.

Maybe she was right. It would be so much easier to move forward with their relationship if they weren't keeping secrets. Regardless of the outcome of his talks with Dr. Young and Dr. Stoker, he planned to camp on Paige's doorstep after everything was out in the open. He'd make an even bigger nuisance of himself than Phillip had, until she took the ring back.

He wouldn't make the same mistake he made with Harper. He loved Paige, and he refused to let her slip away.

"Gabe," Dr. Young's booming voice made Gabe jump. "My medical assistant just told me you wanted to speak to me. I hope I didn't keep you waiting too long." He held out his hand.

Gabe bolted to his feet and shook Dr. Young's hand. "No, sir. I haven't been waiting long." Despite being anxious to get this over with, Gabe wouldn't have minded waiting another hour.

"You can drop the 'sir'. We're colleagues here. Call me James." Dr. Young motioned to the chair Gabe had been sitting in as he rounded his desk. "Have a seat."

Gabe dropped back into the padded chair, certain Dr. Young would change his mind about the first name thing after he learned why Gabe was here.

James rocked back in his chair. "I've heard good things about you."

"You have?" Gabe's shoulders sagged in relief.

"Absolutely. Gladys Murdock swears you're the best thing to ever happen to this town. Travis seems to be making a great recovery, and Paige is doing well also. She keeps telling me how knowledgeable and skilled you are."

Gabe appreciated that Paige sang his praises at home, but he couldn't let himself be sidetracked by compliments. He sucked in a deep breath. "I really appreciate you taking a chance on me and giving me the opportunity to run the office here, but there's something I need to confess."

James' jovial smile faded as his brows arched.

"I've let you down, sir." Calling Dr. Young by his first name in this situation didn't seem appropriate. Gabe was tempted to hang his head, but he maintained eye contact with the older man.

"How so?"

"I've behaved unethically in regard to one of my patients."

James' brows lowered into a single unit. His lips pressed into a thin line, his jaw taking on a hard edge. "Explain."

"I've fallen in love with...one of my patients." Gabe gripped the arms of the chair to keep from tugging at the collar of his shirt. "With your daughter, sir."

James' brows shot up, and his mouth dropped open for a split second before his lips pinched together again. He dropped his gaze to his clasped hands. "How did this come about?"

"Well, sir, I've been attracted to Paige from day one. Not just her looks. Her determination to get better, and her willingness to push through the pain and work hard impressed me. But the unethical part is that she's been pretending to be my girlfriend for the past month."

Probably best not to mention that he'd proposed to her last weekend, especially since she gave the ring back today.

"Pretending?" James' head came back up. A deep crease furrowed his brows. "What do you mean?"

"My mother has pancreatic cancer and doesn't have long to live." Gabe took a deep breath, attempting to steel his emotions. "Her biggest regret is that she never got to meet my spouse—or my sister's. On impulse, I lied to her and told her I was seeing someone in an attempt to make her final days happier." He held up a hand before James could say anything. "I know, I should never have lied to her. But I did. It made her extremely happy to hear that I had a girlfriend, so I felt the need to follow through and find someone to play the part."

"I'm very sorry to hear about your mother, Gabe." James leaned forward and rested his elbows on his desk, his hands still clasped. "As a parent, I understand your mother's concerns for her children. There is peace of mind that comes with knowing your children are in healthy, happy relationships." It almost looked like his lips turned up before he schooled his features. "So, you asked Paige to pretend to be your girlfriend?"

"Not technically. Luke, my assistant, has a big mouth and made it known to some of my patients that I was looking for a fake girlfriend.

Paige made it clear she wasn't interested. Then Phillip showed up, pressuring her to take him back."

James' brows dropped low again, and his clasped hands separated to curl into fists. "Let me guess…you stepped in to play the role of *her* fake boyfriend?"

"Yes, but not before she'd already volunteered to be my fake girl-friend." Gabe couldn't resist any longer; he tugged at the collar of his shirt. Boy, was it hot in here. "I was still undecided whether I'd take her up on her offer when Phillip showed up at PT, making a scene. I felt obligated to back her up at that point."

"He showed up here?" James' brows shot up again as he tapped his desk with a finger.

"I believe it was the day after he first came to town. He kept insisting Paige give him a chance to prove he could be faithful."

Dr. Young snorted. "That snake doesn't have a faithful bone in his body."

"Comparing him to an octopus would be more apt, sir. Spineless and slimy. With tentacles spreading in too many directions."

Gabe considered telling Paige's father about the "offer" Phillip made her the last time he turned up on her doorstep but decided against it. Even though it might paint him in a better light, it would only anger James, and that wouldn't help his cause.

"True." A mask of serious professionalism slipped over the older man's face. "You mentioned unethical behavior. What boundaries have been crossed?"

Gabe squirmed as he searched for the right words that wouldn't cost him his job or favor with the man he hoped would someday be his father-in-law. Technically, he and Paige hadn't even dated, unless hanging out with his mom and sister could be considered dating. But they had held hands and kissed multiple times, which were inappro-priate behaviors for doctors to engage in with their patients.

Gabe opened his mouth to speak, but Dr. Young beat him to it. "You've obviously spent time together outside the office. I assume every time Paige told us she was hanging out with Angie, she was spending time with you?"

"Yes, sir. But we've always spent that time with my mom and sister. We've never even been on a real date. Although we have held hands and kis—"

James' hand shot up. "I don't need the details, unless you've crossed the line...by having sexual relations with my...with a patient." He pinned Gabe with a stare.

"No, sir. Of course not."

"Have you broken professional boundaries with Paige during her PT sessions?"

"No. Luke can vouch that nothing inappropriate has happened between me and Paige during PT."

He bit his tongue to keep from blurting out that he almost kissed Paige at the pool that one day. He felt the need for full disclosure, but he doubted Dr. Young wanted to hear how badly he'd wanted to kiss the water droplets from her lips.

"Good." Dr. Young slowly nodded.

"I'll understand if you want me to step down from running the PT office here. I'm sure Dr. Stoker can recommend another therapist."

"Don't even think about leaving me high and dry with the physical therapy office. We need you too badly here for you to leave." Dr. Young pointed a finger at Gabe. "Dr. Stoker said you're the best Summit has to offer. I'm not interested in bringing in a sub-par therapist."

Gabe couldn't hide his smile as he heaved a sigh of relief. "With this office being an extension of the one in Pasco, I feel obligated to inform Dr. Stoker of my involvement with Paige."

"That's your call." James waved a hand. "If he has concerns tell him to call me." Then he shook his head. "But I suppose it wouldn't be appropriate for you to continue to work with Paige if you guys are seeing each other."

"Paige has already scheduled PT at the office in Pasco."

"By hiring you, I'd hoped to help her avoid having to make that trip multiple times a week." Dr. Young grimaced and shrugged one shoulder. "But it's probably for the best."

Encouraged with how things had gone thus far, Gabe slowly

nodded, sucking up the courage to ask for Paige's hand in marriage. The older man beat him to the punch.

"So, I guess this is the part where I ask: What are your intentions concerning my daughter?" Dr. Young pinned Gabe again with another piercing, blue-eyed stare.

"I love her, sir." Gabe's gaze dropped to the front of the desk for a moment. "I told her a few weeks ago that I couldn't make her any promises because I need to devote all the time I can to my mother for as long as she's with us, but the truth is…I can't bear to face losing my mom without Paige by my side. I want to marry her."

"I suppose there's only one thing to do then." Dr. Young leaned back in his seat and grinned. "Would you like to join my wife and I, and Paige of course, for dinner tonight?" He looked at the clock on the wall. "At Charity's Diner in an hour?"

"Excuse me?" Gabe's jaw dropped.

When Gabe walked into Dr. Young's office thirty minutes ago, he was certain he'd not only leave jobless, but he'd also be devastated, because Dr. Young would refuse to let him have anything to do with his daughter. A dinner invitation was the last thing he'd expected.

"Word will eventually get out that you're seeing my daughter, if they haven't already. People in small towns can be quite judgmental. The best way to combat the gossip about the new physical therapist dating a patient is to show that my wife and I approve of your relationship."

Approve.

Gabe sagged back in his seat and sucked in a deep breath. It was a good thing he was sitting, or he might have collapsed from the sudden weakness in his muscles.

Dr. Young hadn't fired him. He'd invited Gabe to dinner with his wife. And Paige would be there.

How could Gabe possibly say no?

"Thank you, I'd love to join you for dinner. But are you sure your wife will approve?"

James chuckled. "Oh, I have no doubt she will be tickled pink by this development. And I can't wait to hear you and Paige share the details of your *fake* relationship with her." He laughed again as he got to his feet.

Warmth crept up Gabe's neck at the thought of sharing how he fell in love with Paige in a busy restaurant. He rose as well. "I have to say, sir, you've handled this much better than I expected."

"Let's just say I've been in your shoes. I fell in love with Hope the first time I saw her." James clapped him on the back. "Right before I removed her ruptured appendix."

Gabe looked forward to dinner more than ever now. He couldn't wait to hear more about James and Hope's romance. And he couldn't wait to see Paige again. But he needed to go back to the office and finish some paperwork first.

PAIGE GUIDED HONEY, the gentlest horse she'd ever ridden, to the hitching post outside the stables at the Double Diamond ranch. She looked down at how far away the ground was and cringed. She didn't relish trying to get her stiff, achy backside out of the saddle.

Her cousin Jake walked out of the stables, and she breathed a sigh of relief.

"Boy, am I glad to see you back in one piece." Jake had been hesitant to let her get on a horse when she showed up begging to go for a ride.

She'd assured him she had approval from her physical therapist to ride if she didn't trot or gallop. Thank goodness she'd remembered to ask Gabe about riding on the phone last night, because she was way too keyed up after breaking off her engagement to go home and face her mother.

"How was your ride?"

"It was great, but I think I need your help getting down."

Jake reached up to her waist and help her off the horse. "Did you spend this whole time in the saddle? No wonder you're stiff."

Paige had no idea what time it was, but she'd been riding for hours.

"No, I got off and walked a little here and there. But the ride back was the longest stretch, and my muscles all tightened up." She shook first one leg then the other as the pins and needles hit.

Paige had also spent nearly an hour at one of the prettiest spots on the ranch. Where she enjoyed the fresh air, listened to the water rushing over the small waterfall, and poured out her heart to God.

She prayed everything would go well when Gabe talked to her dad and Dr. Stoker. She truly believed Gabe was the reason God brought her home. Now, she needed to have faith that He would work everything out.

At least Gabe's mom knew the truth now. She was certain her parents would be happy for her when she told them she was in love with Gabe, but she couldn't guarantee the doctor side of her father would approve. And she'd never met Dr. Stoker, so she had no idea how Gabe's talk with him would go, but she'd prayed that both men would be understanding.

Jake started unsaddling Honey. "I was beginning to think I'd have to call in a search party to help find you. I didn't look forward to telling your parents I let you go and hurt yourself."

"I'm sorry, I didn't mean to worry you. I should have called or texted to let you know I was okay."

"You probably wouldn't have had any service, you know how the ranch is. Jake gave a sheepish grin as he shrugged. "And you know me, I would have worried anyway, even if you'd checked in."

He managed it well, but Jake had always had anxiety.

Paige patted his shoulder. "I really appreciate you letting me ride. It was exactly what I needed today."

"I'm glad to see you making a full recovery." He studied her face for a moment. "You're starting to look like your old self. You look happy."

"I am happy." Paige beamed. She couldn't wait to tell everyone why she was so happy.

She helped brush Honey down before saying goodbye to Jake and getting in her car. Her phone dinged before she made it to the highway. She picked it up to find a text from her mom.

Dinner at Charity's at 6:30. Don't be late.

Paige glanced at the clock on her dash. It was already after six, and she had a twenty-minute drive to town. She'd make it, but she wouldn't have time to go home and shower first.

It wasn't unusual for her parents to decide to go out to dinner at the last minute, but Mom demanding she not be late was odd. Had Gabe had a chance to talk to her dad already, or did he have to stay late with patients tonight?

She didn't want to step on Gabe's toes, but she vowed not to leave Charity's Diner without telling her parents the truth. Even though she didn't look forward to it, she needed to come clean about everything. She'd rather not do it in a public place, but she was committed to coming clean as soon as possible.

The closer she got to Providence, the tighter her stomach clenched. So much so, she lost her appetite which was surprising since she'd skipped lunch.

She was only a few minutes late by the time she parked beside her mother's car at the diner. She was almost to the entrance when she spotted a familiar blue car that looked like Gabe's.

Did he plan to talk to her dad over dinner in what was usually a crowded restaurant? The prospect made her stomach churn.

Maybe that's a good thing. Dad will be less likely to get angry in public.

She hurried inside and came to a screeching halt. There was no mistaking the broad muscular shoulders and black, wavy hair of the man who sat across the table from her parents. A table smack dab in the middle of the restaurant. Where everyone could see them.

"Ah, there she is now." Her mom's voice rose above the low din of the diner as she waved at Paige.

Gabe stood and faced her. The broad grin on his face sent her heart racing. He winked at her, his impossibly long eyelashes dipping, as he closed the distance between them.

She put her hand in his outstretched one, letting the tension drain from her body. He used it to pull her into his arms.

"In case it's not obvious, my talk with your father went well." His breath against her ear sent shivers racing down her spine. "So far, I still have a job."

"Good." She leaned back enough to see his face. "He wasn't angry?"

"I think he was more concerned about finding a new therapist than he was about the fact that I'd fallen in love with his daughter."

She laughed and leaned in for a kiss. Tingles of electricity zinged through her body as Gabe tightened his embrace and claimed her mouth.

Her euphoria was interrupted, however, by her mom's not so quiet whispers. "What's going on? Did you know about this, James? Why am I the last to know?"

"Hush, they'll tell you everything when they come up for air."

Gabe pulled his lips from hers and laughed. "Your dad is looking forward to hearing us share the whole story with your mom."

"Right." A hint of tension returned to her shoulders.

She peeked around Gabe. At least her dad already knew, and he didn't look upset. Her mom should be an easy sell. She took Gabe's hand and approached the table.

"Surprise!" She gave a cheerful, if somewhat tense, smile as she and Gabe took their seats.

"Hope, our daughter has something she wants to tell us." Her dad gave her a pointed look that held only a hint of the disappointment she'd expected to see on his face.

"I do." Paige fiddled with the edge of the new menu she'd helped Amy design. "But first, I owe you both an apology for lying to you over the last month." She paused, expecting a barrage of questions, but evidently her and Gabe's public display of affection had already answered most of them. "I haven't been spending my Saturdays with Angie. I've been spending them with Gabe and his family."

"Why would you lie to us about that?" Mom's eyes were full of hurt.

Paige's stomach clenched as it dropped. That look. That was the look every child hated seeing on their parents' faces. Paige hated knowing she was the cause of it.

"Because I asked her to." Gabe took Paige's hand, easing her discomfort. "I knew there could be dire consequences to dating a patient, but I needed Paige to pretend to be my girlfriend, so I asked her not to tell anyone."

"*Pretend* to be your girlfriend?" Mom's disappointment changed to confusion, creasing her brow. "Why on earth would a good-looking guy like you need a *fake* girlfriend?"

"That was my thought too," Paige said. She leaned forward in her seat and looked her mom in the eye. "His mom has pancreatic cancer."

Her mother lost a good friend to pancreatic cancer two years ago. It was already well into stage four by the time it was diagnosed, and her friend passed away five weeks later. Mom understood how deadly the disease was.

Mom's eyes grew misty as she looked at Gabe. "I'm so sorry you and your family are going through this."

"Thank you."

When Gabe's Adam's apple bobbed repeatedly, Paige jumped back in. "His mom was heartbroken that she never got to see Gabe and his sister get married."

"Married?" Her parents said in unison, before Dad's gaze cut to Gabe.

Gabe raised both hands in surrender. "I only wanted my mom to see that I was in a happy relationship. I never intended for it to go that far."

Dad's brows hiked up, his eyes widening.

Oh boy, that didn't help.

"You didn't *intend* for it to go that far?" A fresh sheen of tears filled Mom's eyes. "Did you guys elope?"

Realizing how quiet the diner had become, Paige looked around. Every head was turned in their direction. Marie, their waitress, hovered off to the side, uncertain whether she should approach their table to take their orders.

Paige turned to Gabe with a grin. "Instead of rumors flying that you're dating a patient, the gossip mill will be full of the news that we secretly eloped." This was one time she didn't mind being the subject of gossip. As far as she was concerned, the sooner she was married to Gabe, the better.

"What?" Gabe's eyes bulged. Before she could explain to him how fast news traveled in a small town, he rushed to assure her parents. "No, no, no. We're not married."

Deciding to have a little fun with him, Paige pouted. "Only because we've had to keep it all a secret."

Gabe scowled at her before turning back to her father. "We haven't secretly gotten married, but I do want to marry your daughter." His gaze jumped to her mom.

Paige leaned into him to whisper in his ear but kept her voice loud enough her parents could hear. "Do you still have the ring I gave back to you, honey?"

"Ring?" Her father shot Gabe a stern look. "You didn't tell me you'd proposed already."

"Uh...no, sir." Gabe shifted uncomfortably in his seat. "I mean I did propose last Saturday, but Paige gave the ring back this afternoon. So I didn't think it was important to mention at the time."

"It most certainly is important." Dad's words sounded stern, but Paige spotted the twinkle in his eyes. He was enjoying the moment as much as she was.

Paige laughed out loud. She couldn't help it. She was just so happy.

Gabe squeezed her hand. "You're not helping."

"Sorry." She chuckled again. "I figured if our story was going to travel the grapevine, I may as well make sure it was interesting."

"Wait a minute." Mom raised both hands in the air as if quieting a bunch of teenagers. "Would you two please back up and explain to me why Gabe needed a fake girlfriend—and how that came to be you?" She pointed her finger at Paige then Gabe. "And I want every juicy detail that led up to you proposing to my daughter."

Paige waved Marie over, so they could place their orders before she and Gabe took turns filling her parents in on everything that had happened over the past month. She didn't care that dozens of people in the diner overheard their conversation. She was happy, and she wanted the world to know it.

Her mom laughed when she told them about Marisol insisting Paige call her mom the first day they met, since they would be related soon. Then her dad joined in when she recited Marisol's argument that "a mother should never come between her son and the future mother of her grandchildren" to convince Paige to sit in the front seat on the drive to Yakima.

"I should have known something was up with you," Mom said. "I was so glad to see you coming out of the depressive funk you'd been in since the accident that I didn't question it." She grinned and winked. "I should have guessed it had something to do with a man."

When Paige insisted Gabe show her parents his grandmother's wedding ring, he pulled it from his pocket. Warmth rushed through her as she recalled Gabe's sweet proposal and how well the ring had fit her finger.

"Oh, that is pretty." Mom took the ring and studied it. Then her lips turned up as she handed the ring back to Gabe. "I can't believe my baby girl is engaged."

Paige fought the urge to reach out and take the ring. She wanted to insist Gabe put it back on her finger. Despite the positive recent turn of events, she ached for the connection that promised a future with him.

"I'm not. Well, not at the moment," Paige said, her voice full of disappointment. "I insisted Gabe take the ring back this afternoon. I wanted to clear the air with you guys and Dr. Stoker before we made it official."

"Well, I'm thrilled." Mom pressed a hand to her chest. "I'm very happy for you both."

Dad looked at Gabe. "You've worked more closely with Paul than I have, but I've known him for many years. He's a reasonable man. If certain boundaries haven't been crossed, like we discussed earlier..." He gave Gabe a pointed look. "I think you'll be fine. And like I said, I'm happy to put in a good word for you, if need be."

Paige wasn't sure what boundaries he referred to, but she could guess. She blinked back tears as she mouthed, "Thank you." It meant the world to her that her father was willing to help ensure her happiness.

An hour later, she and Gabe waved goodbye to her parents, then she insisted he take a drive with her. She drove them up to the bluff where they could watch the sunset.

Brow cocked, he followed her lead when she climbed out and slid onto the hood of her car. She leaned back against the windshield. He'd barely settled beside her before she burst into laughter.

"Okay, this is not as comfortable and romantic as it was in my head." She sat up.

"Wait. Let's try again." He tugged her back into his arms, his shoulder cushioning her head. "Better?"

"Much." She settled into him, letting the fear and worry drain from her body. "How do you think Dr. Stoker will take the news?"

"If he responds even half as well as your father, I'll still have a job at the end of the day tomorrow." He stroked her arm. "I hate making you drive to Pasco for PT, but it's the best way to combat the gossip mongers and preserve my reputation as a physical therapist."

She angled her head to look at him. "It's okay, I'll do it. I can put up with Toa or Gary if it means we can be together."

"If Dr. Stoker insists you do PT there, I will insist he fit you into *his* schedule."

"Will you call or at least text me after you talk to him tomorrow? So I know how it went."

"Yes." He caressed her cheek. "I'd like to come see you tomorrow evening, but I usually spend Tuesday and Thursday evenings with my mom."

"I'll come to Richland on Tuesdays and Thursdays, if you'll spend an hour or two after work on Mondays, Wednesdays and Fridays with me."

"I hate asking you to do that."

"You say that like it's a sacrifice." She put a hand on his cheek. "It's not, Gabe. I would do anything for you and your mother. In fact, whether we get Dr. Stoker's approval or not, I want to set a wedding date soon. With a short engagement."

"Paige, as much as I would like to have my mother in attendance on my wedding day, I don't want to rush to get married. I only want to do what's right for us."

She pushed up on her elbow and leaned in to press her lips to his. Cupping her head, he quickly took control of the kiss. Before long, her blood pumped a little faster, and her body temperature rose.

She sucked in a deep breath when the kiss ended. "Still think a long engagement is a good idea?"

"Nope. The sooner we get married, the better."

Laughter bubbled out of her. She couldn't remember ever feeling this blissfully happy.

Hello, happily ever after.

EPILOGUE

aige's heart expanded, causing it to ache in the best way possible, as she looked around the table at the smiling faces staring at her.

Marisol and her parents had totally hit it off over Sunday dinner. It was such a relief to have everything out in the open. Paige looked forward to introducing Gabe and his family to Ben and Amy and their kids later this evening when they joined them for dessert.

Mom had been great about including Grace in the conversation, even though most of it centered around the wedding. Paige had even caught her mom making notes on her phone whenever Grace expressed her tastes and what she would do if she was the one getting married.

Paige looked at Gabe to her right.

"Don't look at me. This is your decision, mi amor. I'm done trying to please people." He squeezed her shoulder.

"You're sure you're good with any date I pick?"

"Any date. Although I think you mentioned something about wanting your cousin, Damon, there."

"Yes, we should find out when he's supposed to deploy before we decide on a date."

Damon had said he was leaving this fall, which was only a few months away. It was longer than Paige wanted to wait, but it took time to plan a wedding. Marisol seemed to be handling the new meds well and was doing as good as could be expected, so there was no rush. But Paige had never felt so sure of anything in her life, and she was anxious to embrace it.

She picked up her phone, then paused. She hated ignoring everyone while she talked to Damon.

Mom picked up on her hesitation. "Why don't you and Gabe go into the sitting room to call Damon while we visit?"

"Good idea." She looked at Gabe to ask if he'd like to join her, but he was already standing, ready to pull back her chair.

Less than a minute later, they were settled on the loveseat in her parent's sitting room, Gabe's arm tucked around her.

She lifted her phone, but Gabe gently turned her face toward his. "Damon can wait a minute. I've been dying to do this since I arrived two hours ago." Then he lowered his lips to hers.

She dropped her phone and placed her hand on his chiseled chest before sliding it up into his hair. He'd gotten a haircut earlier this week and there wasn't much there to play with, so her hand soon found its way back to his chest.

He took the time to explore her mouth, in a slow, languorous kiss that simultaneously made her feel like melted butter and utterly energized before ending the kiss.

She sighed and sagged into him. "I will never get tired of that."

"Me either." He leaned his head against hers as he caressed her arm. "I meant it when I said I'm fine with whatever date you choose for our wedding, but I definitely like the idea of a short engagement." Ever since Gabe's talk with Dr. Stoker earlier this week, he'd been eager to press forward with their engagement.

Dr. Stoker had chastened Gabe for initiating physical contact with a patient outside the office, regardless of the pretense. But he didn't believe Gabe had crossed any ethical lines concerning his professionalism inside the office. For propriety's sake, however, he agreed it would be best for Gabe to cease treating Paige. Thankfully, he'd agreed to take her on and decided two visits per week were sufficient.

Dr. Stoker had also told Gabe if he was serious about this relationship, he should commit to it and get married soon. It wouldn't look good for Gabe to trifle with a patient only to end it down the road.

She admired the ring Gabe had placed on her finger again Tuesday evening, with even more sweet words of how much he loved her and wanted her by his side forever. It was all so surreal.

Loving Gabe was effortless. And felt so right.

Paige's phone rang on the couch beside her, making her jump. She picked it up to see a video call from Damon coming through.

Smiling, she answered. "Hey, I was just going to call you."

"What the heck, Paige?" The way Damon had his elbows propped on the table in front of him made his shoulders look bulkier than ever.

Her eyes widened at Damon's greeting.

"I just got off the phone with my mom, and she said you're engaged?" Damon glared into the phone. "When were you going to tell me?"

"I *did* tell you last Sunday. You were the first one I told, remember?"

"I know, but I thought you were keeping it a secret. From the way you talked, everything was up in the air."

"It was." She shrugged and grinned. "But it's not anymore. And it's not a secret. The whole town knows I've been sneaking around with the new physical therapist." She giggled when Gabe groaned at her choice of words. "Damon, may I introduce you to my fiancé?"

"It's about time."

Gabe snuggled a little closer as Paige angled the phone toward him. "It's nice to meet you, Damon."

"I can't believe you, man." Damon's voice turned hard as he peered into the phone at Gabe. "What gives you the right to take advantage of my favorite cousin?"

"W-what?" Gabe stiffened beside her, a slight tremor in his voice. "I swear I haven't taken advantage of Paige."

Damon continued to glare at Gabe for a long moment. "Good. In that case, it's nice to meet you." Then his lips turned up in a broad grin.

Paige burst into laughter as Gabe let out a heavy exhale.

"Sorry, man." Damon shrugged one shoulder. "Ben's a big teddy bear, like Uncle James. He's too nice to play the tough big brother, so it's my job to let you know: if you break my cousin's heart, I *will* rearrange your face."

"Noted." Gabe relaxed as he shook his head. He turned to her. "Do all your family members delight in scaring the stuffing out of the men you date?"

"Wait until you meet my cousin, Robert." Paige blinked innocent eyes at him as Damon snickered. "He's the county sheriff."

Gabe gulped, and Paige and Damon laughed again.

Damon sobered first. "Consider yourself warned, man. Robert *will* give you a hard time, but he's usually joking."

"Usually?" Gabe's wide-eyed response set off more laughter.

"So, when's the wedding?" Damon asked.

"We're still deciding on a date. When do you deploy?" Paige's voice was somber. A heavy, sluggish feeling filled her chest. She always worried about Damon when he deployed, fearing that one of these times, he wouldn't come home.

Damon scratched his jaw. "It was supposed to be the end of October, but they just bumped it up a month."

"So, you leave at the end of September?"

Damon nodded. "I get two weeks leave before deploying, but I have to be back on base no later than forty-eight hours before deployment."

Paige consulted her calendar. "So, we should get married around Labor Day." She looked at Gabe.

"Works for me." He shrugged. "That's only two weeks after school starts. Will you be able to take time off for a honeymoon that early in the school year?"

"It would have to be a short one." Paige winked. "Or we could get married before school starts."

Gabe's eye widened. "In...five weeks?"

"You get married that quickly with rumors already circling that you're slinking around with the new physical therapist, people are going to think you're pregnant." Damon's words made both Paige and Gabe gasp.

"Labor Day weekend it is." Paige said with finality.

They talked to Damon a little longer before saying their goodbyes. After the call ended, Paige turned to Gabe, his face inches from her own.

"Do you think your mom will make it until Labor Day?"

"I hope so." He laced his fingers with hers. "The important part is that she got to meet the woman I plan to spend my life with."

While Paige had been praying so earnestly by the river on the ranch Monday afternoon, she'd also prayed for Gabe and Grace to be comforted. God was answering her prayers.

Gabe didn't struggle to talk about losing his mom as much as he used to. And he seemed to have found a measure of peace and acceptance.

"I would love for her to be there, though." Paige squeezed his hand.

"Me too."

She planned to include Marisol and Grace in every step of the wedding planning, including dress shopping. Marisol might not still be here when Grace got married, so Paige was determined to make sure she got to see her daughter in a wedding dress. She just needed to figure out how to convince Grace to try on dresses with her.

Gabe played with her hand, caressing each of her fingers, sending ripples of warmth radiating up her arm. "I think we should plan the wedding for the beginning of September. If my mom takes a drastic turn for the worst, we'll elope, inviting our parents, of course. Then we'll celebrate with a reception in September with our family and friends."

"Elope? I like the sound of that." Paige gave a broad smile.

She'd been doing a lot of that lately, because she was so happy. She'd spend the rest of her life with a grin on her face as long as Just Gabe was by her side.

~

If you enjoyed Love Remodeled, please consider leaving a review on Amazon.

~

Curious about whether Damon and Grace get their own story?

Be sure you join my newsletter, so you don't miss a new release.
www.jillburrell.com/newsletter

ABOUT THE AUTHOR

JILL HAS always been an avid reader, and romance has always been her favorite genre. If she's not writing or folding laundry her head is usually in a book.

When her father told her, "I've got a story I want you to write," she didn't think she'd ever actually do it.

But after twenty years of being a stay-at-home mom with seven children, the idea of writing and publishing a book sounded less terrifying than entering the workforce again. Boy, was she wrong!

Keep in touch with Jill Burrell
www.jillburrell.com

amazon.com/author/jillburrell
facebook.com/authorjillburrell
goodreads.com/authorjillburrell
bookbub.com/authors/jill-burrell
instagram.com/authorjillburrell

www.ingramcontent.com/pod-product-compliance
Lightning Source LLC
Chambersburg PA
CBHW070810180626
46818CB00001B/188